THE

SYNCHRONICITY

of

ULYSSES

GEORGE SOURRYS

First paperback edition March 2021

Book design by Damonza.com

ISBN 978-0-6450783-8-1 (paperback)
ISBN 978-0-6450783-7-4 (eBook)

www.georgesourrys.com

Thank you to God/the universe for having dreamt up me and for giving me the opportunity to write this book.

It is dedicated to my dog Jack Sourrys who died during the writing of it:

I would gladly trade ever having written this book for just one more week with you, spent going on adventures at the places you love, including The Palmetum and Rowes Bay.

MY PROMISE TO THE READER

On the pages of this book, you will uncover a theory of everything and a secret formula that can guide you to live the life of your dreams.

But they will only work if you see them with the right eyes.

TABLE OF CONTENTS

Chapter 1: The Beginning 1

Chapter 2: Old Sweden 7

Chapter 3: Psychic Powers 9

Chapter 4: The Library. 17

Chapter 5: Oil 23

Chapter 6: Follow The Girl 25

Chapter 7: Synchronicity 28

Chapter 8: Delta's Uncle. 30

Chapter 9: A Great Decision 38

Chapter 10: The Cathedral. 42

Chapter 11: The Shadows. 45

Chapter 12: Ulysses Joins Emit 49

Chapter 13: Journey To Geno 52

Chapter 14: Geno 59

Chapter 15: The Theory. 64

Chapter 16: Present Shadows 75

Chapter 17: Geno's History 80

Chapter 18: The Sage. 83

Chapter 19: Delta's Passion 86

Chapter 20: The Perfect Mindset 92

Chapter 21: Uncover And Hold Your Primary Desires 95

Chapter 22: Luke Loves Her 105

Chapter 23: Have Clear Vision. 107

Chapter 24: The Son Of Ioannis 111

Chapter 25: Be Open To Perfection 117

Chapter 26: You Are Ready Now 120

Chapter 27: The Wife Of Ioannis. 124

Chapter 28: The Geno Martial Arts 127

Chapter 29: The Glowing Ring 130

Chapter 30: The Stars. 132

Chapter 31: The Shadows And The Banks 139

Chapter 32: Surrender To The Chaos With Faith 144
Chapter 33: Discover The Flow State 146
Chapter 34: 14 Fornax Street 150
Chapter 35: Uncover And Create Perfection. 153
Chapter 36: See The Order And Continue 155
Chapter 37: Martial Arts And The Perfect Mindset 158
Chapter 38: Emit's Passion 160
Chapter 39: The Storm. 164
Chapter 40: The Cabin. 167
Chapter 41: The Next Morning 171
Chapter 42: How To Send Dreams. 172
Chapter 43: The Art Of Xiren 177
Chapter 44: Emit Warns Ulysses 181
Chapter 45: Ulysses Sends A Dream. 184
Chapter 46: To Dream To Fail 186
Chapter 47: Magic Powers 189
Chapter 48: Blindfolded Martial Arts. 193
Chapter 49: Enlightenment 196
Chapter 50: Shadows Location. 206
Chapter 51: Self-Actualisation 207
Chapter 52: Stronger Than Ever. 210
Chapter 53: Love Letters 214
Chapter 54: A Member Of Geno 217
Chapter 55: The History Of Geno On File 220
Chapter 56: But It's Not Her 227
Chapter 57: Ulysses Uncovers Perfections. 231
Chapter 58: Girl Of Dreams 236
Chapter 59: The Shadows In The Rainforest. 242
Chapter 60: Luke's Childhood 244
Chapter 61: Delta's Secrets 247
Chapter 62: Sophos Speaks Of Delta 252
Chapter 63: The Golden Moon 256
Chapter 64: Luke Learns 260
Chapter 65: Slowing Time 262
Chapter 66: Orien 267
Chapter 67: A Fight 269
Chapter 68: Healing Hand. 274
Chapter 69: Geno's Garden 279

Chapter 70: Sophos' Vision 287
Chapter 71: Ulysses' Wounds. 288
Chapter 72: Sophos Speaks Of Her Premonition 289
Chapter 73: The Hospital. 292
Chapter 74: Luke Reads The Signs 295
Chapter 75 Tragedy Strikes. 298
Chapter 76: Delta's Blood 303
Chapter 77: The Watch 307
Chapter 78: The Time Traveller 310
Chapter 79: Her Funeral 313
Chapter 80: Ulysses' Decision 317
Chapter 81: Ulysses Prepares For The Quest. 320
Chapter 82: Time Can Be Our Saviour 323
Chapter 83: Darkness Is Not Always Absent Of Light 331
Chapter 84: Blessed Orien 333
Chapter 85: The Missing Page 335
Chapter 86: The Prophecy 336
Chapter 87: Young Delta 338
Chapter 88: Back To The Future 340
Chapter 89: The Past Is Written 345
Chapter 90: A Father's Lesson 349
Chapter 91: The Greater Good And The Time Between Time   352
Chapter 92: Delta's Homeland. 355
Chapter 93: The Future Shadows 357
Chapter 94: Return To The Beginning 359
Epilogue. 361
About The Author 362

CHAPTER 1

THE BEGINNING

IT BEGINS IN the rainforest.

Ulysses gazes upon her as the sunlight plays on her damp blonde hair. Her face is sprinkled with droplets from a rainforest waterfall that splashes them both lightly as it enters a blue lagoon. He has never seen such striking beauty as hers. But his attraction is not just physical – it is more than that.

He can read her mind, something which, although amazing, comes naturally. He sees *her*. He understands her. And it feels as if his whole life has been leading to this, as if it has always been written.

With a desire that can only be fulfilled through the flesh of her being, he leans into her feminine divinity. And as he does, her eyes become brighter to him, the beauty of which attracts him closer still. The tension inside him rises. He reaches forward, pressing his fingers gently against the nape of her neck. And for a moment they do nothing but stare into each other's eyes.

Her blue eyes pierce him, deeply, in a way that is different to how anyone has ever looked at him; they are filled with purity, complete openness and an underlying strength and purpose as if she believes in every part of her essence that what she is about to do is right.

Suddenly, and with great force, she enfolds into him in a sensual embrace, enthusiastically kissing his lips whilst her hands eagerly explore his back. He promptly takes control of her but simultaneously loses control of himself. And like the waterfall beside them, his love flows powerfully. And like the blue lagoon, she accepts his power and envelops it within her being, only to return it by becoming one with him.

Ulysses awakens. The tenderness of the morning seeps between the curtains to gently illuminate the bedroom. He rises in his bed, the white sheets wrapped around the lower half of his body.

It was a dream.

He shakes his head and smiles. *If only it were real life.* This is the eighth time he has had this dream in as many weeks. Who is this young woman, what does this dream mean and why is it recurring? There must be a reason – after all, he believes there is a reason for everything.

Instinctively he feels that he cannot decipher the dream in the present and so he pushes it out of his conscious mind.

He begins his morning ritual, his hand manoeuvring amongst the sheets. He grabs a hold of it and feels its weight. And brings it to his view. His smartphone.

He briefly glances at the performance of the US share markets from Friday's trade. Due to his plane journey and jet lag he missed taking a look yesterday.

He then switches to his social media: photo after photo display beautiful people happily posed in spectacular locations, with expensive cars, luxurious houses, successful careers, perfect physiques and flawless relationships. These are simply snapshots of their lives and not an accurate representation of any overall perfection, yet Ulysses cannot help but feel dissatisfied while looking at them. *Why can't I live the life of my dreams?* He assures himself that one day he will. One day he will be as happy as everyone pretends to be in photos.

He swiftly changes to swiping through a dating app, judging potential partners at lightning speed, simply by the appearance of their first photo. After several minutes of mindlessly doing this, he finally feels ready to face his Sunday.

He stands, his eyes meeting the reflection of a mirrored cupboard. It is the first time in a few months he has looked in this particular mirror and the contrast between his current shirtless body and his previous one is instantly apparent. He is slightly more toned in physique now. This is not surprising as he often loses weight while travelling extensively. He is also pleased that he has maintained his muscle size, probably because he kept up with his routine strength workouts, albeit in the hotel gymnasiums.

Yet even as he eyes what he considers to be a slight aesthetic improvement, he still sees his physical flaws very clearly. His fingers trace over his abdominal muscles – they certainly are not as prominent as he desires; he needs to lose a couple of percentages of body fat to be satisfied there. He thinks how great it would be if he could somehow swipe past his physique to a better option, just like he does with his potential love interests on dating apps.

His attention moves to his face. His previous girlfriend described him as being *the good-looking guy next door, with kind eyes and a charming smile.* She then went on to say *but you're nothing to write home about.* He wishes he could forget this last bit, even though he feels it is an accurate description.

He runs his fingers through his brown hair which is messy from sleep. *No! It can't be!* He rushes closer to the mirror. Just as he suspected! His first grey hair! *Already? At 28?* Furthermore, the lines on his face, while slight, are becoming clearer. Both are harsh reminders that time continues to pass by very quickly and he is still not where he wishes to be in life. *When will I succeed? I'm running out of time.* He gives himself a look of great distaste.

He leaves the bedroom through sliding doors, jumps over a small garden and lands in a decadent resort swimming area. Here luxury is interlaced with natural beauty: palm trees and manicured gardens surround the pool and spa and rainbow lorikeets screech as they fly in pairs overhead.

It is late July, which is winter here on the Gold Coast, Australia. And even though he feels the sun's strength offering warmth to his skin, he consciously wishes he were back in European summer.

He aligns a white deck chair with the sun, lies upon it and looks over the swimming pool. The water instantly reminds him of his dream of the young woman before the waterfall. He has never connected with a person like this before – so naturally, so deeply. The uninhibited openness they shared, the staring into one another's eyes; this just does not happen in normal society. Not like that. People are too guarded to allow themselves to be that vulnerable, Ulysses included.

Yet even still, he believes in the possibility of such a romance. He also believes in the possibility that he can still live the life of his dreams. And there is a good reason for this.

Ever since he was a child, he has felt that the world has a hidden underlying perfection, a magic. Sometimes he briefly encounters it. It might be while gazing at the simple yet intricate beauty of the natural world and suddenly witnessing how everything in it seems to fit so perfectly together. Or while playing a sport and feeling that he is in a great flow with the elements around him, as if he has tapped into their underlying power and is seamlessly using it to manifest his desires. Or when something beyond coincidence happens – a chance meeting or event that leads everything to work out for the best, in ways he could never have envisioned.

But apart from glimpses here and there, for most of Ulysses' life this perfection has eluded him. And while he witnesses it enough to know that it is possible, it is not enough to make his life great. If only he could make these glimpses become his everyday life.

And there is a way.

Growing up, Ulysses' primary heroes were wisdom seekers like Leonardo da Vinci, Albert Einstein, Carl Jung, the Ancient

Greek philosophers and Isaac Newton. People who discovered great secrets. This natural inclination, coupled with his desire to live the life of his dreams, has pushed Ulysses on a grand quest to uncover the greatest of secrets. *A theory of everything.* Like discovering an instruction manual, he hopes that with the secrets of the universe laid bare, he will be able to decipher its magic and then master this wisdom to live the life of his dreams.

It is safe to say that Ulysses' dreams are bigger than some, and perhaps even unrealistic. He knows this, which is why he never speaks of them to others. To most, he is simply a superficial bachelor, with clear perfectionist issues, who frequently travels for his father's financial business, *Prosperity with Purpose.*

Yet privately, Ulysses obsessively seeks to discover this theory of everything. He researches extensively, using his overseas work trips as opportunities to visit shamans, mystics, scientists and philosophers, a quest which has led him on many paths towards great wisdom. And in this present moment, his mind touches upon this.

Yet, no matter how many times he relives these exciting adventures in his mind, they always seem to lead to the same point. Even after all of this time spent and knowledge learned, his sought-after all-encompassing theory remains undiscovered. And now he is home once again without success.

I'm a failure.

He drops his head in defeat and feels the crushing weight of his desires so strongly that it is suddenly hard for him to breathe. He touches his heart. If only he had simpler dreams. Why does he feel so compelled to achieve this vision that he seeks it so devotedly, as if this quest has been deeply ingrained within his very soul? He wishes for reassurance, a sign to let him know that he is on the right path. His head still down, he whispers, "God, if everything will be okay, if I will still live the life I dream of, please give me a sign."

Upon wishing this, Ulysses raises his head. His eyes instantly notice a nearby plant which vibrates from a slight wind. With the sun's rays touching its leaves from above and reflecting onto it from the water below, the plant appears as if it is magically glowing. *Another glimpse of perfection.*

He looks at its individual leaves and sees that they are complete elements in their own right, yet a small part of this greater plant. He then focuses on this plant in its entirety. Ulysses feels deeply connected to this moment and his thoughts intertwine until they disappear. His mind becomes still. Clear. In this moment of conscious emptiness, a single thought enters. An important thought. It takes a moment for the magnitude of it to dawn upon him. But when it seeps into his consciousness his eyes open wide and his mind becomes completely focused. His heart races with excitement and his body begins to tremble as if a greater power has just whispered a deep secret.

I've got it! I can't believe it, but it's true. I've finally discovered the answer I've been searching for!

In an adrenaline-fuelled rush of inspiration he hurries back into his apartment. He glides onto the seat at his desk, starts his laptop and frantically begins typing, his hands shaking as his fingers hit the keyboard. He feels he must write down all that he can about this enlightened thought while it is fresh in his mind, with the foreboding fear that otherwise it will disappear until perhaps some untold millennia when a person, through genius or coincidence, may come to think of this great thought again. He must capture it now...

Eighty-eight minutes pass and Ulysses picks up a newly printed document. *This is it!* In his hands he feels the weight of the paper and while it is light, he knows the power that this document has within it. The power to change anyone's life who comes to learn this knowledge. For Ulysses has finally discovered the greatest of secrets, *a theory of everything.*

CHAPTER 2

OLD SWEDEN

887 – Sweden.

WITH A FLASH of bright light, he appears upon a Grecian pavilion that holds a great significance to the eight Geno members who sit before it. He is tall, with short, dark blond hair, light green eyes and clothes made of a red and black fabric that the members could never have witnessed before.

Their eyes focus on him intently as he saunters down the steps and walks amongst the group, fearlessly, purposefully. Some of the Geno members rise and adopt martial arts stances. But instead of concern, a calm smile comes to his face. After all, he knows what is about to happen next.

Suddenly, there is a loud bellow for attention. It is a male Geno member with long blond hair. And with his powerful arms he lifts a large, ancient runestone high above his head.

The inscription on the stone makes it clear to the members of Geno: this man's coming has been prophesied. It is the will of the Gods, and thus, *this is all meant to be.*

*

Later this same day.

The golden sun beats down upon a town square. A blonde princess, ten years of age, kneels on the ground. She cries desperately as the village burns around her.

He stands and watches. He has finally found her.

CHAPTER 3

PSYCHIC POWERS

The present – Gold Coast, Australia.

ULYSSES, WEARING JEANS and a hooded jumper, walks along a street filled with mansions, parallel to the beach. He often takes walks with no destination in mind. Even when he is on the phone or brushing his teeth, he finds himself pacing back and forth. And this morning, having discovered a theory of everything, he is too excited to sit still.

How incredible to finally know such great secrets of the universe. He can now prove that there is a greater purpose for everything.

That *this is all meant to be.*

Yet, even with his current enthusiasm, as he walks past these luxurious properties his fantasies slowly steal his celebration. He sees one that often draws his attention. It is a white Hamptons-style house with a tennis court and infinity pool, all on a triple-sized block.

A row of hedges hides much of the view of the property from the street, leading Ulysses to daydream about the simple pleasure of privately walking amongst its garden and feeling uninhibited enough to take it all in. He imagines studying the nature and soaking up the elements around him, and the bliss of having the pool all to himself on Sunday mornings – something that is not guaranteed where he currently lives.

He looks up to see the windows in this wooden house are made of one-way glass. This offering of superior privacy is in contrast to Ulysses' apartment where he feels uncomfortable to even have the curtains open in case people were to look in and take an interest in whatever Ulysses is doing. And, more importantly to him, he cannot even be intimate with a woman with any amount of noise without his neighbours hearing.

But here in this mansion... here he could finally live his life properly. He visualises having guests on the mansion's rooftop entertaining area overlooking the ocean, talking and laughing whilst taking in a beautiful sunset.

One day, I'll have a mansion like this and then I'll be living the life of my dreams.

Damn! He instantly realises that while he has finally discovered the theory he has been obsessively seeking for a decade, he still does not feel content. When will he be?

The world around me, and everything it encapsulates, are like words of a sentence. Now that I've discovered this theory, I know how to read the sentence. But I still don't know what the sentence means; this I must decipher if I'm to tap into the hidden perfection of the world and live the life of my dreams.

And so there is more to do, more to do... something which Ulysses has become accustomed to. He feels as if he is forever moving towards somewhere but never truly arriving.

His focus is taken when he notices a small, light brown dachshund, eighty metres away, on a sidewalk across the street. Strangely, whilst looking at this dog a vision comes to him with great clarity: he envisions the dog taking two small steps and jumping from the sidewalk onto the road. It then walks along the bitumen, towards him. Suddenly, a black luxury sedan sharply turns the corner at speed. *The dog's in danger!*

This vision disappears as quickly as it came, but it holds Ulysses' attention. Although he is often in his imagination, it has never run so vividly in his waking hours before. The vision was so clear in his mind's eye that it almost felt as if it were happening in real life. He is unsure what to make of it.

He begins to walk faster towards this dog, keeping a watchful eye as it nears the edge of the sidewalk. The dachshund stops, takes two small steps and jumps onto the road – in the same manner as his vision.

Just in case, Ulysses assures himself and he starts jogging towards the dog.

Suddenly, a black luxury sedan screeches around the corner, travelling directly in line with the dog.

The vision is true!

Ulysses runs as fast he can. His feet pounding the bitumen, he calls out, motioning for the driver to stop.

But the driver does not react.

Ulysses moves diagonally across the road, directly towards the speeding car. His senses work overtime, much faster than the time seems to pass in the outside world. It feels as if time slows down for him. He sees the car slowly moving towards the dog, now only several metres away. He processes everything in what would normally be lightning-quick speed, including where to place his feet to reach the dog in the quickest time possible. He reaches the dachshund and in a smooth and accurate motion picks it up in his arms and carries it towards the sidewalk.

He has reacted quickly, but not fast enough. There is no way he can outrun this vehicle which is now only a few metres away from hitting them both. Ulysses braces for the oncoming impact.

Suddenly the car begins to veer away. *The driver has noticed us!*

A wind hits Ulysses as the black vehicle glides next to him, missing him by a matter of centimetres. Finally, he and the dog make it to the sidewalk.

They are safe.

An elderly lady frantically rushes out of a large house directly in front of them. "Oh my God, is he okay? He got out of the yard!"

"He's fine," Ulysses says, struggling to catch his breath. He gently places the dog on the sidewalk, kneels and pats him as the elderly owner places him on a lead.

The luxury black sedan is stopped twenty metres up the road. The driver exits, slams his car door and approaches them with a stern look on his face. "What were you doing on the road? I almost hit you!" he yells, pointing his finger vehemently at Ulysses.

"This young man is a hero! You almost ran over my dog! Next time watch where you're going," the old lady snaps back at him. She then focuses her attention towards Ulysses. "How on earth did you manage to save little Scamp in time?"

"I just knew it was going to happen. I can't explain it. I had a vision. I started jogging towards the dog before the car even came around the corner," Ulysses replies.

The driver looks at Ulysses very strangely and leaves to return to his vehicle. Ulysses realises how ridiculous he must sound.

"Amazing! Bless you, young man, you saved Scamp's life. How can I repay you?"

"I'm just happy that your dog is okay."

Ulysses gives a last pat to the dog, says goodbye to them both and continues walking.

His mind is filled with questions. *How did I know that was going to happen? How did I manage to save the dog? It doesn't make sense.* But Ulysses does not have long to contemplate. His phone vibrates in his pocket. He pulls it out and discovers that his father, Ioannis, is calling.

"Hey, Dad," Ulysses answers.

"Hi, Ulysses. Just seeing you got in okay last night?" his father says.

"I'm fine, Dad. I told you not to bother."

"I know, I know. How are things being back? Missing overseas?"

"I really am," Ulysses says as he looks towards the sun's rays above a nearby beach house. And for a brief moment his memories drift to his recent adventure, walking through the streets of an old Swedish town, searching. He took a wrong turn and came to a town square. The sun, directly above the buildings, shone so brightly in his eyes…

"Well, I'm sure you'll have plenty of adventures to come. What about those Swedish companies and charities? Did you finish the reports?"

"Yep, I've already sent them through to your email."

"Thanks, son. I don't know if you realise how significant your contributions are. I did some calculations on the Trust and last year's returns were 118 per cent! Some of the charities you have chosen get a good percentage of that."

"Really, 118 per cent?" Ulysses parrots. In truth, he is barely listening. His job is simply a job; his passion lies in his theory. And so, when it comes to the finance part of their conversations, he listens just enough to get by.

"Yes, and it's primarily because of your research. So, well done."

"It's my pleasure. And I think I've found some great opportunities on this last trip."

"Good. I'll look forward to reading them. But I hope you didn't spend your whole trip working, though? Following your dreams, that is far more important."

"As you keep reminding me. And Dad, I have something to tell you… you know the theory I've been working on?"

"The one you're always seeking but never tell me about?"

"Yes. Believe me, the fact that you know anything about it means that I have told you more than most. And great news. I think I've finally discovered it."

"Excellent! Can you tell me a little about it now?"

"I want to work on it a bit more first."

"Okay, but just give me an idea."

"Well, it's a theory that explains everything in existence. It points to everything being meaningful and potentially fulfilling a higher destiny, even ourselves."

There is silence on the line.

"Dad?"

"… Sorry. I was just processing what you said. Very interesting. How do you feel about this theory?"

"I feel like it's the answer I've been searching for, for all of these years."

"Good. Has anything changed since discovering it?"

"What do you mean?"

"Any coincidences in your life? Things you couldn't explain? I know this may sound strange, but it's very important."

Coincidences? Why ask such a thing? "Well… I did kind of have a vision of a dog about to be hit by a car, just a moment ago. And then straight afterwards my vision came true! I managed to save the dog just in time, purely as I foresaw it! It was amazing! I don't know how I knew; I just did. It was like a precognition."

"I see," his father says with a serious tone to his voice. Ulysses knows this tone as he has heard it before: *something is up.*

"What is it?"

There is only silence on the other end. Finally, in what seems like an eternity to Ulysses, his father replies, "I knew this day would come."

"Huh?"

"Ulysses, there's something special about you. It was only a matter of time until you revealed this greater purpose."

"I don't know what you're talking about?"

"Was anybody there when you saved the dog?"

"Just the owner and the driver."

"Tell me about them?"

"I don't know what to say. I've never met them before. The owner of the dog was an elderly lady, the driver of the luxury car was wearing a suit."

His father's voice becomes anxious. "The man in the suit. Did he have a symbol anywhere, say, on his jacket? One of a red triangle?"

"I don't know. I wasn't paying that close attention."

"Ulysses, this is very important. We don't have much time. You need to go to the university library. Do you have a pen? Write this down."

"Okay." Ulysses brings up *notes* on his smartphone.

"You need to find a book. It's in the old books section. Its code is 8888 GE. Turn to page 880 and read what it says. Can you do that?"

"Okay, sure. But what are you talking about? Can't you just tell me what the book says?"

"I don't know what the book says. It's for your eyes only. Did you copy down what I said?"

"Yes, book 8888 GE, page 880."

"Good. Things will become clear as you go. Everything will simply happen."

"What do you mean, everything will simply happen?"

"Things are already happening in preparation for you. The elements of the system will bring synchronicities to lead you."

"I'm sorry?" Ulysses has no idea what his father is talking about.

"It's difficult to explain. Just get to the library. Be careful and whatever you do, don't let anyone know about your psychic powers!"

"Dad, I think you are overreacting! Psychic powers? It's probably just a coincidence."

"Things are rarely ever a coincidence, Ulysses. You will see that soon. Now find the book!"

"Yes, Dad."

"Oh, once you've read the page, take the book with you. You don't have much time, so don't borrow it. The library doesn't own it anyway."

"Okay, Dad."

"Good. Love you." His father hangs up.

Ulysses stands motionless, but blood pumps quickly through his veins. He has never heard his father so concerned. *But why?* Has discovering how the universe works somehow put Ulysses in danger?

A quote attributed to the Ancient Greek Sophocles comes to his mind: *Nothing vast enters the life of mortals without a curse.*

He looks around. He cannot see any sinister reason why he should hurry to the library. Beside him are plants that seem as timeless as ever. The sun is shining onto their leaves just as it has done on plants for many millions of years. He can see the ocean in the distance. Blue skies surround him. Arm in arm, a romantic couple walks past Ulysses in a happy, carefree manner. He feels that his dad is overreacting, just as fathers sometimes do.

Perhaps it is true that since learning the theory Ulysses has started to become psychic. The theory does point to the possibility of psychic powers. It points to many things. It is a theory of everything. But why is that something to cause panic? Does it warrant running after a book? Why is there such a rush?

What have I really uncovered with this theory?

CHAPTER 4

THE LIBRARY

Ulysses feels a great anticipation as he stands at the university library doors. He has finally discovered a theory of everything, has potentially become psychic and now his father has rushed him to this library to find a book. His life is changing at what feels like light speed and perhaps, by simply walking through these glass doors, Ulysses will arrive at a point of no return.

This power of unknowable change leaves an unsettled feeling in the pit of his stomach. While he has not felt any long-lasting contentment in the past, his everyday life feels like a warm blanket; it is comfortable. And so, as he looks upon this three-storey library built with reinforced concrete, he questions whether he should enter.

But then he reminds himself that what he is truly searching for is not comfort, but rather perfection. Since he has discovered the theory, he feels that the flow of the universe is finally leading him towards its secrets. *I must continue to be open to this perfection.*

Believing that he is seeing things with clear vision and that he is ready, he surrenders to the chaos of the unknown and walks through the library doors, whilst holding the faith that somehow, someway, this simple decision will lead him towards his dreams.

The library is unfamiliar, which leads Ulysses to realise that while he has spent so much time in the great libraries of many overseas cities, he has neglected the ones close to home.

Walking with a long gait, he follows overhead signs until he arrives at the old book section. It is a small section of the library, yet he notices that it holds a great deal of obscure texts. There are books on the occult, one on witchcraft that seems very old and falling to bits. *They aren't exactly in mint condition.* One would even question why the library has these old books. He doubts many of them have been read in recent years. They seem like lifeless souls, sitting on rows of metal waiting for people to read them, like puppies at the pound hoping for someone to notice and save them, yet no one ever does.

He walks past several aisles until he comes to a row of books with the numbers on their spine beginning with 8000. His pointed fingers glide past several books. Finally, he finds the one he has been looking for: 8888 GENO. He takes hold of it, throws his backpack to the side and gently transports the book to a nearby desk.

The book does not say it is by an author, nor does it have a title; all it has is a symmetrical symbol on the front cover. It is an eight-pointed star, a regular octagram to be precise, encased within a circle. And inside the centre of this octagram is another circle-encased octagram. It seems familiar to Ulysses. *Where have I seen this symbol before?*

Not wishing to damage this old book, he opens it with care. His fingers shake as he delicately flicks through the yellow-stained pages. *Original, not for reading enjoyment at all.* He notices that every spread of pages is similar. The left page has the symbol from the front cover and a simple sentence underneath it, which is followed by an adjacent page that lists a city's name. Sometimes these pages are written in English, sometimes not. *There is a hidden purpose to this book. What is it used for?*

He finally comes to the page before his desired number. It reads "Gold Coast, Australia." *How would a book this old even mention this city? This book must be hundreds of years older than the Gold Coast, maybe more.*

He closes his eyes in anticipation of seeing something great on the next page, something enlightening to his current situation, something that will explain why his dad was so rushed to get him to the library and why he is encountering psychic coincidences. By simply looking at the next page he expects everything in his life to change even more than it already has on this day and for magic to reveal itself in its entirety. His heart pounds. He holds his breath and turns the page to page 880. Slowly, he opens his eyes. On the page is the symbol. And underneath the symbol reads, "*Follow the girl.*"

Ulysses exhales. His heart stops pounding. *What? This is the answer – follow the girl?* He expected something a little more pro-found. *This is the great wisdom I've been searching for?* Ulysses slams the book closed. He is no longer gentle with it. The book has told him nothing!

Frustrated, he stands and looks around the library, almost as a way to say to his father – *See, there is no girl I'm meant to follow! The book is wrong.* He sees a few women about the library, but none that really stand out to him. *How am I meant to know when I find her anyway?*

And then, he notices her. She grabs his complete attention. She is across the library, with her back to him, sitting down at a desk. Her blonde hair is in a ponytail, a white t-shirt covering her gently tanned skin. She wears blue jeans and white sneakers. He can only see her from behind and his eyesight is not the best at this distance, yet she is familiar.

I must get a closer look.

He places the ancient book into his backpack, straps the back-pack onto his shoulders and hesitantly walks towards her. The young woman gathers her belongings, getting ready to leave. She stands and appears about to turn towards him, allowing Ulysses to catch a glimpse of her profile. But then she seems to decide otherwise and walks into an adjacent book aisle.

Ulysses needs to see more of her. He needs to see if it is *her*. With the guidance of the book, he follows the girl. He walks through the book aisles, tracing the path she took. The library suddenly feels like a great maze to Ulysses as she continues to move away from him and is often out of sight as she walks down new aisles.

As an effort to secretly overtake her, he paces up a parallel aisle to the one she has just taken. He then dashes up a couple more aisles in that general direction until he feels that he must have passed her. He waits at the exit of the aisle he believes she will walk down.

He expects to see her. But she is nowhere to be seen. *Has she already passed this point? Have I lost her?*

He turns and looks down the aisle he just walked. Suddenly, he sees her walking directly towards him. Whilst her head is slightly down and she is not looking towards him, he can now see her very clearly. He gazes upon her in awe. *It's her.*

He follows his first instinct and quickly cowers around a corner, kneeling, making himself invisible behind a desk. *Surely she can't be real?*

After some moments filled with positive self-talk, he regathers his composure and stands. He walks around the corner and discovers her walking farther and farther away.

He moves quickly and soon enough has her closer in his sight as she nears the library exit. But he focuses so intently on her that he does not pay attention to his surroundings and knocks over another student who crosses his path. The student's books fly everywhere. Ulysses stops and helps to pick them up, apologising. But with this delay he loses sight of her again as she exits the library.

Ulysses quickly regains his momentum. He leaves the library and begins to jog along one of the paths that meanders through the eucalypts. The blonde woman is 100 metres ahead. Her ponytail, golden blonde like the sun's rays, sways as she walks. As he nears, he slows to a brisk walk so that he does not make it obvious that he is eager to catch up to her. He wants it to appear as natural as possible, even though it feels very strange to follow her like this.

He edges within fifteen metres of her. He is now close enough to call her without raising his voice too much, "Hey…" He realises he does not know her name. "Hey, girl," he calls out.

She suddenly stops and turns, motioning to herself questioningly.

He has her attention, but he finds that he can barely speak, as his chest is tight from nerves. "Yes… wait!" Ulysses finally catches up with her. "Okay… I've followed you."

"I'm sorry?" she says with a slight accent, like no other he has ever heard, even with his extensive travel.

"I've found you, so can you tell me what this means?"

"I'm not sure this means anything, sorry. You must be following the wrong girl." She turns defensively and begins to walk away.

"Wait…" Ulysses says in a strong voice while he grabs the front of her elbow, where her arm bends. "Please…" His voice softens and he loosens his grip to touch her arm kindly. He gently leads her back towards him, pulls the book from his backpack and shows page 880 to her.

"I'm meant to follow you. I know this seems…"

Her eyes flicker past the words that led Ulysses to her. "I don't know what…" she begins to speak. Suddenly she appears to glimpse the symbol.

She looks up at Ulysses as if it is the first time she has properly looked at him. Her blue eyes seem like water flowing right through his own. He feels as if he is suddenly metaphorically naked and that nothing he has ever done can be hidden from the energy radiating from her.

A smile comes to her so naturally that it seems to Ulysses as if her very being innocently spills out of her. Her dimples become visible. She speaks with an accepting warmth, as if she now realises what this is all about, "Well, I guess you should do as the book says."

She immediately turns and walks ahead. Ulysses moves to keep up with her.

"What does this all mean?" he asks.

"There's one man who can answer that for you. I'll take you to him."

"You know this person?"

"Yes. And it really is no problem. I'm going there anyway."

Although Ulysses does not say anything, he is truly amazed. There is a greater magical perfection in the world than he could ever imagine. It has just been proven to him. As this is the girl from his recurring dreams.

CHAPTER 5

OIL

1901 – California, United States of America.

WEARING A SUIT, he enters a hall filled with various elite and prosperous businessmen. For the next fifteen minutes he has a singular purpose. A large parcel of land where oil has been discovered is being auctioned to the highest bidder. He moves through the crowd, as people bid in the tens of thousands.

"Seventy-five thousand?" the auctioneer asks the hall.

Finally in position, he raises his hand. "Two million," he says in a powerful voice.

The hall instantly becomes eerily silent.

"Are you serious?" the auctioneer asks.

"I have no time for further bidding. Time is very precious to me," he says sternly.

"Two million going once, going twice… sold for two million."

He nods and walks towards the auctioneer, his peripheral vision aware that the crowd of people is watching him intently. They look stunned and begin talking amongst themselves; it is obvious they cannot believe what has just taken place. But he does not care for their curiosity.

He reaches the auctioneer. "My men will take care of everything from here," he says, motioning behind him. Several men in suits move towards the auctioneer, all with tiny red triangle symbols on their suit jackets.

The auctioneer, partly covering his mouth with his right hand, whispers privately, "Who *are* you?"

"My name is Orien."

CHAPTER 6

FOLLOW THE GIRL

The present – Gold Coast, Australia.

ULYSSES AND THE girl walk together through parklands with native grass and eucalyptus trees. He has no idea where she is taking him, but she certainly seems to know where she is going, taking every possible shortcut available.

"Come this way," she says, leading him along another cemented walkway.

He is still unsure of her accent – it reminds him of Grace Kelly's in old interviews, as she speaks so sophisticatedly and articulately that she almost sounds English, *but not quite*. Perhaps it is from somewhere in Europe he hasn't been to, which will be hard going, he considers, as he has been pretty much everywhere.

He glimpses her visually whenever he can without making it too obvious. She is quietly striking and glowing with a natural beauty; her face has the symmetry of a Greek statue. She has light-coloured hair and eyes, which are contrasted by her darker eyebrows. She wears little if any makeup, making it easier for Ulysses to notice what might be seen as imperfections. He notices three small moles that form a triangle on her left cheek. She is also a little puffy around her eyes, particularly around the bottom of them, in a way that is no doubt hereditary. However, to Ulysses, these are not imperfections as he finds these features particularly attractive. Attractive, but he can tell that she is in her early twenties at the most and, therefore, a few years too young for him.

Interestingly, although her physical beauty closely matches that of his dream, there is something slightly different about her. He cannot explain what it is. Perhaps it is because the woman beside him is real, he considers, and not simply a dream.

He notices that in her hand are two books, a textbook on nature and a smaller strange-looking book on magic. *Magic. Why does this not surprise me?*

He also recognises a necklace she is wearing. It instantly triggers a childhood memory for Ulysses as it is the same necklace his father used to wear. As a child, he often asked his father about this necklace, the pendant of which he would see dangling inside his father's open jacket. Commonly, the reply simply was that it was *"from the olden days"*, and his father left it at that. Even so, Ulysses could tell that it was significant to his father, and one day after further prodding, his father told him that it was foremost a personal reminder to do the greater good in the world, and secondly, it was a key to a greater knowledge. He said that maybe Ulysses would understand one day when he was older. Sensing that this was as much information as he would ever gather from his father, Ulysses never asked about the necklace again.

And now, as he looks upon her necklace, he suddenly realises that on its pendant is half of the same symbol that is on the book in his backpack. It now makes sense to him; there was a reason why the symbol first seemed familiar when he looked at it on the cover of this old book. Ulysses has seen half of this symbol since he was very young on his father's necklace.

"So, what's your name?"

"Uhhh," Ulysses responds as he slowly departs his wandering thoughts.

"What is your name?"

"Ulysses," he puts out his hand through polite habit.

She smiles and shakes his hand. "Pleasure to meet you, Ulysses. I'm Delta."

As they continue to walk, Ulysses feels as if he has always been destined to take this path. How could he dream of her, having never met her, and then be led to her through such synchronicity?

CHAPTER 7

SYNCHRONICITY

As HE WALKS with Delta, Ulysses thinks of all that he knows of synchronicity. He believes it to be a term first coined by the Swiss psychologist Carl Jung in the 1920s. However, its roots are possibly much more ancient, for if the concept of synchronicity is true, it is a natural occurrence and therefore has been in existence for an untold passage of time.

He understands the basic tenet is that synchronicity is when two or more events are meaningfully related but are not related through conventional mechanisms of causality. Some people simplify synchronicity as being a meaningful coincidence, which certainly makes the concept easier to understand. However, Ulysses has come to learn that synchronicity is beyond coincidence.

His interest in synchronicity deepened on his recent overseas travels where, whilst trying to discover the theory of everything, he encountered many sages who believe that synchronicity is a sign of there being a deep underlying order to the universe.

And now, today, Ulysses has encountered many synchronicities. He knows that if he didn't dream at night of this young woman, if he hadn't discovered the theory of everything this very morning and become increasingly psychic, if he hadn't received a phone call from his father which led him to arrive at the library at the precise timing he did, he would never have known which girl to follow. If he had arrived at the library just a few minutes later, Delta would have already left and he would not have been able to do what the mysterious book instructed – *follow the girl.*

CHAPTER 8

DELTA'S UNCLE

DELTA CONTINUES TO lead Ulysses. They are now on a quiet suburban street, walking towards a destination unknown to him.

"So how did you know that I'm the girl to follow?" Delta asks.

"I'm sorry?"

"Well, I'm sure there were plenty of other girls in the library. How did you know to follow me and not them?"

Ulysses knows exactly why. It is because she is the girl from his dreams. But he feels that all that has happened today is too unbelievable to explain to her. After all, he had already tried to explain another psychic moment earlier and was looked at very strangely by the driver who almost hit the dachshund. And so, he offers a more realistic solution. "I noticed that your necklace has half of a symbol on it. The same symbol is on the cover of the book and also on the page, just above where *follow the girl* is written."

"Wow, that's very observant of you, Ulysses."

"May I ask, why do you wear that necklace?"

"There's quite a story to it," she says as she stops walking.

"Enlighten me – we are walking for God knows how long."

"Actually, we're here," she smiles as she points at the house adjacent to them.

Ulysses looks at the property. There is a simple, one-level, orangey-red brick home situated on a large block filled with green grass and tall eucalyptus trees.

"Come," Delta says as she lifts her leg and straddles the waist-high fence. She plants a foot inside the yard, lifts her other leg and climbs over.

Ulysses places his hands on the fence and swings his legs to the side, leaping over the fence in one smooth motion. He does this more as a way to show off his athletic abilities to Delta than anything else. Straight after doing this, Ulysses questions himself: *Why do I always try to impress attractive women with physical feats?* Ulysses is too bright not to see through his animal behaviours, but at the same time they are so innate that he has learned to accept many of them.

They walk to the front entrance.

"Do you live here?" Ulysses asks.

"Yes, most of the time. This is my uncle's house."

"And your uncle will know why I am meant to follow you?"

"I already know why you're meant to follow me, Ulysses," Delta replies as she opens the door with her key.

"You do?" Ulysses asks, surprised.

But his question goes unanswered, for as soon as they walk into the house, Delta begins to panic. "Oh my God! Wait here please, Ulysses," Delta rushes through the house. "Uncle Emit!" she calls out with great concern.

Ulysses walks around the lounge room. Papers, textbooks and all sorts of scientific-looking things have been thrown everywhere. A chalkboard has $\pi r^2 \times c$ etched on it, amongst a whole array of other mathematical equations. *Either the place has been ransacked or perhaps a mad scientist lives here.*

Ulysses notices a clock on the far wall. *1:56… that can't be right.* He moves towards it for a closer look and realises the clock has stopped. He then turns and walks into a messy office with a thick wooden desk, three black chairs and a bookshelf overflowing with books. Here he finds something particularly interesting… sitting on the desk are three digital watches and what look like red gemstones spilling out of a little grey sack. He places a couple of gemstones in his hand, studying them.

"Rubies," Ulysses says quietly to himself.

He places the rubies back on the table and picks up one of the watches for a closer inspection. It is an interesting-looking watch, like none he has seen. It appears to be very advanced technologically; with all its inside workings, it certainly doesn't seem to be a traditional watch used simply to tell the time. But even with its technology, it has no screen cover, and it seems to be missing some elements from its inner workings, as there is an empty hole in the lower half, below where the time is displayed. *Perhaps it holds something in there.* Ulysses prepares to put a ruby inside the watch to see if it fits.

"Please be careful when playing with that gizmo," commands a man in an upper-class English accent.

Ulysses quickly turns to see a man looking sternly at him with bright hazel eyes. The man loses his authoritative facial expression and smiles. It seems he was only trying to startle Ulysses for his amusement. Delta comes up beside him.

"Ulysses, this is my Uncle Emit."

"Nice to meet you, Ulysses," Emit says, this time in a more pleasant, gentle tone.

Ulysses now understands where Delta might get her slight accent from. Perhaps her family are English after all.

"Nice to meet you too," Ulysses responds.

They shake hands, the man's grip casually relaxed. Ulysses assumes him to be in his fifties. He is tall, slim, with grey hair that almost reaches his shoulders. He seems slightly effeminate in his movements, which leads Ulysses to wonder if he is gay. His clothing style is neat, in great contrast to his actual living standards. It seems as if he takes care of his appearance but lets his surroundings reduce to almost rubble. Ulysses also notices something else – this man wears the same necklace as Delta and his father.

"I'll leave you both to it. But first, would you like something to drink?" asks Delta.

"Nothing for me, princess," Emit answers.

"Ulysses?"

"Sure, some water will be nice."

Delta nods and leaves the room.

Emit walks behind the desk, picks up the watches and rubies and places them into his desk drawer. His fingers come to rest on the desk and Ulysses notices a silver ring on the index finger of Emit's right hand. It has the same complete symbol that is on the book cover in his backpack.

"Ulysses, please have a seat," Delta's uncle says and motions to the chairs opposite him.

"Thank you." Ulysses places his backpack on the seat next to him. He realises he did not even take notice of this man's name, a habit of his when he meets people. He is often too busy studying people intensely in the initial moments of meeting to remember any name – well, except for women he is attracted to; his mind for some reason works overtime and remembers their names.

He notices on the wall a Ph.D. in physics graduation certificate awarded to an Emit Levart. *That's his name, Emit!* "Thank you, Emit," Ulysses responds as he takes his seat.

"No, it's Emit *(spoken as Emmett)*."

"Sorry, I meant *Emit*," Ulysses apologises, this time saying it correctly.

Emit sits down.

"Apologies about the state of things, Ulysses. My work is becoming very fascinating, all time-consuming."

Ulysses sits silently, studying this man. He gathers as much information as possible, specifically Emit's intentions. Ulysses soon concludes by Emit's body language and the small size of his pupils that there is no intention for ill harm. To the contrary, Emit's eyes speak of warmth and kindness, which puts Ulysses at ease.

"So, you've discovered a theory?" asks Emit.

"How do you know of my theory?"

"All will be revealed. Tell me, has anything changed in your life since this discovery?" he asks intently.

Ulysses cannot help but feel that he is being questioned similarly to what his father was doing earlier over the phone. "What do you mean by…" – Ulysses' attention is momentarily distracted as he notices a clock on the desk has also stopped at 1:56 – "… changed?"

"Has anything amazing happened, anything perhaps you can't explain?"

Ulysses thinks of meeting Delta. "Well, I'm not sure. I have only just completed the theory today."

"I see my niece has done a good job leading you here," Emit smiles as he motions towards the book with the symbol on the front, which partly pokes out of Ulysses' backpack.

"Yes. But why did she lead me here?"

"Delta is serving something greater. Her being in the library at the precise moment that you were was not planned by her, but by a greater power."

"A greater power? What would a greater power wish from me?"

"It wishes only what deep down you have also always wished: for you to realise your greater purpose, Ulysses."

"What makes you sure I have one?"

"You must, otherwise you would not be here. If you are who Delta believes you are, we've been waiting some time for you."

"But I've only just met her today."

"Delta has a unique perspective on life that you don't currently have."

Delta enters the room once more, smiling. She hands Ulysses his glass of water. Ulysses thanks her. He is glad she had the thought to offer him one. Sometimes the hardest thing to do in modern society is to get a complimentary cold glass of water. She turns and leaves the room once more and Ulysses cannot help but wonder why she believes that she knows him. Perhaps she has dreamt of him too, he considers.

"Ulysses, you've discovered something incredible. But you are yet to learn how to control the powers that come with it. We can help you. I'm part of a group that holds the same theory. We have kept its secrets guarded for thousands of years. And over this time, we have come to understand its true potential."

"What is its true potential?"

"It holds the power of all. The world around us is already amazing and filled with magic. The theory just allows us to tap into this magic a little easier."

"Of course! The underlying perfection of the world; you're tapping into it and using its powers!" Ulysses says. He understands this clearly. After all, this is exactly why he had been seeking the theory.

"Precisely. We're discovering new powers all of the time, things that are nothing short of the incredible," Emit says with excitement, his hands expressive. "However, how far one develops their powers on their journey is up to them. Everyone is different. You'll discover your own potential as you go. I'll be very interested to see."

"Are you suggesting that I can somehow gain superpowers, Emit?" Ulysses smirks. And upon saying this he realises how surreal things have become for him. When he first woke up this morning he would have never guessed he could be in this situation right now, having this discussion.

"Yes," Emit answers with a serious conviction. He leans forward, with his index finger raised in the air. "You have more power inside you than you have ever dreamed of, power that must be used for the greater good. Learn how to harness these powers and then, if you pass our tests, become a member of our group."

Ulysses is curious. He wishes to find out what this all means – how this girl is from his dreams, why his father was so concerned that Ulysses had to rush to find the book that led him here, and what this purpose is that Emit speaks of.

"Why should I trust you?"

"Because I'm a good-hearted person with good intentions. You can sense this, Ulysses," Emit says, his eyes sincere.

"I could be wrong," Ulysses smiles.

"A greater force has led you to us for a reason. I'm asking you to take a leap of faith."

Ulysses smile dissipates. "I thank you for your offer, Emit. But I need to speak to my father before I make any decisions. He must know what's happening. After all, he's the one who sent me to the library in search of this book," Ulysses says as he takes hold of his backpack.

"And so it shall be," Emit nods. "If you do decide to come with us, please meet me back here at this house as soon as you possibly can," Emit says and looks down, his eyes suddenly widening as if he has noticed something of great importance.

Ulysses follows Emit's eye line which leads to Emit's ring. It glows a bright red colour, with light blue lines running over the lines of the symbol.

"Delta, come here please," calls Emit in a concerned tone.

Delta enters the room. "Yes, Uncle Emit?"

"The Shadows."

Upon hearing this, Delta appears to become fearful, her face encapsulating a look of trepidation. She touches her temples with two fingers from each hand.

"It's okay," Emit reassures Delta.

"Who are The Shadows?" Ulysses asks.

"We must end this meeting now. We have run out of time."

"Speaking of time, I have noticed that all of the clocks I have seen in this house have stopped."

Emit looks at his watch and realises that it has stopped at 1:56 p.m. He smiles with a large grin, the corner of his eyes becoming wrinkled. He looks at his office clock, then leaps from his chair and runs into the lounge and eyes the other one. He rushes back to his desk, gathering out his watches from inside his desk drawer and discovers that they are all still running.

"It worked!" Emit says with great excitement.

"What worked?" asks Delta.

"My discovery. The reason why my work has become all-consuming since you've been away. The reason why this place is such a mess! My invention has finally worked. At precisely 1:56 p.m. today, my experiment was a success."

"What experiment?" asks Ulysses.

"Time is of the essence, Ulysses," Emit says, holding Ulysses' shoulder and leading him out of the office, Ulysses quickly reaching back to gather his backpack.

"Before I leave, Emit, what is the name of this group you speak of? The group that knows the theory."

"Geno." He pronounces the G similar to the word *gate* rather than the name *George*. Emit pauses to make sure this word has made an impression on Ulysses. It almost seems as if he expects Ulysses to have already heard of the name before.

"Goodbye Delta, nice to meet you."

"Oh, Ulysses, you're not going to come with us to Geno?"

"I'm not sure yet."

Delta attempts to hide it, but Ulysses can see a forlorn sadness in her, as if a big worry, even bigger than The Shadows, has just entered her mind. As he leaves he shares a final intense moment of eye contact with her, savouring it, for it might be the last time he ever sees her. *The girl of his dreams.*

CHAPTER 9

A GREAT DECISION

ULYSSES WALKS BACK through parklands, towards the university. He pulls his phone from his pocket and calls his father.

"Ulysses! Thank God. Are you safe?"

"Yes, Dad. Of course I am."

"Did you find the book and do what's written?"

"Yes. The book said to follow the girl, Delta. She led me to a man named Emit. He is part of a group that supposedly also knows the theory I've discovered. I think their name is Ge…"

"Geno."

"That's right. You know of them?"

"Yes, Ulysses… I am a member of Geno."

"Of course! That explains why you wear the same necklace as Emit and Delta."

"I always knew you would discover this for yourself when the time is right. And now it seems it's time."

Ulysses falls silent for a moment. He struggles to process that there is so much to his existence that he never knew before. The seeds for today were planted long ago. As a child, Ulysses saw the necklace on his father. He has searched to discover the theory of everything for a decade and he first dreamt of Delta two months before he needed to follow her.

He feels as if he was always meant to live this day, as if all of the things that are happening now were always written and it took the theory to push open the doors so that they could finally take place. That bit by bit, through divine fate, he has not only uncovered the secrets of the world but is also slowly uncovering the secret to nothing less than his very existence. And with this, Ulysses is starting to see more clearly the underlying perfection that he has sought to uncover since he was a child.

Yet still, he also cannot help but feel disappointed.

"Are you telling me that I've spent a decade trying to discover a theory that you, being a member of Geno, knew all along? Why didn't you tell me?"

"Well, you never told me what theory you were searching for. Whenever I asked you, you were always secretive."

Damn! He's right. "Tell me about Geno?"

"Geno's a force for good. They use the theory you've discovered to develop their powers and discover great insights."

"Emit wants me to visit this society. What should I do?"

"You have two choices. The first is to go back to your normal life. If you choose this, you must discard the theory. Don't think about it. Just forget you've ever discovered it," Ioannis says with a very serious tone.

"Why do I have to forget it?" Ulysses is considering working on the theory more by himself, and then deciding whether to join Geno or not once he has more clarity about its powers.

"There's a reason why this theory has been guarded by Geno for all of this time. It brings you great abilities. Abilities that attract the attention of those who do not wish you to have them."

"What do you mean?"

"There are opposing forces in this world, Ulysses. It's very important that you understand this. You're bordering on danger as we speak."

"What type of danger?"

There is nothing but silence on the other end of the line.

"I see," Ulysses says.

"Should you choose to delve into the theory more by yourself, the likelihood of your survival is very slim. We can't let that happen," his father says with conviction.

"What's the second choice?"

"It's the one that I prepared you for by sending you to the library. You go to Geno. And under their protection, you learn how to control your powers. And then, if you and Geno both choose, you can join them."

"What do you think I should do?"

"This is not a decision I can make for you. It's only one that you can make."

"Dad, that doesn't help me at all," Ulysses says, frustrated. He needs guidance.

"You know that I've always encouraged you to follow your dreams. I believe very strongly that you have a greater purpose. And I trust that you will naturally be guided towards this. Whatever you choose, I'll stand by you. But please, don't think about the theory anymore unless you're with Geno."

"Okay, Dad."

"Good. Love you. Now stay safe," his father advises, ending the phone call.

Ulysses puts his phone back in his pocket. The large eucalyptus trees that surround the path make him aware of how far he has just walked without realising it. He is now on the final stretch before the library. Only a kilometre further is where, earlier this day, he stood at the entrance of the library, deciding whether he should enter. And now Ulysses is left with another great decision to make.

He can continue in the direction he is going, a path that leads to an ordinary life. The kind of life he would have had if he was not continually searching for the theory. Or he can turn around and take the path back to Emit's. Here he can band with the girl of his dreams and this strange man who reminds him of a mad scientist. Together they can explore the effects of this great theory further. And in doing so, Ulysses has the potential to uncover even more perfection, just like the perfection that has been unfolding before his very eyes all day.

He ponders this decision…

All he has ever wanted was to live the life of his dreams. This is his number one goal. But if knowing the theory is extremely dangerous, then this is an important thing to consider. After all, there is no possibility for the life of his dreams if he is no longer living. Geno is meant to protect him, but how can he be sure they will? Especially if he decides not to join them.

Perhaps this is what people mean when they say to be careful what you wish for, he thinks to himself. All these years he has wished for a theory of everything, to experience the underlying perfection of the world, only to now realise that perhaps he did not truly want this after all.

Ulysses has made his decision. He will try to forget his theory. Instead he will simply live a normal life. A normal life where he will try to make the best of it, just as the average person does… without magic.

CHAPTER 10

THE CATHEDRAL

1303 – Italy.

WEARING A DARK hooded cloak, Orien slinks through the front door of a grand cathedral. Unlike the Gothic cathedrals he visited earlier this day, this Romanesque cathedral is mostly dark, the only external light streaming in through scattered windows.

He strides up the nave, guided by flickering candles that are strategically placed on pillars to assist. His eyes slowly adjust to this low level of light. He can now witness the high ceilings with semicircular arches supported by stout columns. His focus moves to the left side of this cathedral to take in the breathtaking grand frescos, golden statues and other testaments of the great wealth that was spent in creating this place of worship. His eyes then naturally flow to the right side of the cathedral to discover a symmetry with more frescos and statues.

He stops abruptly and stands in the centre of the cathedral. Here the sun shines through a window directly onto him, making it appear as if he shines with light. He extends his palms outward, thirty centimetres from his chest, his thumbs and first two fingers touching to make a triangular shape.

He hears echoic rustlings and looks to see the clergy, who gather in the apse, preparing for worship. Suddenly, they too notice him and seem silently terrified. They quickly divert their eyes in fear, apart from one, the bishop.

Having little time to spare, he walks directly to the altar.

It is obvious that the bishop is the most powerful member in this cathedral. In this time period, great financial riches and power are usually bestowed upon those who are deemed to be closer to God. The bishop proudly wears a mitre and luxurious and jewelled white clothes, while the priests who surround him blend into the darkness with simple long dark gowns.

He thinks of how the Catholic Order is in great contrast to his own. In his Order, everyone is lavished with riches equally, simply for being born into it. This fact instantly makes him feel that his Order is superior. But in defence of Catholicism, he also understands that his Order has a lot more wealth to share around. Certainly not so much wealth that they cannot acquire more, however…

"The time has come," he says to the bishop in Medieval Latin, his deep voice resonating throughout the church.

The bishop nods, turns to one of the clergy, and instructs in his native Medieval Latin, "Errinegedes, get the indulgence proceeds." He turns back and says with a stern look, "Orien, when you go against God, you'll not win. Even if you are immortal."

"God has been my enemy throughout time. But he dare not oppose me. I follow his will as much as my own."

The bishop receives a pot overflowing with a variety of coins from two clergy members. He grunts loudly, his face immediately turning red as he struggles with its heaviness. Orien chooses to put him out of his misery. He reaches over the altar and takes it from the bishop, carrying it effortlessly in his powerful arms.

"From now on I will have others collect this," Orien says. He turns and walks away with the pot.

"Who?" the bishop calls while moving towards Orien.

For the next few seconds all that is heard in the cathedral are the steps of Orien, until he stops in the doorway of the cathedral and faces the bishop once more. "My disciples. They have no name. Purposely. The more invisible they are, the more powerful they can become."

"I shall call them The Shadows then."

Orien pauses and then nods slowly. He removes an item from his cloak. "You will know them by this symbol," he says and tosses a gold pendant the ten metres to the bishop.

The bishop catches the pendant in the palm of his hand, seemingly surprised that he managed to do so. And he studies it. It has a symbol on it – a red triangle.

Orien, his mission complete, leaves this great cathedral with haste.

CHAPTER 11

THE SHADOWS

The present – Gold Coast, Australia.

ULYSSES WALKS ALONG the cemented walkway, nearing the edge of the library building. He is surrounded by eucalyptus trees that inhabit the grasslands to each side of the path.

As he walks, he consciously tries not to think of his theory. However, being immersed in thought as a method to solve dilemmas is a habit of his, especially whilst walking. And besides, the more he tries not to think of the theory, the harder it becomes. It's like when someone says not to think of a pink elephant, all of a sudden a person can't help but picture one.

Ulysses also cannot help but wonder what danger his father spoke of. And why Delta and Emit were suddenly so fearful at their house. *Who are The Shadows?*

Suddenly, his senses are enveloped by a strange vision: he sees two men appear in the distance, amongst the eucalyptus trees. They wear black hooded cloaks over what appear to be black ninja gis. Their bodies are completely covered apart from a slitted opening for their eyes. They rush directly towards him, swiftly and gracefully.

So gracefully that they almost seem like they are floating. As they become closer he notices that each has a symbol of a red triangle in the centre of their cloak.

An intensely ominous sensation flows through Ulysses. *They're coming for me!* Suddenly, he witnesses himself from the third-person perspective. He often notices this switch happens in dreams, just when things get extremely dangerous, perhaps as a way to disassociate himself from the unfolding terror. In the vision, he sees himself panic and run towards the library. But the ninjas are too fast. He has no choice but to turn and face them. One ninja removes the hood of his cloak, draws a sword from behind his back and swiftly strikes it horizontally towards Ulysses' head. There is no way that Ulysses can escape. The sword slices through the air towards him and then... the vision is gone.

What the hell was that? Ninjas? In modern society?

His father did warn Ulysses that he could come into great danger. *Will this vision come true like my last one with the dog?* He certainly hopes not. His heart races as his eyes dart around with great concern, looking amongst the trees for danger. A wave of relief washes over him when he realises that there is no one to be seen. But he is not out of the woods yet.

Desiring the safety of a crowd, he strides towards the library entrance while keeping a watchful eye around him. He sees nothing out of the ordinary. The sunlight trickles through eucalyptus trees. He hears normal bird calls and feels nothing coming towards him apart from a slight wind. His mind must be working overtime. *There is nothing to fear.*

But then he notices them. Amongst the distant eucalypts, two black ninjas wearing cloaks appear.

The vision was true!

Ulysses sprints towards the library. But the ninjas are too fast for him. He turns to face them. He already knows how this will go. He does not wait to see what the closest ninja pulls from behind his back, he simply ducks and screams. The sword just misses him, becoming wedged in a tree.

The second ninja silently moves closer. His hands, covered in black woven gloves, remove his hood and release a powerful sword from behind his back. He lifts it high, ready to come crashing down upon Ulysses. Ulysses doesn't know what he can possibly do. He has, of course, never been trained to defend against ninjas with swords. He simply crouches, placing his backpack before him as a shield. Perhaps the book that has gotten him into all this trouble will block some of the sword's power.

Suddenly the ninja gets a kick to his chest which instantly makes him cease and lower his weapon. Ulysses lowers his backpack to see who this person is. *Delta!* Fighting with a martial art Ulysses has never seen before, she kicks him several more times and throws him onto the ground. The ninja is unconscious. She runs a few steps up the wall of the library and flips over Ulysses to meet the first aggressor. He immediately attacks her, his lightweight cloak flying gracefully with his fluid movements, masking his position and appearing to confuse her. He is extremely fast with his strikes, faster than what Ulysses believes is humanly possible. But somehow Delta manages to fend off this ninja's strikes with blocks and dodges. Finally, she attacks, also bringing him to the ground with a series of lightning-quick blows.

She races to Ulysses' aid.

"Are you alright?" she asks in her strange accent while examining Ulysses.

"Yes, I'm fine," Ulysses replies quickly.

Delta nods and rushes back to the men who attacked him. She places a foot on top of the conscious aggressor's chest. To further make an impression upon him, she shows her necklace, holding it forward so that he can see it. She then kneels and puts her hands together, speaking a prayer out loud.

The once unconscious ninja comes to and looks at her necklace with concern. They verbally signal to one another and rise. One quickly pulls his sword from a tree, the other regathers his sword from the ground. *They are re-arming.*

"Delta!" Ulysses warns her.

But surprisingly, Delta continues to kneel. And the ninjas do not attack her; instead, they swiftly flee, one slightly hobbling as he holds his injured leg and both disappearing into the eucalyptus almost as quickly as they came. Delta stands and walks towards Ulysses.

"Who were those guys!?" Ulysses says in a panic.

"The Shadows! It's a good thing that Emit asked me to keep a watch over you since you left our place. They must know of your powers. We have to get you to Geno as soon as possible. There's no other choice anymore. There is no other decision. It must happen." Delta's voice and demeanour say one thing: *this is very serious.*

CHAPTER 12

ULYSSES JOINS EMIT

Ulysses feels adrenaline pumping through his veins. He does not understand how knowing the theory has put him in such danger. But it is certainly a predicament he does not wish to be in. Thank God Delta was there to save him. And Delta is not all that he is thankful for. If it were not for his psychic vision, he would have been decapitated by the first attacker's sword. His psychic powers are protecting him. This, coupled with having Delta by his side, is leading him to feel a fraction safer.

They return to Emit's orangey-red brick home and notice him in the driveway, packing items into the boot of his car.

"Are you waiting for us?" Ulysses gains Emit's attention. He intended to mask his current anxiety by projecting a cocky bravado, however, he was instantly betrayed with his voice being notice-ably shaken.

"Ulysses! Delta!" Emit says, with a great welcoming smile.

"Uncle Emit." Delta hugs him. She moves her upper body apart from his and speaks with concern, "The Shadows."

"It's okay," he pats her back. They release each other. "Are you both okay?"

"Yes, but I owe my life to your niece," Ulysses answers.

"I think Delta has saved more lives than anyone else in Geno. Perhaps one day you'll pay her back."

Pay her back? Ulysses hopes they are never in an unfortunate situation where he will have to. "Who are The Shadows? And why did they attack me?!" Ulysses needs answers.

"You'll find out in time."

"That's exactly what she said," Ulysses says while motioning to Delta. He is not impressed by all this secrecy. Especially since he is naturally obsessive about finding the meaning for everything.

"Have you decided whether you wish to come to Geno?" Emit asks.

"Do I really have a choice?" Ulysses shrugs.

"I s'pose not. We can collect your belongings on the way."

"Collect my belongings?"

"Geno's in a secret location, deep in the rainforest. It won't be a short trip."

"Great," Ulysses says sarcastically. "Look, I really hate to tell you this but I can't take a long trip. Tomorrow's Monday. I've got work."

Emit laughs, "Ulysses, you've just been attacked by The Shadows. You're in a different world now." He turns and puts some more items in his vehicle. "Besides, I've spoken to your father. He's happy for you to have a leave of absence."

Ulysses does not like the sound of this – travelling to a secret location deep in the rainforest. However, he is comforted that at least his father, someone he trusts, knows what is happening. He is also desperate to get far away from The Shadows, whoever they are. Furthermore, the journey might allow him the opportunity to get to know Delta better and find out why she is in his recurring dreams, a question that often plays upon his mind.

Ulysses nods in acceptance to Emit.

"Goodbye, princess. We shall see you soon." Emit kisses Delta on the cheek.

"Oh, Delta, you're not coming with us?" Ulysses asks, both surprised and disappointed.

"No, goodbye for now, Ulysses. Stay safe. We don't want anything to happen to you. We need you," Delta says, smiling, looking intently into his eyes. He can tell that she is truly pleased he is going to Geno.

He and Emit get into the car, Ulysses keeping his backpack on the floor in the front with him.

"Why isn't Delta coming with us?" Ulysses asks Emit as the car slowly pulls out of the driveway.

"She only just came back to the Gold Coast and wants to do some research here for a theory she's working on – and she mentioned something about needing to buy a brown necklace band?" Emit says with a confused look on his face.

They wave goodbye to her.

"She's creating theories?"

"Yes, of course. She's part of Geno. We're all working on applications of the theory and making great discoveries."

"She must be very smart. And wow, she can fight too. Where did she learn to fight like that?"

Emit laughs. "Delta grew up under much tougher circumstances than you or I, so she naturally has some fight in her. As for the fighting style, it's an ancient martial art that is only used by the people of Geno."

Ulysses is intrigued. An ancient martial art that has remained hidden from the world, and every Geno member is working on applications of the theory. He wonders what other hidden secrets this society keeps from the world.

CHAPTER 13

JOURNEY TO GENO

THEY ARRIVE AT Ulysses' apartment to collect some belongings for the journey ahead.

"Make sure you leave your phone here," Emit instructs.

"Why?"

"The Shadows. They might trace it." He looks into Ulysses' eyes intently.

Ulysses breaks eye contact and simply continues packing. He doesn't say anything in response because he doesn't want to lie. There is no way that he is going deep into the rainforest with a stranger and no ability to contact the outside world. And so, when he has the opportunity, he discreetly puts his phone in his large backpack, albeit turned off.

From Ulysses' home, they drive to Brisbane, the nearby capital city. Here they catch a flight to Cairns, a tropical city in North Queensland.

Throughout the journey, there is a great enthusiasm between Ulysses and Emit. They barely stop talking, discussing deep philosophies. Ulysses thinks this must have been how Freud and Jung were when they first met, enthusiastically discussing theories on topics that modern scientists and experts disregard as nonsense. They speak of synchronicities, of psychic powers, of the theory of everything. However, there are many questions which Emit will not answer and topics he will not go into detail about, always reminding Ulysses that they will be revealed in the right way, the same way it has been for thousands of years to those who come to Geno. And Ulysses will experience this, beginning tomorrow evening.

It is night when they arrive in Cairns. Ulysses feels a blast of intense humidity as they step out of the airplane onto the tarmac. They seem to have left what little there was of winter behind. He immediately takes off his hooded jumper and puts it in his backpack.

Emit laughs, "There are two temperatures in the tropics – hot and hotter."

They then catch a taxi and spend the night at a property which Emit says is indirectly owned by Geno. And the next morning they take a four-wheel drive to the airport. Here, they pick up an unexpected guest.

Delta! She runs up and hugs Emit and then Ulysses. She then pulls back and gives Ulysses a warm smile that etches into his mind.

The three travel in the four-wheel drive, far from the city and deep into the rainforest. Emit drives. Ulysses is in the back seat and Delta is in the front passenger seat reading a book on jewellery making. Ulysses notices this book as being from the overflowing bookshelf in Emit's office.

Delta seems engrossed in this book, only periodically looking up to encourage Emit to slow down so that he does not hit any of the butterflies which fly past the road. They seem to be abundant in this beautiful rainforest.

"This is the Daintree, the oldest surviving rainforest in the world. It dates back to the Jurassic period," Emit speaks, loudly enough for Ulysses to hear in the backseat.

"Does that mean…?" Ulysses begins to ask.

"Yes, this rainforest was once filled with dinosaurs," Emit replies.

Ulysses looks out the window to the trees that completely encase the bitumen roads; he has never seen such a vibrant colour of green. His imagination runs wild as he imagines what this place would have been like millions of years ago.

Eventually, they turn onto a bumpy dirt road and drive as far as it reaches.

"We're on foot from here, Ulysses. This is where the thickest jungle begins," Emit explains.

Following a river stream on their left, they hike upwards through mountainous terrain, all carrying their large backpacks. In the mid-afternoon, they stop at a peak and sit on a long flat boulder that is covered in moss and semi-submerged into the earth. They have some lunch which Delta brought with her.

Ulysses savours the beautiful view from this peak. He can see the tops of many trees. He deeply inhales the pure rainforest air, hearing the wind of his breath so clearly. He is surprised by how peaceful and quiet the rainforest is.

Delta touches his shoulder. "While it's very quiet, this rainforest is richly populated with an abundance of animals," she assures him.

Ulysses looks at her curiously. He tries to read from her if she somehow just read his thoughts. But he quickly realises how futile this is, as in order to read her mind he would have to be able to read thoughts himself.

After lunch, the three continue to hike through the isolated terrain. Delta walks through the forest with grace, her feet skilfully placing themselves in the exact spots to avoid any pitfalls, while Ulysses walks clumsily behind her, often stepping in the wrong places and slipping on things.

However, he soon discovers that there are times when he has a greater natural skill on this hike, compared to Delta. When they take off their shoes and walk through streams of water filled with little stones, he can walk on these tiny stones with ease, whilst Delta struggles.

He thinks of how amazing it is that we all have different innate strengths and weaknesses. If he were ever to be together with some-one like Delta, perhaps their children would be as good walking through the rainforest as they were walking over the little stones in the streams.

But as quickly as he has this thought he pulls himself up. It is true that ever since he first met Delta he has found it difficult not to think of her romantically; after all, he has dreamt about her passionately so many times. But they were just dreams. She's too young for him, he still does not know her very well and he need not indulge in fantasy. Besides, *she isn't quite the same as in my dream. There is something different about her.*

Hours pass into the late afternoon yet onwards they hike. With every step the jungle becomes even thicker and more difficult to pass. Emit leads the way, clearing a path by slashing through the forest with a machete. Delta follows and Ulysses trails her with sweat glistening on his forehead.

Finally, they come to a clearing – a natural lagoon, the most amazing Ulysses has ever seen. Its colour is reminiscent of when he swam in the Blue Lagoon in Iceland, although here the water appears as if it magically glows, with its reflection lighting up the surrounding rainforest. He has read that the Blue Grotto on the Greek island of Kastellorizo has a similar effect, where the mag-nificent colour of the sea water reflects onto the walls inside a cave, but unfortunately his work is yet to take him to the Greek islands.

Suddenly it feels as if time stands still as Ulysses looks upon the powerful lagoon waterfall. He has vivid flashbacks of his dream, of him and Delta standing before it. *This is the waterfall from my dream!* He cannot believe it. How could he dream of Delta and this place when he had never encountered either? Could it be that this dream will become true? He has wondered this ever since he first saw Delta.

He looks over at Delta who drops her backpack. She takes off her jeans, removes her singlet and places them both inside her backpack. She now wears nothing but a red bikini and her necklace. Without hesitation she dives into the lagoon, swims underwater and kicks both legs, swimming like a dolphin. The water glides off her skin as she resurfaces. Her blonde hair is now wet and darkened in colour.

"Come in, Ulysses." She smiles, her head tilted up to him, as she swims on her back. She turns and ducks underwater again, her bottom rising out of the water for a moment as she forces herself to swim deeper.

She resurfaces and swims delicately, with the flow of a dancer. She swims forward and then gracefully spins underwater. It seems as if she is getting all the enjoyment she can from every movement. Ulysses is taken by her playful and carefree nature.

"Go ahead, Ulysses, you look like you could cool down a bit," says Emit as he takes Ulysses' backpack off his shoulders. "This is a way to the base."

"But what about our bags?"

"I can take care of them."

Ulysses nods. He never thought he would wish to swim so badly during winter. He takes off his shirt, puts it in his bag and hands it to Emit. He then casually steps into the lagoon. The water is beautifully clear, but cold, much colder than he thought it would be. It almost makes him change his mind about swimming. However, he is committed now and continues to slowly enter the water, bit by bit. Finally, he is completely immersed in the water and swims breaststroke. His body quickly adapts to the cold and he feels revitalised and happy about his decision to swim.

"Follow me," Delta calls.

She swims towards the waterfall and once she reaches it, she stands on the rocks before it. *Is this going to be the moment from the dream?* Ulysses considers. Suddenly she walks right through the waterfall.

She returns.

"Follow me, Ulysses," she again requests, this time brandishing a cheeky smile.

Ulysses swims towards Delta. As he reaches the waterfall, Delta grabs hold of Ulysses' hand and leads him through. The water splashes them as they pass.

Ulysses is amazed to discover that behind the waterfall is a small cave. Here Emit meets them with a smug smile.

"What took you two so long?" he asks, handing them both their backpacks.

"How did you get here, and you're not even wet?" Ulysses asks.

"The easy way," Emit smiles and points to the path that leads around the lagoon to under the waterfall.

Ulysses cannot be annoyed that he did not know of this short-cut; the cold water has cooled him down, closed his pores and tightened his muscles. He feels invigorated and refreshed.

Delta offers a towel to Ulysses and they both take turns drying off before getting dressed. Once they are ready, they put their backpacks back on their shoulders.

"Geno is not just the name of our group, it's also what we call the location of the Geno base. So, we're about to enter Geno," Emit says. He turns on a small torch and leads them some metres into the cave until they reach a dead end. He takes off his necklace. "Are you ready, Delta?"

Delta nods, removes her necklace up and over her head and takes Emit's necklace from him. She holds them both in her hands, the light of Emit's torch shining onto them. She brings the necklace pendants close together and as if magnetically drawn to each other, they connect, forming the complete circular symbol, the same symbol on the book that led Ulysses to Delta.

Emit follows with the torch as Delta holds the necklaces by the chains and moves the symbol towards a shallow circular impression in the cave wall. Suddenly a blue light shines from the necklaces into this impression. There is a noise that sounds like rocks grinding against each other. The cave walls open.

It's a hidden passage. The necklace is a key, just as his father has always said. A key to a greater knowledge.

"Ulysses… this is Geno," Delta says proudly.

CHAPTER 14

GENO

ULYSSES DISCOVERS THAT beyond the waterfall is a secret paradise, protected and isolated by cliffs.

"It looks incredible!" Ulysses exclaims. He feels a rush of exhilaration from all the visual stimuli.

The sun shines, reflecting the glory of all that it touches. Everything seems different here from what Ulysses has ever laid his eyes upon. The colours of their surroundings are bright and vivid. He is unsure if it is simply because of the great contrast between being in a dark cave and entering back into the light, or if this place is magical.

Emit leads them along a dirt path that winds through the beautiful rainforest. There are giant eucalyptus trees and luscious tropical plants such as tree ferns and palm trees. Birds fly overhead, a green tree frog jumps to a branch nearby, blue butterflies dance through the trees. A rainbow lorikeet flies to Ulysses, lands at his feet and jumps around playfully, as if it wishes his attention. Delta kneels to the bird.

"Ralph, so good to see you," she says enthusiastically, a smile displaying her dimples.

The bird hops around a few more times and then squawks as it flies away.

"Are the animals not afraid of man here?" Ulysses asks.

"Most aren't. Many of the species in Geno have been isolated here since the cliffs surrounding us were first created. The only humans they've ever known have been a part of Geno. The birds come and go, yet they have learned that it's safe here," she replies.

The dirt path turns to marble and the rainforest changes to a spectacular landscaped garden, filled with an array of beautiful green plants and red roses. Scattered purposely through the garden are various manmade items including nude white marble Grecian-style statues, all with plaques underneath. Ulysses notices some plaques engraved in Greek, some in English, and some in a language he believes to be Swedish.

They pass a small grassy oval and then a magnificent water fountain. They walk across a white stone bridge that takes them over a rainforest stream. Here the path turns to dirt and rainforest once more. After a few more minutes they come to a circular clearing of reddish-brown dirt, with coconut palm trees surrounding much of the perimeter.

On the right side of the clearing, there are stone stairs that lead to a majestic circular marble pavilion with Grecian pillars. At the top of the pavilion is the Geno symbol, facing the clearing. Ulysses feels that this pavilion must be of great importance to Geno.

To the left of the clearing is a large grey table with two long bench seats at either side, all made of stone. Further along the left side of the oval is a campfire setting, and further still is a giant fig tree. Running behind all of these objects is a great cliff face.

As they walk across the clearing, Ulysses notices in front of them, at the edge of the oval and a little to the right, is a primitive building that looks like an old shack. Behind the shack is a cabin in the midst of trees and then some larger buildings. To the left of this shack are dirt paths that cut through the rainforest and lead to more wooden cabins in the distance.

On one of the dirt paths hobbles an elderly lady. She is frail, with olive skin. She wears a black traditional widow's outfit with the same necklace as the others hanging prominently on the outside of her dress.

She looks up at them and a smile lights up her face. She enthusiastically waves her arm in the air from side to side and begins to hobble more quickly. Delta and Emit excitedly pace ahead towards her.

"Sophos!" Delta drops her backpack and rushes to greet her.

"Oh, Delta! Emit! You back. Missed you both," the old lady exclaims as she hugs them.

Her attention comes to Ulysses who lags behind. She looks at him curiously.

"Hi, I'm Ulysses," he introduces himself while he studies her. He can instantly tell that her face is kind.

But Sophos does not speak. She simply looks at both Ulysses and Delta together, as if she is considering something very deeply. And then with her brown eyes, she looks into his. "Ulysses! Met before. Must be new one of eight. Pleasure to meet again!" she says in her broken English and an accent that Ulysses assumes to be Greek as she sounds like some of his Greek relatives.

"I'm sorry? One of eight?" Ulysses doesn't recall meeting Sophos, nor does he know what she means.

"Come, Ulysses, I will take you to where you're staying before it gets dark," interrupts Emit.

Ulysses and Emit walk down one of the dirt paths away from the oval. To the left are fruit-bearing trees and a vegetable patch.

"We're self-sustained here, Ulysses. Most of our food is sourced from inside Geno. Our electricity is from the sun; as you can see, some of the larger buildings have solar panels. And there are also small solar lights along the pathways that automatically come on at night," Emit says, pointing at them, acting as a sort of tour guide. "There is no phone reception inside these cliff faces. Nor is there any internet. Besides, those things are strictly forbidden inside Geno."

Ulysses is instantly disappointed. *No phone reception or internet?* He can't help but wonder if maybe this secret society isn't as advanced as he assumed. It also means that he brought his phone for nothing. He doesn't like the idea of being stuck in the middle of nowhere, no matter how beautiful the middle of nowhere is, and being out of contact with the outside world. *What if I just entered a cult?*

They pass over a little wooden bridge that supports them over a small rainforest stream. And then they are once again surrounded by palms, ferns and tree ferns.

"How many members of Geno are there here?" Ulysses asks.

"The members usually only come to the base when they wish to do specific research or cultivate their powers. The exception to this is Sophos, who in her later years has stayed at Geno full time. So, to answer your question, there is only one other member here whom you haven't met – Luke Lukans. He's incredibly gifted," Emit says.

Ulysses hears footsteps patting on the path behind them and turns to find Delta jogging up to them with her backpack. She reaches them, slowing her pace to walk with them.

They turn a corner and in the near distance is a very strong and handsome man standing outside a cabin. He is tall, long-limbed and powerful looking with a muscular stature. His hair is sandy brown, with short sides and length on top. He has a chiselled jaw, strong cheekbones and tanned skin.

"Luke," Emit calls.

Luke smiles upon noticing them. He confidently saunters down the stairs of his cabin and walks towards them.

"Welcome back!" Luke excitedly says in a deep resonating voice. As he reaches them he briefly hugs Emit, patting his back. He then holds Delta delicately.

Ulysses instantly presumes that this must be Delta's boyfriend. After all, it would make sense for a woman like Delta to be with a man who is also in her league. He is also closer to Delta's age. Ulysses guesses he is in his mid-twenties.

Luke leans forward to kiss Delta and she turns her cheek towards him, the side with the three small moles which make a triangle. *A kiss on the cheek but not on the lips; maybe he isn't Delta's partner after all.*

"Luke, this is Ulysses. He has been chosen," Emit introduces.

"*He* is a chosen one?" Luke asks with condescending disbelief. His light green eyes glare down at Ulysses which suddenly makes Ulysses feel quite inadequate.

"I believe he is," Delta says, coming to the defence, which pleases Ulysses even though he is not sure what they are talking about.

"What makes you both so sure?" Luke asks, suspiciously eyeing Delta and Emit.

"He discovered the theory for himself. Synchronicity led him to us. And he is the son of Ioannis," Emit answers.

Luke's demeanour changes from caution to acceptance with the simple mention of Ulysses' father's name. "The son of Ioannis? Well, that's something. Pleasure to meet you, Ulysses," Luke says with a smile and extends his hand.

"Pleasure to meet you too." Ulysses tries to give Luke a firm handshake but has trouble gripping as Luke's hand dwarfs his. With Luke so close to him he realises just how big Luke is. Ulysses is of average height, but Luke must be ten centimetres taller than him.

"Come now, there will be plenty of time to get to know each other," Emit says. He leads Ulysses and Delta further along the path, curving to the left, where they reach a couple of wooden cabins with a shared bathroom in between them. "Here's your cabin, Ulysses." Emit points to the first cabin. Ulysses takes a look inside. It is very basic, with a small desk and chair on the left and a wooden single bed on the right.

Delta walks into the cabin beside his. *She must be staying there.*

"Get yourself organised. We'll have dinner shortly. And afterwards I'll explain Geno to you, in the same way that our Geno members have for thousands of years."

"Do you mean that all of the questions I've asked over the last day will finally be answered?" Ulysses asks with a grin.

"Precisely," Emit says, and he leaves Ulysses.

CHAPTER 15

THE THEORY

AT SUNSET, ULYSSES arrives at the oval. Four flickering bamboo torches stand a few metres from each corner of the stone table. Already seated at the table are members of Geno: Emit, Luke, Sophos and Delta.

Emit welcomes him, "Ulysses, please, take a seat. Sophos has cooked a wonderful feast as a celebration for your arrival and our return."

Ulysses sits beside Delta. She has her hair down; it is the first time he has seen her in this way. She looks just as gorgeous as with her hair in a ponytail, however, now slightly more formal.

Feeling hot and dehydrated due to the humidity of the tropics, the first thing on Ulysses' palate is simply water. "Is it because I am so thirsty or does the water taste much better here than in civilisation?" he asks Delta, instantly feeling stupid for opening a conversation about the taste of water. Surely he has something better to talk to her about.

She smiles, and on the side closest to Ulysses, gently fingers her hair to hook it behind her ear. "It does taste better. It's what I love to drink the most, pure rainforest water. It's sourced from the stream inside Geno," she points to nearby streams of water.

Being seated next to Delta, he cannot help but notice her table etiquette. She sits with perfect posture, keeping her elbows removed from the table at all times. He wonders if maybe this is how they are at Geno and perhaps he should try to be proper too. It is something he knows will take a great conscious effort, as he has not been brought up this way at all. But he looks directly across the table and notices that Luke is sprawling, comfortably relaxed with his elbows wherever he feels like. Ulysses looks at the others. *No, it's only Delta who does this.*

Delta waits for everyone to take their food before she takes hers. She again waits for everyone to begin eating before she does. She certainly appears well versed in table etiquette. He would imagine royalty to have the same social graces as her. Though, upon thinking this, he wonders if royalty would instead take their food and start eating before the others. *Would they, since they are born at a higher status than others?* These are the type of thoughts that continually float through Ulysses' mind, as he tries to figure out absolutely everything, no matter how inconsequential.

As Ulysses thinks about these things that are not particularly important, the Geno members exchange stories of their time apart from one another. Ulysses only sometimes listens, but still finds their joy and openness contagious, so much so that he sometimes finds himself smiling simply from watching them smile.

Delta is quiet most of the time, but whenever she does speak, Ulysses momentarily leaves his thoughts to listen intently. Her conversation flows smoothly as if coming directly from the heart, her topics down to earth. She speaks of the animals she has seen since she has arrived at Geno. Some of them she calls by name as if she knows them very well. She speaks of how she missed the warm night air, and how great it was for her to be under the rainforest waterfall again, even though she has only been gone a few days.

As she speaks, her signature movements and expressions are completely comfortable and relaxed, yet intoxicating in their originality. She does something intriguing with her lips when she finishes speaking, a slight smile that to Ulysses makes her look like a frog. He finds this strangely adorable. He also finds it adorable how when she laughs at the table she completely covers her mouth with her hand, a movement he hasn't seen her do before this evening. This attribute, together with her rehearsed table etiquette, leads Ulysses to picture her as a child in formal environments, trying not to laugh, covering her mouth cheekily to hide her grin and dimples.

But while Delta garners most of his attention, he still cannot figure her out. There are many layers to her. Being an inquisitive person, he certainly finds this interesting about her.

During this dinner, there is a great variety of delicious food available, but everyone only eats small amounts of each dish. They do not gorge themselves at feasts like Ulysses is used to seeing. It is like they eat until they are satisfied and once they are, take no more.

After dinner, they all gather around a now lit campfire, not far from the stone table.

The night sky is cloudy, not even the moon is visible, but the blazing fire brings them light. They sit on logs and pass around a chalice, taking turns drinking the liquid inside.

"What is this?" Ulysses asks, referring to the liquid.

"It will open your eyes. A potion. It's safe to drink," Delta encourages.

He takes a sip. It tastes earthy.

The group becomes quiet, and Ulysses finds himself settling into a comfortable silence as well. After about twenty minutes of simply meditating with his eyes closed, Emit opens them and begins, "Every time we have someone new arrive, we tell the story of Geno and how it began." Emit moves his hands to the front of his body. Suddenly a blue light shines from the palm of his hands. *Magic.* Ulysses can barely believe his eyes.

"First, let's take a step back in time to Ancient Greece," Emit continues, and as he does, inside the blue light appears moving 3D artistic imagery that continually changes in sync with what he speaks of. "Ancient Grecians were seeking great wisdom. In their culture, it was highly prized to discover secrets of the universe and they were very advanced for their time.

"In Ancient Greece, it was asserted that the Earth was a sphere by men such as Pythagoras. The notion that the Earth revolved around the Sun was posed by an astronomer and mathematician called Aristarchus of Samos. Leucippus and his student Democritus, among others, proposed the theory that things are made of atoms, thousands of years before the first tools capable of seeing atoms were invented. And Anaximander developed theories of evolution long before Charles Darwin first published *On the Origin of Species*," Emit says whilst displaying images in the blue light: of wisdom seekers of the past and their discoveries. "Ancient Greece also held a theory which led to the creation of Geno. This theory was discovered by a philosopher…"

The blue light displays moving images of a philosopher. His face is not shown, just outlines of him. He is creating a theory – writing, pondering over many years. He looks at a plant that shines with light, and it comes to him: an epiphany.

Ulysses is amazed! This is precisely how he discovered the theory.

"He was a blue-eyed Greek. Odysseus," Emit says. He stops his visual projection and motions to Ulysses.

"Odysseus is the Greek version of my name."

"Yes. They didn't have surnames in Ancient Greece but if they did his would be Sirius, just as yours is. You see, the theory runs strong in you for a reason. Many of your ancestors have been members of Geno."

Ulysses' eyes widen. There is so much to his ancestors that he never knew before. He knows they too would have listened to this wisdom when they first came to Geno and in this moment he feels deeply connected to them.

"Ulysses, I don't have to pre-warn you that once this theory enters your mind, like Adam and Eve eating the apple, your eyes will be forever opened, since you've already discovered this theory for yourself."

"Yes, only I'm thousands of years behind with my discovery," Ulysses says.

"Thousands of years in the future," Emit corrects Ulysses. "The great formula is: *an element interacts in a system and creates.*"

Ulysses feels tingles in his forehead as this formula enters his mind. He has begun to grasp that it is even more powerful than he first believed.

Emit emits blue light from his hands once again to create a visual projection above the campfire. "Since the beginning of time, this pattern has repeated itself to form everything we see around us. It's in every element, whether it be our hand, a rock, a tree or the sun. As above, so is below. Just as the primary colours are basic yet can be intermixed to create a myriad of colours, this basic formula can explain the entire structure of all that is," he says as he visually displays everything being created in superfast motion; from smaller than an atom, he shows elements creating greater elements all the way up to the known universe.

"Let's go through this process of creation more slowly, with a focus particularly on the creation of a human body.

"Our bodies on a certain level consist purely of subatomic particles. A subatomic particle interacts in a system of subatomic particles and if we were to perceptually switch to a greater level, we would see that this interaction has created an atom," Emit says as he displays this creation.

"This atom interacts in a system of atoms which, at a greater level, creates a chemical element. The chemical element interacts in a system of chemical elements and at a greater level creates a molecule. This formula then goes on to create macromolecules, cell organelles, cells, tissues, organs, until ultimately an organism such as our complete human body is created," Emit says, as finally da Vinci's Vitruvian Man is displayed in his magical projection.

"An element interacts in a system and creates, in this example, through many levels, the human body."

"And just like the human body, everything in existence since the very first elements have been made through this formula. The formula also creates time, gravity, the physical laws, disciplines, ideologies. Even the process of evolution," Emit says as the light from his hands shows a clock, the sun setting over the earth, an apple falling from an apple tree, a chalkboard that seems to be creating physics formulas by an invisible hand, and the rapid turning of several pages in a textbook. Then the projection transforms into what seems like a thousand moving images in one. Ulysses notices monks in a monastery going about their days and countless other moving images, most of which he forgets as soon as they change to the next.

The entire visual then switches to the history of the Earth in super-fast motion. It begins with the Earth being formed in space and then zooms into the Earth. Emit shows how the elements interact with other elements to create things: the earth itself changes, and species of plants and animals are created and continually adapt and evolve into new forms simply through interacting within their systems. The projection constantly magnifies in and out to display these changes in the most amazing way. Changes which may have taken millions of years are displayed in mere seconds. Landmasses move, connect and part, forming new land continents. Lifeforms continually morph and evolve, gaining new features and abilities. Humans are created and the projection ends with a zooming out to see the entire Earth as we would see it today from space. The visual rests with this moving 3D image of the Earth spinning on its axis.

"It's incredible," Ulysses says. He is astounded to see his theory in visual form. It has given rise to the most beautiful creations, including the Earth. While looking at this very lifelike image of Earth, with the blue ocean and continents with clouds moving over them, he cannot help but feel how much love he has in his heart for it, his home.

"Yes, Ulysses. It *is* incredible. All of these forms are created through a simple formula: an element interacts in a system and creates. What's also incredible is that you have discovered this formula for yourself."

"I can hardly believe it. It took me so many years. Yet I feel there's so much more to learn about it."

Delta encourages, "We can help you there. The members of Geno have had the privilege to research it for thousands of years. In this time, we've discovered some incredible insights into this theory."

"Like what?" Ulysses asks.

Delta looks towards Emit as if to seek permission to continue. Emit nods.

"Well… for one, the theory points to elements having greater purposes," Delta says.

"Greater purposes?" Ulysses is curious about her statement. He too has come to understand this. It became apparent to him when he looked upon the plant that was shining in the light. Every part of this plant – the leaves, the stem – were all working towards a greater purpose for the plant. But he is yet to discover his own greater purpose or the meaning of everything for that matter. He believes that he must decipher this if he is to use the theory to live the life of his dreams. Maybe Geno can help with this?

"Perhaps if I explain through using an example," Delta says, and takes a moment to gather her thoughts. "… You and I are both here. We see the campfire, the other members of Geno, the rainforest trees surrounding us. We can look up and see the stars," she says as she points towards all of the things she speaks of. "But there's certainly a lot that we're not perceiving right now. Nor do we usually perceive them in our everyday lives. If it weren't for modern technologies, we wouldn't be aware that inside us are microscopic cells. These cells have their own little world. They have instinctual desires: the desire to live, to consume, to fight off rival cells that invade their territory, to bond with other cells, to reproduce. Each cell goes about their struggles in a way which, if they were conscious to it, might seem to them as being ultimately meaningless and chaotic.

"But we know that their existence isn't purely chaotic, as they have a greater purpose. A meaning to their struggles, *an order*. While they're going about their life, they're creating our hands, our arms, they're protecting us from harmful infections," Delta says passionately, expressively pointing to her palm and then running her finger up her arm and finally making a gesture to her entire body. "You see, their purpose is not just to live, fight, bond and reproduce for themselves. Because while they do this, they also fulfil the purpose of creating a greater element: *us*." She motions to herself and Ulysses. "The cells in our bodies share similar instinctual desires to us as humans. And just as they may not be aware of the greater purposes they are fulfilling…"

"… We may not be aware of the greater purposes we are fulfilling," Ulysses finishes her sentence.

"Yes. But we do have greater meaning. Sometimes as we go about our lives it may seem like it is chaos, but there's an order here. We just can't always see it because of evolutionary design parameters."

"Evolutionary design parameters?"

Delta nods. "We're designed to fulfil our greater purposes. So, we're given the capabilities to help us with this, but not necessarily the ability to perceive the complete overall interaction, such as all of the other interactions, levels and effects of time. This is for good reason. Because, just like the cells, if we were to see the order we are creating, it may actually hinder our ability to fulfil this purpose."

"But this means that I may not learn of the purpose of my life, or the meaning for everything for that matter?" Ulysses says, disappointed. His desire to live the life of his dreams has just encountered a major obstacle, as even Geno who has studied this theory for thousands of years may not have all the answers.

Sophos speaks, pointing her index finger upwards, "May only catch glimpses. And this alright. Don't have to know all. God knows."

"God knows?" Ulysses asks. *Surely this is not Geno's response to such an important question.*

"All systems, levels… arbitrary. Ultimately, one true, all-encompassing system. Alpha to omega. Could call everything. Geno call *God level*. God level, greater purpose of all systems," Sophos answers.

"Wait a minute! Are you saying that God is the ultimate element? And everything is a part of God?"

Delta answers expressively, "We don't know for sure what God is, only that God certainly exists. We call the ultimate level the God level, as it is everything, including God. And so, as Sophos was alluding to, since you're a part of this one true system, you as a single element don't have to know all. Just as a single cell in your body doesn't need to know everything about you. The complete system knows and since you are a connected part of this, you ultimately know too, even if you aren't conscious of it. All we have to do as an individual element is to help fulfil the *greater good* and let the rest of the system take care of the rest."

"What's the greater good?" Ulysses asks and leans forward. "It sounds intriguing."

Luke answers, "The greater good, Ulysses, is what's best for the entire system. It's something I struggle with. It can be very different from what we, individually, believe is good."

"Okay, I think I understand. But how can we tell what's for the good of the entire system?" Ulysses asks.

Sophos answers, "God level communicate us. Many ways. In time, discover."

"Are you saying it's possible to communicate with God?" Ulysses asks unbelievingly.

Delta answers, "Yes, of course. Everything is born of the one source and is ultimately still interconnected in this one system. So, it's possible to connect with other elements in the system, the lower levels and the greater levels. God."

"Really?" Ulysses wants to be sure what he is hearing is correct.

She nods, "Uh-hum. It can be as simple as a cell in your hand communicating with your greater level, asking you to take your hand off a hot stove through sending you a pain signal. You see, to these cells in our body, we would seem like a God to them. The concept is kind of the same."

Ulysses thinks of how all that the Geno members have said is fundamentally the same message that many religions of the world tell us. That there is a greater power called God. God is all-encompassing, the alpha to the omega, the beginning and the end. We are to serve God by doing God's will, which Geno calls the greater good. We can communicate with God, such as people try through prayer. And interestingly, if it is true that God is the ultimate element, then we are literally made in God's image, as we are part of God.

Scientifically, Ulysses thinks, the Geno theory also fits with everything we currently know of the universe. It brings science and religion together, united as one, not opposing forces as they often are in the modern world.

"You know, after I discovered this theory, I had precognitions, visions of the future. I know the theory ultimately points to everything being connected and so I assume this is what makes psychic abilities possible?" Ulysses asks.

Delta nods. "Exactly. Now that you've discovered the theory, you're becoming more aware of how the universe works, which is making your powers stronger. Geno will help you to become even more conscious of these interactions and interconnections and teach you how to control your powers," Delta says.

"I'm looking forward to it." The thought of being able to master his psychic powers is something that greatly excites Ulysses.

Emit speaks, "Ulysses, I think you're now ready to learn how Geno began."

CHAPTER 16

PRESENT SHADOWS

The French Riviera, France.

Leucius sits at a restaurant table. His brown hair is slicked back, his skin tan from being perpetually on holidays. His recent months have been spent in this area of the Mediterranean. His focus glides past his jewelled cufflinks to his diamond watch, both of which have cost him somewhere in the millions of dollars. How much exactly he cannot be sure, as he does not spend much time thinking about small matters. His eyes wander past the luxurious décor until they fixate on an elderly man approaching the table. He has short curly white hair, grey eyes and a white beard. This is Euripedes, and like Leucius, he has a small symbol of a red triangle on the pocket of his designer suit jacket. He takes a seat at the table before Leucius.

"Why did you wish to meet with me, Leucius?" Euripedes instantly questions. Leucius senses by his tone that Euripedes strongly believes his time is more important than Leucius'. Something that Leucius is used to, as according to The Shadows, it is.

"Master of Shadows, one of the general public has shown powers."

"How?"

"He managed to save an animal before it was hit by a car, all because of a precognitive vision."

"And you know this how?"

"He admitted his precognition to the driver of the car. The driver is one of us."

"I see. And was he taken care of?" Euripedes asks as he butters a bread roll.

"Two Shadow Enforcers were sent to his location on the Gold Coast, Australia. However, they were prevented by a female member of Geno. The public member is with her now."

"Who is this member of the public?"

"We're still trying to find out."

"Don't bother, it's too late now. As you said, he's with Geno. They will protect him," Euripedes gives a flick of his wrist and then picks up his bread roll and begins eating it.

"Master…" Leucius leans forward to ensure his point is conveyed. "We rule the world, without question. But there is one threat to our bloodline's prosperity: enlightened people. Yet when it comes to Geno, we do nothing? There's only a maximum of eight Geno members at any one time. Surely, we can overpower and destroy them, once and for all?"

"Geno is stronger than you think. Besides, Orien has forbidden us to ever become involved with any Geno member, or their affairs, without his express permission."

"And why is that?" Leucius leans back again.

"It has always been this way. We keep to traditions here." Euripides, now finished with the bread roll, devours a glass of water.

"Yes, and to our detriment. Maybe if our Enforcers weren't using such archaic weapons we could have defeated this public member before he had a chance to be rescued."

"You must remember that even though we rule the world, it doesn't mean that the world is conscious of our rule. We must be secretive. Swords can be used for many purposes, one being that they leave little evidence behind. They are everything our Enforcers require."

"We have all of the money in the world for research. Couldn't we at least make their swords more technologically advanced? I mean, one Enforcer's sword got stuck in a tree for God's sake! We could create light sabres. If you think swords leave little evidence behind, try tracing light," Leucius smiles mockingly.

"As I said, we keep to traditions here." Euripedes leans forward, his forehead crinkling. "You're still young, Leucius. The young of every generation always wish to mess with the current traditions. They blindly believe that they know the right way and that their elders are completely wrong. I was once like you. I am old now and believe me, I've discovered time and time again that there is a reason why we do things the way we do. It's a flaw of your youth that your will for change is not yet matched with wisdom. The wisdom that we cannot change existing structures without greatly suffering unexpected consequences, no matter how idealistic we are."

"I don't agree," Leucius says.

"Well, agree with this!" Euripedes suddenly points his finger at Leucius vehemently, his voice angry. "Everything you have is because of your ancestors. Your wealth. Your prosperity. Your superior genetics. And many of these luxuries you enjoy are products of traditions that have been kept for thousands of years. Traditions that have been kept for a reason. Because they've been proven to work."

"Yes, but it doesn't mean they will continue to work in the future. Or that they can't be improved upon, for that matter."

"What gives you such desire, Leucius? You have everything you've ever wished for. Yet you still want more?"

"Respectfully, I have never met a Shadow member who didn't want more, not even yourself, Master."

Euripedes immediately looks down and nods solemnly in agreement. His voice becomes quieter and he emphasises his words, "We are all but mortal men... But I have the privilege to speak on an immortal's behalf: Orien. He has a plan. Do not question this. And until he returns we are not to change anything."

"How do we even know Orien exists? A man who has existed for all time – it's hard to believe. It sounds mythical."

Euripedes looks up once again and intensely into Leucius' eyes, "I would expect one of the public Shadows to say something like this, but not you. You hold the symbol of the red triangle because you know the truth about Orien. You've been taught about him since your very birth. You're one of a small percentage of Shadows who have ever heard his name. You've seen photos of him, paintings, statues, all from different periods of history, yet still, you don't believe?!"

"Even if Orien did once exist, it doesn't mean he's still alive. No one has heard from him for almost a century. Well, not unless you believe that silly rumour from fifteen years ago," Leucius smirks.

"He is immortal, he cannot die. Besides, he has disappeared for centuries at a time before, you know. We must maintain faith that he will return and that there is a reason for all of this. Now, I've been entrusted to rule in Orien's place. And you are second in line. Yet I'm suddenly worried about what will happen to the order if something were to become of me."

"Why would you be worried something would happen to you?" Euripedes eyes widen and look at Leucius intently.

Leucius stands. "You've been a great service to The Shadows." He quickly draws a pistol and releases a bullet into Euripedes' chest. The ringing of the gunshot immediately brings forth a chaotic scene with terrifying screams from patrons of the restaurant. Euripedes is killed instantly. Blood seeps through Euripedes' fine jacket, the red triangle symbol becoming filled with blood.

"Well that's really beautiful," Leucius says in great awe. To him, the blood is creating art. He puts in his earphones, instantly playing Beethoven's *Moonlight Sonata*. The sounds take his mind away. He casually walks from the table. And even though there is an ensuing panic in the restaurant, time slows down for Leucius, allowing him to walk through the disorder effortlessly. He misses obstacles that come his way as if he is in a great rhythm with this chaos. And in a matter of seconds, he has left the restaurant and glides into a waiting black luxury vehicle.

CHAPTER 17

GENO'S HISTORY

Geno, Australia.

ULYSSES IS STILL sitting at the campfire with Delta, Sophos, Luke and Emit. Emit enthusiastically explains how Geno began. "Odysseus knew the importance of the theory and studied it deeply, discovering great insights and gaining special powers. He wished to share his theory with others in Ancient Greece, but only where it was of the greater good. He knew that synchronicity is a method to know the will of the other levels, potentially even the God level. So, he created the Geno book. A book that could lead people to him in a structured way which was undeniable in its synchronicity. And therefore, more likely of the greater good."

"The book that led me to Delta."

"Precisely! Even today, it is through this book that we discover our new members. Just as in the ancient world, where seven were led to Odysseus. They were taught the theory and thus a secret society was born: *Geno*. Together this group of eight discovered further knowledge of the theory and the powers that come with it, all in great secrecy."

"Why in secrecy? Why can't Geno share its wisdom with the world?" Ulysses asks.

"The theory gives us great powers, Ulysses. History has shown that those with magical powers are not treated very favourably by others, just as you were put in danger earlier and needed the help of Delta."

"Yes, can you now tell me who those people are and why they attacked me?"

"They are part of an ancient secret society, a related brotherhood. Their objective is purely the success of their bloodline, which they achieve through having mankind, even the world itself, under a deep control."

"What type of control are we talking about?"

"They have power over the economic system, the fossil fuels, the media, politics, the educational system. They have even infiltrated the church. They stop at nothing to gain more power. They pollute the planet. They kill nature. They bend the values of society. They create great division. Some disciples go so far as to create wars."

"Emit, are you saying that the people who attacked me are a part of a society that secretly rules the world?"

"Kings, queens, presidents, prime ministers and emperors are rarely the ones truly in power. For being a figurehead puts you in great danger. Those truly in power keep their identities secret. They are untraceable. Their wealth will never make the rich list; it is hidden from public records. They are like ghosts, and for this reason, they are known as…"

"The Shadows," Ulysses interrupts.

Emit nods. "Precisely. Their biggest threats are enlightened people and thus they seek to end anyone who gains magical powers. Which is why they tried to end you, Ulysses. And why Geno's wisdom must remain hidden until the world is ready for it. We cannot put people in grave danger."

"Do you think the world will ever be ready for the secrets of Geno?" Ulysses asks.

"One day, yes. But we've waited a long time. Millenniums have passed since Geno began in Ancient Greece."

"Tell me more about Geno? How many of you are there?"

"There are usually eight members in any time period, just like when Geno began. There are no leaders. Everyone is equal. And we're all working on new insights through knowledge of the theory. Our current members are Delta, Luke, Sophos and I, as well as three other members who are not present. Your father is one of them."

Ulysses' eyes travel past the members of Geno. He looks at Sophos and Luke. His eyes then rest on Delta. She sits at the campfire with a breathtaking serenity. Her long hair rests on her shoulders. She has a delicate, yet powerful beauty, one in which Ulysses almost loses himself for a moment. He regains his focus. *There's also my father as well as two others.*

"But that is only a total of seven members?"

"Yes, Ulysses, we are looking for our eighth member, the chosen one. And tomorrow we will continue to open your eyes."

Emit stands, and with a quick movement of his hand he creates a powerful gust of wind that magically extinguishes the fire. The meeting is over.

CHAPTER 18

THE SAGE

Ulysses sits on a long wooden log, alone. Only cinders remain of the campfire, lighting Ulysses with a dull glow. *Geno. What an amazing place. I never dreamt that such a place could exist.*

There is perfection here, the same he has been searching for his entire life. Yet he feels uncomfortable. It's like he has discovered perfection, but deep down he wonders if he is ready for it.

"Ulysses," a lady's voice says from behind him; it jolts him until he realises who she is.

"Oh, it's you, Sophos."

"Sorry to startle," she says in her Greek accent.

"That's okay. I was just deep in thought."

"Yes, could see at dinner you think very deeply, not often in present."

"I have lots to think about."

Sophos lowers herself and sits next to him on the log. Her black widow's attire blends into the darkness of night. The flickers of light from the fire rhythmically illuminate different parts of her. "You searching. Often see when people first come to Geno. Habituated to searching, cannot switch off. Always try to get somewhere, don't know what to do once there. Same if modern man suddenly back Garden of Eden. Would search, would wonder if ready for perfection."

"What is the answer, then?" Ulysses asks.

"Every moment lies perfection. No need to search. All around, within. Always been ready to live perfection. Simply need to realise," she says as she gestures towards him. "Here to do good, Ulysses. Everything meant to be," Sophos says.

"How can you be so sure?" Ulysses asks.

"I see everything. Past, present, future, the time between time."

"The time between time? What's that?" Ulysses has never heard of such a thing.

"The time between time, where magic really happens. Eternal perfection. Realm of God. If cannot see, put faith in God, for God can."

Ulysses appears confused upon hearing this.

"Okay if not understand. Soon will. Become as simple to understand as plant shining in sun."

Her words remind Ulysses of how he discovered his theory. There is so much to learn and Ulysses feels like a child again, learning about the nature of the world with a fresh set of eyes and being open to incredible possibilities. His thoughts drift to his father, and he wonders what it was like for him when he first came to Geno.

"Your father great man. One of most magically gifted ever be Geno."

Ulysses nods, speechless that her words led directly from his thoughts. It is like she can see right through him. Every thought. Everything.

"Tell me. How was he when he first came here?"

"Beginning much like you, searching, but grew to love here. Natural philosopher. Run around, discover insights. Always wear jacket even when hot. Brash, break rules, cause troubles. But underlying all, always follow heart. Heart soon focused elsewhere, growing family,"

Sophos says as she briefly points to Ulysses. "Stopped coming Geno. Moved to desert, protect loved ones, help world from there."

"Wait, are you saying that we grew up in the outback as a way to protect us? Protect us from what?"

"Shadows. Just in case." Sophos touches him gently on the shoulder, her brown eyes looking directly into his. "Become clearer every day. Rest now. Just know, I know who you are. I believe in you."

Ulysses is instantly touched by her words. Sophos seems wise, all-knowing, yet also has the power to connect with him so simply. And in this moment, he thinks of how people are drawn in life to those who connect with them. Perhaps it is because we walk most of our lives alone, with hidden thoughts and experiences that only we will ever see. We desire others to share our world view even if it is simply for a beautiful moment. For them to understand what we see, to cherish and appreciate it.

Sophos stands and kisses Ulysses on the forehead. "Good night, Ulysses."

She turns and hobbles away across the oval and towards the shack, along a path lit by small solar-powered lights.

CHAPTER 19

DELTA'S PASSION

THE MORNING SUN has truly risen when Ulysses steps out of his cabin. He walks along the path and comes to the area which is growing fruit and vegetables. Here he sees Delta on her knees, studying plants, taking notes with a small pad and pen. She is so deeply focused on her task that Ulysses hesitates as to whether he should interrupt her.

But as though Delta could sense him, she turns around. "Good morning, Ulysses," she says in her strange accent and smiles welcomingly.

"Hi, Delta," he says as his eyes capture her beauty. Her hair is in a ponytail, glistening with the sun. "Emit mentioned that you're researching something. I'm curious, are you working on a certain aspect of the theory?"

"Yes. I'm using your theory to find discoveries that can help the natural world. You see, I believe that all animals and plants have a place. As Sophos says, *you even need the fly in this world.*"

Ulysses, too, is fascinated by nature. As a child he would walk around his back yard, studying every plant and animal he could find. To find Delta shares his interests makes him more endeared towards her. "I love nature too. I always thought that I would study it one day, but then I reconsidered, as working with nature doesn't pay very well," Ulysses says, instantly regretting his words for they make him sound shallow.

Delta smiles. "Really? That's so great that you love nature too. It's my passion. I'm actually doing a degree in environmental studies, but yes, I'm certainly not pursuing this for the money."

"I'm sorry. I didn't mean to say that. It was very superficial of me."

"That's okay."

"Are you researching anything specific at the moment?"

"Yes, I'm working on how your theory expands on the current theory of evolution. You see, science currently views evolutionary changes as being random genetic mutations, but your theory points to the genetic mutations being caused by interactions between the elements, elements which have greater elemental purposes. Therefore, evolution may ultimately be a purposeful, ordered and meaningful process, where even if some of the evolutions are random, the reason why evolution takes place is teleological."

Ulysses is silent as he tries to process what Delta has said.

"Basically, evolution is meaningful. For a purpose!" Delta clarifies.

"Wow, it will be amazing if you can prove that!"

"I have already begun to prove this. I call this new theoretical aspect of evolution, *eveolution*. It embraces a purposeful, multi-dimensional understanding, in the sense that each evolution and adaptation may involve the interactions and possibly even the desires of many different interconnected elements, systems and levels, both now and throughout time.

"Instincts could also come about in the same way, as could the formation of emotions, even phenomena such as fertility rates," Delta says enthusiastically. She suddenly seems to realise that her passion is taking over and she is speaking very fast, so she looks at

Ulysses intently and slows herself down. "There are so many topics that are yet to be explored and I wish to use your theory to understand and help nature in so many ways."

"You're on such a noble quest, Delta. Geno must be very proud of you. It's incredible how the theory can be applied to so many areas," Ulysses says, recalling the day he first discovered the theory in its entirety and held the printed version in his hands. It felt so powerful.

She nods to Ulysses. "It's a theory of everything. It can be applied to everything."

"Has your work ever been published in a journal before?" he asks.

"My contributions at the university have, but nothing to do with my research here at Geno. I'm unsure if I'll ever be able to publish any of my work here; after all, your theory is a secret held by only us. Maybe one day, the world will be ready. But for now, my research will just be for the advancement of our knowledge here at Geno."

Ulysses glances down at her notepad and notices that her writing is unreadable to him. It seems to him as if it is in another language. Either that or it is very messy. "Is this why your writing is unreadable? To keep your findings secret?"

"One of the reasons, yes. If I were to lose my notepad outside of Geno, it could mean trouble."

"Delta," Ulysses' voice softens with concern, "doesn't it bother you that you're working on potentially world-changing theories, yet you can't share them with the world? I mean, someone else may come up with these theories while you're keeping it secret and then you'll never receive any credit for your discoveries. You'll never be known for coming up with these amazing insights."

"Oh, I'm not doing this work for any recognition. I'm doing this to help the world. When the world is ready for it, the world will know it. Whether they learn it from myself or someone else, it's not important. The important thing is that people will know when the time is right," Delta says, looking up at Ulysses.

Ulysses again feels like a fool for saying something so shallow. His words were in part a reflection of his own situation, as when he first discovered his theory of everything he had every intention to publish it. He had already fantasised for many years about going down in history as a great mind like his personal heroes Einstein, Newton, the Ancient Greek philosophers and so on. *Imagine discovering one of the greatest secrets of the universe.* A secret that may help himself and others to live their lives to the fullest. Surely that is an accomplishment to be proud of and one he would like to be known for.

However, now that he is aware that Geno has already discovered the theory thousands of years before, it would not be right for him to claim credit for its discovery, as he was not the first to discover it. Even if the world does not yet know of the theory, he knows the truth and so he would not feel right.

It is a difficult fate to assign himself to, the prospect of discovering a great theory and never receiving accolades. But with Delta, it comes so naturally. She has the potential to be the most famous girl in the world with her brains and her beauty, admired by all. Yet all she wants is to help the world, so much so that she does not mind if she ever receives any credit for her amazing contributions.

It is clear to Ulysses that even though Delta is years younger, she is far more advanced than him in many ways. He feels inspired and happy with the knowledge that Delta is using her unique talents to change the world for the better, that there is a person out there who cares and is on a quest for good. He just hopes that the world gives her as much back as what she gives it. Looking at her this morning, watching her study nature, he feels that Delta and the world around her have a very beautiful and harmonious relationship.

Suddenly a large wolf-like animal walks with a strange gait from the surrounding rainforest. It has stripes on its back and a long tail that sticks out horizontally. Ulysses is startled until he realises that the animal means no harm. Still, his surprise has not subsided, his body alert with excitement. He eyes it intently as it briskly moves past. It disappears into the forest.

"Was that a…?" Ulysses asks.

"Yes."

"But they're extinct!"

"No, thylacines are certainly alive and well. This region of the rainforest, with cliffs on both sides, had remained undisturbed by man until we arrived. There are many animals here that people believe to be extinct and even some which are new discoveries," Delta says.

"I can't believe it! A Tasmanian tiger!" Ulysses exclaims. He always hoped that the thylacine, the Tasmanian tiger as it is better known, still existed. He never expected it to be so far north of Tasmania. Though he does remember reading that they were once very prominent on the mainland. "What other extinct animals are here?" he asks enthusiastically.

"It will be more fun to wait until you see them by chance. I liked seeing you have such a look of surprise when you spotted your first thylacine," Delta says, smiling.

Ulysses smiles. "I literally can't believe it. I'm so glad to know that some animals we believe are gone still actually exist."

"Me too. Yet so many animals are extinct. We're certainly not in as much harmony with nature as when I was very young. This is why I'm dedicating my life to protecting the environment. My dream is to contribute in whatever small way I can to help mankind to change its ways."

Ulysses nods. And suddenly he becomes conscious that he is taking up Delta's time, time which could be spent on her research, making great discoveries, and living her passions. "I'm really fascinated by your work and I'd love to talk more with you at another time."

"I would love to share more with you, Ulysses. No one at Geno has taken an interest in my work before, apart for Sophos and Emit."

"Well, now you can include me too."

She smiles. "I would love to hear about your dreams too, Ulysses."

Her words lead Ulysses to instantly think of his recurring dream. "I would not only love you to hear my dreams, but also see my dreams for yourself one day."

"Okay, that sounds great," Delta says and chuckles, her dimples showing.

As Ulysses walks away, he briefly looks back over his shoulder to see that Delta has returned to studying the plants. She moves some of the soil around them. To Ulysses, she looks like an angel who is so humble that she is willing to toil on the Earth. And suddenly, in this moment, she physically appears to him to be more like she did in his recurring dreams. More perfect. More divine. *How could this be?*

CHAPTER 20

THE PERFECT MINDSET

IT'S LATE MORNING in Geno. Ulysses sits on the stairs leading to the Grecian pavilion while Emit stands on the soil before him.

Emit speaks in his posh English accent, "In the mornings we'll meet here and I'll teach you how to control your magical powers. And in the afternoons, over there by the big fig tree, Luke will teach you how to defend yourself using the Geno martial arts," he says as he points across the oval to the fig. "Outside of these lessons, you have free time to do whatever you wish."

Free time. Ulysses wonders how he could possibly fill it out in the middle of nowhere. "How long do I have to be here, at Geno?"

"It depends how long it takes you to become proficient with your powers and the Geno martial arts."

"I just want to be skilled enough so that I'm safe to go home," Ulysses says earnestly. As incredible as Geno has been so far, he feels a prisoner knowing that his only choices are to either be in the safety of Geno or perish at the hands of The Shadows.

"And this is precisely what these lessons are designed to achieve. The more you master them, the safer you will be when you go home. We'll begin by teaching you the basics. But if you pass our test and become a member of Geno, we'll teach you our greatest skills, as it is only our members that we teach the most advanced wisdom to."

"And what test do I have to pass to become a member of Geno?"

"Last night I spoke of how the founding members of Geno were led to Odysseus through the Geno book. Thus, they passed *the test of synchronicity*. You are at this precise point, Ulysses.

"But there's also a second and final test. You see, in Ancient Greece, when Odysseus and the other original Geno members learned the theory, they unexpectedly gained magical powers. And much like you, they were unable to control them. So, together, they created a system. Its purpose – to help them to reach self-actualisation."

Self-actualisation. Ulysses is familiar with the term. He researched many disciplines while working on his theory, psychology being one of these. He has learnt that self-actualisation is the state of being where one reaches their complete potential. A concept he has been particularly interested in for one special reason: "If a person reaches self-actualisation, does this mean they'll be living the life of their dreams?" he asks Emit, curiously.

"Precisely! Being self-actualised is the ultimate level of enlightened wisdom. It can give you whatever you truly wish for in life. Contentment, health, wealth, success."

A glimmer of hope comes to Ulysses. All this time he has been trying to live the perfect life. And now it seems that Geno might have the answers after all!

Emit continues, "Self-actualisation also gives us the ability to control our magical powers. This is important as in order to strengthen your powers you must first have them under control.

"Furthermore, self-actualisation is also a direct path to fulfilling our purposes here at Geno. And so, only those that are led to us through synchronicity and go on to become self-actualised can choose to be a member of Geno. Such will be the case with you, Ulysses."

"And you said that the original members developed a system to become self-actualised?"

Emit nods, "*The Perfect Mindset.* Drawn from the theory, it is an adaptable system of eight principles, with each original member having contributed one principle each. You can follow them in whichever order you wish to suit a particular situation. But you must achieve all of these principles continually to attain and keep self-actualisation.

"Are you ready to learn the perfect mindset, Ulysses?"

Whether or not Ulysses chooses to become a member of Geno, he is very excited to self-actualise and learn to control his powers. He also knows that his father, being a member of Geno, must have learned these principles. And he is a great man. A man whose footsteps Ulysses will gladly follow.

"I'm ready," Ulysses answers.

CHAPTER 21

UNCOVER AND HOLD
YOUR PRIMARY DESIRES

EMIT AND ULYSSES are at the Grecian pavilion, deep in the rainforest.

"The first principle of the perfect mindset is: *Uncover and hold your primary desires,*" Emit says.

"What are primary desires?" Ulysses asks. He has never heard of them before.

"You know the theory: *An element interacts in a system and creates.* But there's also what came before this. What existed before time, what exists regardless of time. This is the primary. It underlies all things, even in the present," Emit says as he walks around in front of Ulysses, his hands flowing enthusiastically as he speaks. "The primary cannot be created or destroyed, only uncovered. *An element interacts in a system and uncovers.* And it is through the primary that you uncover your deepest desires."

Emit has successfully captured Ulysses' interest. "How do I uncover my primary desires?"

"Ask the answers, Ulysses."

"Sorry?"

"The primary is already a deep part of you. And thus, whatever you seek to know of it, a part of you already knows the answer. Let me guide you... What's something you desire?" Emit asks, seeming very enthused to play this game, his fingers upright and touching together in anticipation.

"Well, I've always wanted to own a mansion near the beach," Ulysses answers, his reply swift as he often thinks about the objects of his desire.

"I see. And why do you wish for this mansion?" Emit asks, his expression becoming poker-like, as if he does not wish to display any emotion that could lead Ulysses' answers.

"I think it'll be a great lifestyle, waking up in such luxury. I'll feel like I've finally made it in life," Ulysses says passionately.

"And why's it important to wake up in such luxury and to have made it in life?"

"Well, I want to be proud of myself, I want to be admired by others. I want to live a life I love," Ulysses says as he watches Emit curiously, trying to decipher what he is getting at.

"And why do you wish to be proud of yourself and admired by others?"

"Well... it sounds stupid, but I guess I want to love myself and be loved by others."

"Aha," Emit smiles. "Your deepest desires when it comes to owning a mansion are to love yourself, your life and to be loved by others. Do you see the theme here?"

"It's all about love?"

"Precisely! Love is everybody's primary desire. Now, in contrast to the primary is the secondary. The secondary is created through the great formula and therefore is time-based. Buying a mansion, meeting the partner of your dreams and having a great career are all examples of secondary desires. And because secondary desires are created through time, you may only be able to achieve them at certain points in your life," Emit says as he leans on his right leg which he raises on a step.

"Now, listen to this carefully, Ulysses," Emit leans in, his expression becomes serious and his voice quieter. "Because our primary desires often underlie our secondary desires, people in society desperately try to achieve their secondary desires as a way to reach the primary. They believe that once they achieve a career milestone people will love them because of this. Or in your example, once you buy a mansion, you'll have love in your life. But this isn't the best method."

"Are you saying that secondary desires are bad?" Ulysses asks, confused.

"No, certainly not." Emit's voice returns to his normal volume and he walks in front of Ulysses once more. "Secondary desires might lead you to, say, create a great painting, a great relationship and offer many other wonderful gifts in life. Furthermore, secondary desires are necessary to live our purposes in this life."

"So, what's the answer then?"

"The answer is to *hold your primary desires as you move towards your secondary desires.* Remember, primary desires are not created through time, so you can have them your entire life through. For example, if you wish to receive love, there's no need to wait. Love is abundant and exists in every moment. It's all around and within you, simply waiting to be uncovered."

Ulysses suddenly realises that he has been going towards secondary desires his entire life as an attempt to achieve his primary desires. He has attempted to find love through his goals of having the ideal body, of one day getting a mansion, discovering his theory and so on. But there is a problem with this. Because whatever love he receives through secondary desires is conditional love. And what he truly wishes for is unconditional love. It feels like a veil has been lifted from his eyes. "I get it now! You're saying that my experience of life will be greater if I hold my primary desires in every moment. That this way I will feel unconditionally fulfilled and content throughout my entire life. Regardless of what happens."

"Precisely. You're also more likely to achieve your secondary desires and enjoy them once you do," Emit pauses for a moment, his index finger raised in the air. He then looks back at Ulysses. "Okay, I think you're ready. Let's uncover your primary desires."

"What, right now?"

"Yes," Emit replies with a staunch certainty. "Go forth into the garden where the statues are and only return when you have reached a state of complete love," Emit commands while pointing in the direction of the garden. He then gives Ulysses detailed instructions.

*

Ulysses reluctantly walks by himself to the garden, feeling embarrassed to even attempt what Emit has instructed of him. *I have to uncover love? Really?* But despite his protesting thoughts, he wishes so deeply to self-actualise that he is willing to give it a try.

He arrives at the garden and walks towards a beautiful mirror that is encrusted with gold. It is grand and wonderful. He stands before it and closes his eyes, making the wish to be *open to giving and receiving love*, just as Emit commanded.

He reopens his eyes and starts within, desiring to see love in his reflection. But he does not see love. Instead, he sees the usual imperfections he has grown accustomed to. He sees the slight lines on his forehead and wrinkles around his eyes. He removes his shirt and, as usual, discerns that he is carrying too much weight around his lower abdominals. *Damn.* A part of him was hoping this majestic mirror was somehow magical. That by simply looking into it he would transform into something he could love.

But Emit has prepared him for this: "*If you struggle with loving that which you desire, then slowly turn up the good. First, choose to be content. Then turn this contentment into appreciation. And then, finally, uncover love.*"

Contentment. Ulysses wills himself to accept this image reflected at him. Thoughts immediately come to his mind which oppose this acceptance, but he chooses not to debate with them. Instead, he keeps leading his mind towards contentment. Eventually, he loses all judgement and simply accepts himself as he is in this present moment.

Appreciation. Ulysses momentarily moves his focus from the mirror, choosing to begin with the simpler task of appreciating his hands, directly before him. He notices that when he moves his left wrist, he can see a small hard cyst near it, on the back of this hand. The fact that he has never noticed it before is not surprising, as it has been some time since he has really looked at his hands. Yet while he seldom pays conscious attention to them, he knows that they do so much for him. Day in and day out, his hands work tirelessly. *What a blessing they are.* He uses one hand to touch the other lightly. They are perfectly designed to feel touch, a gentle caress. He runs his fingers through the gaps between the fingers of his other hand. He then touches his forearm. It certainly feels pleasurable to feel touch, and sometimes Ulysses forgets this.

His eyes then travel over the rest of his body. He thinks of how things may come and go around him, but the one thing he will always have in this life is his body, comforting and carrying him. For this he feels deep gratitude.

He looks back towards the mirror, hesitantly. But to his amazement, he discovers that he is now pleased with this familiar reflection that stares back at him. He no longer sees flaws in his appearance. His slight wrinkles are not wrinkles anymore, they are smile lines and collections of experiences that make up his life. He looks at his shirtless body and understands the purpose of the extra fat around his abdominals. It is his body simply reacting to the energy he gives it and storing this excess energy as a potential survival mechanism. A great number of times he has hated his body for this when he should simply appreciate it for doing what it is designed to do. It is adapting to whatever he gives it and doing its best purely so that he can achieve what he wishes in life. He now understands his body's purpose. His body is love.

Yet while his body has taken such great care of him, he has not given his body the same care back. He has not loved his vessel as much as it loves him. He notices the tension in his shoulders that he has been holding for some time, and upon this realisation, releases it. *The unnecessary stress I put on myself when I should be filling myself with love. I must begin now.*

Love. Ulysses consciously turns his appreciation into love and instantly sees himself even more incredibly. Yes, he truly loves his reflection, but it is more than that; when he looks in this mirror he suddenly witnesses not only his physical elements but also the energy that is inside of him. It is the unconditional love of all that he is. His entirety.

This love for himself feels like a rediscovery rather than a discovery, as if this love has always been present within him and all he had to do was uncover it.

Ulysses is drawn closer to this magical mirror and looks directly into his eyes. They are striking, blue with tinges of gold inside them. It is as if he can see the beauty of all creation in his eyes whilst simultaneously looking deeply into his soul. A great warmth vibrates in the middle of his chest, as if his heart is glowing. A smile comes to his face. He believes that he finally sees himself as he truly is. A divine creation.

He leaves the mirror and sits down upon a nearby stone seat, the shape of a crescent moon. Successful in feeling great love for himself, he recalls Emit's further instructions. *"Once you discover this love within, take note of it. For this is love which can never be taken from you. Things may try to cloud this love from you, but you will know now and forevermore that it always exists.*

Let this unconditional love flow out and open yourself to the love which also flows inwards. Feel the world touching you, see the beauty, and appreciate that which surrounds you. The more you love and appreciate the world, the more the beauty of the world will be revealed to you."

Ulysses takes in the scenery around him, seeking things to love. He sees the blue sky and the majestic clouds that float through it. He feels the sun's rays as they beam onto the skin of one of his legs. His other leg, partly in the shade of a nearby tree, feels cool and refreshed. He appreciates that the sun gives warmth and that the shade gives cool. Both are pleasure.

He tunes in to the abundance of life around him. The plants, the animals. He hears the musical sound of birds. Butterflies dance as they fly past, ritualistically preparing themselves to mate. The leaves of the surrounding trees glitter with sunlight as they move perfectly with the flows of the wind. He takes in deep breaths of this oxygen, created by nature. He is a part of nature and nature is a part of him. And with every breath he feels blessed, for he is alive.

He has a build-up of energy and stands and walks in the garden. He is deeply appreciative of all that he can see. Even a fly that flies past him. *You even need the fly in this world.*

He smells the aroma of colourful flowers and then touches a plant. Just as it was great to touch his own hands earlier, he finds that this plant is also great to touch. He can sense how full of vibrant energy it is. It reminds him how much he loves nature. And while he often loses his connection with it living in modern society, he realises now how important it is to surround himself with nature, for it is true beauty.

Ulysses realises that everything he is sensing right now was there before he consciously noticed. But now it is as if he is suddenly acutely aware of how incredible the world is. *It's true, the more you appreciate the world, the more beauty it shows you. There is an underlying beauty to everything*, he realises. *A divinity.* Just as Ulysses witnessed earlier within himself.

He feels as if he has been bestowed with great truths. He has uncovered an unconditional love for himself and the world around him. Perhaps this is what Jesus meant when he said to *love thy neigh-bour as thy love thyself.* Perhaps he meant, very importantly, to love yourself, to fill yourself with love. A lot of people miss this first step. And then, in turn, to love the world around you equally as much. One cannot be out of balance with the other. After all, perhaps, fundamentally we are all one.

He recalls further instructions given by Emit. *"Once you have achieved a great love for your surroundings, focus on the love which is beyond the present. How many loving moments have you experienced in your life? You must take the time to still cherish them. As this love is still a part of you and it always will live on inside you. And in times of need, you can draw from this love."*

Ulysses thinks of his family members, his current and past friends, lovers and family pets. Moments of love and perfect moments that he has shared. He finds that there are countless examples of love that have helped him from birth until the present day and many of these visit him through thought. He even thinks of the little things – such as the love that went into creating the clothes on him.

He ponders how we do not get to say thank you to all the people and things in our lives when we die. Not usually. Nor do we get to say thank you when we are born. We must say it throughout our lives. And Ulysses wishes to begin to do so. Right now.

He looks around to make sure that no one can see as he reaches into his pocket and pulls out the device that is banned at Geno. His smartphone. He wishes to call his parents and tell them how much he loves them – now, in this moment, while he feels it so strongly. He turns the phone on and brings the screen up to his eyes. *There's no reception. Damn.* He is hoping that perhaps Emit is mistaken, that certain parts of Geno can receive reception. He turns the phone off and places it back in his pocket, making the promise that he will tell his parents when he gets the chance, in the future.

His focus returns to the present and he recalls Emit's final instruc-tion: *feel the love of God.* Ulysses did not need this last instruction.

He can already sense God in the underlying beauty of everything, as if God is the true source of this love. In prayer, Ulysses expresses his gratitude to God for everything that is and for everything that has ever been in his life.

Confident that he has reached a state of great love, Ulysses walks back to the oval where Emit waits for him.

"How do you feel, Ulysses? Do you feel great love?" asks Emit.

"I do," Ulysses says proudly.

"Good. This love that you are feeling, everyone wishes for it, it's one of their primary desires. But most don't realise that it is already inside them. And it surrounds them in every plant, in every tree and every sunset. It always exists, always has and always will. And thus, they can feel love in every second of their lives."

Ulysses nods. He is amazed that he has gone so long without uncovering this love that has always been at his fingertips. It seems foolish to have even tried to live the life of his dreams without first unconditionally loving himself, his environment and his life. He now understands that he must feel this love for the rest of his life and only do things which reflect the beauty of his eyes that he saw through this magical mirror. "Do the primary desires exist in the time between time?" Ulysses asks.

"How do you know about the time between time?" Emit asks curiously, with a quizzical smile.

"Sophos told me last night."

"Ah! Yes. While the elements may change forms, due to our formula, there's an eternal part of them that remains unaffected by time. This is the realm of the time between time. And where the primary can be sourced."

Ulysses motions towards his chest. "And when I wish to uncover my primary desires, do I simply follow this same process as today?"

"Yes. You can begin by asking the answers what your primary desires are. Remember, deep inside you already know the answers, so when you ask, they will come to you. Personally, I ask the answers while rubbing my chest where my heart is, as I find the answers quickly come this way.

"And then once you have a primary desire in mind, let go of whatever is currently preventing you from uncovering it. You can do this by simply knowing that whatever you seek in the primary you already have. Furthermore, it is seeking you.

"For example, do you wish to be great, Ulysses? You already are great. Do you wish to feel significant? You already are significant. Do you wish for an opportunity to live a great life? You already have this. Do you wish to be blessed? You already are blessed. Everything you desire your entire life through, all your primary desires, you already have. Really understand this, Ulysses: *The deepest things you truly want, you already possess.* The kingdom of God, is within you. You just have to uncover it and hold it throughout your life."

Ulysses nods. He cannot wait to uncover and hold all his primary desires.

Emit continues, "As you advance you can uncover all of your primary desires in a moment by simply being in the present, in the state of *no mind.* After all, as Sophos says, everything we teach at Geno can also be understood in an instant, as it is as simple as seeing a plant, shining in the sun."

Ulysses does not quite understand what Emit means by this, just as he did not when Sophos made mention of this the night before. He realises that there is still much to learn. He finds it amazing that this is only one of the eight principles in the perfect mindset, yet he has already discovered so much. He imagines how self-actualised he will be by the end of Emit's training and is very eager to learn more wisdom. And so, he sits back on the steps of the Grecian pavilion.

CHAPTER 22

LUKE LOVES HER

Luke delicately holds a bunch of yellow flowers in his hand, a collection of different species, which he secretly picked from Geno early this morning. He patiently stands behind her, watching as she studies nature. She turns and he moves towards her, kneeling and handing the flowers to her with a warm smile.

"Oh, thank you, Luke," Delta says, keeping her head down, seemingly unwilling to look at him as she takes the flowers from him.

His smile quickly dissipates. "You don't have to say anything. I can read your mind."

"It's just… I prefer flowers to be on the plants, where they belong," she says as she looks at his gift.

"Yes, but that's not all that's on your mind. It's okay." He stands again.

She finally looks up at him and into his eyes, which he savours. *Her beautiful blue eyes.*

"I'm sorry. It's just that when we look into each other's eyes, there is something that tells me it's not meant to be."

Her words instantly wound him, deeply. *Eyes are the windows to the soul.* And in this moment, he feels that she is rejecting all that he truly is. He nods and leans in to kiss her goodbye. She turns her cheek to him, the side with the three tiny moles that form a triangle. *She always turns her cheek*. He kisses it gently, envisioning that he is kissing her red lips.

He moves his head back and they look at each other once again, only this time he purposely keeps his face like stone. It is only when he turns from her that he lets the cracks in this stone appear.

He walks away, sincerely hoping she cannot read his mind, otherwise she will know that she has hurt him once again. Furthermore, she may even discover that he is losing his self-actualisation.

Why is he so obsessed with seeking love purely from this one source? It is against everything he has learnt in the perfect mindset teachings. Yet still he is bound to possessing her.

Is this pure romance? To courageously go after the object of your desire even when its thorns wound you?

HAVE CLEAR VISION

EMIT CONTINUES TO teach Ulysses the perfect mindset at the steps of the Grecian pavilion.

"The next principle I will teach is: *Have clear vision*," Emit says. "Clear vision is the optimum state of clarity. It's being able to see yourself and the world around you as close to true reality as possible."

"Now that would be an amazing skill," Ulysses says. For many years he has encountered a great deal of internal suffering, desperately trying to figure out the nature of the world around him, who he really is, and what his role is in all of this. "How do I achieve clear vision?"

"There's no set method. But as with the primary desire of love, let's start within. *See thyself with clear vision*. And one part of knowing yourself is to know your desires," Emit says and motions towards Ulysses. "Now, we've already started to uncover your primary desires. Holding these will offer clear vision with your secondary desires. For example, do you still wish for the secondary desire of a mansion now that you're fulfilled with your primary desire of love?"

"That's a great question. It certainly isn't as important to me as it was before. Now I feel like I could live just as great of a life without one."

Emit nods. "If you find that you no longer wish for a secondary desire after holding the associated primary desire, then this secondary desire is what we call an illusory desire. Illusory desires are to be discarded.

"Alternatively, while uncovering and holding a primary desire, you may still wish for a secondary desire. For example, if a person uncovers a deep love for themselves, they may be even more determined to achieve a secondary desire such as quitting smoking or living a healthy lifestyle, as this secondary desire is in line with their primary desire. These desires we call *true desires*.

"Once you know your true desires, you can gain more clear vision by seeing if there is anything internal that is limiting you from achieving these desires. One way a person can limit themselves is through having *limiting beliefs*. You see, beliefs can empower you or they can limit you. Limiting beliefs are false beliefs that limit your potential to achieve your true desires."

"What's so bad about having a few limiting beliefs?"

"They can mean the difference between life and death, Ulysses. You may have heard of a book titled *Man's Search for Meaning*, by Dr Viktor Frankl. Dr Frankl was a psychologist who endured the misfortune of being a Jewish captive in a Nazi concentration camp during World War II. He discovered there were a high number of deaths in the concentration camp the day after Christmas and the day after New Year. The reason for this, he concluded, is that many of the captives believed they would be home by Christmas or the New Year. They used this belief, this hope, as a way to push through every day, to keep fighting in such harsh conditions, with death all around them. However, once these dates passed and this limiting belief did not ring true, they simply gave up the will to live and thus died.

"Their belief served a purpose; it helped the captives to keep fighting with an end goal in mind. It was empowering in this sense, but only to a point. It had an expiry date where it became limiting. And once it became limiting, they suffered the consequences of it and passed."

"Wow, that's intense."

Emit nods. "Another example of a limiting belief can be found in the tribes of Australian Aboriginals, like the ones near where you grew up in Mount Isa. A Kadaitcha man is a powerful figure in Aboriginal culture who punishes those who transgress Aboriginal law by simply pointing a bone at them. Many Aboriginals believe that this pointing of the bone by the Kadaitcha man symbolises that the recipient will die. And thus, because the recipient believes it, they often do."

Ulysses feels as if he has just been bestowed with great wisdom. "I didn't realise a belief could be so powerful before."

"As I said. A belief can be the difference between life and death. And so, you must discard any limiting beliefs."

"Okay. I can know my desires and rid myself of limiting beliefs. How else can I see myself with clear vision?"

"There are many ways to know thyself, Ulysses. Some meditate. Some use psychodynamic and other psychological methods. In time you will become a master at reading yourself."

"Okay."

"Now to look at things outside of yourself with clear vision. Knowing thyself will give you some insight into others, as fundamentally we're all much the same. Soon you'll become a scholar at the art of reading other people. You'll know that every movement, every scratch a person makes, everything, means something. You'll know that others, like you, also have primary and secondary desires, illusory and true desires, sometimes conscious and sometimes hidden to them. They may also have limiting beliefs. It's possible to become so good at reading others that to them you might even appear as if you are psychic, even without using your psychic skills. And you'll also learn to see the world around you with such clear vision that you can predict what will happen next. You are connected to all, Ulysses. You have great powers. And these skills, interlaced with your actual psychic abilities, will offer you even greater clear vision."

"I can't wait," Ulysses says with enthusiasm. After all, this is the reason he is here at Geno. He wishes to control and strengthen his psychic powers so that he can protect himself from The Shadows.

Emit continues, "This being said, there are limitations to knowing all. You, being a human that has evolutionary design parameters, don't know everything. Thus, you must always be open to being correct, but not bound by your version of reality. Knowing your limitations will strengthen your clear vision, just as knowing thyself *is having clear vision.*"

Ulysses looks confused.

"Put simply, also know what you don't know, Ulysses."

"Which is a lot at the moment," Ulysses laughs.

"It'll come. Eventually, you'll reach a state we call *the clear light.* In this state, everything becomes clear. You don't need to think at all. You'll simply know. Everything becomes as clear as looking at a plant…"

"… Shining in the sun," Ulysses interrupts. "Perhaps I've already experienced this. Literally. When I discovered my theory I had a moment of no thought."

"Yes, it's possible that you were in the clear light in this moment. Imagine what you could discover if you reached this state often."

Ulysses' thoughts drift to the possibilities in Emit's last sentence. He cannot wait to master all of these perfect mindset teachings.

CHAPTER 24

THE SON OF IOANNIS

The French Riviera, France.

IT'S 2.15 A.M. Inside a luxurious mansion is an office where, by the sheer grandness of it, one would be excused if they suddenly believed they were in a wing of the Vatican Museums. There are high ceilings with frescos and gold motifs, priceless paintings on the walls, antiques and ancient sculptures scattered around the room.

The artefacts in this office were gathered in such secrecy that many outside the order believe them to have been lost through the course of history. Certainly, if these items could speak, they would tell a terrible story. There are antique guns and weapons that have been chosen specially because of their prior use in the most poignant moments in battle, great turning points in history. These are priceless artefacts acquired through both bloodshed and acts of uncompromising power. There are stuffed animal heads on the walls: a lion, a polar bear. A pelt of a thylacine, various ivory pieces including jewelled rhinoceros horns, elephant and mammoth tusks, some sculptured, some plated with precious metals.

In the centre of this office, hanging from the ceiling is a small wooden birdcage. At the front of the cage is a jewelled clock, specifically designed to never stop ticking. And inside this cage is a live bird that spends most of its time frantically trying to find a way out of its prison, as if it is doing a painful dance which is completely out of rhythm with the classical music that flows through every corner of this office.

Below this bird is a grand mahogany desk. And here sits Leucius. He is usually up at this hour, emphatically writing with his favourite gold pen barely leaving the pages of his journal. He captures details of his previous day, his inner feelings and, most importantly to him, his plans.

Leucius has been taking great pleasure in making and executing plans since he was very young. They are always very intricate and deep. He still remembers his first written plan with this gold pen. Growing up, he went to one of the most prestigious all-boys boarding schools in all of England. Here he lived as a boarder in a dormitory with a dozen other boys. His plan was simple. Every day, Leucius would secretly move a tissue box from one boy's desk and place it in the boy's doorway. A very slight change. But sure enough, every day this boy would come back to the dormitory and become instantly frustrated and confused, questioning why anyone would do this. It simply did not make sense to the boy. Over several consecutive days, the boy's questions turned to screams and yells. Weeks passed of this, until one day this boy had a particularly bad day at school. He arrived back at the dormitory and as usual, found that the tissue box waited for him in his doorway. The tissue box was the straw that broke the camel's back. The boy burst into tears, sobbing uncontrollably. And as he sought to dry his tears, surely everything made sense to him. The tissue box was there all along just for this occasion. Its purpose was not only to slowly break him down but also to dry his tears once it did.

Leucius never moved the boy's tissue box again after this day. There was no need; his plan had proven to be a success. Instead, he created new plans. Each more daring.

As a fourteen-year-old, he successfully robbed a great bank in London. It was a brilliant plan. Whilst his armed men held up this bank, he also had accomplices, dressed as police officers, who interceded. These policemen pretended to save the day, calmed the public members inside the bank, heroically arrested the criminals and took the bank money as evidence, with the promise to return it. It was such a convincing act that the real police were never called. It took the bank several weeks to realise they had been swindled. Leucius didn't need the money. The Shadows owned this bank anyway. He simply loved witnessing his plans as they came to life.

He successfully carried out dozens of other plans over his formative years, all written with this very gold pen. Each one deeper. Each one more ingenious. For a purpose. For practice.

But practice time is over. His ancestors were very accomplished and thus he has heavy shoes to fill. And in this moment, the plans he writes are to be his life's greatest work. Something which will set him apart from those who have come before him. Especially now that he holds the prestigious title of...

"Master of Shadows," a voice echoes through the room.

Leucius casually looks up from his journal and sees a Shadow member at the doorway, some twenty metres away. The man is middle-aged with grey hair and thick dark eyebrows; he wears dark pants and an emerald tweed blazer with a small red triangle on the breast pocket, and holds a magnificent golden cane. "Yes, Anomonet?"

Anomonet raises his free hand before him, respectfully motioning to his inconvenient interruption. He then bows as best as he is physically able and walks towards Leucius, his cane clopping heavily against the brilliant natural stone floor until he comes to a luxurious rug that softens its sound. He continues to project his voice so that it will reach Leucius from his distance, "I am sorry to bother you, Master, but I have news. We have the name of the man with precognitions."

"Good, who is he?"

"Ulysses Sirius."

"*Sirius.* That name has come up far too much in Shadow history. The most recent, I believe, being Ioannis," Leucius says, leaning back in his chair, the point of his gold pen pointed upward in his hand.

"Yes, he is the son of Ioannis."

"Of course, it makes sense. The great Ioannis Sirius. A man's name I haven't heard since I was a child. A man my late father should have ended many years ago."

Anomonet, now having reached the desk, lowers his voice to a normal tone. "Yes, Master, but as you know, Orien forbids us to become involved with the Geno members without his permission."

Leucius suddenly becomes angry and drives his gold pen towards the desk forcefully. He stops just millimetres short of hitting the desk; after all, it is his favourite pen. His composure rapidly changes to being calm once more. "You're as naïve as Euripedes!" he laughs mockingly.

"As naïve as Euripedes *was.* Your honour, there are Shadows of the inner red triangle who are not happy with the way Euripedes' blood was spilt. He was one of our own."

"Euripedes had served his purpose. Besides, he believed in fairy tales, just like most of the inner triangle. Orien doesn't exist and we must forget all about him."

"Yes, I see this is your plan," Anomonet says, motioning towards a large blank space on the wall where until recently hung a great 16th-century painting of Orien.

"And I also have another plan. See this cage above my desk... you are well aware of what it represents. The cage, the bird, the clock, all purposely serve as a metaphor to how The Shadows rule mankind."

"I am aware."

"Yes, but you are missing something, Anomonet. You understand that this bird will try all it might, but it will never be free of its own accord. Of course. No lateral thinking needed there. But there is a way it can escape. All it needs is for someone from outside the cage to intercede. And the bird is free."

"Yes, and what is your point?"

"Geno is outside of the cage. They are not part of the society that we control and thus they have the power to intercede. And as the Master of The Shadows, I will implement a new rule – from now on we are not to spare any Geno member."

"Master, this is not just about Orien. Throughout history, even when instructed to battle Geno, we have never succeeded in finishing them. There may only be eight of them, but they are very powerful."

"Yes, powerful, perhaps. But don't you find it a coincidence that every time we are instructed to fight Geno they end up winning the battle? Surely if Orien did exist, a man who is immortal, he would be better with his battle plans? If you ask me, it's almost like we are purposely being set up for failure."

"That is a preposterous supposition."

"Yes, it is preposterous, simply because Orien doesn't exist. But either way, perhaps in some way we don't yet understand, we have given Geno far too much credit for far too long. So much so that they have become almost mythical to us in their powers. Even our Enforcers are afraid of them. But this is all going to end with me. Now, what information do you have on Ulysses?"

"Very little at present."

"Make this task your priority. Find out everything you can about him. He may lead us to the other members of Geno. To Ioannis. To the Geno base."

"Yes, Master. Surely he has a phone. Perhaps we can use it to trace his whereabouts. And if he has used it to contact his father, we can use the phone records to track Ioannis too."

"You have the world's entire intelligence system at your fingertips."

CHAPTER 25

BE OPEN TO PERFECTION

Geno, Australia.

It is now late morning. The sun blazes sideways through the trees at the Grecian pavilion in Geno. Being seated for the entirety of the last principle makes Ulysses feel lazy. He casually sits on the marble steps, his elbows resting on a step, his legs outstretched to his left.

Emit stands before him, continuing to teach in his English accent. "The third principle of the perfect mindset is: *Be open to perfection*. Being open to both your primary and secondary desires: how do you wish to be in this moment? What do you wish to do right now that has the possibility for perfection?" Emit asks as he touches his left index finger with his right index finger, the sun shining past his hands which makes a flicker as he moves them. Ulysses realises that Emit is not wearing the ring he wore when he first met him. "And being open to experiencing perfection with the world around you: what gifts do you wish to experience in this moment?" Emit asks as he touches his left middle finger with his right index finger.

"I've always believed that perfection is attainable. But how can we be sure?"

"Ulysses, let me tell you an amazing truth. The entire history of the universe has led to this very moment. All of its interactions, all of its creations. Everything culminates at this precise point in time where, incredibly, you and I are alive, sitting here, magically flying on a little blue planet through the galaxy. Surely this shows that perfections are possible." Emit smiles. "But still, you may find yourself struggling with the idea of perfection. If so, then as you did earlier with love, start smaller and build your way up. Be open to good, then once you are comfortable with this, be open to greatness. And finally, be open to perfection."

"How will this help me to self-actualise?"

"Due to the interconnection of all things, when you know what you wish for and you're open to receiving it, you communicate these desires to the other elements and levels. And thus, you increase your chances of receiving your desires," Emit says, his arms flowing, his voice fervent. "You'll be amazed by what desires you can receive when you're open enough to express them to others and go directly towards them.

"Contrastingly, if you're not open to your true desires, you're less likely to receive them. Nor will you enjoy them if you do receive them for that matter, because you can't enjoy what your heart is not open to."

"That's true. I'm sure that many people in life secretly wish for things whilst also not being truly open to receiving them. Why do you think this is?"

"Because being open can make us feel vulnerable. Yet we must embrace this feeling of vulnerability and still be open to perfection anyway."

These words instantly remind Ulysses of something he once read on social media, back in what feels like his previous life:

It is important to let your true self shine. Your true gifts. The beauty that dwells in your mind and your unique perspective on life needs to

be heard. You will suffer criticism. But their opinions do not matter,
because you HAVE to be you. And by being you, you will attract the
right people into your life and repel the wrong people. And soon you will
predominately be surrounded by people that love you for you. Which,
after all, is what you desire.

Ulysses thinks how his dreams are his own for a reason. If he
does not believe in them strongly enough to be open to them, even
when it makes him feel vulnerable, then who else will? He is dedicated to being open to his desires from now on. "How can I make
sure that I'm open to perfection?"

"You can behave in a way that shows you are open to your true
desires. You can discard any limiting beliefs. You can ensure that
your inner dialogue is in line with being open to perfection. You
can ask the universe or God for what you seek. You can visualise
achieving your true desires."

"And can I get whatever I wish for by being open to it?"

"What you *truly* wish for, yes. You see, it's being *open to perfection*.
This doesn't mean your vision of perfection will come true. After all,
your vision of perfection is limited by evolutionary design parameters, by your own mind. And so, the system may overrule your wishes.
The perfection that God wishes, in the bigger picture, not just in the
moment, may be greater than you could ever imagine in your mind.

"The wishes of God, as you are aware, we call *the greater good*.
This is what perfection truly means. These are your *truest desires*.
They overrule what you believe to be your desires. So, you must
be open to your vision of perfection, your true desires, but not
attached. As you are only bound to true perfection, the greater
good. Your truest desires."

Ulysses nods. He looks forward to using this principle in his
daily life and seeing what desires he can manifest.

"And now, Ulysses, it is time to learn the next principle."

CHAPTER 26

YOU ARE READY NOW

EMIT AND ULYSSES continue the perfect mindset lessons at the Grecian pavilion in Geno.

"The last principle of the perfect mindset I will teach today is: *You are ready now,*" Emit says. "You see, the truth is that very few people are living to the fullest. Instead, they are putting it off for the future, to some distant time. They believe that they will be great once they have reached some goal, learned some great wisdom or arrived at a destination in life. When the truth is, as we discussed, every moment holds perfection. And we're all ready to live our lives to the fullest right now."

Emit's words remind Ulysses of what Sophos told him by the campfire the night before: *"Always been ready to live perfection. Simply need to realise."* Her words have been in Ulysses' mind and today he has questions. "I understand that perfection is possible. But sometimes, don't we have to grow before we're ready for perfection?"

Emit smiles as if he were expecting Ulysses to ask this. "A seed is just as perfect as a tree."

"Sorry?"

"I'll give you an analogy, Ulysses. Do you see this tree?" Emit says as he points to a bottle brush tree, tens of metres away. "Follow me," he motions at Ulysses to follow as he walks towards the tree.

Ulysses catches up with Emit. Once they are within a few metres of the bottle brush tree, Emit picks one of its seeds from the ground, holding it in his fingers. He draws Ulysses' attention by raising it towards him. "This tree began as a seed just like this, then it sprouted and became a seedling, then a sapling and finally it grew into a mature tree. It has gone through many developmental stages. Did this tree become any more perfect as it grew? Or was it perfect at being whatever it was in the moment?"

"I guess it was always perfect."

"Precisely. When it was a seed, it was perfect at being a seed. When it was a sapling, it was perfect at being a sapling. Its destiny was always to become a tree, this was written deep into its being. Does this seed have to wait until it can become a tree? *Yes.* Does it have to wait for perfection? *No.* It is ready now. A seed is as perfect as a tree," Emit says as he leans down and places the seed back onto the ground. He then rises and focuses his attention solely on Ulysses. "Now with you, Ulysses, you've been seeking perfection for most of your life and little did you realise that you've always had it. It's always been right in front of your eyes. You simply had to be open to perfection and believe that you were ready now."

Ulysses thinks about Emit's words. Maybe he does have the ability to live the life of his dreams now. After all, if he is to live a perfect life, then logically, he must already have the skills he needs to have perfection in every moment.

Emit continues, "You'll come to realise that your life, the world itself, is all perfect for you. That you've been given all you need to live the best life. That even the challenges you face are there to help you, to guide you. That your past, present and future are all perfect." Emit becomes more and more passionate with every sentence. "Really understand this, Ulysses. The biggest regrets come from not holding your primary desires and going towards your true secondary desires. From not believing you are ready now," Emit says earnestly and looks down, his eyes sad.

Ulysses can sense that Emit has made this very mistake in his past, something Ulysses finds easy to empathise with; after all, he too has been guilty of not believing he is ready now. Very few instances of Ulysses' life has he truly lived, embracing the moment. Those moments where he has, he cherishes and keeps close to his heart. But still, he has questions. "If I believe that my life is already perfect then why would I have any reason to achieve any goals, to become better?"

Emit's thoughts seem to return to the present moment. He looks at Ulysses. "Well, Ulysses, it's true that you'll no longer desire to *become better* in the sense that you have to desperately fill some void that is missing. Instead, you'll naturally achieve great things simply because you value and appreciate them so much.

"Let me give you an example: If a partner were to tell you that you're a perfect lover, does this make you wish to rest on your laurels and declare that you no longer wish to love them anymore? *Of course not*, not if you value this relationship. If anything, it will make you want to put even more effort into this area. To please this person even more. To see what other greatness can be uncovered with them. You see, when you love and value something greatly and you're experiencing perfection with it, you'll wish to continue with this trajectory."

"Yeah, I guess so," Ulysses says while contemplating his own experiences in life.

"You don't need to focus on becoming *better*. You are ready now, Ulysses. You are ready now to be the person you wish to be. You don't have to try to be someone, *you already are.* You don't have to build up to a perfect moment, you are already there. The growth will happen naturally. Just as it did with this tree," Emit says, pointing to the bottle brush tree once more.

Ulysses nods. He understands now.

Emit continues, "This concludes today's lesson. I will teach you the final four principles of the perfect mindset tomorrow. Then you will know all the principles you need to self-actualise.

"Have a break now and then see Luke. He also has a lesson for you," Emit says.

CHAPTER 27

THE WIFE OF IOANNIS

Mount Isa, Australia.

MOUNT ISA IS a small city which appears as a man-made oasis in the harsh desert-like environment of the outback. Here, at 14 Fornax Street, is a large corner block that is full of life. A cassia fistula tree is on the far-right side of the property, with a poinciana and another large tree on the left; Ulysses loved climbing that tree the most as a child. There is a tall eucalyptus tree and a hibiscus tree with beautiful yellow flowers with pistils that seem like tiny magical wands. There are several trees of the fruit variety dispersed throughout the yard, including a small banana tree that has never grown since it was planted here. There are ferns, shrubs, a variety of plants and lush green grass. The birds routinely visit during the day and at night the fruit bats visit for the fruit of the Java plum trees. Nocturnal green tree frogs are living in the squared hollow poles of a lattice at the very back of the yard. There are also pets on the property: two dogs – Pepe and Cindy. Two cats – Suzy and Cleo. And in a large aviary are two cockatiels – Moses and Beauty.

In the centre of this property is a simple, small three-bedroom, single-story wooden home. And inside this house, in what used to be Ulysses' bedroom, is an office. Here sits a man with dyed dark hair, thick glasses and a dark jacket. He opens a small jewellery box. He pulls out a necklace and dangles it before him at eye level. It is silver, and on the pendant is a regular octagram within a circle. *The Geno necklace.*

"That old thing?" his wife, Lel, says at the doorway, startling him. She has long grey hair and a kind, beautiful face.

"Yes… this old thing," Ioannis answers.

"You haven't worn that for many years."

"No, but it has always remained close."

"You know, you never have told me what this necklace means?"

"It's a key…"

She interrupts, "Yes, a key to a greater knowledge, I know. But what is it really?"

Ioannis is silent.

Her eyes travel downwards and then back up to look into his eyes, "You know, it isn't always easy being with you. Not understanding why we're out here in the middle of nowhere."

"You'll know when the time is right, my love," he answers sincerely.

"I've also heard this many times, ever since I first met you. We are old now. Maybe the time will never be right? Besides, I thought you were always a person that believed that you are ready now?" she smiles cheekily.

He looks at her curiously, trying to figure out how much she knows. A part of him has always hoped that she somehow knows. Carrying these secrets has been such a burden to him. "It's for the greater good, Lel. But I believe the time will be right soon. Ulysses is a part of all of this. Right now he's doing something very important. If he succeeds, the time will finally be upon us."

"How do we know that he will succeed?"

"He must succeed."

"I trust so," she says. She turns and begins to walk out.

"We have to leave soon. Just for a while," Ioannis says, stopping her in her tracks.

She turns back for a moment, nods, and then leaves the room.

CHAPTER 28

THE GENO MARTIAL ARTS

Geno, Australia.

THE AFTERNOON SUN blazes onto Geno. Ulysses stands with Luke on the oval, near the big fig tree.

"Why do I have to learn this?" Ulysses says as he looks up at Luke, who towers above him.

"Emit told me The Shadows attacked you. *This* is why it's important to learn to defend yourself. Knowing this theory is dangerous. And if you ever want to survive outside of Geno again, you must learn this. After all, you will not always have Delta around to take care of you," Luke answers with a strong conviction, his voice powerful.

"But Emit just taught me that love is part of the perfect mindset and now you're teaching me how to fight. It's contradictory."

"I'm teaching you how to defend against attack. Not everyone in this world is showing their love in the best way. But you, even when you fight, must be full of compassion," he says, pointing to Ulysses' heart. "Everything you learn here must only be used for a good purpose. You must never permanently hurt or kill another.

Just as I don't doubt that Delta let those who wronged you free, with superficial wounds. You must do the same. Always. Even though it might seem easier to get rid of them, to end them, know that another will simply take their place. Because evil is a symptom of something deeper. And if your plan is to kill all that opposes you, you will only create more enemies in the process. Instead, treat others as if they are a part of you. And since we are all part of the same system, *they are*. If inside them is anger and you wish to stop it, then defend yourself from this rage, control them and then fill them with better emotions, such as love."

Ulysses wonders if this is why Delta blessed the assassins after the attack. Perhaps she was trying to fill them with love. And by letting them go, they may have realised that she is not an aggressor, but a force for good in the world.

Luke squints, appearing to study Ulysses' physique with great scrutiny. "You have muscles built from the gym, but they're not functional for martial arts. Your core and your legs are weak," Luke says as he slaps Ulysses in both of these areas. "I will help you to strengthen them through training. And not only will I make your body strong and able. Not only will I teach you the skills you need. But I will improve all of your senses," Luke says, his light green eyes looking intently at Ulysses.

"How could you possibly improve my senses?"

"People are only as good as their environments, or the previous environments of their forefathers through the qualities they have inherited. *An element interacts in a system and creates*. If you don't need quick reflexes, chances are you won't develop them. Why does a bird have better eyesight than us? Or a fly quicker reflexes?"

Ulysses shrugs.

"Because *they need to*, Ulysses. And in Geno, you will develop superior powers – because you will need them. I will make sure of that. Now, the martial art you'll learn here is secret and known only to Geno. But you may notice that some of the philosophies in it are similar to other martial arts. For example, in Tai Chi, they learn to move with the energy of the opponent until they are so in sync that they can predict what they will do, before they even do it. We sometimes do this in Geno," Luke says as he demonstrates some basic free-flowing moves against an imaginary opponent. "In Judo they use an opponent's energy against them, and in Geno we sometimes do the same. But even with these similarities, our martial art is impossible to beat when it comes to any other known fighting skills. Because above all, there is one thing that Geno's martial art has which none other does."

"What's that?"

"Magic."

Hearing this excites Ulysses. He would love to finally learn magic.

They begin the lesson. And as the time passes, Ulysses unfortunately discovers that this first lesson, while physically tiring, is basic in technique and similar to the teachings of other martial arts, in the sense that no magic is used.

Ulysses will have to wait.

CHAPTER 29

THE GLOWING RING

EMIT WALKS THROUGH Geno's garden, passing many statues. He is alert to the sounds around him. There is water trickling down a little stream that passes a nearby small bridge. There are the sporadic bird calls of kookaburras, which if he did not know better, would lead him to believe that monkeys live in the trees of the Geno rainforest. And, importantly to him in this moment, he finally hears what he has been listening for – the sound of shears steadily chopping away.

It is Sophos. He has found her.

She is hunched over, using gardening shears to slowly prune the bushes. As usual, she wears her black widow's clothing but parts of her arms and face are bare and glow in the sunlight, making her appear even more orange in colour than usual.

"Sophos… I have grave concerns about him," Emit interrupts her, sternly.

"How so?" Sophos asks as she continues to prune, only occasionally glancing at Emit.

"This," Emit says as he pulls a ring from his pocket. "It's a very technologically advanced ring I created. It alerts me by glowing when a Shadow member is within a specified distance, currently set at 250 metres."

Sophos stops pruning and rests the shears on top of the bush. She moves to take a close look at the ring. It has the Geno symbol on it which glows red and blue. "Ahh, it glow now."

"Yes. The ring glows because of him. I've had to stop wearing it while at Geno."

"Where he right now?"

"He is doing martial arts training on the oval. His skills will only grow with every passing moment. If we are to act on this, the sooner the better."

"I see," Sophos says, her emotions as steady with this revelation as she was while cutting with shears.

"You know what this means, Sophos. He is related to The Shadows. We have let a Shadows descendant into Geno!"

"Yes."

"So, what do we do?"

"Not worry. He led here by Geno book. Meant to be. Already written." She waves her right hand in the air as a gesture to dismiss his concern.

"But we might be in great danger."

"Meant to be. Let happen, whatever danger may," Sophos says while touching Emit's shoulder with her right hand, just for a moment. She then picks up the shears and begins pruning again.

CHAPTER 30

THE STARS

It is the evening, 8:40 p.m. Ulysses is the last to be sitting at the campfire. He looks over his shoulder to see Delta, alone, near the pavilion. She lies on a thin blanket, her hands behind her head, her right leg slightly bent. And although he cannot see her face since she is facing the pavilion, he assumes she is gazing up at the heavens.

Ulysses has looked towards her periodically, thinking how he wishes to join her. To share a moment with her. However, he is also nervous about rejection. *Maybe I shouldn't bother her,* he reasons. *Maybe she wishes to be alone.*

He has been in many situations similar to this before, that is, finding excuses not to face his fears. But then he recalls what he has learnt today from the perfect mindset: his desire is to share a moment with Delta and to get to know her better. But he also knows he must not be bound by this version of perfection. For clear vision says that he does not know if she will or will not welcome his advances. Luckily, he has also learnt today that either way is fine, for even if he is rejected, he still holds his primary desire of love. And so, he has nothing to lose. He is ready now.

He walks towards Delta and is soon within a few metres of her.

"Ulysses," Delta says. She raises herself and turns her body to greet him. Again, it was as if she already sensed he was there.

"What are you up to?"

"I like to look at the stars before I sleep."

"May I join you?"

"Sure," she smiles and makes room for him on the blanket.

Success. The blanket touches his underside as he lies down next to her.

Ulysses discovers the night sky is beautifully tranquil in the rainforest, undisturbed by the light of civilisation, allowing him to be instantly mesmerised by the stars. He spends some moments taking them in before he breaks the silence. "Looking at the stars… there's a beauty here… this is what life's truly about."

"Aren't they incredible?" Delta replies.

"They really are. While everyone has retired to their cabins, you seem to have spent your entire day outdoors. You must love to be with the beauty of nature."

"Yes. I really love to be outside. To touch the naked ground with my feet first thing in the morning. To be a witness to the sunrise and then immerse myself in nature throughout the day. In the early evening, on a clear night, I take in the beauty of the stars near the Geno pavilion as the cool night air caresses my skin. To me, it feels like home," Delta says fondly "And I guess it's true that I see beauty more easily out in nature. As if it is a direct source. But I can see the beauty of nature in everything. Because, to me, everything is a reflection of nature's beauty."

Ulysses was open for perfection and Delta so eloquently gave it to him in a single sentence. "That's the most perfect thing I have ever heard. *Everything is a reflection of nature's beauty.* If only everyone could see the world like this."

"I wish they would because if everyone could see nature as the true source of beauty, they would want to protect it as much as I do," Delta speaks with conviction as she rises to a seated position.

Ulysses believes that the wisest people have a deep affinity for nature. He has read that one of his heroes, Leonardo da Vinci, would spend hours in nature, studying it, just like Delta seems to. He would purchase birds in cages just to let them free. Ulysses can imagine Delta doing the same. And from her words, he is discovering that the depths of her mind are much greater than he could have ever imagined.

She continues, "It's not that hard to see this beauty if they wish. If they appreciate God's work in the perfection of nature, all of its beauty will be revealed to them," she says while motioning with her right hand in a semi-circle, past Ulysses and towards the stars.

God's work in the perfection of nature. Ulysses certainly sees the perfection of nature in this very moment. He looks at the stars and sees perfection. Then he looks over at Delta. She seems to notice his attention which leads her to smile, her white teeth and red lips a perfect complement to the blonde strands of her hair. She looks beautiful. And in her, Ulysses sees an equal perfection to that he just witnessed in the stars. He feels honoured to be looking at the stars with such an amazing woman. For the universe to have her with him right now, a girl he dreamt about. Surely this is proof of a great perfection being possible. *Maybe there is perfection all around us. Just as Sophos and Emit believe.*

Although the forms of the elements may change, an underlying perfection is always there. This perfection exists in the time between time, just like love. It's eternal. It's within everything, including us all. The theory and the perfect mindset open our eyes to see this perfection more clearly and allow us to live this perfection in every moment.

Ulysses matches Delta by also rising to a seated position. "Sophos taught me about a concept called the time between time. And Emit has taught me a little more today. I'm still learning what they mean by it, but I'm starting to believe that the time between time, the beauty of everything, already exists within us all. That…"

Ulysses pauses, "... the love of all time exists within here," he says with sincerity as he points to her heart.

Delta looks intently at Ulysses and suddenly her eyes fill with tears.

"What's wrong?" Ulysses asks. He reaches out and puts his arm around her, attempting to comfort her with his gentle touch.

"Oh, you wouldn't understand even if I told you, Ulysses. Just trust me, it will all make sense one day," she says as the tears seep out and run down her face like the little streams that meander through Geno.

Ulysses holds her closer and begins to caress her with his fingertips. He is not sure what to make of what she just said, but he trusts her completely when she says that he will understand in time.

Delta lifts her arm and dries her tears with her sleeve. "I apologise for being so emotional, Ulysses."

"You don't have to apologise."

"These were tears of joy. But it's not always like that. Sometimes it's very hard. But then I look at the stars and I feel that everything will be okay. They guide me. Which is amazing as they could just as easily make me feel vulnerable."

"What do you mean?" Ulysses asks.

"Well, when I look at the stars, I realise how small I am compared to all that is. That I have little control over the fate of the universe. Yet, amazingly, the beauty of the stars also whispers that there is a greater purpose for all of this. I don't quite know how to explain it."

"Let me try." Ulysses takes a moment to gather his thoughts. And when he speaks, it is with such passion that he feels it comes deep from within him. He points up towards the heavens. "Delta, do you know that if we were close enough to a star we would see only constant chaotic explosions? Yet we are far enough away to see a star's true beauty. The stars from our vantage point are perfect. I feel that life is also like this sometimes. Sometimes the events in our life may seem like chaos, but it's only because we are so close to them. If we were to view these events, through time, in their completeness, we might realise that they too are perfect. That our lives are truly beautiful, like the stars," he says and motions past them both with his right hand.

"Wow, that's so beautiful," she says as she looks at him with soft eyes, as if she has been deeply touched by his words.

"So, the stars hint at how beautiful our lives are. But the heavens tell us even more than this. Because yes, you're correct, our bodies are small in comparison to all that is. We are indeed very vulnerable through our physical design. Which is exactly why it's incredible we are alive here on this little blue planet. With all the odds against us being born, all the trials and tribulations that our ancestors went through to make our existence possible. Even the trials and tribulations our father's sperm went through to win the race and enter our mother's egg. The odds were improbable for us to exist. Yet, despite these odds, it has happened. You and I, in our current form, are alive. Because the universe wishes us to be. At any moment, a meteorite could strike and end it for mankind. We are only flesh and bone. Thousands of meteorites enter the Earth's gravitational field every year. But most meteorites can't hurt us, as life on Earth has created the ozone layer, a force field that protects us from harm. Almost as if this magical protection were pre-ordained in life's design. Just as a sperm instinctively knows to swim towards the egg, just as a bird knows to make a nest, and a caterpillar knows to make a cocoon so that it can turn into a butterfly, there is a hidden intelligence here. So, while we are vulnerable, we are also secure and beautifully happy on this amazing planet. Because we are more than just ourselves, Delta. The universe's intelligence has chosen to create us. It wishes for us. It protects us. Because we are here for a reason, a purpose."

"That's so incredible. How blessed we are for the universe to come up with us, to create us and to offer us divine providence. It must mean that we are for the greater good," Delta says and leans in closer to Ulysses affectionately.

Ulysses is delighted to have a girl who is on the same wavelength as he. He deeply wishes her to be amazed by his thoughts.

"I love the way that your mind works, Ulysses. Such treasures come from it. You're a modern-day philosopher," Delta says, almost as if she can read his wishes.

"I feel the same about you. It isn't often that I find someone that I can speak deeply to," Ulysses says.

It feels as if they complement each other's deepest thoughts. Which leads Ulysses to believe that just as this is a perfect moment in time, perhaps just like his recurring dreams, they really are also perfect for one another. Regardless of their age difference.

"Delta, do you believe in soulmates?" he asks as the fingers of his left hand run through his hair.

"Yes, I do," she replies, and she also begins running her fingers through her hair. It is like they are in sync, willing to match one another, even if it is subconsciously.

"What do you believe soulmates are?" he smiles.

"I believe it's when two souls are destined to be together. No obstacles, not even time, can keep them apart."

"As you wish," Ulysses answers with a cheeky smile. He is inferring that even with their age difference, perhaps not even time has kept them apart.

Delta's eyes open wide, "I'm in awe. You just quoted my favourite line from one of my favourite books, *The Princess Bride*! Do you believe in soulmates, Ulysses?"

Ulysses nods, "Yes. I'm starting to believe that it's when you meet the partner from your dreams. And when you look into the other's eyes, it feels as if you could look into them for an eternity. As if your love has always been written," Ulysses says, his words merely an expression of how he feels in this moment.

Delta's dimples show as she smiles and continues to look into his eyes. "I love what you believe soulmates are, Ulysses."

They share what feels to Ulysses an incredibly intense moment. It is like he can see the eternal beauty of all time within her eyes. He becomes lost in them. And although no words are said, he can read her purely: her eyes also have a strong desire burning inside them.

Delta suddenly looks down. But what has just happened cannot be undone. It only lasted a few seconds, but their connection felt powerful. She raises her eyes to meet his again and she speaks nervously, "I must go to sleep, Ulysses. I have to wake up early tomorrow and continue my research." She stands. "I'm sorry. Have a good night." And she leaves in such a hurry that she does not even take her blanket with her.

Ulysses cannot help but think that he has done something wrong.

CHAPTER 31

THE SHADOWS AND THE BANKS

Paris, France.

Leucius walks into a large open-plan office surrounded by fake plants and other features designed to give the illusion of a less artificial environment. The sounds of classical music play through his earphones. He wears slacks and a casual designer blazer with a small red triangle, his favourite golden pen on display from the pocket of his white long-sleeved shirt. In his left hand he has a yellow A4 envelope with the symbol of the red triangle on it. And inside the envelope are very important documents he has prepared.

He feels energised by the ambience of this towering bank skyscraper. To him, it is his church. A place of worship. Ever since he was a child and first learned he was in line to control the world, The Shadows' system of power has fascinated him.

The plan is so ingenious. Even he, a master of plans, could never have dreamed up such a thing.

What a brilliant system.

Leucius studies the men and women in business attire as they work busily at their desks. He cannot help but smile. They are his worker ants. Slaves who do not realise they are slaves, for they were born into this system and so they have little to compare it with. Leucius, however, having learnt the history of The Shadows, the true history of the world, understands the vast amount of freedom that has been taken from humanity. Little by little, bit by bit. Like a frog being boiled in a pot, so slowly that it does not notice the water is heating up.

Compared to Leucius' lifestyle of great leisure and the choice of whether to work, the worker ants live in a completely different realm. The ants have set hours per week; however, with everything added in, much of their waking lives are simply a focus of their occupation. Some of the most hard-working ants hardly see their friends and family and when they do, they are either too exhausted or do not have enough time to have meaningful relationships.

To justify this commitment to each other, the ants allow their occupation to define their identity. Which is why one of the first personal questions a worker ant will ask when meeting another is, "What do you do?" A question Leucius has always despised. After all, he has no answer to it. And nor should he. Yet these damn worker ants keep asking him! On the positive, however, he knows that the more they believe this work is an intricate part of them, the more they will embrace being a slave.

It's a brilliant system.

Most worker ants get paid just enough to survive each week, and thus, they are forced to continue this cycle of labour. They work so hard that they feel stress which, coupled with other lifestyle factors, causes many of the ants' health to deteriorate. They then, personally or as a group through healthcare, spend whatever money they can, desperately trying to get back to being as healthy as they would be if they were not so stressed to begin with.

Yet still the belief that they are doing the right thing is so entrenched in them that any worker ant who does not conform to this lifestyle of excessive labour is despised by the others.

But it is not all doom and gloom for the worker ants. The Shadows have continually fed their desire for greed, so much so that they deeply admire the lifestyle of The Shadows. And ingeniously, the system is designed so that a small percentage of ants can prosper and live a lifestyle almost as well as The Shadows. These few prosperous ants help The Shadows to blend into society much more easily. They also give hope to the many worker ants who are struggling, by making it seem that it is fair to struggle, as one day, with hard work, a smart idea or maybe even a stroke of luck, they too may be in a better position. Thus, the ants have no obvious reason to revolt.

Humorously to Leucius, the truth is that if every single ant tried very hard it would do them little good. Again, the system has this under control. The more they collectively succeed, the more they earn, the more disposable income they have to spend and the more inflation rises. The more inflation increases, the less these worker ants can afford with the money they have earnt. And ultimately, with a cohort of hard-trying ants, the only thing that changes is that the next cohort of worker ants then has to continue to produce and consume at a great level just to keep up with what is the new acceptable level of production, making them like hamsters on a wheel that are unwittingly increasing their own pace with every step.

And so, day by day, these ants continue to sacrifice their time in this pursuit of labour until eventually they are too old to physically work any longer. And even though they know this is their fate, not once do they protest the truth that by sacrificing their time along the way, they are sacrificing their very life.

And the real irony of all of this is that the worker ants believe that this is what they choose. That they are free. *But they're not free. They just think they are.*

The only real winners of this game are The Shadows. For they secretly control much of the economic system and have convinced the majority of these worker ants to embrace a lifestyle of excessive toil, capital expenditure and unfavourable debt.

What a brilliant system.

Did The Shadows invent this? A system where the majority slave tirelessly for a select few? No, it was created long ago. It has been around since the first leaders of groups, the first tribal leaders, the first kings and queens. It is evident in nature, in a pride of lions, in groups of apes. No, The Shadows didn't invent this system. They are merely using a system that has been there for a very long time to their advantage.

A system is simply a tool and like all tools is neither good nor bad. It is how a tool is used that makes the difference between good and evil. Leucius knows that this system is not currently being used for the greater good. Which is exactly why he is so deeply concerned about The Shadows' most powerful enemy: Geno. If humans were to become enlightened with the knowledge the members of Geno have, The Shadows and all others like them would no longer have power over them. The masses would be free to create a better balance between the man-made and natural world, between work and play. And with a few adjustments they could use this very same system for a greater path to the greater good.

This certainly cannot happen, Leucius thinks to himself as his fingers run along the yellow envelope he holds in his hands.

A man comes into Leucius' view. He is middle-aged with grey hair and thick dark eyebrows; he wears dark pants and his signature emerald tweed blazer with its small red triangle, and holds his golden cane. *It's Anomonet.*

Anomonet appears to notice Leucius and bows awkwardly. He picks himself upright. "Master, we have received some news," he calls as he moves closer, hurriedly, clip-clopping with his cane.

"I'm listening," Leucius says, removing his earphones.

"We have Ulysses' phone number."

"Very good. And you have tracked his phone?"

"Yes. But it is either turned off or is out of coverage area. His last known location was on the Gold Coast, Australia," he says, finally reaching Leucius and resting on his cane for balance.

As a man in a suit walks past, Leucius stops him by grabbing his arm.

"Leucius?... Anomonet?" The man seems surprised to see them. He bows to Leucius.

Leucius simply hands the man the yellow envelope.

The man nods. "Thank you, Master."

Leucius waves his fingers to signal the man to leave. Without skipping a beat he is back in the conversation with Anomonet. "I see. Geno would have made sure he didn't take his phone. It's very smart of them."

"Yes, we will continue to monitor it, just in case. Flight records show that Ulysses has flown to a small city in northern Australia known as Cairns."

"Could this be where the Geno base is?"

"It could be."

"Is this all of the information we have?"

"No. I have been saving the best for last. We have used Ulysses' phone records to track his father."

"The great Ioannis? Where is he?!" Leucius feels an intense wave of excitement.

"14 Fornax Street, Mount Isa, Queensland, Australia."

"Send our Enforcers there immediately. And make sure they don't spare him or anything close to him. I'm talking all his loved ones, even his pets – destroy the lot. We need to send a clear message," he says as he makes a fist and reopens his fingers quickly, as a way to show the destruction he wishes.

Anomonet nods. "Your will be done, Master."

CHAPTER 32

SURRENDER TO THE CHAOS WITH FAITH

Geno, Australia.

THE NEXT MORNING, Ulysses awakens and leaves the cabins. As he walks to breakfast, he discovers Delta in the distance, already busy at work, studying nature and taking notes. He wonders how long she has been awake. Her level of passion towards her work, towards life itself, greatly inspires him.

He also wonders how she will act around him today – after their encounter the night before. He still feels bad about how it ended.

*

An hour later, Ulysses sits on the marble stairs of the Grecian pavilion. And just as the previous day, Emit is before him, preparing to begin his lesson.

"Today we'll finish our introduction to the perfect mindset. Yesterday you learnt the first four principles. Uncover and hold the primary desires, have clear vision, be open to perfection and you are ready now. The fifth principle is: *Surrender to the chaos with faith,*" Emit says. "Surrendering yourself to what may appear as chaos, with the faith that all things ultimately lead to order."

Ulysses instantly understands Emit's words. His moment with Delta last night has prepared him well for this principle. When Delta was looking at the stars, alone, Ulysses did not know whether she would welcome his approach. But he surrendered to the unknown, to this chaos, and walked bravely towards his desires. He did this while putting his trust in a higher power that no matter the outcome, he would still receive perfection in some way. But still, he has questions. "How do we know that everything ultimately leads to order?"

"Our theory. It shows that there's an underlying order in all of the elements known to man, in the form of a greater elemental purpose. So, we certainly know that order exists. But do we know that everything ultimately leads to order? That the God level is ordered? No. This is why it's surrender to the chaos with *FAITH*. Having faith is important. We must have faith in ourselves, our ability. We must have faith that the other interconnected levels are doing their bit towards our shared greater good. Faith that everything works out for the best because the universe is on our side. And that, ultimately, there is an order, a greater good, taking place."

Ulysses nods. "But as our psychic abilities grow at Geno, wouldn't we eventually reach a point where we already know what will happen next? And therefore, nothing will seem like chaos?"

"That's a good point. But I'm unsure if it's possible to know all. Fundamentally, our psychic abilities are there to help us. And sometimes knowing things, especially when it comes to our futures, can get in the way of our greater purpose. But you might wish to ask Sophos this question. She's certainly Geno's most powerful oracle. If any human knows all, and yet is still fulfilling her greater good, it's Sophos. But, in the meantime, until you reach this level, know that things will sometimes appear as chaos, but you must simply have faith that there is a greater purpose at play," Emit says.

Ulysses nods. He understands.

Emit continues, "And now for the next principle…"

CHAPTER 33

DISCOVER THE FLOW STATE

EMIT CONTINUES HIS lessons.

"The next principle of the perfect mindset is: *Discover the flow state*.

"You see, there are flows of energy. You can cultivate the flow of energy within you to be in line with your true desires," Emit says as he motions up and down his chest. "And when the flow of energy outside of yourself is in line with this flow within, they become in sync and everything you desire manifests easily," he motions outwards to the world around him. "When you reach this point, you are in *the flow state*."

His words instantly lead Ulysses to think back to his high school days, where in certain moments he would throw shot after shot in basketball and continually get it in the hoop. It felt that everything was very fluid for him and that he was unstoppable. "Is the flow state you're referring to the same which people talk about in sport?" Ulysses asks Emit.

"Precisely! The flow state occurs when you have the greater power of the elemental forces on your side. You can encounter it in sports, in everything."

"I have definitely experienced this before!"

"And you have also experienced synchronicity too. The only difference between the flow state and synchronicity is that with the flow state an element is consciously using its powers to achieve its desires. While with synchronicity, desires are fulfilled outside the conscious powers of the element experiencing the synchronicity, and so it seems coincidental."

"Huh?"

"Let's use an example. Assume that you wished to catch a bus. This was your conscious desire. But as you waited for the bus, you were momentarily distracted and missed it. Luckily, another bus was due in five minutes. On this second bus, you met someone who ended up becoming your life partner. Meeting your life partner was your greatest desire in this situation, but as you didn't purpose-fully strive for this to occur, you didn't plan to miss the first bus, it appeared to you as being synchronistic."

"I get it now! When I discovered this theory, I realised that synchronicity is when the other connected elements, in the systems and levels, are working in concert to bring about our desires.

"But I never realised that the flow state and synchronicity were so closely related. Or that the flow state was so within our control. I personally have only experienced the flow state in a few small moments, here and there, with no idea how to stay in it. How do I get in the flow and stay in it?"

"You can begin by first discovering the flow within yourself. You already partly achieved this yesterday, when you discovered the love within yourself. This love already existed, you simply had to uncover it. It is the same with the flow. It is already within you, you just have to cultivate it.

"Once you have done this, discover the flow external to yourself. Now, sometimes this flow is moving towards your true desires and sometimes it is not.

"If the flow is moving towards your true desires, then simply get into sync with the flow state and your desires will manifest before your eyes.

"If the flow is not moving in line with your desires, then pay attention. Sometimes, the greater forces of the elements don't wish the same as you. And sometimes this is a good thing. Just as when you are open to perfection, you must not be bound by your version of perfection. Sometimes what we believe are our desires are not our truest desires. And thus, the flow leads us away from these desires.

"Other times, we aren't yet ready for a secondary desire, so the flow doesn't lead us to it until we are ready. Perhaps we need to learn, to grow, or for the circumstances to be right. Don't rush God in these latter cases. For, as discussed, while we are always ready to live a life of perfection, sometimes we have to become ready for specific desires to manifest in our life. As it is through time that a seed becomes a tree."

Ulysses nods his head. These concepts he recalls from the previous lessons.

Emit continues, "But there's also a third option: sometimes the flow isn't moving in line with our desires, yet we are ready for them. And we have the power to lead the greater elemental forces to change the direction of this flow. Here there comes a choice. In these cases, use the other principles of the perfect mindset to help with your decision on whether to change the flow."

Ulysses nods. "And what happens if I change the flow?"

"Sometimes as you receive your desires you will realise that you didn't truly want these things after all. They were not your true desires in the present moment. Have clear vision so that this does not happen often. But if it does happen, it's okay not to accept these gifts. To step out of the flow which leads towards them.

"However, when you are offered your true desires, always take them. For if you communicate your desires to the system and then you don't take them when they are offered to you, you show that you are either not ready for them or that you do not truly desire such gifts. Therefore, these gifts will stop flowing to you.

"In comparison, when you accept gifts from the universe with appreciation, more will come."

Ulysses understands what Emit says. "Before I started to work for my father, I noticed that when I wished to get a job, sometimes I would get no job offers at all. But then once I got one job offered to me, many more offers would come my way all at once. Or sometimes a girl would like me, I would be intimate with her and suddenly many more would be interested in me. They were all independent of each other and I couldn't understand why it was happening. All I knew is that when it rains, it pours."

"Yes, these are examples of where, through receiving a gift, you showed the interconnected elements that you were worthy of them. And thus, you attracted other similar gifts to you, leaving you to decipher which gifts were your true desires to accept."

"I can imagine that this is something which also makes holding our primary desires so powerful. Because when we already hold what we are seeking, we attract more of the same."

"Precisely! The secret of having all you dream of is in the perfect mindset. The more you develop it, the more you will realise this. And now we move on to the second to last principle…"

CHAPTER 34

14 FORNAX STREET

Mount Isa, Australia.

THE STREETS ARE bare as a mid-afternoon dry heat scorches the small outback city of Mount Isa. It is normal to have temperature changes of almost twenty degrees Celsius over the course of the day and night, especially during the winter.

And in this heat, two Shadow Enforcers arrive at 14 Fornax Street. They wear black ninja gis, with dark cloaks that are covered with patches of red dirt that were incidentally sourced from the surrounding landscape. The ninjas have one mission: find whoever is in this house and kill them. Simple.

They gracefully jump the waist-high fence, their cloaks gliding with them. And with stealth, they swiftly make their way through this beautiful yard.

There is nothing of interest to them so far. No sign of any guard dogs. *Nothing to stop them.* They separate, one moving to the front door of this one-story wooden house, the other walking up the stairs to the back entrance. They both discreetly pick the locks on the doors, slowly turn the doorknobs and walk inside.

One moves through the kitchen, the other the lounge. There is no one to be found. They then collectively search the main bedroom, the bathrooms and the second room. Finally, they meet in the office, the last room of the house.

There is no one here. There is no one anywhere.

A Shadow Enforcer notices an empty necklace box on the desk. And next to this necklace box is a mobile phone.

*

Forty-five minutes later – The French Riviera, France.

Sounds float past Leucius. There is the beautifully hypnotic whisper of classical music drifting through this grand office. The frantic movements and tweets of a bird, in its tiny cage, trying desperately to get out. And the rustlings of Leucius' gold pen as he fills a page, obsessed with his ideas.

The phone suddenly rings, sending Leucius a jolt of energy. He was so deeply immersed in his work that he had lost track of time. Frustrated, he reaches across his grand mahogany desk.

"Hello! Hello!" Leucius answers the phone angrily.

"I'm terribly sorry, Master of Shadows," a meek voice responds on the other line.

"Why did you interrupt me, Anomonet?" Leucius bellows, his gold pen still in his hand. He was working on something very important.

"The Shadow Enforcers have arrived at 14 Fornax Street, Mount Isa."

"Okay, this is good." Leucius calms.

"Actually, there is bad news. There is no one there. Furthermore, Ioannis' mobile was left here, so we have no indication of where he might be."

"Damn!" Leucius says, driving his gold pen towards his desk. But he stops short, as usual. After all, it is his favourite pen. "They must have somehow known we were coming."

"The Geno are psychic, Leucius. As I said, they are not as easy to destroy as you hope."

"Leave the Shadow Enforcers in Mount Isa, just in case the great Ioannis Sirius returns."

"Yes, Master of Shadows."

CHAPTER 35

UNCOVER AND CREATE PERFECTION

Geno, Australia.

At Geno, Emit continues to teach Ulysses the perfect mindset.

"The next principle is: *Uncover and create perfection*," Emit says. "As discussed in previous principles, there's an eternal perfection in every moment. A sunset always changes forms, yet it is truly the same perfection. This is the same with the elements. They change forms, but their perfection always exists. We must tap into this perfection, to uncover it. And then there is also to create… Like a great work of art that changes in each passing moment by using the same paints, this life is your masterpiece. You can create whatever you wish from the elements that are already here. Not because you love any moment more than another. But purely because you wish to create. This is, after all, the way of the universe through time. *An element interacts in a system and creates*."

"I thought about this deeply last night," Ulysses says. "That underlying every moment is a perfection which already exists in the time between time. And it is changing forms through time itself."

"Precisely! All that the elements, combined, are doing is creating new forms of perfection. Such as a seed becoming a tree."

"It's incredible."

"You too can help uncover and create new perfections in the universe. I want you to really enjoy this principle when you use it, Ulysses. Start within. Is there anything internal that is keeping you from experiencing perfection? If so, remove this obstacle. And focus on the flow within you: your enjoyment, your enthusiasm. And project this outwards.

"Enjoy the perfection around you. Bask in every new moment as if it is eternal and all you have is right now. Life is an adventure and perfections are waiting to be uncovered. And there is no greater joy than uncovering perfections and creating beautiful moments in life. For certainly a life of beautiful moments is one that is blessed."

Ulysses' thoughts drift to how he will use this principle with Delta when he is next with her. He wishes to be in the moment with her and for them to share perfections. Not with the desire that it will be even greater than last night. But with the desire that they will create a new moment of perfection.

Emit continues, "And now for the final principle of the perfect mindset."

CHAPTER 36

SEE THE ORDER AND CONTINUE

EMIT CONTINUES TO teach Ulysses at the steps of the Grecian pavilion.

"The final principle of the perfect mindset is: *See the order and continue.*

"To see the order is when you see that everything has meaning. That everything has worked out perfectly and that the greater good has taken place. It's seeing the order from the chaos. It will feel literally like staring right in God's face, for God's divine work is on display for you."

Ulysses already understands this step of the perfect mindset. It is deeply engrained in him, something which he has always known. Only now can he put it into words after learning the wisdom of the perfect mindset. "It's the underlying order which may begin as faith, but eventually becomes perceivable."

Emit continues, "Precisely. And the final part of this principle is *and continue.* You may have heard of the Ancient Greek phrase *never rest on your laurels?*"

"Yes."

"Not long before Geno began, laurel wreaths were given as symbols of victory. And so came the lesson to never rest on them. To continue. Because, each moment, as you know, offers the seeds of perfection. And so, while we appreciate our achievements and we may bask in them, we must also always continue to do the greater good and continue to uncover and create new perfections. We must continue on this trajectory and step up levels if we are to live the greatest life possible."

Ulysses has also often thought about this part of the principle. Too often in life he sees people lose their motivation and their hunger to stay on top and then they lose everything. People who are so happy to enter into relationships yet later become complacent, who start to neglect their partner and become bored with what they have. He already realises that continuing is very important. To keep growing, to keep stepping up levels. And Ulysses in this moment feels very dedicated to do so.

Emit speaks, "I can sense that you already understand this concept as well, Ulysses. And so, that concludes our teachings of the perfect mindset."

Ulysses nods. "Thanks for teaching me. They're incredible principles! I was wondering, have they always remained the same, ever since they began in Ancient Greece?"

"Yes. But as I said at the very beginning, they are adaptable. The first members of Geno mentioned this explicitly. So, if we ever find better ways to become self-actualised, we can do this instead. That being said, Ulysses, in all of the history of Geno, we still haven't improved this system. So, embrace these principles fully."

Ulysses nods. "So now that I have been taught the perfect mindset, when do I become self-actualised?"

Emit leans on the step with his foot. "Once you fully grasp these concepts and use them in your life. As you begin to use them you may discover in certain situations that even one principle alone can lead you to perfection. However, when you use the principles together in unison, you'll have all of the power of the universe."

"I see."

"After a while you won't even have to think about these principles. They'll become a part of you. You'll be completely in the present moment. One with God's will. And in this moment, you'll self-actualise."

"And how will I know when I'm self-actualised?"

"You'll simply know, Ulysses. And we'll know too, as those who are self-actualised can tell when others are."

Ulysses is eager to become self-actualised and to live the life of his dreams. He feels that he is closer to this than he has ever been.

CHAPTER 37

MARTIAL ARTS AND THE PERFECT MINDSET

IT IS MIDDAY. Ulysses stands with Luke on the dirt oval by the fig tree, ready for Luke's martial arts lesson.

"Now that you've been taught the perfect mindset, you can understand how it relates to Geno's martial arts," Luke says in his deep, powerful voice. "The perfect mindset will make you better in combat. For example, uncovering and holding your primary desires will be a great source of strength in tough moments. Even in battle, you must still hold the primary desire of love. Such as no doubt Delta held by blessing your assailants.

"Clear vision will help you to see things as they are. Yourself, your environment, your opponent. You'll clearly see how to use all of the elements to help you in the battle. To the point where you'll be able to anticipate what will happen next.

"Being open to perfection means that you'll be open to succeeding in combat.

"Being ready now means that you'll move quickly and not hesitate," Luke says as he moves his body with quick martial art strikes. "Surrendering to the chaos means that you will be brave in entering battle, even though you don't know what will happen next. Coupled with faith, it will make you stronger and give you belief in your movements.

"By discovering the flow state in yourself, your opponent and the environment, you'll become fluid. You will know when to strike and when not to strike. You'll know how to use an opponent's flow of energy against them, how to use the flow of energy within the environment to your advantage and much more.

"Uncovering and creating perfection is achieving perfection in battle, such as Delta did when she protected you.

"And finally, seeing the order and continuing. This is seeing the greater good behind the combat and continuing to protect what you love… But anyway, enough talking, let me show you."

Luke and Ulysses immediately begin physical training. During this lesson, Ulysses learns further insights into how the perfect mindset helps the Geno ancient martial arts.

As the lesson progresses, Ulysses cannot help but be in awe of how strong and powerful Luke is. Luke's muscles are perfectly balanced on his body and as he moves he appears to be in tune with every muscle fibre. Ulysses considers him to be the perfect masculine identity. And it is not just his physical body. Luke is certainly far ahead of him in every way that he has so far witnessed: with skills and intelligence. Ulysses is very thankful to have him as a mentor as he wishes to aspire to be more like Luke. Even though he also feels that he could never actually compete on the same level.

There is a moment during training where Ulysses notices Delta walk past them. Ulysses purposely shows off some of his newfound skills, hoping she watches admiringly. But she does not seem to pay any attention. *Why do I always try to impress Delta with physical feats?* He realises that he does not have a clue how to get her to like him.

CHAPTER 38

EMIT'S PASSION

AFTER THE MARTIAL arts training, Ulysses decides to walk to his cabin. But as he is so deep in his mind thinking about his learnings of the perfect mindset and the Geno martial arts, he mistakenly takes the path that leads to Emit's cabin. He only realises his error when he sees Emit on a cabin balcony, wearing spectacles and with chalk in hand, feverishly writing formulas on a blackboard. Emit stands back to contemplate his work.

"Excuse me, Emit. Are you working on something to do with the theory?" Ulysses asks, gaining his attention.

"Ulysses! Precisely. I'm interested in the implications our theory has on the discipline of physics," Emit says as he points to his chalkboard.

"Of course. I remember seeing your Ph.D. in physics hanging on the wall of your home office. What exactly are you working on?"

"The holy grail of the physics world," Emit says as he removes his glasses and places them on the duster holder.

"Sorry?"

"Currently, there's a great inquiry into how to reconcile the different physical models. Our theory at Geno proposes possibilities which may impact on these efforts."

"Really? How?" Ulysses knows a little about physics as he studied broadly to help him to devise his theory of everything. He recalls reading that there are competing physical models that seem to be correct individually but are also incompatible with each other. But he is certainly no expert.

"Well, firstly, our theory points to physical laws being created purely through the interaction between the elements. And thus, while the same general constructs can be universally true, in the sense that they are repeated in many interactions and on many levels, this is not always the case. This change in thought may significantly affect the way we currently view physics. And it may explain why the existing physical models are not compatible at every level.

"Secondly, there is the possibility that our discovery of physical laws may currently be limited due to evolutionary design parameters. For example, we're not evolutionarily designed to see the quantum world naturally, so maybe, even with the use of current technological instruments, we're still missing the ability to see certain aspects of the interactions in the quantum levels."

"That's so insightful, Emit."

"It's a work of fervent passion. But, you know, there is something which has even greater implications than this holy grail… Do you remember, on your first night here, how we discussed how Geno's theory may point to God being the ultimate system?"

"Yes."

"Well, Geno's theory can bring together science and religion."

"Yes! I realised the theory had this potential! Have you proven it?"

"No, not me, previous members of Geno. Listen to this… many physicists currently believe that the universe started as a singularity. What if this singularity was God? And God, through Thyself, created all that is? Religious people would call this moment Creation; physicists would call it The Big Bang."

Ulysses is amazed at what he is hearing. He never realised this connection before.

Emit continues, "And it gets deeper than this. The more I delve into science and religion, the more I see that they're both telling the same story."

"The possibility is incredible."

"It certainly is. Thankfully, past members of Geno have greatly contributed to this discipline already. And so, I'm standing on the shoulders of giants."

Ulysses nods. He suddenly realises that he is taking up Emit's time. Time which could be better spent deciphering great secrets of the universe. "I'll leave you to get back to writing feverishly, Emit. But I'd love to learn more some time."

"I'll teach you everything I know, bit by bit. Thanks for taking an interest, Ulysses." Emit smiles and goes back to working on his theory.

Ulysses walks away from Emit's cabin, feeling inspired. Everyone at Geno seems to be working on ground-breaking theories that could change the world. He cannot help but wonder what other great discoveries past members of Geno have made. And if there have ever been any famous historical figures that were secret members of Geno.

Perhaps Geno has also collaborated with non-members for the greater good. This thought leads him into a daydream where he imagines Geno collaborating with Einstein. That perhaps Einstein did come up with great theories later in life but chose to simply leave them with Geno after seeing how his theories unintentionally contributed to the creation of the atomic bomb. *Perhaps Geno is the gatekeeper of many grand theories, and not all created by them. There are so many possibilities*, Ulysses thinks.

He makes it back to the oval where he sees Delta with Luke. She has a bow in her left hand and her right hand reaches behind her back and pulls out an arrow from her quiver. She lines the arrow and pulls it back with her bow.

She looks entirely focused on the target ahead, a bullseye on the cliff face. She releases the arrow from her fingertips. The arrow moves fast and strikes just outside of the bullseye, becoming lodged in the dirt of the cliff face. Ulysses is surprised. *A great shot, but not perfect.*

This is the second time he has ever seen Delta do anything without absolute perfection. The first time was when she tried to cross the river on the journey to Geno and she struggled over the little stones.

However, realising that Delta is not perfect in every task she attempts does not lead Ulysses to think any less of her. To the contrary, it attracts him even more. It hints that maybe he could complement her talents in one way or another.

And so, her imperfections are still perfection to him. And therefore, Delta is still very much perfect in his eyes. Again, it reminds him that perhaps perfection is all around us, it is just that we need to have the right eyes to see it.

CHAPTER 39

THE STORM

Taking a wrong turn through Geno has brought out curiosities in Ulysses. He is amazed that he has been here for two days and does not know his surroundings better. With this in mind, he purposely explores, walking along the meandering paths through the rainforest of Geno.

He walks over the white stone bridge, passes an ancient fountain and arrives at the garden near the entrance. Surrounded by rosebushes and white Grecian nude statues with plaques underneath, he takes a path to an area of the garden he has never been before.

And then he sees *her*. He becomes transfixed. The white marble nude statue appears completely accurate to her proportions. It is the most beautiful work of art he has ever seen. "Delta" is engraved on a plaque at the base of the statue.

Suddenly, while looking at this statue, he has a vision, a vision of Delta standing naked before her statue.

"I would like you to get as close to me as possible, Ulysses. As deep as you can get," Delta speaks in this vision.

The power of her beauty intoxicates him. Ulysses is drawn towards this apparition. He moves closer. But then, as quickly as this vision appeared, it is gone.

Ulysses is brought back to reality. *Was this another premonition?* Ulysses certainly hopes this one will come true. He continues to study this nude statue, questioning when he is going to become self-actualised so that he can control these powers.

Suddenly, he notices a drop of water hit the base of the statue. And then a few more. He looks up and sees the clouds sprinkling droplets of water, which begin to lightly hit his face and shoulders.

He can hear heavier rain battering the rainforest trees a short distance away and moving towards him at a fast pace. *A storm.* He immediately starts running towards the centre of Geno, trying his best to outpace the rain. But it is of no use. The rain catches him and becomes heavier and heavier. Soon it is so hard that it stings when it touches his bare skin. He runs past the oval and takes cover in the first shelter he finds – the kitchen shack.

He ducks through the door, thoroughly drenched. And he is not alone. Delta and Sophos are also taking refuge here. However, unlike him, they are both completely dry. *Their psychic powers have probably protected them. When will I develop mine?*

Sophos is sitting on an old chair. Delta is leaning against a bench with her bow and arrows beside her. Ulysses cannot help but think of Delta's statue as he says hi. He feels rather uncomfortable, as if he is hiding a secret. He avoids eye contact with Delta and simply leans against a bench, switching between looking out the doorway and a nearby window to take in the intensity of the rain as it hits the outside elements. It turns into a torrential storm. The coconut trees across the oval bend with the mighty wind. Hail pellets the kitchen shack from above. As the roof is made of tin, it sounds even more frightening than it would otherwise. There are also powerful bolts of lightning striking Geno, rapidly followed by deafening thunder that groans for what seems like an eternity afterwards. Even if Ulysses wanted to speak in this moment, he knows that they would not be able to hear him.

But despite its ferocity, within twenty minutes the rain ceases and it becomes peaceful again. Ulysses hesitantly walks outside to inspect things. Delta joins him and they both walk towards their cabins. On the walk he notices the humidity in the air strengthens the pleasant aroma of the rain soaking into the elements. *Everything is peaceful again.*

But when he arrives, he is visually shocked. A large eucalyptus tree has fallen over both Ulysses' and Delta's cabin, destroying the roofs.

Delta calls out to Emit who walks nearby.

"What is it, Delta?" Emit asks as he walks closer.

"Look at our cabins. What do we do?" Delta points to the damaged cabins.

"Hmm, I see," Emit says, his temperament not changing at all. "It will be dark shortly. Grab your personal belongings and put them somewhere dry. I will prepare some backup accommodation you can both use. It'll be basic, but it'll do for one night. And tomorrow we can fix the roofs," replies Emit.

CHAPTER 40

THE CABIN

IT IS THE evening. Ulysses and Delta sit on slightly damp logs, the soil around them still moist. The sky is overcast, no stars visible. Delta has her knees curled up to her chest, her arms delicately wrapped around her legs. And before them is a fire which steadily burns through dry timber blocks that had been stored in Geno's kitchen for a rainy day.

Ulysses suddenly realises that with the storm ruining his cabin, he does not know where he will be sleeping tonight. He never asked. And now Emit, Sophos and Luke have retired to their cabins.

"Do you know where we're sleeping tonight?" he asks Delta.

"Out here by the fire," Delta responds cheekily. "Just kidding, we're sharing a room. There's a spare cabin with bunk beds."

"Oh, okay," Ulysses says nonchalantly, hiding the fact that he is pleased to have the fortune to sleep in the same room as Delta.

*

Ulysses enters the spare cabin. It smells of fresh toothpaste. Delta is already on the bottom bunk, the sheets pressing against her. He adores seeing her in this moment, so much that he does not want to make the room dark. He savours her a couple more seconds, which he feels is as long as he possibly can without making his attraction overtly obvious. He turns off the light. The room instantly darkens. It takes a moment for his eyes to get used to the darkness, but once they adjust, he moves towards the bed and climbs onto the top bunk. He gets settled and then breaks the silence.

"Delta, were you born on the Gold Coast?"

"No. I was born in Sweden, I lived there until I was ten."

"That explains why your accent is so different."

Ulysses noticed from her very first words that Delta had an accent. One of his natural reactions when he first meets someone with an accent is to ask where they are from. But he did not do this with Delta. The reason being that while travelling overseas for long periods, he purposely got into the habit of not engaging in the same conversations over and over. He would get asked this question, of where he is from, so many times a day. Knowing that other travellers must be the same, he consciously stopped asking this question. Instead, he would keep the conversations novel, knowing that the standard questions would eventually be revealed naturally if you get to know a person well. And now with Delta, this standard question is finally being revealed.

"Haha, yes, I grew up in Sweden, but I think an accent depends on where and when you grew up, your social class and so forth, as I have noticed that the Swedish accent of most travellers in Australia is very different to how people would speak where I grew up. When I was ten, I moved to Australia to live with Uncle Emit, who is, of course, originally English. So, I have a real mix of an Australian, Swedish and English accent. Nobody can ever pick it."

"I just came back from Sweden. I loved it. What was it like growing up there?"

"It was great. I lived in a small village. My family had a simple house with a large piece of land. Every day I would ride my lovely white horse, Salt."

"That sounds really magical." He envisions Delta as a young, modern-day peasant girl, living on a small farm and being happy with the simple pleasures of life.

"It was such a magical place. It really was. I miss it so much. How about you, where did you grow up?"

"In Mount Isa, a small city in the Australian outback. We too lived in a modest house, where three bedrooms housed five of us, including my sisters. We made friends with the neighbourhood kids and played freely, roaming the streets. It was such a great place to grow up. My parents still live there and I visit them often. Are you close with your family?"

"I try to be. I think of them every day. I love them so much. Family is the most important thing," Delta says.

"I believe so too." Ulysses instantly realises that this is an opportunity to share some of his romantic beliefs with Delta. "I feel the greatest gift you can ever give someone is to get married and have kids together. By getting married you are offering the one you choose to become a part of what is most important to you – your family. And when you have children together, you entwine in one another's genetic code for eternity. A bond that can never be broken."

"Wow, that is such a beautiful way to look at it," Delta says, her words, whilst earnest, slowing as if she is becoming sleepy.

Ulysses wishes to learn everything he can about Delta. What her childhood was like. What her favourite tree in her backyard was when growing up. Her deepest thoughts. Everything.

"Delta, why did you move to Australia and live with your uncle?"

But Delta does not answer. Ulysses rolls to the edge of his bed and looks down to discover that she has fallen asleep. She looks comfortably at peace. He has never before seen someone sleep with such perfection. *A sleeping beauty.*

And as he looks upon her, he notices that the darkness brings out features of her face he does not usually see in the light. He has often thought of how it will be great to find a girl who he is attracted to in all shades of light. Delta has this embodiment. He has found that she looks just as breathtaking in the sunlight, as under a flame, and in the dark. Different, but equally gorgeous.

He settles back into his bed, this time lying on his front, with the image of Delta below him still fresh in his mind. He can imagine that he is lying on top of her, knowing that there is only a mattress and some vacant space making it not a reality. And if this situation is not hard enough, he also has the vision he had while viewing the statue to contend with.

Ulysses delves into this fantasy. Every move Delta makes in her bed stirs lustful feelings inside him. His body tells him not to rest, it tells him to give in to his urge to envelop Delta.

He spends most of the night tossing and turning in his bed, feeling overly sexual and occasionally dreaming that he and Delta are together.

In parts of the night, he even contemplates going down to her bunk to be next to her. If only he could control and strengthen his psychic powers, he thinks. That way he would know what Delta's desires are. And he would know whether she would welcome his advances, without taking a chance.

CHAPTER 41

THE NEXT MORNING

DELTA AWAKENS, FRANTICALLY checking her stomach by lifting her sheet. *There isn't any blood.* She relaxes. *It was a dream.* The same dream she has been having since she arrived back at Geno. *It felt so real.*

She rises from her bed. As usual, she is up at first light. Being an early riser comes naturally to her, but there is an element of habit too, as where she grew up, the entire village was up at the break of dawn. It was a necessity for them, as making the most of the sunlight was vital for their survival.

She looks over at Ulysses, seeing that he is deep in sleep. He looks so handsome to her. She studies his broad shoulders and his pretty boy face, which are free from the blue sheets. She visualises climbing into bed beside him and touching his chest. But just as quickly as she imagines this, she scolds herself. She knows that she cannot be with him in a romantic sense. *This is not meant to be.*

CHAPTER 42

HOW TO SEND DREAMS

Ulysses awakens. He rolls over and looks down to the bottom bunk, but Delta is gone. As usual, she has awoken before him.

*

Later, in the mid-morning, Ulysses sits on the stairs of the pavilion. Here, just as the days before, Emit stands in front of him, giving him a lesson.

"Ulysses, today I wish to teach you more applications of the theory and great discoveries from past members of Geno," Emit says enthusiastically.

"Emit, with all respect, you promised to teach me how to control and strengthen my psychic powers. But I'm yet to learn," Ulysses says, expressing his frustration.

"That's because it's important for you to first master the perfect mindset and become self-actualised."

"But I believe I'm ready to learn now. After all, I discovered the theory for myself. I'm capable of things that previous members are not. Give me a chance."

Emit looks upwards and appears to be thinking very deeply. Ulysses would love to know what exactly is going through Emit's mind. Perhaps when Ulysses masters his psychic powers he will be able to read minds in moments such as these.

Emit looks back at Ulysses and ends his contemplation by speaking a simple sentence, "And so it shall be."

"Thank you, Emit. You won't be disappointed," Ulysses says, feeling a rush of anticipation.

"I hope not. Now, let's begin. You must first understand Geno's distinction between psychic and magic powers. Magical powers have an external effect that can be obvious to a witness as being magical, say, moving an object from a distance just by willing it. Meanwhile, psychic powers are internal and therefore can be kept more hidden – such as reading minds, seeing the future or communicating telepathically.

"But apart from this subtle difference, both psychic and magic powers are in essence the same thing. They both involve interacting with the elements in ways not currently understood by science. Yet they're understood by our theory here at Geno, as due to the interconnection of all things, interaction is possible between all," Emit explains.

"Yes, I gathered that the unseen forces and interconnections create psychic abilities," Ulysses says, leaning forwards. He finds this topic fascinating. *Finally I'm going to learn magic!*

"Precisely. And ever since you have discovered this theory, you have become more open to this, causing your psychic powers to be uncovered. But still, you lack the ability to control your newfound powers. Which is one of the reasons why you have been taught the perfect mindset. This mindset will help you with everything you do, not the least of which is to become in control of your powers. So, whatever I teach you today, remember to also use the perfect mindset."

"Understood."

"Good. I'll begin by teaching you one of the more basic psychic techniques: sending dreams. You see, dreams serve many purposes.

They can help us to learn, they can be tools of wish fulfillment, vessels for our deepest desires and fears. But it's important to know that not all dreams come from the mind. Some dreams give us insights communicated from other interconnected elements, systems and levels. They can also be telepathic, preparing us for the future. And just as the elements and systems can communicate with us through dreams, we can also communicate with others through sending them dreams," Emit explains.

"Why would we want to send dreams?"

"There's also a lot of power with this ability, Ulysses. Dreams persuade people greatly. Even if they don't consciously remember their dreams, they seep into their unconscious, shaping their desires, their plans."

Ulysses' mind darts to how Pontius Pilate's wife was warned through dreams that Jesus was an innocent man. Because of this dream, she felt a strong desire to warn Pontius not to be involved with his death. Ulysses wonders if the dream was sent to her. And if it was, why was it sent? Maybe some of the other elements tried to prevent Jesus' death, he ponders.

Emit continues, "Sending dreams is also a safer way to send psychic messages to people. For example, if you were to send visual or auditory messages to a non-member of Geno in the waking hours, they might think they have lost their mind."

"That's true."

"Furthermore, sending dreams is a good place for us to begin, as it's easier than most methods of psychic communication. It's simpler because as the receiver sleeps, their minds are not always self-imposing the limitations that they do in their normal life. Which is the same reason why many psychic and enlightened insights happen whilst people are not consciously thinking, in a moment of no mind, in the clear light."

"So, tell me, how do I send dreams?"

"A method we use at Geno is as follows: connect your hands in prayer, with the intention to send a dream," Emit says as he connects his hands in prayer and closes his eyes. "Have the person in your mind you wish to send the dream to. Visually display and feel their energy in your mind's eye. It's easier to send dreams to those you know well, as you know their energy and are more easily connected to them. Once you feel their energy strongly, in your mind, hold an image of yourself and your own energy. Then interact your energy with the energy of the person you wish to send the dream to, in whichever way you please, but importantly give these images in your mind heightened emotions, which portray the message you wish to send. Once you have reached the point where these images in your mind are very strong, request the help of another interconnected element that has the power to send the dream. You may choose to ask God. Or something else altogether. Use the interconnected element you feel will work the best. I find that asking a spirit is a good method as some people who have passed are in tune with the interconnection of things. Especially a specific spirit whom the receiver knows and that you feel you can connect with," Emit says while being very expressive with his hands. "Ask the element to send your dream. Wish for the receiver to receive the dream and that it will be so powerful that they remember it in the morning, themselves awakening with heightened emotions. While your hands are still interlocked in prayer, kiss your right hand by simply drawing your connected hands towards you and the dream shall be sent. You may then release your hands," Emit says and he finally opens his eyes.

"Wow," Ulysses says. He is amazed to learn such practical wisdom. But even still, there is something troubling Ulysses. "I'm not sure if this is right. Isn't sending dreams very invasive?"

"Yes, they are invasive. So, you must use this power wisely and only use it when necessary. If you use the perfect mindset, it will guide you on whether you should send a dream or not. And to calm you, it's important to know that a person will only receive this dream if it is the will of the elements that you use to send it. Furthermore, it's easier to be sent if the receiver is open to it."

Of course, Ulysses thinks. Perhaps this is why Pontius' wife received the dream, not Pontius himself. Maybe she was more open to receiving it.

"Tonight, I want you to test your skills by sending me a dream of something. And then tomorrow we'll see if I've received it."

Ulysses has finally been given a task which will help him to control his psychic powers.

CHAPTER 43

THE ART OF XIREN

LATER THIS DAY, Ulysses meets Luke for the martial arts lesson, on the oval near the large fig.

"There are ways to manipulate others and their thought patterns," Luke says.

"Such as through sending dreams?"

"Yes. But in the waking world too. And without the use of psychic powers. How do you know about sending dreams anyway? Has Emit already begun teaching you?"

"Yes, just today."

"That's strange, normally he saves this for when a member is self-actualised," Luke says as he squints his eyes and seems to study Ulysses.

"I believe I'm ready," Ulysses says.

"Believe me, you're not ready, Ulysses," Luke smiles. "No one's ready before they self-actualise." Luke looks intently at Ulysses. "I wonder what he sees in you that he's willing to take this risk?"

Ulysses shrugs his shoulders.

"I'll have a chat with him later and see if I should introduce psychic and magical elements into the martial arts training. But for today's lesson, I'll show you a powerful psychological trick. The Art of Xiren."

"Xiren?"

"It's where you confuse your opponent to the point where they are unable to move, effectively freezing them. It allows you to have complete control of them."

"How does it work?"

"Ulysses, I want you to listen very carefully. This is important," Luke says in his powerful, deep voice as his arms and hands move gracefully, similar to a cobra moving in time with a flute. And as his arms move, Luke makes intricate hand movements and gestures. They seem to come fluidly and naturally. He speaks words that he chooses purposely, as if he knows exactly what to say to penetrate Ulysses' subconscious. "This isn't real," Luke says with such conviction that it strikes Ulysses.

"What isn't real?"

"Do not you know? This world. This life. This is not real. You have always known this. You are simply afraid to awaken."

Suddenly Ulysses feels more present, more awake than he ever has been. He is so alert that he can hear a faint humming in his ears. It feels as if every element in his body has suddenly been caught out playing a game. That, deep down, every part of him knows that this life is not real. And with this realisation he becomes incredibly fearful. Ulysses worries that if he does not go back to being unconscious to this fact, he could leave this reality forever. And he does not want to leave. He prefers to be asleep. He wants to be with the beauty of the world that he knows. With Delta.

Luke begins to move his arms fast and then slow, fast and then slow, continually and in repetition. He seems to create a hundred arms to Ulysses. "Because you do not remember it is easy to forget. Do not you know who Delta is?"

Ulysses hears the words, though Luke's hand movements subconsciously take energy away from his concentration. Everything is becoming harder for Ulysses to process. It is like he is more conscious than he has ever been while his mind is simultaneously becoming like stone. Ulysses only just manages to answer the question, almost on autopilot. "Who?"

"She's Jesus," Luke says and then his hands become still, his right hand upright and close to Ulysses' face.

Ulysses becomes stunned at this point, unable to speak, unable to process anymore. He is at the will of Luke.

"I want you to regain control," Luke says as he brings his hand, palm face up, to his mouth and slowly blows wind onto Ulysses.

With a jolt, Ulysses suddenly comes back to his normal functioning. "How did you do that!?" he says to Luke, feeling confused and in a panic, his heart now beating very fast. *How did he just lose control, while being both completely conscious and powerless at the same time?*

"When we have clear vision and are in the flow state, we can summon the powers of Xiren and use this flow of energy to seduce others. Through using the perfect mindset, words come to our lips. We instinctively know exactly what to say in order to Xiren. They are words which are personal to the receiver and on the topic of their desires, their fears, their deepest thoughts. Or simply words that feel right in the moment, as if they have been given to us by the greater connected elements.

"Once you reach the state of Xiren they are unable to think rationally. To them, it feels similar to waking from a dream, but their body is still asleep, unable to move. They are frozen and you have complete power over them."

"How's this even possible?"

"We transform the energy within them. You see, every element has potential inside it. Every lion has the potential to roar. Every butterfly the potential to fly. It's how we interact with an element that brings out these potentials. Every person has the potential to fight, freeze or flee. These instincts come from the most primal regions of their mind and can be activated very easily. No one has ever withstood Xiren before. It's one of our strongest psychological tricks. It always succeeds."

"So, it's kind of like a Jedi mind trick?" Ulysses asks with a smirk.

"Yes, Ulysses, I guess you could say that," Luke says while laughing.

CHAPTER 44

EMIT WARNS ULYSSES

Ulysses arrives at his cabin to discover Emit standing on a ladder, hammering a nail into the roof with Delta standing next to him. Delta seems to be just leaving.

"Bye, Emit."

"See you, princess."

She greets Ulysses with a smile. "Hey, Ulysses."

"Hi." Ulysses savours a moment of eye contact with her as she walks past. His attention then moves to Emit. "Do you need a hand?"

"No thanks, Ulysses. We've just finished." Emit steps down from the ladder. "It's all fixed. You don't have to share a cabin with Delta anymore."

Ulysses feigns a smile. He is unsure whether he is happy that his cabin is fixed or not.

"There's something I wish to talk to you about," Emit says, his facial expression suddenly stern.

"What's that?" Ulysses' pretend smile quickly dissipates.

"Have a seat," Emit says, and they both sit at the stairs that lead to the cabin. "It's about Delta."

"Delta?"

"Yes, I've noticed that you're developing feelings for her."

Ulysses nods. "Well, can you blame me? She's amazing."

Emit places his hand on Ulysses' shoulder. "I know. And I think Delta likes you very much. I've seen the way she becomes shy around you. The way she gazes at you when you're not looking. But you don't know the entire truth about her, Ulysses. Her past... she keeps a secret wall around her heart. And for good reasons."

"What reasons?"

"There's no easy way to say this. But Delta has been receiving signs that you're not meant to be together. She must listen to these signs."

"What do you mean *signs*?"

"It isn't my place to go into great detail. But I believe they are signs from the greater levels. Perhaps from God."

A pain instantly pierces Ulysses heart, like a sharp arrow. If God does not wish them to be, then he cannot possibly have her. After all, he is not more powerful than God. "How do you know these signs are from God? How do you know you're not mistaken?"

"It's complicated. You have to trust me."

Even though Ulysses is confused by Emit's vagueness, he does trust him. He believes that Emit would never say anything he did not believe to be true. "I just don't understand."

"Delta is starting to open her heart to you. But if she does, her life will be in danger. You must decide if you love her so much that you're willing not to be with her. Because this is *very serious*. Your love could destroy her."

"Destroy her?"

"She could die."

Ulysses puts his head down, silently overcome with emotions.

Ulysses then looks up, directly into Emit's eyes. "I don't want her to die." And he does not say another word. There is no point; he is powerless. He stands and strides from his cabin, away from Emit.

"It's for the greater good," Emit calls after him.

As he walks away, Ulysses feels as if he has been internally wounded. Here is a man so wise, telling him that he must not be with the girl he is beginning to love. And what is most painful of all is that God does not want Ulysses to be with her. And God knows all.

CHAPTER 45

ULYSSES SENDS A DREAM

In the late evening, Ulysses lies in his wooden cabin bed. But there is something different to the last time he was here on his bed, as now he is heartbroken.

He was beginning to believe that Delta was romantically destined for him. After all, his intimate dreams led him to her. *How could these synchronicities occur if they were not for a reason?*

Now he has been warned by Emit not to pursue her or she may die. That it is the will of God. Ulysses struggles to comprehend how God would not wish to share the gift of Delta with him when everything Ulysses feels so deeply inside urges him to be romantically with her. What if Emit is mistaken? There must be a way he can become certain that this is truly God's wishes.

Suddenly, a great idea comes to Ulysses. Perhaps he can still show his feelings to her from a distance. Feelings that he is not allowed to show her in person. Emit, without realising it, has just given Ulysses the powers to do such.

And it makes perfect sense. He may not be able to show his affection to Delta in public life. But he can send his affection to her in a dream. Like a kiss through a veil. Their love may be forbidden in the waking world, but Ulysses can grace her at her most intimate, while she is sleeping so beautifully in bed. Just as he saw her on the bottom bunk the night before.

And *there's nothing wrong with this plan*. For if he uses God as the interconnected element, then it will only be sent with the consent of God. And therefore, Ulysses will discover whether it is the will of God for him not to be with Delta, or if Emit is mistaken. If she receives it, then God wishes her to receive it. If she does not, then God does not wish their love to be. Ulysses will know once and for all.

This is the answer!

Excited, he begins. He envisions Delta, her beautiful image which he has come to know, her energy. He then visualises himself, his energy. He then projects them together at Geno's garden, near her nude statue, making passionate love. He does not spend much time on the exact details of the dream but instead focuses more on the emotional intensity, which Ulysses feels so strongly within him as if it is truly happening. He prays to God to send her this dream, to make it a dream that portrays the emotions he has just felt, and he adds the wish that Delta is so sensually touched by this dream that she remembers it in the morning, awakening with an overwhelming feeling of love and pleasure.

Ulysses, certain that his desires have been expressed, with his hands still interlocked, kisses the closest side of his right hand and releases his hands from prayer. *It has been done.*

CHAPTER 46

TO DREAM TO FAIL

DELTA AWAKENS. EVER since she has arrived at Geno, she has had the same recurring dream: a dream of her and Ulysses kissing under a waterfall. This is followed by a second part to her dream, where great tragedy strikes. She dreams that her stomach is covered in blood. She is dying.

Last night, however, she did not dream this recurring dream. She dreamt simply of Ulysses and her making love in Geno's garden. His seductive eyes looking into hers, his strong arms holding her. She awoke with a feeling of great sensual excitement. But it has also left her feeling confused. She cannot make sense of it. Why are her dreams warning her away from Ulysses, whilst drawing her in at the same time?

Half an hour later, Delta and Ulysses meet at breakfast on the large stone table on the oval. Delta is surprised as Ulysses is not usually awake at this time. It is the first time they have ever met at breakfast. She looks at him as he takes his seat, but instead of her normal warm welcoming greeting, she simply says hello and then instantly looks down, diverting her gaze from him. It is as if suddenly she is completely shy by Ulysses' presence. She can barely talk to him or even look him in his eyes. After all, here is a handsome man who has attracted her so deeply in her sensual dreams.

"Did you have a good sleep?"

His words lead Delta to think even more of her dream. She becomes even more demure. "Uh-hum," she simply replies. The truth is that this is all she could muster to say.

*

Ulysses looks into her eyes, searching for clues that his dream has been received. But as they sit across from one another, he notices how indifferently she behaves towards him. Most of the time she looks down, eating her breakfast. She hardly ever brings her eyes up to meet his. She does not seem to have any interest in him at all, though with Luke, who joins them at the table, she immediately talks vibrantly, with much conversation.

She mustn't have received the dream, Ulysses reasons.

Ulysses is deeply disappointed. Not by the prospect of being unskilled at controlling his psychic powers. But rather, because of another possibility.

He does not want to believe it, but this possibility becomes even more proven to him as the time passes at this table. As just as he is about to speak to Delta again, Luke interrupts this intention by talking to her first. Ulysses waits patiently until their conversation finishes and when it does, he seizes the opportunity and motions towards Delta. But she does not notice because at the exact same moment she is called by Sophos to join her in the kitchen shack.

Ulysses, filled with doubt, still makes one last attempt to garner her attention. As Delta leaves the table, he stands and walks towards her.

"Wait…" He gently grabs the part of her arm in front of her elbow, where her arm bends. "… Please." Ulysses' voice softens and he touches Delta's arm kindly. She turns back towards him. His touch appears to instantly bring down her guard. He knows that he is touching her just as he did on the day they first met outside of the library.

"Yes?" Delta asks, looking into his eyes.

"Delta, I…" Over her shoulder, Ulysses suddenly sees Emit walking towards them. He cannot be caught pursuing Delta. He cuts it short. "Have a good day," Ulysses says.

"You too," Delta says, looking confused. And with this, she turns away from Ulysses and continues towards Sophos.

As she leaves, Ulysses feels hurt. It hurts that he believes she has not received the dream. It hurts that he believes that she has become cold towards him. And it hurts that the flow is against him this morning, that many times when he tried to speak with her things got in the way of his intentions.

But there is one thing that hurts Ulysses far more than any other. It is what all these signs point to. And that is, the greater force of the elements, God, does not wish for him and Delta to be.

CHAPTER 47

MAGIC POWERS

It is the mid-morning at Geno. Ulysses sits on the bottom stone stair of the Geno pavilion while Emit stands before him. Ulysses is not ready for this lesson. He feels mentally closed off and struggles to think of anything apart from Delta and how their love cannot be.

"I didn't receive any dream last night?" Emit asks, waking Ulysses from his thoughts.

"Oh… I forgot to send you one," Ulysses answers. This is true, he did forget; he was too busy sending one to Delta.

"That's okay, we'll move on. Today is the day you've truly been waiting for. I'll be teaching you how to perform magic. And unlike the psychic ability of sending dreams, this is the kind of magic which has no delayed effect so you can witness its power instantly."

"Wait a minute!" Ulysses stops him with a great realisation. "Why did Delta use martial arts to protect me from The Shadows? It would have been easier to use magic. Why didn't she simply put a spell on them?"

"We try not to use our magic powers outside of Geno. That's not to say we haven't in the past, but only as an absolute last resort.

Instead, we use martial arts, discreet psychic powers and psychological tricks. This way our magic abilities are kept secret."

Emit throws a leaf in front of himself, only briefly looking at it as it floats to the ground at his feet. He puts his hand out and with seemingly very little concentration, he begins to move the leaf back into the air, just by willing it. It dances in sync with the movements of his fingers and rises back up to his hand.

"How did you do that?" Ulysses asks. He stands to look at the leaf in Emit's hands with amazement.

"Magic. Everything is interconnected, this is how magic is born. Have a try," Emit says as he again drops the leaf to the ground.

Ulysses excitedly places out his hand and attempts to make the leaf move with his mind.

But the leaf simply continues to rest on the ground.

Ulysses tries again. He closes his eyes and visualises the leaf moving upwards. He then reopens his eyes and tries again for real. But still it does not move. He brings his hand back to his side. *Perhaps I need to focus more.* He puts his hand out again and uses all his mind power, concentrating very intensely. Still *nothing*.

"I can't do it," Ulysses says. Giving up today is very easy for him.

"Ulysses, you're doing what most people do when they first try to move an object at Geno. They concentrate on moving the object with their mind. But this isn't the correct way. Magic is more than your mind. Besides, it's your mind that thinks it's impossible for you to move this leaf. Instead, use the elements. Everything is connected, so you can move this leaf by wishing the other elements to move it for you. Begin with the perfect mindset principles. And then use the same techniques as sending a dream: picture the element as you wish it to be and harness the power of an interconnected element to fulfil this wish."

"Luke showed me Xiren yesterday. He said that it's achieved by transforming the energy which already exists. Is this the same with magic?"

"Yes, Ulysses. Magic is simply a key. Have you ever noticed how listening to a certain song may give you a certain energy? Or looking at a sunset? These things simply decoded an energy that already existed inside of you. They served as a key. In the same way, magic decodes the energy of the world around you. It lets the elements know your wishes and requests those elements with the power to turn the key for you. You see, in every leaf there is the ability to fly with the wind, and there is the ability to fall with gravity. What you ask of the leaf is nothing it's not designed to do. So, for example, you can get the wind to move the leaf for you, up to your hands."

"And what about elements that the wind cannot move?"

"If the element can move itself, then this is a method. Otherwise use elements that do have the power to move it. If nothing else can help you, allow God to do it. For God can do all if it is for the greater good."

Ask God? God doesn't wish for the same things as I. Ulysses suddenly feels an affinity to Ulysses in the Ancient Greek mythology. He, too, was in opposition to the Gods as their good was not the same as his. "I can't ask God."

"Then ask another element which has the power. You can do this; I believe in you."

Ulysses closes his eyes and begins with the perfect mindset. But he simply cannot focus. He quickly opens them again, "I can't do it, the perfect mindset doesn't work for me," Ulysses says, giving up before really trying.

Emit touches Ulysses' shoulder gently. "Maybe we're moving too quickly. After all, this magical training is usually reserved for those who have self-actualised."

Ulysses nods. He has tried to rush things only to realise that he was not ready. Perhaps he will never be ready for them. Just like he never seems to be ready for his version of perfection. And with this thought his mind drifts back to his problems.

"Don't be disheartened. You'll grasp the perfect mindset soon. And when you do, you'll find moving objects to be easy. After all, as you're connected to everything, when you move something you're not really moving a foreign object, but rather a part of yourself. And thus, it's not much harder than moving your hand, once you master it. With practice you'll become very quick at this process, where moving objects is instantaneous. Especially when you learn to slow down time."

"Slow down time?" Ulysses' attention refocuses.

"That is a lesson for another day. First you need to truly have faith. You don't believe yet."

And with these words, Ulysses' attention flitters away once again. It is true, he does not believe. He does not believe the world is amazing and magical. Not truly. It may have magic in it, which very few get to experience, but it is not magical for all. The world chooses those who it deems worthy to give its gifts to. Those which are of the greater good. Like the others at Geno.

I'm not good enough for Geno and I'll never be as good as those here. I'm a fool to think that I could be, that Delta could like me as I do her. She's far better than me. She's strong, beautiful, intelligent, caring. She has the perfect mindset and magic. All I've ever accomplished is the theory. A theory which was already discovered by somebody else, millennia before.

CHAPTER 48

BLINDFOLDED MARTIAL ARTS

It is the early afternoon in Geno. The sky is becoming increasingly overcast and the humidity sticks to Ulysses' skin. He stands on the dirt oval with Luke, about ten metres from the fig.

Luke begins his lesson, "The Geno martial arts are very quick and complex to a person who has not yet self-actualised or mastered psychic abilities. We must build ourselves up to the level required. And so, for now, I'll simply teach you a taekwondo move. But with an added element. Put this around my eyes," Luke says as he hands Ulysses a black blindfold.

Ulysses ties the blindfold around Luke's head, as best as he can. Luke then immediately walks away from him, towards a coconut that hangs on a rope, tied to a high overhanging branch of the fig, about ten metres away. Ulysses is amazed how Luke blindly walks directly towards it. *He must be powerful in his non-visual senses.*

Luke ceases walking, with the coconut now about a metre from him and twenty centimetres above his head. Suddenly, he jumps in the air, spins his body 360 degrees and kicks the coconut. He lands gracefully back on the ground, with complete balance. Still blindfolded, he walks directly back to Ulysses, the coconut swaying back and forth behind him.

"Amazing!" Ulysses says. He cannot believe that someone could be so skilled.

"Your turn, Ulysses," Luke says as he takes off his blindfold.

"There's no way I could even do that, let alone blindfolded. I'm a visual person. Let me practise without the blindfold, to begin with."

Luke shakes his head. "You're missing the point, Ulysses. I spoke to Emit yesterday and he said that we can start working on your psychic powers. So I'm teaching you this not only for the move itself but also so that you can begin to build and control your psychic powers with the Geno martial arts. If you become too practised at the move, you'll use less of your psychic powers."

Ulysses hesitantly nods his head. Luke ties the blindfold around Ulysses' eyes.

It becomes pitch black. *Here we go*, Ulysses thinks to himself. He knows there is no chance he can accomplish this.

Ulysses begins to walk blindly towards where he believes the coconut is. He feels so disorientated without sight. He has no idea where he is or how far he has walked. He fears walking too far and running into the fig tree or the cliff face. He decides to stop. Perhaps he will get lucky. He jumps in the air and ungracefully tries to spin around whilst doing a kick. He lands back on the ground, loses his balance and falls over into the dirt, tasting some of it. He pulls his blindfold off and sits up. He is a good five metres from the coconut and not even facing it. He feels a fool. "I can't do it. It's impossible when I can't even see it," he calls to Luke, and brushes the dirt off himself.

"You may not be able to see it. But some of the elements can. Let them be your eyes. And try again, Ulysses."

"No, I can't," Ulysses says with conviction as he brings himself to stand again. He walks back towards Luke.

"What's wrong with you today? You don't have the strength of will."

"I'm not good enough," Ulysses answers, a sentence which equally represents how he feels with Delta and Geno as it does his training. As he reaches Luke, he hands him the blindfold.

Luke's voice softens, "You are good enough, Ulysses. It's okay, we can continue this later. But know that you'll master this in time."

CHAPTER 49

ENLIGHTENMENT

ULYSSES IS INSIDE his cabin, sitting at the end of his bed. He puts his head down in his hands. The blood rushes to his forehead. He thinks of how only a day before everything in his life seemed to make sense. All the trials he had endured while discovering the theory appeared to lead to something greater.

Now, he realises this glimpse of order was simply an illusion. Just because he has discovered the theory, it does not mean that he will be able to use it to live the life of his dreams, as what he desires may not be God's greater good. This is what Luke was talking about on Ulysses' first night at Geno, when he mentioned his struggles with the concept of the greater good. Something which Ulysses finds hard to believe, as Luke, like everyone else at Geno, just seems too perfect. He imagines that they could get whatever they wanted in life.

Ulysses needs someone outside of Geno to talk to. He sorts through his belongings, finds his smartphone, turns it on and sits back on the edge of the bed. *There's still no reception. Perhaps if I go elsewhere in Geno,* he considers. He puts the phone in his pocket and leaves his cabin. He walks through Geno, along the meandering paths, through the rainforest and past the statues. But still, there is no phone reception.

He arrives at a dead end, the stone entrance to Geno. He notices on his right is a large stone that has a button with the Geno symbol on it. *So, this is the way to exit Geno.* He presses the button. There is a rumble as the stone doors to Geno open.

The cave before him is dark. Luckily, Ulysses has his phone with him. He uses its inbuilt torch and walks inside. Soon he arrives at the beautiful lagoon, the one from his recurring dreams. Then he realises something! He cannot get back into Geno without two necklaces joining as one! He is now stuck out in the rainforest, with no way of contacting anyone inside Geno. *Damn! If only I had mastered my psychic powers, I could have communicated with them psychically.*

He looks at the surrounding cliffs of Geno, seeing that there is no possible way he can climb them. His only options are to wait here until someone finds him, or follow his original intention: find phone reception and call for help.

He walks into the lush green tropical rainforest, following the same path as when he arrived at Geno, intending to reach higher ground in case there is phone reception. As he walks through this isolated terrain, the emotions he has purposely kept hidden begin to seep out. It is not simply the heartache from Delta that Ulysses feels, but from all the moments in his life he has felt this very same way. Moments where he has had great expectations, only to discover the world does not match the beauty he envisions in his mind. He finds that with every new heartache, every expectation crushed by the world around him, it does not become easier for him, it becomes harder.

*

Meanwhile, at Geno, Delta searches for Ulysses. She asks around if anyone has seen him. She feels psychically as if he is getting further from her. It would not make sense for him to have left Geno, as there is no way for him to get back in. *Unless he is leaving for good.* Her heart sinks as she gives attention to this possibility. She so wanted him to become a member of Geno. She needs him here.

*

Ulysses walks beside a stream of water that leads to the top of a hill. Finally, he arrives at the peak. Drenched in sweat, he takes off his shirt to cool down and places it on a nearby tree branch. He walks and stands on the edge of a cliff face to see the expansive view.

The ocean, which is various shades of blue, encases a love heart-shaped rock lagoon that is several metres wide and filled with aqua-coloured ocean water. A sandy white beach snakes along the coastline and meets this lagoon by the shore. On the other side of the beach, a lush green rainforest pushes against this sand and greets it with coconut trees that scatter along the beach. The view, he knows, should be breathtaking. But it is not. Not for him. He is too consumed by the inner chaos within his mind. It suddenly dawns on him that there is no place where he can be comfortable when feeling this way. *I really need to talk to someone.*

He pulls his phone out of his pocket. *Success! He has reception!* He quickly types in his father's number and it begins to ring. Suddenly, everything changes.

*

Delta instantly gets the feeling that Ulysses is in great trouble. *It's urgent.* "Something is wrong with Ulysses, Emit. We must go and help him," Delta says in a panic.

"Are you sure?" Emit asks.

"Yes!" Delta says as she touches her temples with two fingers from each hand; she feels it even more strongly now.

*

Ulysses screams as he slides on his back down the cliff face, feeling excruciating pain. Suddenly he comes to a stop. A tiny ledge prevents him from falling further. He loses his phone on impact and watches as it tumbles down the rocks to eventually land in the sand below.

He looks up. A part of the cliff gave way, right where Ulysses was standing! He is now stuck, ten metres from where he once stood and thirty metres above the rocky and treacherously jagged earth below. One wrong move and Ulysses will fall to his death. And since he has lost his phone, he cannot even contact anyone for help.

He feels an intense fear. And just as he is sure that things could not get any worse, the heavens open. *Rain.* It intensifies. A storm is brewing and he is precariously stuck on a dangerous ledge!

The rainwater collects on this ledge and his feet begin to slip. He feels around with his hands behind him, desperately trying to find something he can grip on to. But there is nothing. Anxiety flows so strongly through his body that he struggles to breathe. He knows that with this increased anxiety there is even more chance of him falling to his death, which in turn makes him even more anxious – a vicious cycle.

Suddenly memories flood his mind. Little things. *Perhaps this is what it is like just before death, perhaps your life flashes before your eyes.*

All of his memories share the same theme – they are moments where he did not truly live his life to the fullest.

He has a memory as a young teenager where he was playing tennis with his father. Beside the court, there were people waiting for their turn. Ulysses should have cherished this moment with his father, but as these strangers were watching them play, he felt too self-conscious to enjoy himself. He remembers wishing his time away in this moment, wanting the game to be over. *What a wasted gift*, as not long afterwards his father became too old to play tennis with him anymore.

He also remembers a couple of years later, on an extremely hot day, that he desperately wished to swim in the local pool with his friends. But he refrained as he was not happy with his physique. *I will swim when I become more muscular,* he thought to himself at the time. And so, he forwent the pleasure and pushed through the unbearableness of the heat, imagining at the same time how much fun his friends were having.

A memory surfaces of the morning he discovered his theory. He looked at his reflection in the mirror and was deeply unhappy with what he saw. He was so harsh on himself. He should have simply appreciated being himself and being alive. If only he were back there now rather than on this cliff face.

Ulysses' memories make him realise that while he may have lived for twenty-eight years, he has not *truly* lived for many years at all. The pain of knowing this, in this moment, is very intense for him. If only he could have his time over again and do things right.

But instead, here he is on this cliff and it is only a matter of moments before he will certainly fall. How cruel it is that he should die this way. After preparing all these years, hoping for a life that never manifested for him. What makes it worse is that the reason the life of his dreams never manifested is simply because the perfection was already there. It was always there. He just did not have the right eyes to see it. And now his time has run out.

If only there was a way to survive.

The wind begins to pick up and the rain becomes harder. Ulysses feels he has only seconds left. In this moment of utter helpless desperation, he does the only thing he can do. He prays to God. It is completely an internal prayer. He does not put his hands together as he is too scared to lose his balance on this cliff face.

"Please God, help me out of this situation. I promise if you do, that from now on I will live a life that reflects the gift you have given me. Please God, guide me."

Something amazing happens. Immediately as he finishes this prayer an answer comes to Ulysses. It is very clear in his mind as if God has spoken it directly to him with a great force, bringing order through the chaos like a blanket covers the cold: *Use the perfect mindset.*

Ulysses obeys and instinctively begins by *surrendering to the chaos with faith.* Instead of fighting internally with the situation at hand, he accepts it. He accepts that he is stuck on a cliff face with the wild weather around him. With this acceptance, strangely, his anxiety fades. His breathing slows. He becomes calm. For some reason, his anxiety cannot continue unless he opposes his situation. And as he becomes calm, he begins to have faith, faith that somehow things will work out for the best in this situation.

He then consciously *uncovers and holds his primary desires.* He feels grateful to be alive as himself and forgives himself for not living his life to the fullest. He promises that he will make every second he has left a reflection of who he truly is. With this promise, the pain of his past mistakes disappears. This pain, he realises, was a lesson to push him in the right direction. Now that he learns, accepts and is appreciative of this lesson, it is as if God says to him, *Good, you have passed the test,* and this painful energy has turned into its true form, *love.*

And with this great love, Ulysses also begins to see love around him. He looks over to the mountains beside him. There is a powerful stillness to them. He sees the serenity of the rainforest covering these mountains. His eyes move to the water of the ocean; it is breathtaking. It always was, he just had to be open to experiencing its beauty.

While he continues to look upon the beauty of the world which holds him, his mind suddenly becomes still. This stillness is followed by an epiphany, a great thought: *the universe is connected to me and is a part of me. The air that I was trying so hard to breathe in is me. The space between myself and the rocks below is a part of me.*

The entire world which I desperately don't wish to leave is me. I have a deeper I. I am a part of God and God is everything.

And with this realisation his eyes begin to fill with tears. Being part of God is no longer just an abstract concept. He feels it to be literally true now. He suddenly sees the world as it is and he realises the power of his eternalness. *Clear vision.*

A raindrop falls on him right where his cheek is, intermixing with his tears. It is symbolic, he feels, signifying that as he is part of the system, when he cries, the whole system does too.

I am the system. The system is I. And this is how I will control the elements around me.

The rain intensifies even more. Clear vision says that if he is to get off this cliff face he must first stop it raining. He must use the elements. He *opens himself to a perfect moment* and is *ready now.* He stretches out his right arm and commands the sun to shine.

Magically, at this same precise moment, the clouds begin to part and the rain stops pouring directly above him, even though the rain continues elsewhere around him. A ray of light beams down through the circular parting in the clouds, its rays shining directly onto him, touching Ulysses with a delicate warmth as if a direct omen from God. *It's incredible.*

Ulysses commands for the clouds to part even more. And they do. The sun increases its light over the area surrounding him, making everything brighter moment by moment. The tree's leaves become greener, the edges of them beginning to shine with a bright light. There are blue flowers in the distance that hang from their branches, and their colour becomes even more vibrant from the sun. The sun also makes the water of the beautiful ocean become even more colourful.

As the sun's rays continue to envelop his surrounds, he thinks of how the sun has given so much to the Earth. He can intensely feel how sad it will be when the sun eventually burns out. With this thought, he thinks that while we are all the one true element, the individual creations are powerful and to be cherished. This is precisely why he must get off this cliff face. He is an important element that has much more to give and be given.

Ulysses looks above and sees a hand-sized rock on top of the peak above him. It is resting on the cliff, part of it dangling over the edge. He thinks back to what Emit said about magic – that it is purely getting the elements to do what they are already designed to do.

"Rocks can roll down cliffs," Ulysses says to himself.

He notices there is some water flowing, near the rock. He commands the wind to change the direction of the water so that it moves towards the rock. To his amazement, it does. But the flow of water is still not strong enough to make the rock move.

Ulysses commands the strength of the wind to increase and it does. This has the ill effect of leaving him to struggle to keep his balance with the strong wind flowing and swirling around him, whilst also having his arm outstretched and focused on this stone. Finally, the water hits the rock with more force and the rock rolls off the cliff face. Ulysses catches it in his waiting hand.

He immediately uses the rock as a tool to uncover other rocks in the damp cliff face above him. He does this by digging the dirt around the rocks until they are exposed. Through this process he creates suitable rocks to hold onto and climb up. He places his digging rock in his pocket, and climbs up the cliff face, gripping onto the uncovered rocks with his hands and feet. He repeats this process, using the rock to uncover more rocks until he climbs further. It is very difficult and dangerous and he moves at a pace of only one rock at a time. He knows that if he were to have attempted this moments earlier in the pouring rain and without the perfect mindset guiding him, he would have fallen.

He continues to climb upwards, using all his strength and will to survive. Some rocks are already protruding from the cliff and do not need to be exposed, while others do. Soon he *discovers the flow state* and the process becomes easier. He moves up the cliff fluidly.

He gets to just over an arm's reach of the top, but unfortunately on this part of the cliff face there is no rock to uncover or hold onto. He looks for other opportunities and sees that there is a bunch of grass that has firmly planted itself on the side of this cliff. How amazing that this grass would grow at this precise location. *It's synchronicity. The elements are on my side. The universe wants me to survive.*

Ulysses grabs hold of the long strands of grass and pulls himself up, praying that these interconnected elements hold strong for him. He moves quickly. He knows the grass cannot hold his weight for very long and so he purposely keeps enough momentum so that his free hand can reach the top of the cliff without putting too much of his weight on the grass. *It works!* He grips the top of the cliff with his left hand and quickly follows this with his right hand. He pulls himself upwards with all his might.

He feels the intensity, knowing that if he fails this last moment, all will be for nothing and he will perish down the cliff face. He grunts. His muscles are in agony. It requires all his remaining strength. And finally, he pulls himself over the cliff ledge.

He has made it!

Slowly he stands, walks a few steps and then drops to his knees. He is spent of energy. His bare back is bloody from the rocks. His fingers dig into the damp ground. He picks up some soil into his hands and raises it to the heavens, some of the dryer dirt slowly seeping through his fingers. He cherishes being back on solid ground so greatly.

Where there was chaos, he now *sees order*, an order which feels akin to staring God directly in the face. He understands now why he is on this mountain. He understands the whole experience. The pain he has felt over the last day is a blessing in disguise, because he needed this experience. He needed the unrequited love. The falling down this cliff. It all held a greater meaning which gave him the impetus to grow. It was not just God's greater good. It was his as well. They were in line all along. He needed to learn that he has the power to have the perfect mindset and it is his responsibility, not his environment's, nor anyone else's to achieve this. That he must hold the perfect mindset regardless of anything around him, even on a cliff face in a storm.

Ulysses can sense as Emit and Delta arrive on the mountain top. But they are too late to rescue him; he has already conquered the cliff face. They watch while he kneels, looking into the sky with serenity.

"He is enlightened," Delta says.

CHAPTER 50

SHADOWS LOCATION

The French Riviera, France.

It is morning. Leucius sits at a rounded ivory table, on the balcony of his mansion. The purple flowers of a nearby jacaranda tree litter the balcony. On the table is the remainder of his breakfast, a half-filled glass of orange juice and remnants of a croissant with jam, all of which were prepared by his private chef. Beside this is an A4 yellow envelope and his mobile phone which suddenly begins to glow.

"Yes, Anomonet," Leucius answers.

"Master of Shadows, we have tracked Ulysses' phone. He tried to use it to call his father's phone which we have in our possession."

"Excellent. Where is it?"

"It's deep in the rainforest, north of Cairns."

"You know what to do; get the Shadow Enforcers there as quickly as possible."

"It is already underway."

"Good." And with this Leucius hangs up, places the phone in his pocket and picks up the yellow envelope.

CHAPTER 51

SELF-ACTUALISATION

Geno, Australia.

IT IS A new morning. Ulysses looks at his eyes in the bathroom mirror. They are striking, a deep blue and powerfully glowing. He has never seen himself so handsome. He looks at his entirety, witnessing masculinity in his current form, the perfect creation that is man. He can also glimpse his divinity, as with the love of God he has been created and therefore he holds the light of God within him.

"I love you," he whispers to himself in the mirror. This is his new ritual; every morning before he leaves the cabin he has decided he will look in the mirror and tell himself this. It feels similar to when a person kisses their partner before leaving to go to work in the mornings. From now on, he wishes to keep the love for himself uncovered.

He leaves his cabin. As soon as his eyes hit the sunlight, he takes a moment to pray to God. Ulysses thanks God that he is alive and promises to do God's will – the beginning of another new morning ritual.

He then walks, tall and strong, confidently relaxed. He feels a great power within every cell and a deep pleasure flowing through his body. His heart holds a vibrant warmth. His head is buzzing, with pins and needles in his forehead. Yet his mind is clear. He does not need to think often, instead, he simply knows. He is at a new level of sensing things. Clear vision. Calmness of mind. Clarity.

This must be the clear light.

It feels as if the clear light is the natural state of being. That the clouds have parted and uncovered what truly is.

He continues to walk through Geno, holding a complete inner peace – the feeling that he will be comfortable in any environment, with any circumstance. He does not fear anything, but rather, he has the security in knowing how beautifully the world works and complete faith that everything will work out in his life. He is completely present and pleasured. In touch with the synchronicity and flow. In harmony with the universe.

"This is self-actualisation," Ulysses whispers to himself.

Ulysses thought that it would be harder to reach self-actualisation. Whilst it is true that he almost died in the process, a part of him thought that it would take years of monk-like reflection and dedication to reach such enlightenment. But now he realises that it makes sense that it can happen so quickly. *We are ready now. We are always ready to live the life of our dreams.*

And with this self-actualisation, the real fruits of the Earth are offered to Ulysses. He sees the beauty in nature even more vividly than he ever has. The colours. Nature's breathtaking designs.

He walks to a nearby stream and drinks the clear water. It is even more delicious and refreshing than any water he has previously tasted while at Geno. The water has not changed since then: he has. He savours it as he walks to a nearby tree. He touches the tree with his left hand and feels its energy powerfully flowing to him.

Suddenly, he notices a Ulysses butterfly on a plant to the right of him. It is magnificent, with striking, deep blue wings. Yet it moves around on this leaf in a panic – it has a broken wing and can no longer fly. Ulysses instantly feels a deep empathy for this butterfly. A oneness. How could he not, since the day before he was just like this butterfly, stuck on a cliff face, unable to raise himself.

He walks towards it and puts out his hand. *Love can heal*, he thinks. Ulysses has not been trained how to heal, but in this state of self-actualisation he feels he can do it. He summons the interconnected energy of all the beauty of the world. All the love he has ever encountered. And through using these interconnected elements, he feels a great invisible power coming out from his hands. In a matter of seconds, and even to Ulysses' surprise, the butterfly's broken wing magically heals and straightens. It immediately begins flapping its wings and within seconds, flies away.

*

Delta is nearby, studying nature. Through the trees, she notices Ulysses. She stops and secretly watches him. Suddenly, she is amazed as she sees him healing the butterfly.

"He is the one!" she says to herself. "And he is ready."

CHAPTER 52

STRONGER THAN EVER

IT IS THE mid-morning. Ulysses meets Emit at the edge of the oval, near the kitchen shack. Emit nods his head, signalling Ulysses to begin.

Ulysses closes his eyes and immediately goes through some principles of the perfect mindset. *Primary desires. Clear vision. Open to perfection. Ready now.* He then opens his eyes and places out his hand above a leaf that lies on the ground before them. *Surrender to the chaos.*

A few seconds pass and nothing happens. But then suddenly, the leaf begins to slowly levitate. It seems to dance as it rises, sometimes smoothly rising, sometimes jerking higher in the air. *Find the flow state.* The leaf's journey smooths in a spiral pattern. Finally, it reaches close to Ulysses' hand. *Uncover and create perfection.* He turns his palm and places it underneath the leaf. And the leaf slowly and beautifully floats downwards into the palm of his hand. *See the order.*

"You've done it! I knew you could!" Emit says, bursting with enthusiasm and putting an arm around Ulysses.

"I can't believe it!" Ulysses says, his body shaking. First, he healed the butterfly and now this. He can do magic!

"You're self-actualised, Ulysses," Emit says as he releases Ulysses and places an outstretched hand on his shoulder. "I could sense it as soon as I first saw you this morning."

"I am self-actualised," Ulysses says strongly. "And there's someone I must speak to you about." Ulysses leads Emit to sit on the stairs of the pavilion with him.

"Delta?" Emit asks as he takes a seat.

"Yes. What led you to believe that God doesn't wish for me to be with her?"

"I can't answer that, Ulysses. That's for Delta to say."

"And this I can accept. I know that I'm not privy to the things that Delta and you know in this situation. But you also don't know the things that I do. I feel in every essence of my body that Delta and I are meant to be together. Being self-actualised, having clear vision, doesn't detract from this belief – to the contrary, it magnifies it. Don't misunderstand me, I believe that God didn't want me to be with her before. I too felt the flow against us. But I don't feel this will be the case any longer. You have seen how much my powers have grown since the other day. I feel that I can protect her now from whatever might harm her."

"Ulysses…" Emit says in a concerned tone.

"Hear me out. All I wish is to show her my heart and then let her decide. Surely, she is better off having all of the information at hand, including my feelings? Surely this is the right path?"

"I'm not in the position to know what is the greater good. All I know is what Delta told me and my interpretation of this. I can't stop you both from doing anything. Ultimately, the choice is and always will be yours and hers."

"That's right," Ulysses agrees.

"But Ulysses, please, if you do pursue her, can you honour one thing?"

"What's that?"

"Can you keep your courting a secret to only yourselves?"

"Why?"

"Just trust me on this. If nothing else, just this."

"I'll keep it secret. I promise," Ulysses says sincerely.

*

A couple of hours later, Ulysses stands on the dirt of the oval. Luke places a blindfold over Ulysses' eyes. Everything becomes black.

Ulysses knows what he must do. He blindly walks towards the coconut, comes to a halt and lines himself up to where he senses the coconut to be. He jumps and spins in the air, kicking. But he does not feel the coconut. He must have missed it. At least this time he lands steady. He takes off his blindfold and looks up to see that he must have been very close to hitting the coconut.

But it is still a failure.

"Good try, Ulysses. A very good improvement," Luke says.

"Let's go again." Ulysses walks back towards Luke.

Luke puts the blindfold on Ulysses and once again it becomes black. Ulysses takes a moment to calm himself and get used to the dark. He then walks towards where he believes the coconut to be. He jumps and does a spinning kick. This time he feels that he slightly clips the coconut with his right foot!

"Well done, Ulysses!" Luke calls from his distance.

"Again," Ulysses requests. Ulysses feels that he can do even better. He does not bother taking off the blindfold. He simply walks to where Luke is and back, completely blind. And he tries again. And then again. But while he grazes it every time, he does not succeed in hitting it with his full power. He finally takes off the blindfold.

"Come, Ulysses. You've tried your best. You've touched it. That's a success. The lesson is complete."

Ulysses concedes and they walk away together. But as they come to the very edge of the oval, Ulysses turns to look at the coconut once more. "One more time," he says to Luke.

"Ulysses, you've tried enough."

"Trust me, Luke. This will be the last time, you have my word. I know what to do now."

Luke pauses, but then seems to reluctantly nod. He places the blindfold on Ulysses for one last time. "You're too far away, Ulysses. You'll never do it."

Ulysses refuses to listen. In complete darkness, he walks across the entire oval towards the coconut. He must walk forty metres when suddenly, he stops. Amazingly, he knows that this is exactly where he needs to be. He can sense it. He visualises the coconut. And although he is blind, he can see it in his mind's eye very clearly. Suddenly he jumps in the air, vocally exhaling out his breath. He spins around and kicks with such a force that he can feel and hear the coconut cracking open. He lands gracefully, bending his knees to absorb the impact of the landing.

Ulysses can hear Luke running towards him. "My goodness, Ulysses! How did you do that?" Luke excitedly congratulates Ulysses by shaking him by the shoulders. "You didn't just hit it, you broke it in half! I've never seen anyone do that before." He removes the blindfold from Ulysses. The light instantly reaches Ulysses' eyes.

CHAPTER 53

LOVE LETTERS

IN THE LATE evening, Ulysses lies on his bed. He is awake, but his thoughts rest on Delta.

Ulysses desires her greatly, but he has no expectations of having his love requited. He understands that she may desire him, but she also may not. And even if she does desire him, she still may not choose to be with him due to her signs from God.

Still, he wishes to be open to perfection. And to accomplish this, he must be open to being with her. *Open but also secretive,* just as Emit wishes.

Ulysses does not dare try to send her another dream. Instead, he decides on another method to inconspicuously show his feelings to her. He rises from his bed to sit at his desk. And here he pens her a love letter.

Delta,

There is a secret I wish to share: I dreamt of you. Even before I first met you. This is the true reason why I knew to follow you in the library. We had already met in a dream which recurred for me.

I dreamt of kissing your lips and connecting with you. It was incredibly deep as it felt like we already had shared history.

Now that I have discovered you to exist in real life, it is natural for me to be curious about you.

I wish to know you as deeply and romantically as I do in my dreams. I would love to learn everything you feel comfortable in sharing. Your favourite romantic books, your childhood fantasies of your future partner. Anything. And through time, I wish you to also know me deeply.

Please keep this letter a secret.

Love, Ulysses

That evening, he places this letter underneath Delta's cabin door. He knows that he is taking a risk. He knows that she could reject him. But he feels deep down inside that taking this chance is right and it is his true desire.

The next morning, Ulysses awakens and rises from his bed to find a note under his door. *It is a reply!* He feels the letter's light weight and opens it delicately, unsure of what he will read:

Dear Ulysses,

There too is a secret to my dreams which I will tell you one day. I accept your request to get to know me better and I will do my best to tell you who I am.

When I was younger, I would sometimes visit Sophos for the weekend. She taught me so much wisdom, including how to cook and garden. In the bedroom where I would stay, at the foot of the bed, there was a painting of a couple. I would fall asleep looking at them, wishing it were my partner and I one day. The painting was just gorgeous. The male and female were in an embrace. The male is behind her, holding her as she is leaning back and kissing him.

For books, I have always loved The Princess Bride. *I still do not know how you managed to say my favourite line from that book. There have been so many coincidences. Another book I love is* Sleeping Beauty. *As a young girl I would read these novels over and over. Both for enjoyment and also to improve my English reading skills.*

I wish to learn about you too, Ulysses. I will keep this secret.

Sincerely, Delta

A great response. She has accepted his wishes to get to know her. And she has given him clues on how to love her!

Ulysses instantly wishes to start enticing into reality her romantic imagery. But first, he must learn more of her romantic fantasies; he must learn of these books that she loves.

CHAPTER 54

A MEMBER OF GENO

THE TIME IS 12:08 p.m.

Ulysses stands in the ancient circular pavilion. The sun is directly overhead. It shines through a circular opening at the top of the arch, illuminating the Geno symbol on the front of the pavilion, and travelling through to the base of the pavilion.

Emit, standing beside him, instructs Ulysses to move under the light of the sun, which he does. With this bright light surrounding Ulysses, he gazes out to Delta, Luke and Sophos, who all sit on their personal blankets on the oval, looking upon this ceremony. Delta has put extra effort into her appearance for this occasion. Her golden blonde hair is braided majestically in a curly waterfall braid. A classy white top hugs her upper body and tight grey pants reach down to her upper ankles. He has never seen her looking anything but casual before. He is unsure if she dresses like this because of the letters they shared and her wish to make an impression upon him or if it is purely an indicator of the importance of this moment.

Emit reads out words in Ancient Greek, words which he previously informed Ulysses had been passed down from the very first members of Geno. And as he speaks this foreign language, he uses his hands to bless Ulysses.

Emit then speaks in English. "Ulysses, you were brought to us through synchronicity and have learnt the ways of Geno. You have become self-actualised through learning the perfect mindset and are ready to be taught the deeper ways in which the founding theory of Geno can be applied. You are worthy of becoming our eighth member of Geno. So, on this day, you are given the choice. Ulysses, will you join Geno and become a force for the greater good?" Emit asks.

Ulysses has only been at Geno for seven days, yet what he has learned thus far is incredible. He has never felt so enlightened and fulfilled. He finds the members of Geno to be deeply inspiring and is beginning to understand how powerful the gift of Geno is. Furthermore, being a descendant of many Geno members, he feels that it is now time for him to rise and do his ancestors proud. "I will."

Ulysses is presented with a Geno necklace, the symbol in half. It shines brightly as it comes into the stream of light from the ceiling of the pavilion.

"You are now a member of Geno," Emit says as he places the necklace over Ulysses' head, the chain resting it on the back of his neck, the pendant above his heart.

There are cheers from the oval.

Ulysses touches the necklace with warmth and as he does he instantly hears his father's voice in his mind, *"A personal reminder to do the greater good in the world."* Ulysses makes the conscious decision that this necklace will be a reminder to him, to stay self-actualised and to continue to do the greater good.

He looks down onto the oval and sees Delta. She has a warm smile and her hands together as if she had been praying. He proudly walks down the stairs to be amongst them.

Delta excitedly greets him. "Congratulations, Ulysses," she smiles and warmly touches the side of Ulysses' shoulder.

They share a moment of eye contact which feels powerful, though he doesn't keep it for long as he wishes to hide his feelings from the other members.

Ulysses walks past Sophos. "You now one of eight," she says while kissing him on the cheek.

Luke congratulates Ulysses by shaking his hand. "Well done, Ulysses. I'm proud of you." But there is something in Luke's smile that seems forced, his congratulations laboured. Before Ulysses can question this, Luke turns his back on him and walks away.

Emit comes down the stairs. "I'm glad that you've decided to become a member, Ulysses."

"Thank you, Emit. Ever since I first became self-actualised, I knew that becoming a member of Geno was my true desire. The perfect mindset is serving me well. Thank you so much for teaching me."

"It's my pleasure."

"Also, there's something I need to ask you. I'd like to find some books to read in my spare time. Does Geno have any?"

"Yes, the Geno library," Emit points along the path. "It is the first right after you walk past Sophos' cabin. There aren't many *normal* books there compared to most libraries. That's why Delta often visits libraries on the Gold Coast, such as the one where you first met her."

Ulysses nods, "Thank you. I'll have a look this afternoon."

CHAPTER 55

THE HISTORY OF GENO ON FILE

An hour has passed since Ulysses became a member of Geno. He opens a heavy door and enters the Geno library, the door's weight making it inevitable that it will close itself behind him. He instantly finds the temperature cooler inside the library.

He walks through the library slowly. It's such a magnificent room and he wants to take it all in. Before him are several rows of old books. On the side wall are glass cabinets with what appear to be important manuscripts on display. He passes the rows of books and comes to an open area. Suddenly he realises that he is not alone. There is a man, seated at the table, his back facing Ulysses.

"Ulysses," he says, not turning, but simply sensing Ulysses' presence.

"Luke… I never knew of this place."

"The Geno library. It's fireproof, waterproof, climate-controlled."

"These books must be very important," Ulysses says as he walks around the table and comes face to face with Luke.

"They are. This collection began at the provenance of Geno in Ancient Greece, even before the great library of Alexandria. We have extremely rare scrolls, codices and books by various authors throughout history."

"Amazing," Ulysses says as he looks around.

"However, most of the works in our collection have been written by past Geno members. Every great idea, every discovery made by Geno can be found in these books. There are books on how to perform different types of magic, books on theories, detailed diaries written by past members that chronicle their lives. The wealth of knowledge in these walls is invaluable. Each and every book could change the world."

Ulysses releases one of the books from the shelf. "I would love to read them all."

"You can't. Not unless you understand Ancient Greek. But perhaps soon. I'm helping to translate these works into English. And I'm making the library digital, so that in the future we can easily search for whatever we're looking for," Luke says. He buries his head back into his books which Ulysses now realises he is translating onto a laptop.

Ulysses refocuses on his purpose for being in the library. He hopes to find the books that Delta loves here. But as they are not written by previous Geno members, he realises that it is merely a hope.

He searches for *The Princess Bride* and after a while he is surprised to find it. He holds it delicately. He knows that this could be the actual book Delta read while growing up. Her hands may have touched it, her mind and passions ignited by it. He then searches for *Sleeping Beauty* and is amazed that it is also here in the Geno library. His mission is a success.

On his way out, he notices that Luke's face is pained, his forehead crinkled.

"Luke?"

Luke looks up from his work.

"Is everything alright? It's like you have something troubling you," Ulysses asks.

"Well, Ulysses... I've become utterly consumed by this library, reading over all of these books. And, well... I've learnt so many things. But this morning I read something that completely shocked me. And the more I read, the more I knew it to be true."

"What's that?"

"The other members of Geno have purposely been keeping something from us."

"What?" Ulysses asks, deeply concerned.

"Not what, who... Orien."

*

Ulysses arrives at Emit's cabin. Here he finds Emit, writing intensely on his chalkboard, chalk in hand.

Ulysses interrupts, "Emit, who's Orien?"

Emit looks over to Ulysses and his eyes widen with surprise. He nods his head and puts down his chalk. As important as whatever he was writing appeared to be, it seems that the topic of Orien is far more so.

"Come, Ulysses." Emit leads Ulysses to walk with him through the grounds of Geno, near the cabins. "We don't know a terrible lot about Orien. But he seems to have existed for all time. Our records in Geno mention him at many points throughout history," Emit explains.

"Existed for all time? That's impossible! Surely no man is immortal."

"We have no other explanation for it."

"What can you tell me about him?"

"Orien believes the world to be chaos. Survival of the fittest. That one is to fight for resources, compete to pass on their genetics and ensure that their offspring have the strongest likelihood of survival and replication. And because of these beliefs, he desires to make his bloodline the most powerful in the world. He selects girls from each time period, the most beautiful there are. He showers them with material riches when they procreate with him. And because of this, Orien has had many children throughout history. These descendants make a powerful dynasty, rich beyond measure, with the chosen men of his lineage becoming his disciples… The Shadows."

"So, the Shadows who attacked me – Orien is their leader and their creator?"

"Precisely."

"But, I'm confused. How do we know that The Shadows are wrong? They seem to be doing on a much larger scale what people in society are naturally doing anyway. Most people have the survival of the fittest mindset. We all compete with each other for success. We try our hardest to amass as many resources as possible so that we and our children have the best chance of survival. It's been happening since life began, every animal does it. In some ways, it seems that Orien is purely the most successful at doing such."

"Yes, this is true. Orien isn't the first to seek out that which he is. But in order to contemplate discerning right from wrong we must first discuss the greater good." Emit motions for Ulysses to stop walking as they arrive on top of a small bridge. "The greater good is the will of God. And thus, it always prevails. Just as the chaos always leads to order. But just because each day is destined to turn to night, that doesn't mean that what happens during the day is unimportant," Emit says. "The greater good can come about in many different ways and forms. And this is where we, the elements, have free will and a choice."

Emit points to the stream below them. "Imagine that this stream leads to the greater good. We can be the stones in the riverbed that slow down the stream as it flows past," Emit says as he points at the rocks that poke out of the stream, diverting the water around them. He then points at a small coconut floating down the stream. "Or we can be the coconut and let our journey become one with the desires of the stream. Either way, the stream will flow towards the greater good. It is designed to do so. How it flows, how soon it reaches its destination, we all play a part in. Whether it reaches there in one tide or many."

"I think I'm starting to understand," Ulysses says, without any confidence or conviction in his statement.

"On your first night here at Geno you learned that God communicates with us. He instils within us true desires, both eternally and through time. He talks to us through dreams. Through life experiences. He teaches us and pushes us towards where we know we are meant to be until we as an individual element are truly in line with his will. And, therefore, on the greatest path to the greater good."

"But if God wants us to follow his will, then why does he give us free will? Why even give us a choice?"

"I assume that choice is for the greater good of the system. It helps a species to adapt, to master many types of environments. To break free from their instincts if they are not serving them. Furthermore, what is the better way of teaching? To force? Or to simply guide while letting them make their own choices?" Emit smiles. "God is the perfect teacher. He guides you towards where you are meant to be and gives you the wisdom you need. But he also allows you the choice. It's always up to you to turn the key."

"I've never thought of it being like this before."

Emit nods, his right index finger raised. "Now to what separates Geno from The Shadows… We believe that the greatest path to God's wishes is through self-actualisation. We know from experience that when we use the perfect mindset we are operating at a very high level, our enjoyment of life is greater and we can achieve our true desires easier. Because of this, we believe that self-actualisation is what God wishes for mankind. That through being self-actualised we will best achieve our elemental purposes.

"Meanwhile, The Shadows are unable to self-actualise. They simply cannot on their path. And so, even after all the control that Orien and his disciples have amassed and all the power and riches, they are still not satisfied."

"But how can we know for sure that self-actualisation is the will of God? I mean, I feel it is, just from being self-actualised. I have never felt closer to the divine. But how can we know for certain?"

"We can't. Not for certain. We have beliefs here at Geno. But ultimately beliefs are simply beliefs. Only God knows what's true. And make no mistake, The Shadows also believe they are on the greater path and that they are doing the greater good."

"What's the purpose of having beliefs then, if everyone could be wrong?" Ulysses smirks.

"If I were to ask you what colour the sky is and you had no beliefs, how would you answer?" Emit says as he points towards the sky.

"I would answer that I'm not sure what colour the sky is."

"And that is still a belief, a belief that you are not sure. Don't try to escape beliefs."

"I remember reading that Socrates once said something like *the only thing I know for sure, is that I know nothing for sure.* Which of course he understood to be a contradiction. He was pointing towards the lack of certainty one can have with beliefs. And I realise now that he was also pointing to it being impossible not to have beliefs."

"Precisely, Ulysses. And so, we have our beliefs here at Geno. But more important than any beliefs are actions. Unlike The Shadows, we at Geno don't seek to end those with different beliefs to us. Instead, we simply do what we believe is good and hope that one day others will learn of our discoveries and insights and decide what to believe for themselves. This is why we bless our rivals and let them free after combat. Because we love them unconditionally. We know that what is our reality isn't always the same as theirs. We don't judge them. We simply show them our way and then let them decide. Just as God may do for us – we guide them, but we allow them to turn the key for themselves."

Ulysses takes a moment for this to sink in. Once he understands he nods his head. "I have one more question, Emit. Why did you keep Orien a secret from us?"

"Well, most members of Geno already know of Orien. It is only yourself and Luke who hadn't learned of him. And there are two reasons why. Firstly, as you must appreciate, there is much to learn at Geno. Revealing him is not a priority as there are very few occasions in recorded history where Orien has been a direct threat to a Geno member. Supposedly even The Shadows haven't seen or heard of Orien for almost a century."

"I see, and what's the other reason?"

"It can be very demotivating to learn that there is an immortal enemy."

The gravity of these words hits Ulysses.

CHAPTER 56

BUT IT'S NOT HER

1873 – London, England.

IT IS A July afternoon and very warm by English standards. Inside a luxurious, palatial estate is Orien, towering over the middle-aged Shadows member who stands beside him. Their eyes focus purely on what is before them… twelve young women, all nude. The women are here willingly – they always are. Willingly, but not without the promises of potential riches.

"These are the finest in all of Holland, sir," says the Shadows member.

"And for this evening?" Orien asks in his deep voice.

"Germany."

"Hmm, I believe I'll feel more like Spain by then," Orien says. He finds that each nationality has their own flavours and intricacies when it comes to having sex, and his taste changes with his moods.

"Very well, sir."

Orien walks towards the women and studies them closely, one at a time.

He points to the first two girls – two slim brunettes who look like sisters. And with a flick of the first two fingers of his right hand, he directs them to the bedroom. They will begin there, in the bedroom. But they have all afternoon, so they may end up anywhere on the estate, including around the swimming pool.

He walks past a couple of women, their faces unable to hide the disappointment that he has not chosen them. He then selects a lady with dark hair and a voluptuous hourglass figure. She smiles beautifully. He passes a few more and stops to select a girl with brown curly hair and brown eyes. *Exquisite.* He passes two more. Finally, he comes to a beautiful girl with blonde hair, blue eyes and dimples in her cheeks when she smiles. He walks towards her and becomes so close that he can feel her energy. He smells her neck. This one he likes the most.

Having done this many times, he already knows that she will be the lucky one to win his seed. He knows this because she reminds him of a girl he once knew. A girl who still holds his heart. *It's incredible. She looks so similar... But it's not her.*

Orien has had his men search the world for hundreds of years, yet he has never found another in the same league as the girl he loves. She truly is an original blessing. He desires her so deeply that he would happily trade all of these girls, including this blonde before him, for one special moment with her. To feel the touch of her skin. To possess her. He would go so far as to hurt her just to hear her screaming his name. This is how much he craves her.

He motions towards the blonde girl with dimples and she becomes ecstatic. She walks with a spring in her step, almost dancing towards the bedroom. *Of course she's happy.* Orien is the most successful male to have ever lived. He is handsome, he is rich, he is powerful. And because of this, he has the reward of mating with the most beautiful girls in any time period.

"That is all. I will simply have five for now," Orien says.

"Very well, sir," nods the Shadow member.

Orien saunters towards the bedroom. He will take his time to get to know the chosen women, building a beautiful connection with each of them. None of their interactions will involve talking, however. After all, they will not be able to speak English anyway. Instead he will learn about each female through another language – their body language. He can learn more in a brief encounter through reading their eyes, tasting their scents and uncovering their inner physical passions than a person can through a platonic conversation that lasts for a week. After all, *people lie in conversations, but their bodies never do.*

He feels moderately satisfied that every heterosexual male would deeply desire to be in his position, even though many may pretend they would not have sex with these beautiful women given the opportunity. But they just say that because they are too weak to have them. And society, especially desirable women, hates it when weak men try to reproduce with them.

He arrives in the bedroom and is instantly greeted by the women. He can sense their nerves, their excitement. He knows exactly what will happen next.

If the average man were to watch Orien's encounters, they might be surprised how uninhibited and wild even the most shy and timid of girls become. *Perhaps it's because there are other females around,* Orien has often considered. They naturally compete with one another. They see who can pleasure him the most. Even the most seemingly proper and sophisticated of women become absolute animals when in the throes of an orgasm. And Orien takes great pleasure in witnessing a side of them that he knows very few others will ever see. It makes him feel special, enlightened even.

We're all animals with basic animalistic desires, no matter how much we try to cover them. Sex has evolved over a long time period. A time period I know too well is deeply written in blood. Perhaps this is why so many women wish to have violence in the bedroom under the guise of play fighting. They wish to be dominated aggressively by a male who is worthy, just as they wish to succeed over the other women present. Sex is ultimately a representation of the brutal realities of life itself.

The women who were lined up just a moment ago were chosen by The Shadows from a pool of tens of thousands of women, all in Holland. Orien will now have sex with his chosen ones, all together, in this one session. However, only one will be the victor by receiving his seed.

He will then select a new group of women from a new country. This will continue every four hours, three times a day. Over the next few weeks he will have sex with so many women, he will lose count.

The victor of each group will stay in the mansion and eventually be made into groups with other victors. Orien will then spend time with these groups of victors. They will fight hard in their sessions, trying their absolute best to make him orgasm, to have his seed for themselves at every opportunity. But ultimately there will be only one main sexual victor, who will accompany him for ten days at her most fertile and will be the only woman he will have sex with over this time.

There is one aim in all of this – for women to bear him a child. Any girl who, through the entirety of this game, succeeds in this will forever be lavished with riches, both for her and her child, as long as she never reproduces again with another from outside of his Order, The Shadows.

CHAPTER 57

ULYSSES UNCOVERS PERFECTIONS

The present – Geno, Australia.

OVER THE NEXT four weeks, Ulysses uncovers more perfections. He has continued with his morning ritual of saying *I love you* in the mirror before he leaves the cabin every morning. He finds that this love amplifies and returns to him, every single time. He also says a prayer to God when his eyes first greet the sunlight outside the cabin. And then throughout the day he appreciates the beauty of everything around him. *It is true, the more you appreciate the world, the more of its beauty it will show you.*

Ulysses also becomes more skilled at magic. He learns from Emit how, through belief alone, he can become invisible to most, no matter how plain in sight he is. He also learns how to zoom in on far away objects with his eyes, making them appear closer, such as an eagle can do.

Emit also teaches Ulysses some of the history of Geno and the amazing discoveries that previous members have made. He learns that the Geno pavilion was once in the centre of a grand temple in

Ancient Greece, and that it already existed before Geno was created, but was left abandoned by its previous occupants. The only change Geno made to the pavilion was by putting the Geno symbol on it.

Sophos is also a great source of wisdom for Ulysses. He seeks her out every day and often finds her gardening or cleaning. Ulysses helps her with these tasks as she teaches him in her fragmented English about many topics he has found fascinating since he was a child. He learns that ghosts exist in the *heret* – both the here (our reality) and there (the afterlife). She also speaks of what heaven, the realm of God, might be: that it could be the coming together of the time between time – the eternal unchanging beauty – and the order – the greater good which is created through the interaction between the elements. In heaven, an eternal soul lives only the perfection, the order. Not the chaos, the breakdown of all, like we do on Earth.

Through Sophos, Ulysses also learns of possible direct paths to the greater good for mankind. For example, she speaks of how we have all been created as individual elements as it is for the greater good. That we are amazingly unique with special talents and gifts that must be cherished. But at the same time, we are also very much a part of the one system. And so, when we pollute the rivers, we are polluting ourselves. She speaks of how mankind has distanced from these beliefs and that we need a return to this. That we need to treat every element as being beautifully unique, but also an important part of ourselves.

With Sophos, Ulysses also takes the opportunity to sneakily add in questions about Delta. He finds that Sophos is a great source of knowledge about her and with Delta being often on his mind, Ulysses cannot help but discuss her.

Luke successfully teaches great martial arts skills to Ulysses. Through this, Ulysses becomes very athletic, learning how to use every muscle in his body. He also learns how to use his surroundings, so that the world around him seems like an extension of himself, one he is in complete rhythm with. He fluidly swings from the branches of trees, flips himself and lands gracefully on the ground in a martial arts position, ready to attack. He even learns to run up stone and dirt walls, just like Delta did on the side of the library building when she rescued Ulysses from The Shadows.

The Shadows. They are another reason to train with such ferocity. He needs to learn how to defend himself should he come across The Shadows again. Or even worse, Orien. In some ways, Ulysses wishes he had never learnt of Orien. It is true, it is rather demotivating to know that there is an immortal enemy out there who can probably never be beaten, no matter what skills Ulysses learns. *How could I possibly learn enough skills in a few weeks to defeat someone who has had an eternity to master his craft?*

In the evenings, after training, Ulysses devotes his time to romancing Delta. He reads the books Delta adores. The first book he reads is *The Princess Bride.* He then follows it with *Sleeping Beauty.* Through these books he concludes that Delta wishes for a man who will symbolically save her. But, even more important, a man who is her true love.

Every night, just after the others have gone to sleep, Ulysses pens Delta a beautiful love letter and places it under her door. Every morning Delta awakens and replies to Ulysses, placing a letter under his door.

In the letters, Ulysses learns what Delta's childhood was like…

"As a child I had tutors during the day. My parents hired the best in the land. I learned about all sorts of things – including many of the great philosophies of the world. In the afternoon, I would spend much of my time riding my white horse, Salt, and exploring the woods with him. When I came to Australia and grew into my teenage years, I attended school like everyone else. My favourite leisure sports were tennis and swimming. And I would spend a lot of my spare time studying nature and caring for injured animals."

She also asks of Ulysses' life before Geno and Ulysses writes about his family life. How his mother is a great nurturer, always selflessly helping the family. How great it is to grow up with his sisters. And how his father has been a great supporter of his dreams by giving him paid work whilst also encouraging and making it possible for Ulysses to pursue things close to his heart, such as discovering the theory.

Ulysses writes how he works in his father's investment advisory business. They only have one client, which Ulysses has gathered is an extremely wealthy trust. Ulysses has never met the beneficiaries of the trust and his father has always refused to reveal to him who they are, telling Ulysses that they insist on the utmost secrecy.

His father is in control of choosing the trust's investments as well as liaising with the trust's beneficiaries to distribute income to them and their charitable causes, while Ulysses performs various administrative tasks, as well as researching new investments and charities – the latter sees him often travelling the world.

Delta's reply to Ulysses' letter surprises him. She mentions that his father is in charge of Geno's wealth. And suddenly Ulysses realises why he has never been told who the beneficiaries of the trust were sooner. All this time his one client has been Geno.

Coincidences start to happen in their writings. Synchronicities. Ulysses mentions how sometimes when she smiles she reminds him of his favourite animal – a frog. And then on the very same day as she received this letter something very uncommon happens. While studying nature, a green tree frog jumps on her shoulder. She laughs thinking that perhaps Ulysses is right as she seems to be attracting frogs.

The coincidences work both ways. Delta mentions specific philosophical ideas in her writing and then, coincidentally, Sophos brings the same topics up to Ulysses on the same day. It appears the letters they write to each other are creating magic in the world around them. As if there is a deeper purpose to their letters and the whole universe is smiling at their courting.

Ulysses consciously begins to synchronise his sleeping pattern with Delta's. This way he can have more waking hours where he has the possibility of seeing her, even if from afar or just momentarily during his daily tasks. In doing such, Ulysses soon discovers no matter what time he sets an alarm, he always manages to wake up just before it is set to go off, with just enough time to turn the alarm off before the noise of it, which he dislikes, disturbs him. He finds it amazing, as it shows how aware of everything he is, even as he sleeps. He is truly becoming more and more in control of psychic powers.

When Delta and Ulysses meet in person, it is usually within a group. So, they do not speak of their love letters. It is their secret. Ulysses also tries to keep his deep attraction to her a secret to others by not looking upon her as much as he desires. He finds this hard, however. It is unnatural not to look upon someone of great beauty. And so sometimes their eyes do magnetically attract each other's now and again.

He realises that being around a person he loves makes every daily activity more exciting. And he finds himself completely enamoured by her. He wishes there were a way they could become even more intimate.

CHAPTER 58

GIRL OF DREAMS

IT IS THE first day of spring. Sweat glistens on Ulysses' forehead as he slowly practises his martial arts moves alone on the dirt oval. He moves smoothly, gracefully, while feeling a great inner power. He is completely in the flow state.

A smile comes to his face as Delta enters his line of vision. She walks barefoot towards him from one of the dirt paths that lead to the oval. As she reaches him, she grabs his hand with a cheeky grin on her face.

"Come," Delta says. She guides him, past the oval and towards the garden.

"Where are we going?" Ulysses asks. He is amazed how brazen Delta suddenly is – holding his hand so openly inside Geno.

"You look like you could cool off." She gently releases his hand so that she can cup water out of a nearby fountain. Ulysses assumes that she is about to take a drink. But instead, she looks at him, smiles and throws the water onto him. She bursts into laughter and runs towards Geno's entrance. A smile comes to Ulysses' face. He chases after her.

She arrives at the Geno exit. With her left hand she quickly presses the button on the large stone while her right releases a torch from her pocket. She waits for the doors to open, looking nervously behind her as Ulysses closes in on her. This is his chance. He almost reaches her when she just makes it through the stone doors. Ulysses, suddenly blind in the darkness of the cave, is forced to slow down. He follows the light of Delta's torch ahead, flashing back and forth as she runs.

Finally, he reaches the sunlight. He sees her. She finishes running along the path at the furthest side of the lagoon. She quickly takes off her clothes to reveal her red bikini underneath and dives into the water. Ulysses, following her path, knows that it is too late to get revenge; she has already done the honours in making herself wet. And so, he gives up the chase and slows to a walk.

"I'm sure you'll do better next time," Delta says, again with a cheeky smile, swimming a stationary breaststroke in the water below him.

Ulysses purposely ignores her and casually takes his shirt off. He places it on a boulder beside him. He looks down at himself, where he now has the six-pack abs and muscular physique he always desired outside of Geno. The training with Luke and clean diet of Sophos' cooking has helped here. And he feels that loving himself has been an important factor too. When he stopped seeing himself as having flaws, his whole identity changed. And with this, his physique has followed.

He looks over to see Delta looking up at him, in such a way that Ulysses can only read as being her admiring him. And even though it must be obvious to her that he catches this admiration, she still does not look away. It is as if she loves seeing him with his shirt off and does not mind telling him how handsome he is with her eyes.

"Come in, Ulysses," she says as she swims towards him.

Ulysses walks and stands at the water edge, procrastinating. He knows very well how cold the water will be. Delta, seeming to notice this hesitation, climbs out of the water and comes behind him. Here she quickly gives him a little playful shove so that he jumps in. She then joins him back in the water and they play-fight. Ulysses *really* has to get even with her now.

But his attention is suddenly diverted as he notices a honey bee drowning in the water, fluttering its wings, close to the waterfall. He reaches out his hand. The bee climbs onto his finger. And after drying its wings, it flies away. It has been given the gift of another day.

"That's so nice of you, Ulysses. How did you know it wouldn't sting you?"

"Honey bees die after they sting. It has already shown a desire to live, by climbing onto my hand to escape drowning. And given that I'm not a perceived threat to the bee or its hive, it's logical that the bee wouldn't sting me. Clear vision," Ulysses says.

"Well, I've actually been stung before doing that," Delta says and laughs. "Still, I'm touched that you would save what I care so deeply about: nature. You're such a nice guy, Ulysses."

Again, Ulysses can see great admiration in her eyes. "I know," he smirks.

Delta chuckles at his arrogance. She then cups her hands under the waterfall. Ulysses is sure that she is about to splash him again, as she did at Geno. But instead, she draws it to her mouth and drinks it. She smiles and then simply splashes Ulysses with water from the lagoon as if she knew what he was originally expecting.

They then swim together, continually teasing one another by splashing water and play-fighting. Ulysses often becomes very physically close to Delta, so close that their chests almost touch, but then at the last second, she pulls away backwards in the water, her eyes still locked with his, as if they are dancing together.

She stops and turns. They swim towards one another. But once again, at the last moment, Delta changes direction, swimming backwards, trying to get away. Ulysses continues to move towards her. She soon finds herself before the waterfall. Here she moves partially out of the water, trying to escape as Ulysses closes in. He swims up to her as she leans back on some rocks. He is in a dominant position. He moves his body on top of her, with his arms supporting him to be careful that he does not put his entire weight on her. He feels the sexual intensity, their athletic bodies pressed against one another. But then Delta suddenly splashes him and he backs away, treading backwards in the water.

Now she chases him. They swim in circles until once again they are both under the waterfall. Here they rise out of the water, both equally dominant. And they stand in front of one another.

The waterfall cascades down the dark rocks before them, splashing them both lightly as it enters the lagoon where they have been swimming. Ulysses looks upon her. The sunlight plays upon her damp blonde wavy hair and the water trickles down her face.

With a desire that can only be fulfilled through the flesh of her being, he leans into her feminine divinity. As he does, her eyes become brighter to him, the beauty of which attracts him closer still. The tension inside him rises. He reaches forward, pressing his fingers gently against the nape of her neck. And for a moment they do nothing but stare into each other's eyes.

Her blue eyes pierce him, deeply, in a way that is different to how anyone has ever looked at him; they are filled with purity, complete openness and an underlying strength and purpose as if she believes in every part of her essence that what she is about to do is right. And it is in this precise moment that Ulysses realises that this moment was in his recurring dreams. *It was a premonition.*

He realises that he now can see the true beauty of her. All this time he found Delta to be physically gorgeous, but there was something different about her to his dream. Now he realises that it was not her that had to change. It was his own eyes which had to uncover her beauty even more by appreciating and getting to know her. Now he can see her beauty, inside and out, and she is the most striking girl Ulysses could ever possibly see.

Ulysses feels like both touching her gently and sensually, whilst grabbing and holding her forcibly close at the same time. So many contradictory emotions stir inside him. He wants to taste her, to kiss her, to consume her. But he also wishes to protect her.

Suddenly, and with great force, she enfolds into him in a sensual embrace, enthusiastically kissing his lips whilst her hands eagerly explore his back. He promptly takes control of her but simultaneously loses control of himself.

A wave of sexual tension that has built so beautifully is finally being explored. He wishes to taste her completely and gently kisses and bites her neck. He feels her hard nipples press against him through her bikini. He too becomes hard and he pushes against her through his shorts.

Suddenly, Delta stops and pulls back from him, looking a little alarmed. "We have to go back to Geno, Ulysses. You wish to keep this secret and if we stay longer I sense that we'll get caught," Delta says.

While Ulysses finds it difficult to stop during such passion, he believes in her psychic powers. They swim back to the edge of the lagoon.

As they gather their clothes, Ulysses looks back to the lagoon. What a perfect location for their first kiss. From this angle there is a rainbow in the waterfall. Two rainbow lorikeets fly past the waterfall and in this moment they seem to directly relate to both the rainbow and this waterfall. As if they were also born from this same great source of water and all-powerful sunlight.

Ulysses looks at Delta and notices her eyes widen as she finds a blue gemstone at the edge of the water. It is almost six centimetres long, a tetragonal prism and pyramid shape. She kneels, picks it up and looks at it closely, and it brightens her eyes as it reflects the different corners of them. She turns it with her fingers and it suddenly becomes so bright that she must close her eyes for a moment. "Wow. Oh my God," she looks at Ulysses and smiles.

"It's beautiful," Ulysses says.

"It is more than just beautiful!" She takes it in her hand, stands and cuddles up to Ulysses. He witnesses such perfection in the moment: a rainbow in the waterfall surrounded by the natural beauty of the rainforest, man and woman who have shared their first kiss, and a beautiful blue gemstone. How beautiful the world's design. He appreciates that he has the right eyes to see it. "We should go," she says again.

They then walk through the cave to the entrance of Geno. Here they must put their necklaces together to enter. Delta does the honours, explaining as she does, "The need for two necklaces to join as one to enter Geno is both purposeful and symbolic. It's symbolic as we have a need for others in life. Just like the bees need the flowers, the pandas need bamboo and a newborn needs its mother. This is what needing two keys to get into Geno represents. No one can enter Geno alone. Just as no one truly enters the world alone. We are all important, we all have a purpose and are significant, but we also need the other elements."

Delta's words remind Ulysses very much of Sophos' teachings on the paths to the greater good for mankind.

A blue light shines from the necklaces and the cave wall opens. As they enter Geno, Delta stops and stands before Ulysses. She looks as if she glows from his love, and she is as beautiful as ever. Here they hug for what could be an eternity, because time for Ulysses seems to stand still. It is as if their hug takes place in the time between time.

They share a final kiss and Delta hurries ahead.

*

Right at this moment, two men arrive at the lagoon. They wear cloaked black ninja gis and have a symbol of a red triangle on the centre of their cloaks.

CHAPTER 59

THE SHADOWS IN THE RAINFOREST

The present – Monaco.

IT IS A perfectly sunny day. Leucius lies on a deck chair, tanning himself on his superyacht. His chest is bare. He wears black wayfarer sunglasses and white shorts. His white linen shirt with a small red triangle symbol at the breast is resting on a nearby chair.

Suddenly his peace is disturbed when his mobile phone rings. He fumbles around trying to get to it. His sunglasses fall off his face and onto the deck of the yacht. Eventually, he finds his phone underneath the chair, in one of his boat shoes.

"Oh, what now, Anomonet?!" Leucius answers angrily. *How dare he ruin my leisure?*

"Sorry to bother you, Master. The Shadow Enforcers have just contacted me via radio. They have found fresh footprints in the rainforest which could only be from the members of Geno."

"Okay, this is good. Where do the footprints lead? It might take us to their base," Leucius says excitedly. He had grown impatient as

The Shadows searched within the thick rainforest fruitlessly for the past month. *Finally, there is hope.*

"There is some confusion, Master. The footprints surround a lagoon and are also inside a cave which is a dead end. However, there are no prints elsewhere."

"They can't have disappeared into thin air! Have them continue searching in the area. And prepare my private jet."

"Your jet?"

"Yes. The Enforcers must be closing in. I'd like to be there when they discover the Geno members. It's something I've been looking forward to my entire life. Arrange two Shadow Enforcers to accompany me on this journey."

CHAPTER 60

LUKE'S CHILDHOOD

Twenty years ago – Public housing.

LUKE SITS ON an old grey carpet in the lounge room. His beautiful mother is seated beside him, watching as he plays with toys she has just given him for his fifth birthday. Luke has a yellow truck in his hands, driving it across the carpet, making motor noises.

"Luke, I'm afraid I'll have to go work shortly," his mother says while looking up at the clock hanging on the wall in the adjacent kitchen.

"But it's my birthday, you promise to spend day with me," Luke says, saddened.

"I know, Luke. And I have spent most of the day with you."

"You been working so much, Mummy, I never see you."

"I know. It's just that things are very difficult at the moment, and we need to pay the rent. Margaret from next door will come over and mind you. And you can show her your new toys," she smiles.

"I don't want to play with Marg. I want you."

"I know. But I can't, Luke."

Luke feels the tears roll down his little cheeks. Deep inside his heart he feels a hurt he cannot describe. "But Mummy."

"I can't."

Suddenly Luke feels a powerful surge rising inside him. He stands and yells, "I don't love you anymore! I hate you." Then he runs out the door.

"Luke! Wait!"

Sometimes he feels that he cannot control his emotions, such as his anger in the moment. It consumes his little body. He runs down the cement steps which to him feel very large, jumps on his little yellow bike and goes as fast as his feet will pedal. His mother calls out to him. But he quickly rides past the jacaranda tree with purple flowers and around the corner.

It makes him feel a little better knowing that his mum will miss him and that she called out to him not to leave. It shows that she cares. But even with this, he still feels sad.

He feels sad that it is his birthday and he is by himself. *I'm always by myself.* He wishes he had friends like most other boys.

He rides around his lower-class neighbourhood, with no particular destination in mind. He needs time to himself when he feels such emotions. Finally, after two hours he feels calm enough to return. And he rides back.

He arrives at his home and looks inside the closed window. He can just make out his mum in the frosted opaque glass. She did not go to work after all! Maybe she stayed behind just for him. To spend his birthday with him. He cannot wait to see her. He wants to make it up to her. He truly does love her.

He raps on the door repeatedly with his little fist. The door opens and he smiles, ready to see her beautiful face. But it is not her, it is a lady he has never met before.

"Luke?"

"Who are you?"

"I work with your mother."

"What are you doing here? Where is Mummy?"

"Something has happened to her."

"Huh? Wh… wh… what happened?"

The lady sits down on a nearby chair and leans forward. "It's her heart. It failed."

Luke immediately bursts into tears. Sometimes he cannot control his emotions.

"Her heart broke?"

"Yes, her heart broke."

"I broke her heart and now she is died'ed?"

"I'm sorry, Luke. Your mother had been trying to manage her high blood pressure. But she's been working so hard lately."

"What can we do to save her?"

"There's nothing we can do. It was just God's will. She's in heaven now."

Luke instantly feels wounded. He drops to his knees, feeling an intense pain in his stomach. One he has never experienced before. He does not want her to be gone. He did not mean to break her heart. He did not mean it when he said he did not love her anymore. And now she has died from a broken heart. He killed his own mother. The only person he loves and who loves him in the entire world.

"There was nothing you could do, Luke," she continues.

"I could have! I just broke her heart and now she is gone!" he screams.

CHAPTER 61

DELTA'S SECRETS

The present – Geno, Australia.

FIVE DAYS HAVE passed since their first kiss. In this time, Ulysses and Delta have increasingly spent time together, both in person as well as continuing to communicate through love letters.

On this afternoon, they walk along the meandering paths that journey through the rainforest that thrives inside Geno. Ulysses finds himself acutely aware of how amazing Geno is. No matter how much time he spends here, it never becomes less enchanting.

On their walk, Delta often pauses to greet the animals that come to them, many of whom she greets by name. She also educates Ulysses about the species of trees and plants that they pass. He already knows that her passion is so deeply in the natural world. It is one of her favourite topics to talk about.

He finds that she has a natural grace that Ulysses hardly ever comes across. Most people have had this side knocked out of them from a young age. They are told to behave a certain way and because of this they become restricted. Ulysses can only sense a stiffness in Delta when she is at the dining table; in all other areas, she is completely natural. The way her eyes look upon things, like a signature which is only hers. The way she speaks openly and smiles freely about the things that touch her heart, to such an extent that it seems she does not have any inhibitions at all. Her ability to show who she really is and wear this on her sleeve, Ulysses realises, is extremely attractive. In today's often-masked society, realness is more valuable than diamonds, he thinks.

He and Delta also play-fight a little as they walk, only to end in a caress each time. Delta makes a branch she walks past swing back and lightly hit him, teasingly. Ulysses repays the favour by slightly tripping Delta when the time is right, only to catch her before she falls. He certainly does not feel his age around Delta.

Besides, things like age just do not seem relevant to him anymore. It is amazing how many limiting beliefs he once had. Before Geno he never would have thought he could have a great romance with someone more than a couple of years younger than him. But here he is with Delta and he could not be happier. He wonders how many gifts in life he has forgone just because he did not realise they were gifts.

The playfulness and sexual tension rises between Ulysses and Delta moment by moment. But suddenly Delta stops. She turns to Ulysses, about to say something. She pauses and looks down, as if she suddenly finds it difficult to bring herself to look at him.

"What's wrong?"

Delta looks up, showing her watery eyes. Her lips start to quiver. "There's something I must tell you. I've been holding it in for too long."

"Yes?" Ulysses asks, concerned.

"I've been having a dream. A dream that if I'm with you, if we're together, I will die. I'm sorry I've kept this from you." She sobs and moves into him in an embrace.

"Tell me about your dream."

She pulls a little away from his chest. "I began to have this dream not long after we arrived together at Geno. I dreamt of our kiss by the waterfall, and that you and I are in love. Then the dream flashes forward and I'm murdered."

"By who?" Ulysses asks, determined to protect her should this dream ever begin to materialise.

"I believe it's Orien."

Orien. The name fills Ulysses with anxiety. *How can I protect Delta from a man who is immortal?* "Are you sure it's Orien?"

"His appearance is never shown in the dream, but I sense that it's him. And I don't know how, but there's an overwhelming feeling that the two parts of the dream are linked in some way. That the first part causes the next. That you and I are in love and somehow, because of this love, I will die."

"I understand," Ulysses says, the back of his hand drying her tears from her cheek. "Emit warned me to stay away from you. Is this why?"

"Yes. He knows of my dreams and is worried they are prophetic. That the system is warning for us to stay apart. I didn't tell you as I didn't truly wish for you to stay away from me."

"Everything makes sense now," Ulysses says, his mind having a great realisation. "No wonder Emit was worried. Orien hasn't been seen in a century and now suddenly because of me, he will reappear."

"Wait, there's more to this... after the day you fell down the cliff and returned to Geno, I started to have another part to this dream. A third part. The dream flashes forward and I'm walking in a beautiful garden with you. It's so vivid. You have roses in your hands and there are white doves in the tree."

"What do you think this part means?"

"I don't know," Delta replies.

"Do you think this part of your dream could be heaven?"

"I'm not sure. But I know that no matter what happens, in the end we will be together. The dream tells me so."

Ulysses releases Delta from their embrace. "Delta, Emit warned me to stay away from you, but he never told me exactly why. I wanted to be with you so deeply and it felt so right that I foolishly thought I could protect you from whatever harm would come. But now that I know the entire truth, that it's because of Orien, we can no longer take this risk. Orien is immortal, I can't protect you from him... I shouldn't have pursued you." Ulysses turns himself from her.

"Yes, you should have," Delta says with conviction and pulls him back towards her.

"I've put your life in danger. I'll not allow you to die for me. If I must make the ultimate sacrifice, to never be romantically with you again so that you can live this life to the fullest, this is what I choose. You're too beautiful of a creation for the world to lose you."

"Ulysses." Delta grabs him by his shoulders. "I would rather die than not be with you."

"I won't let you die."

"Don't you wish to be with me?" she says as she looks up at him and gently kisses the bottom of his neck.

"I wish to be with you more than anything. I wish for us to be so close that we're one. This is how deeply I wish for you. But it's because I love you that I can't let you suffer."

"Ulysses, we must be pure and courageous in following our hearts. I've already made my decision. I made it the day we first kissed under the waterfall. You see, I've waited my whole life for you. And I would rather spend a few beautiful moments with you in this life and then see you in heaven, than to live a lifetime without you. Please, give me the gift of these moments."

Ulysses looks into Delta's moist blue eyes. He feels torn. His heart tells him to be with her but his mind tells him that it is foolish. He reluctantly nods in acceptance to her wishes. The perfect mindset says that he should be open to perfection. Perhaps there is still another way. That somehow they can be together and he will be able to protect her from Orien.

"Ulysses, there's something else."

"Oh, Delta, not more."

"There's one more secret. Only I and the other members of Geno know. No one else have I have ever told and for good reason. But I believe that you're ready to know now."

"What is it?"

"If you don't love me once you find out, I understand."

"Please, Delta, tell me…"

"I'm from another time."

CHAPTER 62

SOPHOS SPEAKS OF DELTA

Ulysses feels overwhelmed with his recent revelations: He is in love with a girl from a different time. He never envisioned this could happen. But he knows that God works in ways that are more amazing than he could ever envision. And Delta is more amazing than any girl he has ever met – she is the girl of his dreams. But what to make of her dreams? He must find out more. And there is one person who Ulysses believes has the answers to everything.

He finds Sophos in the small kitchen of Geno. As usual, she is wearing her black widow's outfit. Her forehead glistens with sweat as she hobbles around, sweeping the floor with a broom.

"Please, let me do that for you, Sophos," Ulysses interrupts her.

"Very well, Ulysses. Thank you."

Ulysses gently takes the broom from her and begins sweeping. Sophos has a seat on an old chair in the corner of the room by the wooden bench. Her right hand rests over the front of the chair arm.

Ulysses finishes sweeping, grabs a dustpan and brush and kneels to collect the rubbish. "Delta has told me her secret. That she is from another time," he says nonchalantly.

"Yes. Must be very special to her. Thinks greatly you, trusts dearly. How you feel about her?"

Ulysses knows that his and Delta's love is meant to be a secret. He promised Emit. Yet he also cannot lie to Sophos. She knows all. *Surely she will see the truth.* He feels conflicted on what to do. And so, he simply does not answer, pretending instead to be pre-occupied with putting the dustpan rubbish in a nearby bin.

Sophos smiles. "That okay Ulysses. I already know. Know from very beginning that destined for one another. Since you first come to Geno and saw you standing together. What you share powerful, even time itself not stand in way. This why together, in present day."

"How could this happen? How could she be from another time?"

"Have to tell bit about her."

Ulysses takes a seat on another old chair in front of Sophos and listens intently.

"Delta born in what call old Sweden, to royal family."

"She's a princess?" Ulysses asks. He noticed that Emit often calls her princess. He thought it was just a term of endearment.

"Yes, princess. But more than princess. You, I, learn to be pure. But Delta, born pure. Continues to live without sin."

"She has never sinned?"

Sophos nods. "Delta, most pure girl ever exist thus far," Sophos says enthusiastically.

Ulysses is astonished. *How could she be without sin?* Yet as incredible as it is, he knows it to be true. He has studied her; he knows how warm-hearted she is. It just would not come into her nature to ever purposely wrong another. *Delta is pure.*

"She on direct path to greater good. From beginning, parents knew something special about Delta. Did best to keep protected from evils of world. But, protecting not only task, also kingdom to rule over. Know someone's true colours when in position of power, whether abuse power or rule justly. Life very tough in old days, but parents ruled justly. Good people. And not only royalty… also members of Geno."

"Just like us?"

Sophos nods. Her face is alive with wonder. She seems to relish speaking of Delta's upbringing. And to Ulysses, it seems like a true to life fairytale. "Geno's base at this time in Sweden. Base move every time Shadows discover location, must remain hidden. Also spent time in Greece. Now Australia."

"So how did she travel through time?"

"Age ten, tragedy struck village. Burned around her, she in great danger. Rescued by gallant gentleman, member of Geno, taken to safest place for her. *Future*."

Ulysses can hardly believe what he is hearing. *Delta was rescued from her homeland and taken to the future!* His emotions are torn. He feels such sorrow for Delta that she had to leave her home like this. But at the same time, he feels blessed that she was taken to this time, for if she were taken to any other period in time, he would never have met her.

"So, time travel's possible?"

Sophos nods.

"But how?"

"Even Delta don't understand how. But happened."

"Tell me more."

"Delta raised in her future, our past, by another Geno member, Emit. He taught ways of living in modern time. She went to school, did everything young girl do. But deep down she very different. And because this, never fit in well other girls. Instead, spend much her time with nature. With animals. And with two people who know her secret. Emit and I.

"School holidays, she spent Geno. No need to learn perfect mindset, already innate. Self-actualised. This why without sin. Why on direct path to greater good."

"Of course. Because one can't purposely sin when they're self-actualised."

Sophos nods. "Because of natural gift, advance quicker than any Geno member in history. Great achievements. But still, all the while, deeply longed for parents. And something else too," Sophos says while looking intently at Ulysses.

"What's that?"

"Desires no different from birds or butterflies she study. Often male searches for female and female searches for male. Just how life is." Sophos becomes very expressive with her hands. "Ever since male and female first separated from single entity, deeply desires to find other, find missing part which nature separated. Desire to meet, dance, love and forever be entwined as one. Delta same, her heart beats for romance. She give love freely to all God's creatures, but inside heart… special place for only one man. Gentleman who understand her secret and complete her." Sophos looks at Ulysses. "You gentleman, Ulysses."

Ulysses is honoured to be. "I promise I'll spend my life fulfilling her romantic desires and will do everything I can to help her loss as a child," he says with great strength and conviction.

"This you will. Love powerful, Ulysses. And hers for you. Her hopes, dreams since little girl finally become true. Delta open secret garden to you. Now you begin to learn the secrets she holds."

"Yes. Such as the recurring dream she has been having, the dream of Orien. What does it mean?"

Sophos' eyes open wide. Her wrist pointing inwards, she raises her right index finger in the air. "Dreams serve many purposes, Ulysses. Some forewarn you. This such dream. Prepare. Many trials ahead."

Ulysses nods. "Thank you, Sophos." And with this, he stands to his feet with a quiet determination. He must find Delta.

CHAPTER 63

THE GOLDEN MOON

The present – Geno, Australia.

THERE IS A Golden Moon this evening. It is full, large. Ulysses notices Delta engaging in her nightly ritual, looking at the night sky, alone. She is standing on a small wooden bridge, on the path that leads towards the cabins. Small solar-powered lights contribute soft lighting to the path. There is a narrow stream of rainforest water that leads directly to her and travels underneath the bridge she stands upon. She faces the large Moon, seemingly transfixed by its wonder.

Ulysses comes behind her. As if instantly sensing him, she turns her head back towards him. He reaches forward and holds her around her waist, embracing her. She moves her neck back and kisses him, just like the couple in the painting from her childhood which her heart so deeply adores.

Their lips part. He continues to hold her. Bathing in the glow of the Moon roots Ulysses to the present. He feels deeply drawn to it.

"Isn't it beautiful?" Ulysses asks looking into the night sky.

"Our love or the Moon?" Delta responds.

"Both."

"You know, when I see the Moon, I think of you. As you're awake late into the night, whilst I fall asleep early and rise with the Sun. It's like you're ruled by the Moon and I'm ruled by the Sun," Delta says.

"I agree. But while the Moon chases the Sun and the Sun chases the Moon, they never meet. I don't wish us to be assigned to such a fate. That's why I've been trying to synchronise my sleeping pattern with yours. I want to change what rules me."

"Wow, I've been trying to synchronise with you too! Little by little. But you know, we don't have to change how we naturally are. As the Sun and the Moon do secretly meet. At night when the Moon glows, it's the Sun touching him that makes him shine. Look at the Moon's reflection on the water of the stream. That's the Sun," Delta says as she points to the Moon's light which sparkles on the water as it moves down the stream towards them. "Like liquid gold dancing towards us. The Moon and the Sun, together as one. Even time can't keep the Sun and the Moon apart."

Ulysses brings her closer to him. "I love you." Immediately upon saying it, he is surprised that these words left his lips. It was almost like every cell in his body forced his guard to come down so that he could express his heart to her.

"Do you love me even though I'm from another time?"

"Yes, my love for you is all-encompassing, it transcends time."

She holds his hand a little bit tighter. "Then I'm glad that my deepest secret has been revealed to you. And I love you too." She turns towards him, smiling, her visible teeth shining in the low light. And they kiss.

Their lips part and Ulysses speaks, "Sophos told me about what happened to you as a child, how you were separated from your parents and came to live in the present."

"My wounds from not seeing my family again have never healed."

"I don't wish you to be wounded. I find it incredible that you can suffer such misfortune and still manage to be the amazing girl that you are. You're so strong."

But as Ulysses speaks these words, Delta's face becomes forlorn and her emotions seep out. Tears run from her eyes.

"Oh, Ulysses, don't you see that when I look at the night sky it's not just to see the marvels of the universe? As a child, I would look at the stars with my mother and father. I know that some of the stars in the night sky must be the same that we would look at together. This is how I connect with my parents while we're apart. This is all I have to hold onto them. I don't have photographs. I don't have videos. All I have are the stars," Delta cries. "I look up at them, knowing that somewhere in time, my parents and I are both looking at the same stars and our hearts are filled with love because we have each other."

Her vulnerability has engaged Ulysses' protective side. He holds her tighter, wishing he could wrap her up in the security of his love and cure her with his kisses, one heartfelt kiss at a time. But he also knows that none of these offerings could truly make up for her loss. He touches her face with the back of his hand, drying a tear which runs down her cheek. He then kisses her forehead gently.

Delta turns and leans back into his chest, looking again at the heavens. "I know that I may not be able to see all of the stars we once looked at, as Australia is in the Southern hemisphere and Sweden is in the north, but surely some of the stars are the same," she says, reaching to the night sky, as if she is trying to grab a collection of stars.

"You would have seen *Sirius*. It's the brightest star in the sky," Ulysses says as he places his hand on top of her outstretched arm and guides it to point to Sirius. "It can be seen in locations of both hemispheres."

"The Sirius star… isn't it amazing, that a star which bears the same name as you connects me to my past," Delta says. "I do believe, deep inside, that everything that has happened, as painful as it is, is perfectly designed for some greater reason. Just like your theory points to. One day I hope to discover what this reason is."

"I know you will." Ulysses nods.

She turns back towards Ulysses. "Your belief means so much to me. I'm filled with belief also, but I'm not as strong as I may outwardly seem. Your belief fills me with this strength that I lack. I guess I'm not as perfect as you say I am after all."

"Sometimes what seems like imperfections can be perfections when you look upon them with the right eyes. Maybe I've been perfectly designed to complement all that you are. To be your guiding star, so that you have no weaknesses."

Delta nods. Her eyes look up to Ulysses with a warmth and faith that he has not seen before.

"I promise that I will heal your wounds in time," Ulysses says with a deep conviction. He is unsure how this will be possible. But he knows he must.

CHAPTER 64

LUKE LEARNS

THE SUN HAS risen when Luke walks from the Geno library. He has spent all night there, working on translating the old books. It is becoming an obsession of his. Every moment he spends reading these books in the Geno library he becomes further fascinated by the secrets that Geno holds.

His plan now is to get a few hours' sleep. But first he wishes to see Ulysses. He has just learned something in the Geno books about Ulysses' ancestors which Ulysses will find very interesting.

Luke walks to Ulysses' cabin and knocks on the door. There is no answer. He begins to turn to leave when something grabs his eye. Poking from underneath Ulysses' cabin door is a letter. He knows whose handwriting it is – *it's Delta's*.

He picks up the letter and studies it. *It's a love note*. He suddenly feels as if he is winded. He drops to one knee, his stomach in great pain.

*

A short while later, Luke finds Delta. As usual for this time in the morning, she is in nature, kneeling and studying plants. He confronts her.

"I've found your note," he throws it at Delta.

"Luke, that's not for you."

"I know. I know who it's for!"

"Please don't tell anyone. It's meant to be a secret," Delta says, her arms waving before her, a worried look on her face. She stands.

"You choose Ulysses, even though you know that you will die?"

Delta nods. "I can't help who I love."

"Yet you've never even given me a chance!"

"Luke, we've been through this before."

"I'm smarter than Ulysses. I'm stronger. I'm everything better than him. And I've always loved you, since the moment we first met. You don't even know him. You've known me for years!"

"Yes, but I just feel that it's right in every part of myself. I've dreamt about him."

"Yes, dreamt that you will die because of him. Is that what turns you on?"

"No, that's not what turns me on," Delta says, as tears start to fill her eyes.

"Why can't you simply give me a chance?"

"I just don't feel that way."

"You don't *feel* that way? You can't just act on feelings, Delta. Feelings are fleeting. I feel too. And I feel angry right now. Does this give me the right to show my anger? Should I too be ruled by my feelings? Should my feelings cause someone's death? Because you could die because of him and yet you're still ruled by your feelings," he says and then pushes past her angrily, almost knocking her to the ground. And he leaves.

CHAPTER 65

SLOWING TIME

Ulysses awakens and excitedly walks outside his cabin door. But to his surprise he discovers that there is no love letter from Delta. It is strange, especially considering that they shared such a beautiful moment the night before. *I guess she doesn't have to write to me every morning,* he reasons. He sincerely hopes that her feelings have not changed overnight.

*

Later in the morning, Ulysses meets Emit for his lesson at the Grecian pavilion.

"Today, I'm going to teach you how to slow down time," Emit says.

Slowing time. Emit made a brief mention of this on the day Ulysses was having troubles with Delta and was unable to master magic. Ulysses thinks of how incredibly things have worked out since that day. It feels like a lifetime ago to him. There was so much he was yet to learn. And now, bit by bit he is learning Geno's secrets. "It is actually possible to slow down time?" Ulysses asks as he takes his usual seat on the stone stairs.

"Yes, perceptively for yourself. Imagine this for a second. Imagine if nothing in our solar system moved. If the Earth didn't rotate so there wasn't a day approximately every twenty-four hours. If there were no morning or night. If nothing inside our world moved at all. If a clock's hands didn't move. If even yourself were completely still, with no thoughts at all. How would you perceive time?"

"I couldn't."

"Exactly. You see, time is perceived by humans purely through the interaction between the elements. If there were no interaction between the elements – there would be no perception of time."

Ulysses suddenly realises the great truth in Emit's words. "I think I understand what you're getting to. You're saying that we can change our perception of time by simply changing how we view the interactions?"

"Precisely! You may be surprised to know that you've already done this in the past. Have you ever noticed how some moments in your life seemed to last forever, while others went by very quickly?"

"Yes, I think everyone has."

"And more specifically, have you ever been in danger and realised how slow time felt during this moment?"

"Yes!" Ulysses says excitedly.

Ulysses can remember a moment as a child so vividly. He was on top of a bedroom cupboard when he suddenly fell backwards. As he fell, it felt to him as if time had slowed down and he was floating down from this cupboard like a feather. It was taking him an extraordinarily long time to land. And when he did, it did not hurt him at all. It seemed as if the slowing of time cushioned his fall. He will never forget that experience.

And yes, *of course!* He also experienced this on the day he discovered his theory, when he saved the dog from getting hit by the black car. He put himself into danger by running in front of the vehicle and suddenly everything became slow for him, helping him to save the dog and carry it to safety. Ulysses is amazed how so many of his experiences have perfectly prepared him for the future, for being self-actualised and helping with his learning at Geno.

"You slowed time in these circumstances as your consciousness was working at a faster rate than usual. So fast that the elements seemed to slow down. But they didn't really slow down. Time remained constant for them. It's just for you, personally, time ran slower."

"Wow, this is incredible!"

"Yes, and when the world around you seems slow compared to the speed of your consciousness, you'll be able to do the seemingly impossible. You'll gain the ability to process things faster. You'll have faster reaction times. Your reflexes may become so quick that to others you'll appear to have super-human powers. You'll be able to land safely from greater heights than you'd ever think possible, as you'll have time to fall in such a way that it minimises your impact – just as a cat does when it falls from a great height but still lands perfectly and unharmed."

"Tell me, how do I slow time?" Ulysses asks enthusiastically. He wants to get straight into the practical.

"Well, you already do it naturally. So, all we have to do is bring these skills to the conscious mind. And one way to learn is through jumping."

"Jumping?"

"Yes. The stairs that you sit on," Emit points to the row of eight stone steps leading to the Grecian pavilion. "You are to jump over these stairs and continue to do so until you can consciously slow time."

Ulysses nods, stands and turns to look at the stairs before him. Eight stairs are not easy to jump over. He knows that if he fails, he could greatly injure himself. Yet maybe this is the idea behind it – after all, time seems to slow when he is in danger. Still, as he loves himself, he decides not to try to jump over all eight straight away. He walks up the first three stairs and jumps over them onto the dirt.

Nothing. Time seemed to run as usual. He tries again. *Still nothing.*
"Try a little higher," Emit encourages.

Ulysses jogs back up to a couple of steps higher than previously, literally stepping out of his comfort zone. He jumps. Suddenly it works! It was very subtle but Ulysses felt as if the jumping over these stairs lasted briefly longer than it should. Meanwhile, the speed of his awareness seemed as usual. *Amazing!* The outside world slowed, but his consciousness has remained the same.

He tries again, this time jumping from an even higher step. Success – time seemed to slow down even more on this jump.

Ulysses enthusiastically runs back up the stairs, this time to the very top of the pavilion. He looks at the ground below him. He knows that if he fails he will surely hurt himself. But now that he has tested his physical capabilities, he believes he can do it. He runs along the base of the pavilion and jumps as far as he can. Suddenly, time slows down for him, immensely. It feels as if the world is in super slow motion. He glides over the stairs elegantly, slowly putting his feet in the exact right position to land properly and safely. After what feels like perhaps three times as long as it should, his feet touch the dirt. He immediately performs a roll that Luke has taught him in the martial arts training. The roll lessens the impact through gradually slowing his momentum rather than abruptly coming to a forceful stop. He completes the roll and is immediately back on his feet. He did it! "Wow! That was incredible!" Ulysses exclaims, feeling on a high.

Emit pats him on the back. "Time waits for no man, but it can slow down for them. With practice, you'll be able to consciously slow down time, like flicking a switch, whenever you need it," Emit says.

"I can't wait, this is one of the best things ever!" Ulysses says, feeling so high on energy.

"Luke will have many great things to teach you now that you have this skill. You'll find that through slowing time you can learn martial arts a lot easier. And once you start using this skill coupled with magic, you'll be ready to learn the most powerful Geno martial arts skills."

"I'm looking forward to it."

"Good. Because it's important. We're not the only ones who have mastered this skill. The Shadows can also slow time."

"How do you know?"

"There are ways of telling if others are slowing time around you. They're very graceful with their movements, their reaction times are enhanced. The more you learn it yourself, the easier it is to tell in others."

Of course, Ulysses thinks. This is exactly how The Shadows were when they attacked him. They were certainly very graceful with their movements. Ulysses feels he has much to learn to get to their level of fighting skill. And as for Orien, he hopes to never see what the fighting skills of an immortal man are like.

CHAPTER 66

ORIEN

The past – Lithuania.

"I AM A god and into this chaos my child is born." Orien blesses his newborn child in this same way every time a woman bears him one. He leaves the baby with its beautiful mother to nurse and walks out the front door. He knows that he will never return inside again.

He sits on the steps of this small house, his mind as vacant as his stare. In the yard before him is a flock of chickens. He watches as they frantically chase after a grasshopper, each attempting to subdue it as it jumps about in a panic, trying its best to live. The battle is violent. The chickens are possessed by their primal instincts, *by evil*; they even attack one another while competing for this meal. And they tear the grasshopper to shreds.

While the grasshopper is a shadow of its former self, it is still alive. But not for much longer. A rooster wins the final piece.

The world is a very cruel place.

Orien, having seen many centuries, is in a good position to pass judgement. He has witnessed the great cruelty of life, a thousand times in a thousand ways, regardless of what time period he is in. It always begins like a rising tide. He can sense it in the air, the bad disintegrating the good. It takes hold of the elements as if they have breathed it in and now have suddenly turned pure evil. They become possessed. Like the chickens with this grasshopper.

And what saddens Orien the most is that this cruelty is inside of him too. It is inside everyone. And it has been ever since time began.

I am a God and into this chaos my child is born.

From the moment a man is born into this world, he is given no choice but to play the cruel game of survival. For him to live, it is at the expense of other creatures who ultimately will become like the grasshopper. Once he matures, he learns that he must compete with other men for reproductive partners. The more he conquers other men and the environment around him, the more power, the more resources and the more women who desire to mate with him. The more children he fathers and helps to also conquer, the more chance his genetics will be passed on. This is what nature wants of beast and man. This is to live.

Orien has played this game better than anyone, in all of history. Compared to even the most successful men, he is a god.

And as for the real God – to design such cruelty into the system, this is not a god that Orien could ever worship.

Yet he also knows that there is only one way to rebel. And that is to *give God everything that HE wants.*

Orien stands. He knows what he must do. *There is an important destination to travel to.*

CHAPTER 67

A FIGHT

The present – Geno, Australia.

IN THE AFTERNOON, Ulysses stands with Luke on the dirt of the oval. He is excited to use his newfound skill of slowing time in his training. He is also looking forward to learning the true Geno fighting, with magic. Perhaps by combining these skills it will be possible to protect Delta, even from someone like Orien, he considers.

"Is there a way to defeat Orien? An immortal man?" Ulysses asks Luke as they begin to spar, practising martial arts moves.

"You're asking the wrong question, Ulysses. You're not to defeat Orien. You're only to help him to have the desire to change."

"But how can we possibly change Orien when he believes such things about the world? Wrong things?" Ulysses answers as he ducks a strike.

"He doesn't believe wrong things. He believes the truth," Luke says and looks at Ulysses seriously. As if he knows something that Ulysses does not.

"But he believes that the world is chaos. Look around us: the world is beautiful and magical. Purposeful," Ulysses says as he motions around Geno.

Luke stops sparring, leading Ulysses to lower his fists. "Geno is like the Garden of Eden, it's quite easy to believe and see all of the good in the world here. But the real world, outside of Geno, is tough. It's survival of the fittest. There are rapes, murders and wars. There is starvation. Believe me, inside all of us is good and bad. All of mankind."

"Maybe so. But I believe that we can learn to become good and do only good."

"Ulysses, how can you be so ignorant?" Luke sighs. "Imagine that you live in a perfect world. Every day is perfect. And everything is perfect. But there is one dark street that people tell you not to walk down. No one knows what is down this road. But it looks dark and scary. As you go about your perfect life you will be drawn to this dark street. Your curiosity will want to walk down it. Just to see what is down there. And one day you will. You will sacrifice your perfect life, just because your curiosity wishes to see and feel the dark side. A part of mankind is attracted just as much to the chaos as we are the order."

"But the theory says that the chaos isn't truly chaos. It is ordered."

"Exactly, Ulysses. The chaos creates the order. But at our level, we must function in the chaos. And on this level of chaos, there are things that we would consider to be evil. Because these evil things are necessary to create the order. Why do you think *live* spelt backwards is *evil*? To live is to have evil. We are designed to be both our human version of good and bad, for they both serve us. Our human understanding of bad is sometimes the greater good. Just as the chaos is truly order."

"Evil can't be for the greater good. What about someone like Hitler, how was he a force for the greater good?"

"Let me tell you something about Hitler!" Luke says, his finger dominantly pointing at Ulysses. "Do you know how many times his opponents tried to kill him, yet seemingly, by simple coincidences he managed to escape? I do. And believe me, they weren't coincidences. Synchronicity was protecting him. The interconnected elements wished for him. *Why?* We don't know. Maybe mankind had to learn this lesson before our technology increased so much that a future Hitler had the power to destroy the whole planet? Maybe he was the lesser of two evils? A catalyst for change? We can't be sure. But I suspect that his appearance on this Earth was for the greater good."

"I don't believe we had to go down that road. I've spoken to Emit about the greater good. He said there are many paths to it. And just because evil can reach the greater good, it doesn't mean we had to take that route."

"You don't understand. What you or Emit consider to be evil is immaterial."

"Why?"

Luke stretches his right leg out and leans on it, the striations on his thigh becoming visible. "Let me ask you. What do you believe is worse, killing and eating a human or raping a human?"

Ulysses is thrown by this question, and doesn't see its relevance. But he answers Luke, "Well, killing and eating a human would get a greater penalty in a court of law."

"Now, what's worse, killing and eating an animal or raping one?"

"Raping an animal is bestiality. So that would get a greater punishment."

"Exactly. See the contradiction? Much of our human good is purely what is best for the survival of our species. And so, we can't judge good and evil through the eyes of our species, when there are evolutionary design parameters at work. It's what God believes is evil that matters." Luke starts to spar with Ulysses again.

"Yes, but as Emit says, surely the greater path that God wants for us is to be self-actualised," Ulysses says as he dodges Luke's strikes. "And we can't self-actualise while doing what we as humans consider to be evil."

Again, Luke stops sparring. He looks as if he is becoming annoyed. "Ulysses, we've been metaphorically cast out of the Garden of Eden, heaven. The greater path for man *IS* to operate in the chaos.

This is what the theory at Geno is truly about. Even though life may appear to have bad moments, it is still for the greater good. The bad moments seem to be chaos, but they're truly order. Should a lion stop hunting an antelope because you understand it is evil to kill? Evil is inherent to this level. It's part of the greater good." And with this point, Luke begins to spar again, leading Ulysses to raise his fists. "Besides, we don't have to be self-actualised to best serve our purpose. Sometimes, self-actualisation will hinder us."

"I disagree," Ulysses says as he dodges Luke's attack.

"Why?"

"I can feel how important self-actualisation is for mankind. We need it to evolve."

"You're delusional, Ulysses. Just like Emit." As Luke's conviction gets stronger, so do his martial arts strikes at Ulysses.

"No, Orien is."

Luke suddenly hits Ulysses so hard that Ulysses flies across the air. Ulysses somehow manages to still stand and adopts a defensive martial arts pose. Luke steps towards him.

"Don't you say that about Orien! Orien is working for the greater good. You don't understand. You haven't read what I have."

"Why did you hit me like that for?"

"Hit me back then."

"No."

"Be one with the chaos, Ulysses. Hit me, I dare you."

"Why?"

"Because you have evil inside you too. And I'll prove it to you. If you don't hit me, I'll hit you."

Luke begins to throw a series of fast strikes. Ulysses uses his newly learnt skill and slows down time, thus managing to just evade this attack. However, he is finding that he cannot hold out for much longer – Luke is much better at fighting than he. Finally, a strike succeeds in hitting Ulysses and he is knocked to the ground.

Luke strides towards him.

"Luke! What are you doing?" Ulysses yells, defenceless on the ground.

Luke stands above him and points at him sternly. "It's what you're doing that's the problem. You're trying to take what doesn't belong to you. It belongs to me. I've wanted it far longer than you have," Luke answers and walks away.

CHAPTER 68

HEALING HAND

Ulysses lies on the dirt of the Geno oval. Spent of energy, he slowly raises himself from the ground and dusts himself off. His hands are shaking; his altercation with Luke has left him tense and filled with adrenaline. Thank God Luke ended up storming off to the Geno library, as Ulysses would be no match for him in a fight. He does not understand how a person who is self-actualised could possibly attack him like that. *What did Luke mean when he said that I am trying to take what's his?*

Ulysses walks through Geno and arrives near the fountain in Geno's garden. This has recently become his regular meeting spot with Delta. *But Delta isn't here.*

He realises that it must be because he has arrived earlier than usual, due to the martial arts training being cut short. He continues walking through Geno, searching for her. Finally, he finds her in the forest, sitting at the edge of a pond with her side towards him.

He wishes to read her mind, a skill which comes and goes, but one that he is slowly becoming better at as his connection with her deepens. And in this particular moment, he can read her very clearly:

She looks at the pond, in awe of how the water reflects the sunlight to create a beautiful flow of colours onto an overhanging branch. She looks at the fish swimming in the water. To her it is almost like they exist in another world. How different it must be to live under the water, she ponders, turning her head to the side, her lips closer to the sky.

Ulysses loves to see Delta in her natural element, sitting in nature, filled with wonder. She takes in so much beauty that many others would simply miss.

He comes closer to her, now only a couple of metres away. He wishes to quietly observe her for a moment longer. But he can read that she has already noticed his presence, not in his reflection on the water of the pond, or by looking to her side, but as usual, simply by sensing him. She turns, giving him the warm-hearted gaze of meeting her loved one and a smile of contentment coupled with excitement. Ulysses walks to her and lowers himself in front of her. He leans forward, closes his eyes and moves in to kiss her softly on the lips.

But he kisses thin air. He opens his eyes and to his surprise she has disappeared. Suddenly, Delta walks from a tree behind him and kisses Ulysses with such a great force that he almost falls over backwards. Ulysses regains his balance and returns her kiss.

"How did you do that? How did you disappear?" Ulysses asks, wondering whether she teleported herself or if she is just very skilled at slowing time. And with this question he realises that he did not read her intentions before she did this. It is like suddenly he cannot read her mind again. *It comes and goes.*

"There's much to learn about magic, Ulysses. I'm looking forward to you learning, we'll have so much fun," she smiles, her dimples on display.

Suddenly there is a look of alarm on her face. "You're bleeding? What happened?" she says as she attends to his finger.

Ulysses did not realise his finger was bleeding. Though he can guess how it may have happened. *If I escaped with just a small cut on my finger after an altercation with Luke, then I am truly blessed.*

"Umm... it's just a finger," Ulysses says as she examines it.

"It is not just a finger," Delta disagrees as she puts her lips around it, purposely putting pressure on it to stop the bleeding while soothing it with her mouth.

Ulysses finds it strange that Delta is doing this. But he reminds himself that she is from a different time and perhaps this was normal back then. When Delta releases Ulysses' finger she has licked and sucked all the blood away.

"The cut is still there. But it should stop bleeding now," Delta says.

"Thank you, Delta," he says with appreciation. Appreciation, not because he was at any great risk of danger with simply a bleeding finger, but because it shows that Delta cares for him so much that even a small cut to the finger is a reason for her concern. It reminds him of his mother when he was a child. So attentive to his needs. As a child, there is nothing that can heal as quickly as a mother's love and attention. Now Ulysses has found a girl outside of his family who also feels a great level of love and care for him. He knows that one day, like his own mother, Delta will be a great mother as well.

The more he gets to know her, the more he becomes in awe of her, and the more he deeply knows that she is the partner he has always dreamt of being with, both literally and metaphorically. Which is why he needs to ask her...

"Delta, there's something I wish to talk to you about."

"Yes?"

He knows that for now they must keep their love affair secret. Yet he still wants to solidify their relationship, even if it is just to each other. He holds her shoulders gently. "Fate has brought us together, love has joined our lips and destiny will entwine our souls forever," he leans forward and kisses her forehead. "Will you be mine?"

She smiles, "Do you wish me to officially be your girlfriend?"

"Yes, I do," Ulysses says. He smiles. He already knows that he wants more than this; he desires to one day marry her and have a family with her. But "girlfriend" will do for now, he thinks.

"You already own all of my kisses, all of my sensual touches. But now you own me in word and promise. Yes, I'm yours, Ulysses." Delta smiles. "And you're mine too."

*

It is now late in the evening at Geno.

Ulysses does not write to Delta. He assumes that their relationship has moved on from this, as he did not receive a letter from her this morning. Instead, he spends time in his cabin, relaxing. He looks down at his finger. It has stopped bleeding and is completely healed. Almost as if the care from Delta has magically healed it.

As he studies his hands, he again notices the hard cyst just above his wrist. The cyst he first discovered on his day he uncovered his primary desire of love in front of the majestic mirror in Geno's garden.

A thought comes to him:

I wonder if I can heal myself of this cyst now that I'm mastering magic?

Ulysses believes that physical ailments are sometimes symptoms of deeper causes, often psychological. Perhaps he can discover the true reason for the cyst. What this ailment is trying to tell him. To gain clear vision. And what better way to find out than by *asking the answers.*

Ulysses, in his mind, asks why the cyst is there. And straight away an answer comes to him. It is caused by anxiety and stress. He receives the internal message that every time he has felt stress, unbeknownst to him, he unconsciously has stored all of this stressful energy into this part of his body. With this new understanding, he realises that this cyst is not something bad, but rather a sign of love. It is his body showing him that something is wrong. He thanks his ailment for showing him this. He touches it lovingly and with his mind he tells the cyst that he appreciates it. He promises that he will stop putting so much stress onto his body and thanks the cyst for teaching him this. And now that he has made this promise, he lets the cyst know that it has done its job and can move its energy to other places.

And he wishes for the interconnected elements in his body to help this process.

*

The next morning, Ulysses awakes and looks down at his hand. He is amazed! The cyst has completely disappeared. *It worked!* He has healed himself!

CHAPTER 69

GENO'S GARDEN

As ULYSSES' AND Delta's love continues to blossom, they naturally become more daring, spending more time together inside Geno.

It is midday and they lie on the grass in Geno's garden, near the statues at the entrance of Geno. They are surrounded by rose petals the wind has blown from the rosebushes. Delta is on her back, wearing a white dress, her feet bare. Ulysses is on his side, his upper body raised slightly over hers. He wears dark shorts, a green polo and aviator sunglasses.

"How come you haven't told me about your deepest desires, Ulysses?"

"You are my deepest desire," Ulysses quickly replies.

"Apart from me," Delta chuckles. "I've learned so much about you. Through observation, through your love letters, your words, your touch, your kisses," she says, looking up at him with admiration. "I can tell that you're an amazing, handsome and gifted man. But I know so little of your dreams in life. Why haven't you told me?"

"I'm more interested in you than talking about myself."

"But I'm interested in you. I want to know the deepest parts of you."

"Well, there are secrets I haven't told you."

"What?" Delta sits upright, immediately concerned.

"Don't worry," Ulysses smiles and leads her to lie back down. "I don't think my secrets could possibly be as big as yours."

"I sure hope not. Will you tell me?"

"Well, my deepest desire has always been to live the life of my dreams. Just like most people, I guess. And this is why for so many years I searched to discover a theory of everything. Now that I've discovered it, I've uncovered my primary desires and have self-actualised. And I feel like I am living the life of my dreams. But with this, a secondary desire has surfaced. You see, I've realised it isn't enough for me to simply live a great life. As all of these beautiful moments I've experienced, all of these thoughts… I'd feel sad if the world didn't learn about them. Life is short and I don't want everything I've come to know to simply be a whisper in time. I want others to be inspired by the wonders I've witnessed so that they can experience it for themselves," Ulysses says. Delta reaches to touch his chest, where his heart is. She holds her hand there as he continues to speak. "This is why I want to be a writer. I want to speak my heart, documenting moments and amazing insights. To write a book which will serve as a key, a key to a greater knowledge, one that can unlock the beauty of the universe for those who wish to see it." Ulysses takes off his sunglasses and looks into her eyes.

"What great timing. Right at your most intimate, just at the pinnacle of turning me on mentally, you unleash your beautiful eyes, your soul, onto me."

Ulysses smiles.

"Sorry, I just had to say that. Please continue," she urges him.

"It's okay, I appreciate it. My writing can live on as a legacy for good. People can read my book in a thousand years. And I will know that I've touched the world in a grand way."

Delta sits up and speaks with great enthusiasm, "You *are* a writer! I could tell from the moment you first penned a beautiful love letter to me. You will inspire dreams within souls. Expressing not only the beauty you see outside but also the beauty you have inside. The beauty that I witness when I'm with you. I'm sure of it."

"I know I'll be a success with you by my side."

"And you'll always have me by your side. You're going to write a great book. Even greater than the books I've always adored reading," she says with a deep sincerity. "I can tell that you're going to help the world, Ulysses… I can just tell." Delta leans over and kisses Ulysses' chest.

"I'd really love to write about Geno. I know it's a secret. So, if I'm not allowed to make what I write public, I'll simply put my book in the Geno archives, with the hope the world will one day be ready for it. Even if it's centuries from now."

"You're so incredible. To be willing to wait for your dream to be realised, all for the greater good."

"I learned this quality from you. It's the same with your theory of eveolution."

"I didn't realise that you've been paying such close attention to me."

"I've been taking in everything. I'm going to use a lot of this for my book," Ulysses says, motioning to Delta and himself.

"Are you?"

"Yes. The way you look at me. Your beautiful insights. What it's like to be romantically intimate with you. I want to base a main character on you. And even use some of your exact lines."

"Really?" A smile lights up her face.

"Yes. *Everything is a perfect reflection of nature's beauty.*"

"Oh, I'd be honoured if she said that," Delta says with tears welling in her eyes.

"My book will not only be a vision of mine for a long time, but also a symbol of our love. People will be able to witness our love through this book, forevermore."

"Wow. The idea that you are documenting our love so that it can last for eternity is beautiful. I love your romantic vision," she smiles and wipes a tear from her eye. And suddenly she looks at Ulysses with a determination. "Let's give the book some excitement." She stands and pulls Ulysses' hand, leading him to also stand.

"What do you mean?"

She delicately removes the straps to her white dress from her shoulders and her dress drops to the ground, revealing her naked body. Ulysses is instantly enamoured. Some women look even better naked than with clothes on. They are the ones that got the raw end of the deal with clothes being invented. Delta is such a woman. She steps out of her dress, removes her necklace and places it on top of the dress. "Come, Ulysses," she says with a playful grin as she starts to walk away from him.

"Inside Geno? Out in the open? What if we get caught?"

She turns back to him, "Ulysses, you're forgetting, we're psychic! We'll sense if someone is coming. So don't think about that, just think about you coming with me," she smiles, her beautiful dimples on display.

Ulysses accepts her logic. He takes off his clothing and walks with Delta through the beautiful garden. It takes him some moments to embrace being naked in a public area. But soon it becomes very natural. He enjoys the sun's late afternoon rays. It is not often that he can feel the air and sun on his entire body, free from the restrictions of clothes.

"See, people at Geno embrace nudity," Delta says as they walk past nude statues.

"Yes, why does Geno have these statues?"

"They are current and past members of Geno. Unfortunately, we don't have all of the past members' statues here. Many of them have been destroyed or lost through the course of history."

They arrive at Delta's nude white marble statue, the one Ulysses secretly admired on the day of the thunderstorm. Delta purposely stands next to it, an invitation for Ulysses to simultaneously consume both her and her statue with his eyes. He realises how amazing it is to be urged to freely absorb her being. To look upon another with no self-consciousness. He becomes sexually aroused just by studying her. She looks down and notices, and smiles.

"When I first saw your statue…" Ulysses begins.

"You got aroused? I hope so! From now on I want you to be aroused whenever I'm around," she says, smiling. She moves her hand forward as if she is about to touch him but then stops short and brings her hand back to her side. "Do go on… You were about to tell me what it was like when you first saw my statue?" She looks at Ulysses cheekily, as if she is well aware of the power she has to cause him to lose his concentration.

"I thought it was the most beautiful statue my eyes have ever laid upon. But still, more important than any representation of you, *is you*," Ulysses says. He moves closer and touches her face with his fingers. "You're a living, breathing human being. You're the most beautiful work of art there is, nature's creation. Better than any imitation could ever be, for you are flesh," Ulysses says as he looks upon Delta. Her lightly tanned skin is shining in the daylight, her striking face and captivating eyes looking up to him. The contrast to the white hard statue beside her is obvious. He leans close to her neck, consuming her alluring scent.

"What's your favourite part of me?" she asks.

"You become more beautiful the less you wear and the deeper one gets. Your soul is the most beautiful of all."

"I would like you to get as close to me as possible. As deep as you can get."

Suddenly, as Ulysses looks upon Delta, naked, next to her statue he realises that this is the vision that he had on the day of the storm. *It was a precognition. It has come true.*

"What is it?" Delta asks.

"I have seen this moment before. In a precognition."

"So, this was always meant to happen?"

Ulysses nods and touches Delta's shoulder, circling his fingers so sensually that she shudders. Seeing this effect makes him feel as if he has a magnificent power within his hands, greater than any magic he has performed. "One of the most amazing things is giving, whether it be a loving touch, a present or a kind word. It's incredible, for if the gift is welcome, it feels great simultaneously to both the giver and the receiver. And when you have two people both giving and receiving at the same time…"

"… It's the most amazing thing in the world," Delta finishes his sentence and reaches forward to touch Ulysses' arms, caressing him.

"Through wonderful design, the intimate parts of our body are the most sensitive to touch. Our lips…" Ulysses says.

Delta instantly moves to kiss Ulysses, but he holds her lips back with his index finger. He is purposely teasing her. He touches the side of her neck and moves his chest to touch hers. Her hard nipples press against him, her heart beating fast. She exhales deeply as he moves completely into her arms. Her hands explore his back with loving touches. She keeps trying to kiss Ulysses, but he purposely moves his lips from her.

"Ulysses!" she protests.

But Ulysses knows what he is doing. He has found that sex is not just the act itself. It is also the build-up, the tension. It starts with every look, every innocent touch, every word and teasing game that you play. The more two people delve into this sexual tension, the more pleasurable it is to succumb to. Eventually, this tension greets sex like a powerful waterfall. It washes away all inhibitions. And what is left uncovered is a shared moment deeply in the present – where every touch and every sensation is cherished. Where nothing exists apart for the creation of an art most others will only ever witness as a fantasy.

He lifts Delta with his strong arms onto the white base of her statue.

"Are you going to put this in the book?" Delta asks.

"I just might."

"I find it cute that you believe you have the willpower to tease me," Delta says as she reaches out, holds his face still and looks deeply into his eyes.

She gives him a lifetime of words with this one look. A whole universe, a whole existence. It will take the rest of his life to express in words the beauty he sees in her eyes. And so, he surrenders to the moment, knowing that for now, all he must do is simply look back.

Suddenly and with great force, she pulls him close and they kiss passionately. And from this moment onwards, she takes control.

*

Delta and Ulysses lie together, naked, on the grass of Geno's garden. Both are spent from immediately finishing making love. Her cheeks flushed, Delta leans over him and caresses his chest, "You know, in past times, like the time I am from, sex was much more out in the open than it is today. Of course, I was too young to partake, but it was considered so natural and important to society that it wasn't hidden. In fact, sex and fertility were worshipped... semen was revered as a great elixir," Delta says.

"An elixir, really?"

"Yes. It's a very magical liquid when you think about it. We sensed it back then. Modern science is proving this even more now. Inside this liquid is your DNA," she says as her finger touches some of the semen which remains on his chest. "So, it's a deep part of you."

"I will always be all for you," Ulysses replies.

"Good," she says as she looks deeply into his eyes and playfully licks a drop off his chest. She then collapses on top of him, giggling. They are both a sweaty mess.

Ulysses has never made love like that before. It felt so natural, passionate and animalistic. Yet also romantic, meaningful and magical. *So, this is what having sex with a girl who comes from another time is like. One with magical powers.*

CHAPTER 70

SOPHOS' VISION

SOPHOS SITS, ALONE, on the Geno pavilion stairs. She is hunched over a crystal ball which she holds close to her bosom.

She raises the crystal ball to her eyes and looks deeply into it. Images begin to form inside the crystal. She sees the Geno members. And then suddenly there are great visions of terror. *No, can't be true.* But it is true, the crystal never lies. Tears stream down her sagged cheeks. The visions are so terrible that she cannot stand to look at them any longer. She closes her eyes and tries to mentally will herself to accept what she has just seen. *There is much pain to come.*

Her hands shaking vigorously, she accidentally drops the crystal ball onto one of the stone stairs and it smashes into many pieces.

CHAPTER 71

ULYSSES' WOUNDS

IT IS THE evening.

Ulysses is inside his cabin. Resting on the bed next to him is a sharp knife that he secretly took from the kitchen earlier. He knows that what he is about to do is a very hard thing for him, as he loves himself so deeply. But he feels that he must. He grabs hold of the blade. He closes his eyes and breathes deeply as an attempt to calm himself.

He raises the blade to his shoulder. With his eyes still closed, he slices his shoulder just above his bicep. The pain leads him to instantly open his eyes. He witnesses the blood rushing out and quickly applies pressure with his hand and closes his eyes again. He uses all his powers. He uses magic.

He opens his eyes and slowly lifts his hand. But his shoulder is still wounded, his hand now covered in blood. *It hasn't worked.*

He applies pressure to his shoulder again, drops his head and sighs. How did he manage to help the butterfly, yet he cannot heal his own shoulder? He feels as if he is running out of time.

CHAPTER 72

SOPHOS SPEAKS OF HER PREMONITION

THE NEXT MORNING, Ulysses visits Sophos at her cabin. Unlike the other cabins, this one has no stairs and is more like a shack. As he walks in, he notices that she is busy sorting through her belongings.

"Hi, Sophos!"

"Hi, Ulysses." Although Sophos welcomes him, he can read in her eyes that there is something concerning her.

"What's wrong?"

"Ulysses…" she pauses and sits down on the side of her wooden single bed. "May I tell little about life I come to learn?" she says, leaning forward.

"Of course," Ulysses says. He sits next to her on the side of her bed. He always loves to hear wisdom from Sophos. In many modern societies, the elderly are often treated as being useless and unproductive when they have finished their working lives. But Ulysses finds this to be false. Apart from sharing their love and energy with things they deem to be important, the elderly also have vast reservoirs of untapped wisdom. Wisdom which many of them also love to share.

Sophos speaks with raw emotion in her voice, "Meaning of life… many things, just look around." She moves her hands as if to expressively encompass everything around her. "Sometimes not meant to know all meaning. Just as flower no witness the beauty it creates. But I tell you insights, help decipher meaning of life…"

"Okay, Sophos," Ulysses says, feeling excited to hear Sophos speak about such a mystery.

"Must live way you know meant to, Ulysses. Every moment precious. Deep down inside you know how wish moment to be. Make sure do everything you wish. Be as true and open as you can. Live life of dreams. Do not hold back. Only one chance at life. Where one second of real engagement worth lifetime of falsehood," Sophos says, her voice trembling. "Have tests in life to pass, challenges that allow you to serve purpose. Must pass tests while stay true to pure and perfect self. Simple as this. And if fail, must learn, grow and do things right if ever in situation again.

"If you wounded emotionally during life, must heal with love. Do not leave this life with wounds… I very blessed and lived life to fullest. Lived through many shades and still pure and perfect self. And so, have done everything need to in life," Sophos says as she taps herself on her chest repetitively with two fingers of her left hand.

"You're talking as if you're going to die. You're not going to die."

Sophos looks at Ulysses glaringly. A stare that speaks a thousand words.

"No! You can't die."

"I have foreseen death."

Upon hearing this, Ulysses feels a wave of shock flow through his veins. Sophos is wise and all-seeing. He knows that it is possible for a person who is deeply connected to the universe, like her, to know the day they are going to die. But still, even though he believes her words, he hopes that she does not have to resign herself to this fate. "There must be another way. Tell me, what did your vision tell you?"

"Geno betrayed, one of our own."

"Betrayed? By whom?"

"No matter."

"It does matter. Maybe I can stop it. Maybe I can protect you."

"You promised to save Delta. Can't save both. I die so love may be. Besides… it's time, can't save someone when it's their time."

Ulysses eyes well up and he puts his head in his hand. He does not want this to be true.

"Come, Ulysses. Wish to show something," Sophos says and leads Ulysses to just outside her cabin, to an area of grass. "Be careful where walk, Ulysses," Sophos says, putting an arm out to stop Ulysses from walking ahead.

"Late husband, Joe, buried here. He was member of Geno too. I often spend time here, visit him. See rosebush?" she says as she points towards a lone rosebush, with no roses, to the right of his grave.

Ulysses nods his head.

"He planted for me as romantic gesture. Always said I as beautiful as rose. Wished me to have roses every day, near cabin door at Geno. Funny how life work out. Rosebush never flowered. Not once in forty years! But that okay, no need roses, all really wanted was him." She stops and looks into Ulysses' eyes. "I ready to see Joey again."

"No, Sophos, you can't, aren't you afraid to die? How do you know that you will be okay in the afterlife?"

"I promise I find heaven, Ulysses. And once I do, will give you sign."

CHAPTER 73

THE HOSPITAL

Fifteen years ago – A children's hospital.

THERE ARE THREE single beds spread out in this room. Luke lies on one, his only privacy is a thin hospital curtain which currently surrounds him. Stacked on his bedside table are encyclopedias and books on history. This is how Luke spends his time. Reading all that he can about world history.

At only ten years of age, he has read every single history book he has been able to come across. And now, he is re-reading them while he waits for more to somehow, and often synchronistically, come his way. Recently, a tall man donated some to the hospital and gave Luke words of encouragement. If only everyone was as nice to him as this man.

Suddenly, Luke's curtain is drawn. He sees two nurses. One is the head nurse and the other is a new nurse Luke has not seen before.

"And this is Luke," the head nurse says.

"Luke Lukans?" the new nurse reads from her paperwork.

"Well, we aren't sure of his surname. He has spent many years in orphanages and foster care. We just put it down as that."

"I see."

"He's an amazingly gifted young child. Aren't you, Luke?" the head nurse says as she gestures towards him and smiles. "You can ask him any date in history and he will tell you what happened."

The new nurse displays a crooked smile and unconsciously lets out a *hmpf*. Luke can tell that she is sceptical. "Okay, Luke. Let's see how good you are. What happened in 1494?" the new nurse asks.

Luke does not say a word, he simply contemplates.

"Oh, it's okay, I don't expect you to know," the new nurse smiles knowingly, giving Luke a chance to gracefully concede.

"Do you want me to answer or not?" Luke says in his soft pre-pubescent voice as he sits upright in his bed. He looks directly at the new nurse. "In 1494, the House of Medici were expelled from Florence. Also, in Florence, the Italian war began, which lasted four years. Charles VIII of France started an invasion in Florence. Charles VIII also purchased the right to the Byzantine Empire in the same year, although historians argue about the exact date. Meanwhile, across the ocean, Christopher Columbus first sighted Jamaica. And the Aztec forces conquered Mitla." Luke pauses as he notices that the new nurse's mouth is wide open with disbelief. "... Would you like me to go on?"

"That's fine, Luke," answers the head nurse.

"Please, if you ask me again, can you make it a prime year?" he asks the new nurse.

"Why a prime year?" asks the new nurse.

"Because there's magic in prime numbers. Even some of the simplest creatures know this. Do you know that there are species of cicada that only appear in prime intervals? The rest of the time they live underground. They do this so that predators are unable to predict when they will reappear."

"How do you know so much about cicadas and world history?" the new nurse asks curiously.

"With my sickness, I've a lot of time to read. And I especially like to read anything to do with time and history."

"Yes, we know, Luke. But why this particular fascination?" the head nurse asks.

"Because it shows us who we are. The same common themes are often repeated throughout human history. We can learn from them."

"And what's something you've learned?" asks the new nurse.

"I've learnt that I'm not alone. That my suffering has been felt by others throughout time."

"Suffering?" the head nurse asks.

"Yes, there's much suffering. No one escapes it. It's part of being human. But it all has a purpose. *We* have a purpose," Luke says as he looks around at the white walls surrounding them.

"A purpose?" the new nurse asks as she chuckles.

"Yes, I've realised this. There's a reason for everything. Just as there's a reason for my sickness," he says as he points towards himself.

"And if there isn't?" the new nurse asks.

"Then I will create the reason. I'll use time to become as good as I can be. You'll see, I'll get out of here. I'll be great. I'll be strong, healthy and handsome. And people will treat me better."

The head nurse lowers her head and talks quietly to the new nurse, "He often speaks like this. He doesn't seem to realise that the chance of his recovery is extremely unlikely. The poor boy, he has no family. And he's either a genius or has lost his mind from the medication."

The head nurse looks up and smiles at Luke, not realising that Luke has heard everything she has just said.

"Luke," she continues, this time at a normal volume. "Let's keep quiet about history from now on, okay? You can keep reading your books. But let's not speak of it again."

"But... she asked me," Luke protests, motioning to the new nurse.

"Luke, that's enough. We're all tired of it."

CHAPTER 74

LUKE READS THE SIGNS

The present – Geno, Australia.

IN THE EVENING, Luke purposely pays close attention to Delta and Ulysses at dinner. He wishes for one final sign, just in case he is not seeing things with clear vision. But unfortunately, his greatest fears are confirmed. *It's true.* He can tell by simply looking at them. He can sense it in every cell of his body. *They're in love.*

It hurts deeply because *Delta is not like other girls.* Ever since Luke became strong, healthy and handsome, just like he predicted he would, girls have thrown themselves at him. Yet no matter who he becomes, he has never been able to win the affection of Delta. *Why does she always say that my eyes repel her?* He fears that somehow she sees beyond his current form and to the sickly child he once was, a part of himself that he knows he will always hold. And a part of him which he desperately wants to keep hidden.

This unrequited love of Delta has Luke wishing even more to withdraw socially. Lately, he has spent most of his time in the library. And it is here that his old passion of world history has returned. He is so obsessed with reading Geno's history books that he either

misses meals or eats less than usual. He neglects all other training and exercise. And with this, his physical wellbeing is gradually
deteriorating, almost as if the sickly child is making a comeback.
Furthermore, he is beginning to lose his self-actualisation and the
powers that come with it.

The Geno library, Delta, training Ulysses, everything here is
bad for him. *I must leave here. I must leave Geno.*

*

Later that same evening, a dozen questions race through Luke's
mind pertaining to the unjustness of his predicament. Why does
God keep the gift of Delta from him? Why isn't his good the same
as God's greater good?

All of these questions are, however, unanswerable. And now he
stands at the exit of Geno, feeling as if he has been cast from the
Garden of Eden when he has not even sinned.

He whispers into the night sky, *"My God, my God, why have
you forsaken me?"*

He picks up his backpack and places it on his shoulders and
presses the Geno symbol. The cave doors make a rumbling sound as
they open. His torch lights up the nearby vicinity. Luke walks into
the cave, intending to never return.

He passes the beautiful blue lagoon which is darkened by night
and rounds a corner on the path. Suddenly, he hears some rustling
ahead. He is on alert to see what type of animal it is and whether
he should be alarmed. A crocodile will be the worst possibility, but
unlikely for this part of the forest. He shines his torch into the dense
undergrowth. And is shocked as he sees several figures. *Out here in
the rainforest?* They are moving towards him.

The darkness of their uniforms camouflages them with the
night. Luke can just make out that they wear black ninja gis. Nothing good can come of this.

The Shadows.

One of the ninjas alerts the others with a loud grunt. Suddenly, they all pull out swords from behind their backs.

Luke drops his backpack and walks to them, fearlessly. He has nothing to lose. The ninjas prepare to attack, their swords outstretched. Luke gracefully adopts a Geno martial arts pose, his torch still shining on them.

"Stop!" yells a voice. Another man comes out between the Shadow Enforcers. This man does not wear a gi. He has his hair slicked back, an expensive-looking safari-style outfit and a gold watch encrusted in diamonds which reflects the light from Luke's torch strongly. He waves his own torch towards Luke.

Luke yells to this man forcefully, "Are you here to destroy Geno? I won't let you do it." Even though Luke does not want to be a part of Geno, he also does not wish it to be destroyed.

"What? What?" the man asks as he continues to move towards him. It is as if Luke's aggression is completely disregarded by this young man.

"That is exactly what Nikel Romanov said just before he was killed by the Bolsheviks. Are you too saying your last words?" Luke says, instantly realising that he is letting his secret passion of world history known. *Who cares now?* he thinks. He has nothing to lose anymore, he might as well be who he truly is.

"Oh my God. It's you," the young man says as he comes closer, studying Luke's face with a great terror.

"Okay, your last words are getting better," Luke says, noticing the fixed blade knife in this man's belt and looking for other possible dangers to overcome.

"But you're not real? How could you be here?"

Luke is confused by this young man. Why does he believe that he knows him? He looks into his eyes, trying to understand. And then… he does. Everything makes sense.

CHAPTER 75

TRAGEDY STRIKES

EARLY THE NEXT morning, Delta and Ulysses meet at their usual meeting place, by the fountain near Geno's garden.

Delta arrives carrying her thin blanket. "Let's take an adventure today, Ulysses. Let's go to that beautiful beach we discovered on the day you gained enlightenment on the cliff face."

"The one with the love heart lagoon?"

"Yes. This way we can make as much noise as we want," she smiles cheekily.

"Okay, you've convinced me."

They exit Geno and walk through the thick rainforest. Their path seems to have become overgrown since they last walked upon it, five weeks before. Ulysses moves the vines and branches that are in their way, simply by putting out his hand and willing it. Every day Ulysses is becoming more powerful at magic. And his powers are being displayed in many ways.

Delta walks with her blanket in hand. She has the posture of a gymnast, a signature style of walking.

"I love your walking style," Ulysses says.

"Really?"

"Yes, you're very natural with your movements. Perfectly fluid with great posture. I can't describe it, but it's just sexy."

Delta smiles, "You know, I really like your compliments, Ulysses. Most people just say to a girl how beautiful she is. Yours are specific. When you say them, it's like you really mean them."

Delta suddenly puts her arm with the blanket before Ulysses to stop him from walking forward. "There's something I wish to tell you." She guides him to turn towards her.

"Oh no, here we go again," Ulysses says, concerned. He has heard too many secrets from Delta. Her being from another time, her having dreams which warn her against him.

Delta smiles and calms Ulysses' frustration, "No, this is good. Ulysses, I want to open my heart to you. I've been waiting for you to come into my life since I was a child. You're my handsome saviour and I wish you to know that I love you, deeply, with all of my heart." Delta reaches into her pocket. But she does not appear to find what she is searching for. She becomes flustered. "Oh no, I've lost my gift for you. I planned to have it for you as I spoke my heart. I must've dropped it on our way here."

"Delta, it's okay about the gift. The only present I truly wish for is right here," Ulysses says while holding Delta's hips. He thinks of how Sophos' late husband planted roses for Sophos when all she truly wanted was him. With his right hand he then touches Delta delicately on her neck. His hand appears to calm her as if his touch has become so familiar a companion on her skin. She closes her eyes, leans her neck to the side and appears to almost lose herself to the moment. But then she stops herself...

"No, I must get this for you. I want you to have it. I made it just for you, for an important reason."

"What is it?"

"It's a surprise."

"Well, we can go back and look for it."

"No, I don't want you to see the gift before I give it to you. I must've left it behind when I took a drink of water from the stream. It isn't far. Wait here, I'll be back in just a moment."

Ulysses nods his head in acceptance.

Delta hands her blanket to Ulysses to hold. She then turns and runs as quickly as she can through the jungle. Her feet perfectly place themselves to take advantage of the natural curves of the path they have just taken, whilst avoiding all the branches and rocks that lay along the way.

And then she is out of sight.

Ulysses' mind wanders. He has been thinking a lot about Sophos' premonition. *She will die as a member will betray Geno.* Suddenly, he has a great realisation. *Everything makes sense. Delta's dreams, Sophos foreseeing her death.* Ulysses is instantly filled with a great dread.

*

Luke sees Delta run towards a stream of water. She stops, and with her back to him, kneels to pick up something. He walks towards her and purposefully stands behind her. She rises quickly and turns, about to begin running again, when she runs into Luke, the impact causing her to almost fall over. Luke catches her and steadies her with his strong arms.

Delta looks at him. "Luke?"

"Delta," Luke feigns a smile.

"What are you doing out here? Why did you leave Geno?"

"I could ask you the same thing but unfortunately I feel as if I already know the answer. Anyway, I'm returning to Geno now, just for a bit, to do what has been written."

"Written?"

Luke nods. He eyes the necklace around her neck. "Yes, but there is something I have to do first."

"What's that?"

"This," Luke suddenly reveals a fixed blade knife and lunges forward with it. Delta tries to block, but her reaction is too late and he successfully stabs her in the stomach. She instinctively holds her wound, falling to the ground.

Luke stands above her. "Oh, and I'll be needing this," he says and forcibly rips the necklace from her neck. He then walks off, leaving Delta helpless and bleeding to death.

*

Suddenly Ulysses has a feeling of great despair. *Something just happened. Something is terribly wrong.* He begins to run as fast as he can.

*

Luke connects Delta's necklace to his own and enters Geno. He knows that The Shadows he met the night before will be long gone by now, he has made sure of that. But they have given him a gift of a great realisation. By simply having this encounter with them, they have helped Luke to understand his greater purpose. A purpose which has led him back to Geno to get something important.

He walks to Emit's cabin and without knocking, goes inside. Emit's cabin is always a disorganised mess, but Luke soon discovers what he is looking for in a clothes drawer: the ruby watches. They look very technologically advanced, digital with rubies in the middle of them. He picks one up, studying it. *It's such an amazing invention.* He is completely mesmerised by this watch, knowing that everything in his life has led to this moment. *It isn't just the past* that *is written, the future is written too.*

"Know who you are, Luke," a lady's voice says behind him.

Luke turns quickly to discover it is Sophos.

She continues, "Knew I would find you here. A wonder didn't sense me coming. But noticed you losing powers for some time. Slowly losing who truly are. But you do have choice, Luke."

Luke becomes angry, "No I don't have a choice. It has already been written. Do you think that I wanted to become this way? It's God's choice! I never had a choice."

"Are what you wanted to become. And do have choice, Luke. Charge of destiny in next few moments. Present yet to be written."

"Even if I were in charge of my destiny, I would still choose what I'm choosing right now. The world is inherently cruel, I cannot change this. So, I might as well have the ultimate pleasures in life."

"But will this give true pleasure?"

"Yes," Luke says as he swiftly lunges forward and stabs Sophos in the stomach, just as he did Delta moments before. She struggles for breath. But even amongst this struggle, she manages to say a few breathy words to Luke. "May die... at hands... but will never kill Delta. She has... synchronicity of Ulysses."

"If she survives it will be a miracle, for what you don't know is that right now she is bleeding to her death."

"I know everything!" Sophos replies in such a powerful manner that it gives Luke a shiver.

He turns his back on her, places the watch on his wrist and then walks out of Emit's cabin, only to turn back briefly to see Sophos collapse to the ground, her frail body appearing to feel the weight of itself as she hits the earth. And she writhes in pain on the wooden floor. Luke walks down the path that leads from Emit's cabin.

After a very brief detour to the Geno library, he strides towards the Geno pavilion and walks up the stone stairs. And within seconds, he disappears in a flash of light.

CHAPTER 76

DELTA'S BLOOD

Ulysses can see a great fear in Delta's eyes. *This is why Emit forbade their love.* This is why he told Ulysses not to pursue her. Because if their love was to be, tragedy would strike. Ulysses did not listen and now this is all his fault.

Delta speaks softly and laboured as she lies on the ground, "Although I've dreamt this many times, I didn't realise it would be so hard. The pain I feel… is excruciating."

"I want to save you," Ulysses says in a panic as he kneels beside her and holds his hand against her wound in an attempt to stop the bleeding. He cannot let this beautiful essence die. He watches the blood pour from her stomach. Even her blood to him is beautiful, for it is her. He wishes so deeply that it was not leaving her body.

"I don't want to die. But I also want you to know that I don't regret anything. My whole life I've wanted a beautiful love like the one we share. And to experience these few moments of love with you, it's all been worth it."

"Oh, Delta. What can I do? How can I save you?" Ulysses asks desperately as he helplessly watches the love of his life dying. He grabs hold of her thin blanket and presses it against her, trying to stop her from bleeding. The blanket quickly fills with blood. In this moment, he can see how mortal and vulnerable she really is. Her eyes close. He touches Delta's fingers, and they feel as if they are becoming lifeless. Out of her hand drops the gift Delta returned for. A clear blue gemstone, held by a long, thin brown band which wraps around it. He recognises the gemstone as the one that Delta found in the Geno lagoon, the day that they first kissed. It has been polished and now appears to reflect light even more strongly than before, so much so that Ulysses can faintly see his reflection in its surface. Written on the gemstone is "The love of all time exists within here." The words that Ulysses spoke to Delta when they first lay together looking at the stars. *She remembered.*

"Oh, Delta." Tears come from his eyes. He cannot live his life without her. He loves her, he needs her. She is his soulmate. And he believes that the world needs her too. Surely the elements do not wish her to die. For such a natural beauty to die, it would not be fair. It would be like witnessing the sun burning out.

He must save her.

The past weeks Ulysses has been secretly trying to learn how to heal so that he could try to save her should Orien ever appear. He was not successful with his shoulder recently. But still, he must try.

He holds his hands above Delta's wound and wishes to give energy to the elements that can heal Delta from injuries. He closes his eyes and builds his inner strength, through using the perfect mindset. He finds the love inside him, the power running through his veins. He thinks of all the beautiful unconditional loving moments of his life, the loving feelings he has shared. The love of his family, of his family pets, of those who are no longer living, of everything. He thinks of Delta and the beautiful moments they have shared. He uses the elements around him. He draws strength from all the love of the world, the love from the time between time. And he channels all this unconditional and true love. He uses this power. It fills him so that he becomes shining with light. At its peak, he lets the energy pour out. Bright light shines from Ulysses' hands and covers Delta's wound. And this energy fills her.

He then moves to her lips and kisses them. Delta's eyes open.

She slowly comes to. "Ulysses!" She raises herself and kisses him back. He puts his arms gently around her, but she hugs him tightly.

"Oh my God, Ulysses!" She rises with him and touches her stomach where she was wounded, "I feel… fine." She looks at where the knife entered her; while her clothes are bloodstained, her blood has stopped pouring and the wound has completely healed. "I was willing to die for your love, Ulysses. But you have saved me! Just as in one of my favourite books, *Sleeping Beauty*, my prince has saved me with his kiss."

"It wasn't just my kiss that saved you. I used the help of all the elements, the help of God. We all need you here."

Delta nods, "Thank you."

"Tell me, how did this happen?" Ulysses asks.

"I was stabbed."

"By who?"

"Luke!"

Ulysses cannot believe it. *How could a member of Geno do such a thing?* "Are you okay to stand?"

"Yes, I'm fine, Ulysses," Delta says. She gathers the amulet and places it in her pocket and stands. "Come, we must make sure Emit and Sophos are safe!"

"I'm not letting you out of my sight," Ulysses says as he stands.

*

Delta and Ulysses make it to Geno. However, they cannot get back inside as they do not have two necklaces. *Luke has taken Delta's.* Delta calls to Emit and Sophos using her telepathy.

"I'm very worried about Sophos," she voices to Ulysses, with a worried look. "I cannot reach her telepathically."

More time passes until Emit finally opens the cave door and meets them at the edge of Geno. He looks deeply saddened.

"Oh no, what's wrong?" Delta asks.

"Sophos. She's no longer with us," he says with tears.

Delta immediately begins to sob. As Ulysses holds her, he feels an overwhelming sadness and despair. *Sophos' premonition was true.*

Furthermore, Ulysses feels a great deal of responsibility. He knows that if it were not for Delta's and his love, Sophos would still be alive. If they had not left Geno together on a love tryst, Luke would not have been able to get back in. A great beauty has died because of the love that they share. "This is all my fault, Emit. I didn't listen to you when you warned me not to create a love affair with Delta. And now because of it, Sophos is dead," Ulysses says.

"Ulysses, I warned you for Delta's safety, not for Sophos'. And while I see blood all over your clothes, Delta seems fine."

"Yes, but Sophos died," Ulysses rebuts.

"And that is not your fault. It's Luke's. When I saw him disappear in a flash of light on the Geno pavilion, I knew that something was horribly wrong. I soon discovered Sophos on the floor of my cabin. I wish that I could have saved her. I really tried, but she pleaded with me to simply savour the last seconds we have together. She said it was her time and she was ready to see Joey," Emit cries. "I kissed her forehead and held her as she told me how much she loves all of us. When she finally passed, I saw a mist leave her body as if her soul had departed," Emit says in between sobs and Delta wraps her arms around him to comfort him.

CHAPTER 77

THE WATCH

THE SUN IS setting at Geno and the mood is very sombre. Ulysses and Emit stand at the front of Sophos' cabin. Delta sits on a log nearby. It is obvious that the death of Sophos has damaged everyone greatly.

"You said that Luke disappeared in a flash of light. Where did he go?" Ulysses asks Emit.

"I'm not sure. But don't worry, he's long gone, Ulysses," Emit says as he continues to look towards the ground with sadness.

"Why did this happen? Why did Luke kill Sophos and try to kill Delta?"

"He was after something very powerful," Emit's hazel eyes look up at Ulysses.

"What?"

"One of these," Emit says as he pulls a digital watch out of his pocket. In the centre of it is a ruby.

Ulysses comes closer and raises Emit's hand to study the watch. "I've seen these before. On your desk, the day that I first met you."

"Yes. This is no ordinary watch. When Delta first arrived on my doorstep, I became inspired with the concept of time travel. I didn't know if it was possible. But with my passion for physics, the answers started to come to me. Eventually, I knew exactly how the watches should be."

"Are you saying that this is a time travel watch?"

"Precisely."

"Incredible! How does it work?"

"There are two parts to this watch. The first is the technology.

"From the outside it might look like a retro watch from the 1980s, but if you were to see the inner workings, you would see that it is very technologically advanced," Emit says as he circles his fingers around the watch face. He then presses a button on the left and the screen changes from displaying the time, to displaying the date including the year. He then presses it once more and it is back on the time.

"The second part is the Geno ruby," he says as he points to the encased gemstone which sits perfectly in a hollow, just below the digits of the time.

"The Geno ruby?"

"Yes. Discovered in Ancient Greece and blessed through magic, these eight secret rubies were hidden for centuries."

"Where?"

"Many places. By the time I discovered them they were in a collection of crown jewels on display in Sweden. I guess if you want to hide something, hide it in plain sight... Years passed until I finally perfected the watches, the very day you came to my house."

"Of course. So that is why the clocks had stopped? You were experimenting with a time travel device!"

Emit nods and smiles. "My experiment was a success."

He seems chuffed with his accomplishment. Ulysses realises that it is the first time he has seen a positive emotion in Emit since Sophos' death. "And you said that Luke took one of these watches and disappeared in a flash of light?"

"Yes. From the Geno pavilion. You see, the Geno pavilion has remained relatively unchanged for millennia, so it acts as the perfect safe portal. Therefore, Luke can travel to any time and location where the Geno pavilion has been. That is, until he creates another portal. Which I'm sure he has by now."

"But why would Luke be interested in time travel?"

"Luke has been spending most of his time in the library, poring over the history of Geno. Learning of Orien and The Shadows. He already knew that these watches were time travel devices. But I'm guessing that everything only just clicked for him."

"What do you mean everything clicked for him?"

"Don't you see, Ulysses?" Emit looks at him intensely. "*Luke is Orien.*"

CHAPTER 78

THE TIME TRAVELLER

887 – Sweden.

ORIEN WALKS PURPOSEFULLY along a stone paved street that is barely wide enough to fit a couple of horses. He wears red and black, the fabric of a material the local villagers could have never witnessed before. On the chest of his uniform is a symbol of a red triangle inside a black circle.

There are wooden buildings and stalls to either side of him, many overflowing with villagers who are enthusiastically buying and selling goods. They have no idea that their village is about to burn. But Orien knows. And as he strides through the crowd, he reflects on what has become his constant over the equivalent of nine years.

Time travel.

Orien wishes he never began such a journey. Most people, given the opportunity, would travel through time and be content with simply being a spectator. Orien, however, has purposely meddled with the hands of time. And now, all of this time travel has left him time-worn.

He has greatly shaped world history. Things like politics, the man-made world around him, are all just pieces of a board game in his mind. A game he has played so many times and wins far too easily. How can anyone compete with Orien when he can travel through time? He has the greatest evolutionary advantage ever given to an element. And yet for his great successes he receives no accolades, as a time traveller must be shrouded in secrecy.

Orien is silent most of the time. He does not bother talking – he receives no pleasure from that. He does not receive much pleasure from anything anymore. He has lived in so many different time periods and experienced so many things that all his superficial desires have been fulfilled.

Yet while he has succeeded on every superficial front, he still does not feel inner fulfilment. And he knows exactly why. He feels it deeply in his heart in this moment. It is because he has collected many wives, but no love. Many children, but no experiences of being a father. He has money and power, yet still lives in a world of chaos. A nightmare. Wherever he travels through time, whatever he achieves, he cannot escape one thing: Orien. When you were created in the dark, even when you step out of the dark, the darkness still follows you around.

If only he could become Luke again.

And there is a way… Delta.

She is the most incredible woman in all the times that Orien has witnessed. One whom he desires more than anything. He knows that he can never have her of her own free will. After all, God does not wish Orien and Delta to be. *No*, he cannot have Delta. But he can have the next best thing: for Delta to have never existed in his eyes.

All he has to do is find her as a child in old Sweden and rid her from this Earth. Then he will free himself of the eternal chaos and pain of knowing her. She will never travel into the future. Emit will never have known Delta and therefore will never be inspired to discover time travel. And without time travel, Orien will still be back in his Garden of Eden – Geno. And as who he was, not who he became. *As Luke.* The Shadows will no longer have the world under their control. And Luke will never do something which he will greatly come to regret – murder Sophos.

As Orien walks along these narrow streets, he knows that he has an opportunity which is the equivalent of Adam going back in time to prevent himself from eating the apple.

Delta must die for his sins.

And this is exactly why he is in 887, Sweden, searching for her.

CHAPTER 79

HER FUNERAL

The present – Geno, Australia.

IT IS THE afternoon, the day after Sophos' passing. All the members of Geno, apart from Luke, are present for the solemn occasion of Sophos' funeral. For the first time, Ulysses meets a part-Papua New Guinean, brown-skinned man named Fabian and a brunette Spanish woman in her forties called Leire. There is also another Geno member who arrives especially for the funeral: Ulysses' father, Ioannis.

"Dad!"

"My son!"

"So good to see you," Ulysses hugs his father. He notices inside his father's open jacket that he wears the Geno necklace, the same that he used to wear when Ulysses was a child.

"Good to see you too! How are you coping with things?"

"It's shocking about Sophos and Luke."

His father nods and looks down sadly. "Sophos was like a mother to us all."

He touches his father's shoulder in empathy. "I know… Come. There's someone I wish you to meet."

Ulysses has never introduced past girlfriends to his parents as he has never felt that they were 'the one'. But on this occasion, he cannot wait for his father to meet her. Ulysses just wishes it were under better circumstances. He walks with his father to her.

"This is Delta."

Delta steps forward to greet him. "Ioannis, I love Ulysses. And I owe my life to him."

Ioannis, his mouth open and his eyes wide, seems surprised at the directness of Delta's words. But this look quickly turns into a smile. "Pleasure to meet you, Delta, *finally*. I've heard about you since you were a child."

"And I've heard much about you. The great Ioannis," she replies.

They hug and as they do Ulysses realises that his father and Delta are much the same height.

The mood quickly becomes sombre as Emit calls that it is time to begin Sophos' funeral. They stand at her unmarked grave which is directly in front of the rosebush her late husband planted for her, the one that has never bloomed. To the left of her grave is where her late husband rests.

Ulysses recalls what Sophos said to him the day before she died: *do not hold back. Only one chance at life.* This truth has never been more apparent to him than now. He will never see her beautiful self again, or hear her wisdom. He wishes he could go back to just days before, just so he can spend a few more moments with Sophos. But, even greater, he wishes he did not waste any moments of the time they originally had together.

Emit is the first to speak at the service. He has been mostly quiet all morning. The death of Sophos appears to have affected him greatly, as it has Delta. But Emit seems to have dealt with his waves of anguish silently, in contrast to Delta who has cried openly and talked constantly to Ulysses about her.

"We are gathered here today to commemorate the life of Sophos. I remember hearing from her late husband how physically beautiful Sophos always was to him, from the day they first met as teenagers. Many of us did not witness her youth, but we were still enamoured with her beautiful energy, an energy that stayed with her throughout her life and is the reason why, to her late husband and all of us, she was always as beautiful as any flower. When I became a member of Geno, she took me under her wing. Her caring nature knew no bounds; she was always thinking of others first. Even just moments before she died, she asked me to tell the members of Geno that she loves us all very deeply. And that she will live on with her late husband.

"It seems that she wanted us to feel okay with her passing. But a part of me dies with her today," Emit says as tears come to his eyes. "I know that the universe knows what it's doing and that there must be a greater good here. But still, I pray that she lives on in some way. Because if Sophos doesn't live on, then it's not right. It's not right that an energy as beautiful as hers can just disappear forever. All I can say is, we love you, Sophos."

Delta sobs loudly and then rushes forward to hug Emit and comfort him.

After Emit, Ioannis and the other members of Geno take turns speaking eulogies. It is a very emotional day with many tears shed.

In the evening, the loss of Sophos is felt again at dinner time, as for many years Sophos has been preparing meals for those at Geno. Delta takes the lead and everyone pitches in to help prepare the meal. Luckily, Delta has been learning cooking from Sophos since she was ten. And so, Sophos' knowledge in this area will be passed on.

After dinner, the members spend their time around the campfire. Ioannis and Delta talk to each other for hours about Sophos and her amazing achievements both at Geno and in the world. They also talk about many other topics of the universe. It becomes clear to Ulysses, by how deeply in conversation they are, that his father greatly approves of the woman he loves.

While the other members chat amongst each other, Ulysses spends most of the evening deeply in thought. Everything has finally become clear to him. Tomorrow he will tell Delta what he plans to do.

CHAPTER 80

ULYSSES' DECISION

It is morning in Geno. Ulysses finds Delta sitting on a log by Sophos' cabin, her hands wiping her tears. She would normally be studying plants at this time. It is obvious that she still mourns the passing of Sophos very deeply.

Ulysses finds that all her emotions, positive or negative, make him adore her even more. He comes behind her and kisses the right side of her neck gently. She closes her eyes and appears to lose herself in the moment, giving in to his sensuality. He then moves to the front of her and kneels. There is something important he must tell her.

"Delta, I'm going back in time."

She looks up at Ulysses, confused, "… Ulysses, I'm sure Sophos would appreciate your beautiful gesture, but we cannot save her. It's been written now. And we shouldn't change what has been written."

Ulysses strokes her face and dries her tears with the back of his fingertips. He speaks softly to her, "I know. I'm not going back in time to save Sophos."

"Then why do you want to go back in time?"

"I must bring you to the future."

Suddenly Delta's eyes become bright. She hugs him tightly and speaks excitedly, "Oh, Ulysses, I knew it was you! I've always known it to be you. I knew it from the moment I first looked into your eyes outside of the library. I knew you would be the one to save me and bring me to the future. I have wanted to tell you for so long."

Ulysses nods. He only recently realised what his destiny is. He was blind to it all this time. But now, everything makes sense.

She continues, "But still, I'm torn about it. What if you don't succeed?"

"I must have already succeeded; I must have saved you. Otherwise, you would never have been taken to the future. We would've never met and we wouldn't be together right now. But here we are," Ulysses smiles confidently.

"But what if you don't succeed in making it back?"

She has a point. His smile dissipates. Just because Delta makes it to the future, it does not mean that Ulysses will make it back safely to the present day.

"I'll do my best to make it back into your arms."

"But how can we be sure?" Delta asks.

"We can't be sure. Which is why we must surrender to the chaos with faith."

Delta nods her head, "Yes, I know that it's important to be courageous in following our hearts. But still, I'm fearful of what may happen."

"Even if I don't make it back to this time, we'll still be connected. Just as you're still connected to your parents. For when I look at the stars or the moon, you will one day look upon the same. That is how we will connect throughout time."

Tears well in her eyes again, "I don't want our love to be long-distance."

Ulysses laughs and Delta, realising the humour in what she has just said, joins Ulysses in chuckles in between sobs. He hugs her.

"I'll make it back, Delta. Please believe."

Suddenly, Delta leans back from Ulysses with a look of certainty, as if she has just realised something. "I do believe. I really do believe in you. Let me give you something for your journey."

"What is it?"

"It's the gift that I intended to give you when we went on our walk in the rainforest. It's an amulet. It will keep you safe, Ulysses," Delta says as she pulls it from her pocket. "I found the gemstone here in the lagoon at Geno, the day we first kissed. I believe it to be special and I've blessed it with magic."

Ulysses studies the blue gemstone once again. It reflects the light so strongly that he has to squint his eyes.

"No, have it this way up," she says as she turns it to a side where the light no longer shines in his eyes. The side with the beautiful inscription that Delta wrote for him.

"I love it, thanks Delta!"

Delta nods. "I want it to be a symbol of myself giving my heart, body, mind and soul to you. And for now, it's also a symbol that I am waiting for your return."

They kiss passionately. And afterwards, Ulysses looks into her beautiful eyes which are filled with tears. The same beautiful eyes that he fell in love with in his dreams. He knows that even if he had pre-planned his life before he was born, he would still choose Delta from the infinite number of choices. She will always be his choice. And he hopes that he will be able to continue to look into her eyes forever.

CHAPTER 81

ULYSSES PREPARES FOR THE QUEST

LATER IN THE morning, Ulysses and Emit sit at a desk in the Geno library. With the help of Emit's expertise in translating Ancient Greek, Ulysses learns about Luke's/Orien's time travelling from the Geno journals. They pay particular attention to one moment in history – 9th-century Sweden. As Sophos once mentioned to Ulysses, Geno was located in Sweden for a period of time and Delta's parents were not only rulers but also members of Geno. Ulysses learns from the Geno journals that Orien and his Shadow members invade their village in search of a blonde princess, Delta. But the journal is incomplete. It is missing a page. *Where is that page?*

Suddenly, Ulysses realises that Orien has a great power, for whatever Ulysses learns from these readings, he knows that Orien will also know. But perhaps Orien also knows more than Ulysses. Maybe he has taken this last page and therefore has the complete history of Geno. And now Ulysses does not know the outcome of this moment in old Sweden. The outcome of whether Ulysses lives or dies.

He speaks worriedly to Emit, "There's so much that I still don't know. There's a page missing in the Geno journals. I don't know the outcome of my quest."

Emit nods and takes off his reading glasses, placing them on the desk. "Yes, but God knows. So put your faith in God, Ulysses. God will watch over you."

"I will. And this I understand. But this isn't just about the future. There's so much I don't understand about the past. Our past. How long have you known that I will be the one to save Delta as a child?"

"Delta told me, as soon as she first brought you to meet me."

"Then why did you warn me not to pursue Delta? If this was my destiny?"

"She was having those dreams. So we didn't know if Delta would be safe in the present. Let me explain…" Emit becomes more expressive with his hands. "You didn't have to change in order to be worthy of Delta's admiration, as you received this unconditionally from the moment she first met you. But you had to develop as a person before you could be together. If your relationship blossomed too greatly, too prematurely, then perhaps you would not be able to heal her if tragedy were to strike earlier.

"This is the way life is, it has to happen when we're ready and not a moment before. We work to the timing of God and nothing else. If you rush God, he may oblige, but you will quickly learn through the outcomes to never rush God again," Emit says with such conviction that it leads Ulysses to believe that Emit has rushed God before and learnt his lesson.

"I understand this. And I have another question. How long have you known that Luke is Orien?"

"See this ring, Ulysses?" Emit says as he points to the ring on his finger, the one Ulysses saw glow red and blue on the day he first met Emit. "It warns me when a Shadow member is close by. You may notice that I haven't always worn it at Geno. It's not because we're safe here, with these high cliffs surrounding us. Rather, it's because I knew that it would shine in the presence of Luke. I knew this because it has before. This made me realise that Luke is related to Orien, to The Shadows. But still, I didn't realise he was Orien. It's only when I saw him disappear through a flash of light that it all made sense to me."

Emit continues, "As you know, Luke knows our martial arts and he has disciples. Their symbol is of a red triangle inside a black circle, so keep watch for it. I'll give this ring to you for your journey, so that you'll know when Orien and The Shadows are close," he says as he hands the ring to Ulysses.

Ulysses places it on his index finger with the determination to be brave even though he realises he is about to be in great danger.

CHAPTER 82

TIME CAN BE OUR SAVIOUR

IT IS TIME. Ulysses nervously walks towards the Geno pavilion. He wears his time travel watch, Geno necklace and ring. In his pocket is a spare time travel watch and the gemstone amulet Delta gave him. Three other members of Geno are gathered at the base of the pavilion – Emit, Delta and his father, Ioannis. They are all that is left at the Geno base; the other members have gone home.

As Ulysses reaches the stairs of the pavilion, Delta runs up and stops him. She hugs him tenderly. He embraces the moment, feeling the warmth of her body against his. He does not want to stop holding her and he can tell that Delta does not want to stop either.

He thinks of how caring and amazing Delta is. And again, he thinks of how she will make a great mother. What a blessing it would be to be entwined forever with her, through Delta bearing their child. To have such a beautiful future with her is his greatest dream of all. *I must return.*

"Please come back to me," she says.

Ulysses nods. "I have to, Delta." He touches her cheek delicately with his hand and then releases her. He walks up the stairs of the pavilion and stands under the ray of sun which enters the circular opening in its roof.

The time travel device works through a mixture of technology and magic. Ulysses has pre-programmed his watch with the date he wishes to travel to. And the magic is already within the device, in the red ruby which is in its inner workings. He holds down a button on the right side. He does this for four seconds. Suddenly, light travels down through the pavilion and shines onto him. It seems to lift him a couple of centimetres off the ground and then Ulysses lands instantaneously in the past.

*

887 – Sweden.

Ulysses looks around. He stands on the same Geno pavilion, though the Geno base before him is void of buildings. There are also no Geno members here. And although he cannot tell where he is, if everything worked to plan he knows he must be in Sweden, on July 7th, 887.

He walks through a circle of trees to the edge of Geno. There is no hidden entrance to Geno back in the past, no two necklaces needing to be joined as one. Just a path leading into the deep woods. He takes this path.

As he walks in this nature, it does not feel much different to the present. For some reason he expected the past to seem like a different world. But he still feels the same sunlight, the same wind. The nature may be slightly different, with spruce, birch and pine trees, and the weather is slightly colder, but it is as he would expect it to be in a different country. He can understand now why Delta said that being out in nature makes her feel like she is home. It is the closest thing to her past that she can experience in present day Australia.

Ulysses comes to an open field and sees a village in the distance. And it is on fire. *This is the village in the Geno writings.* He begins to run towards it.

As he gets closer, he realises that the village is familiar. *I've been here before!* Ulysses visited this town, albeit a more modern version, on his recent holiday in Sweden. As he enters the village he realises what a blessing it is that he has been here before, because the village layout in this time is much the same as it is in the future, allowing Ulysses to be instantly orientated, despite being back many hundreds of years. He recognises some of the same buildings, albeit now centuries newer.

Ulysses runs through the village at speed, dodging people, ducking, weaving. Being in the flow state allows him to do so gracefully without needing to slow down. His eyes search for Delta, but he cannot see her anywhere. The village is crowded, the villagers in a panic, fire blazing around them. He hopes that he will magically recognise Delta when he sees her, but he does not even know what she will look like. All he knows is that he seeks a ten-year-old blonde-haired girl. And there are many blonde children in this village. He suddenly realises how futile his task is. *There are too many people here to find Delta.*

He moves into a town square, his eyes quickly scanning across it. Suddenly Ulysses notices a girl in the distance. She grabs his complete attention. A young girl, with braided blonde hair, in a white dress. She has her back to him, kneeling on the ground. He is instantly reminded of how he first saw Delta from a distance in the library. Even though he could only see her from behind, he just knew it was her. And again, Ulysses just knows it is her now.

Ulysses' ring begins to glow red and blue. *The Shadows.* He runs towards Delta. He has to get to her before it's too late. Suddenly Orien (Luke) walks into the town square just metres from Delta. Ulysses uses a skill he learned in his training: he zooms in with his eyesight, blinking every time he wishes to magnify. He sees that Orien wears red and black and on the chest of his uniform is a symbol of a red triangle inside a black circle. Orien draws a knife.

"Luke!" Ulysses screams as he runs towards them as fast as he can. *He must slow down time.* He focuses, using the techniques he learnt at Geno, and suddenly the world around him moves very slowly. In contrast to the external world, he finds that his perceptions are still operating at a normal speed. He must think of what to do, quickly, for he only has seconds. How can he save her? He knows that he cannot run there in time… he must call upon the interconnected elements.

Ulysses begins to take in all around him, as if his filters have suddenly switched off. He hears a bird's call on top of the building. He cannot see this bird from his position, but it does not matter; the system can see where his eyes cannot, so he has the power. This is his chance. He is not meant to use magic in public, but he believes this moment must be an exception. He focuses all he can, communicating with the system to do his bidding, in particular, with this bird that he hears the call of.

Orien walks closer to Delta, with his knife still drawn and pointing at Delta's throat, only a couple of metres away. Suddenly, an eagle flies above the building, its spectacular wings outstretched. Orien moves to enter the knife into her, when the eagle dives down and begins swooping at Orien. It attacks him, slowing him down.

Ulysses is close now. He jumps into the air and with a flying kick precisely knocks the blade from Orien's hand. Ulysses then lands, bends his knees and touches the ground with a hand to balance himself. He communicates psychically with the bird, telling it that it has fulfilled its purpose. And the bird flies away.

"Ulysses!" Orien says in his deep voice. "How did you command that bird to attack me?"

"A bird will attack when it needs to, such as protecting its nest, I simply unlocked the potential which could already be. You taught me this," Ulysses says. He studies Luke, who is older than when Ulysses last saw him. His face is weathered. His body is not as muscular as it was at Geno. No doubt he has been time travelling for all this time.

"Your powers are becoming very strong, Ulysses. But you're still no match for me," Orien says, his facial expression twisted.

"Luke, you have a choice. Don't do this."

"Sophos said the same thing to me before she died. But this is my choice, Ulysses. You will see that." And with these words, Orien strikes at Ulysses using martial arts. He is so fast with his assault that Ulysses has to slow time again just to process his attack. Ulysses blocks several of his punches and his kicks, but Orien still manages to throw Ulysses to the ground. Ulysses quickly stands but is kicked hard in the chest. He buckles over. He is not standing a chance. With every blow Ulysses is becoming weaker. And he has not even had the chance to fight back yet.

Ulysses dodges and blocks as best as he can as Orien continues his offensive. But he is again knocked down, this time near Delta who still kneels on the ground. She prays with her eyes closed and seems too frightened to open them. Tears stream down her cheeks.

"Why would you want to kill Delta?" Ulysses yells from his position on the ground.

"Don't you see, Ulysses? This is my one chance. If I kill Delta now then she'll never arrive at Emit's door in the future. Emit will never be inspired to make time travel devices. There will be no time travel. I'll never have the heartbreak of knowing her. You'll never follow her to Geno and therefore will never join. Sophos will still be alive. I'll go back to being a member of Geno. And the whole world will not have the influence of Orien and The Shadows and therefore will be a better place. The nightmare of this current reality will not exist for anyone," Orien says.

As Orien passionately speaks, Ulysses continually looks over to Delta. He can read her innocent mind. She does not understand the reasons why this is happening. She is simply a ten-year-old girl whose village has been invaded. She does not understand the language the two men are speaking, except she hears her name. She knows they are talking about her. She opens her eyes and looks at Ulysses. He can see in them hope, hope that he will protect her from Orien who only moments ago had a knife pointed at her throat.

Orien continues, "Delta is the reset button. She is perfect, without sin and she must die for our sins."

"Delta is not a sacrifice for your sins. She'll come to the future with me – it's been written," Ulysses says with conviction as he stands.

"You know not what has been written," Orien says as he pulls a piece of paper from his pocket and holds it before him.

It is a page from the old book in the Geno library. The missing page!

And with this, Orien kicks with such force into Ulysses' chest that it sends Ulysses flying back and he hits the ground with a thump. Ulysses writhes in pain, unable to breathe. He watches on powerlessly as Orien grabs Delta's arm and picks her up by it. She struggles. She has a great deal of fight in her for a little girl. But Orien is overpowering her. He walks, carrying her, towards the knife that was previously kicked out of his hand by Ulysses.

"You may have healed her once, Ulysses. But you cannot heal her when she is dead."

Ulysses lies on the dirt, holding his chest, helpless and hurt as Orien picks up the knife. It is becoming clearer to Ulysses that this was destined to happen. To fail his mission. For Delta to die here. For it to have all never happened.

He touches his Geno necklace, thinking of his recent past, savouring it for one last moment, knowing that all that he has come to know will soon disappear. He thinks of meeting Delta for the first time. Of when she recognised the symbol in the Geno book and then looked at him so beautifully in his eyes and smiled. He remembers being led to Geno and swimming with her in the lagoon. Seeing her sit at the campfire with her knees tucked up to her chest. Kissing her under the waterfall for the very first time. Seeing her naked next to her statue, while she flirted, hoping to make his future novel more interesting. Making love to her. And hugging her just before he left on this quest. He knows that if Orien kills Delta, none of these beautiful memories will have ever happened. Ulysses will have never experienced any of this.

Instead, Delta may simply exist in Ulysses' recurring dreams and nothing more. A remnant of a love they shared in the time between time.

Delta continues to resist Orien, saving herself seconds more life, but she cannot prevent him forever. Ulysses closes his eyes; he cannot watch on.

*

Back in Geno, in the present day, Delta prays with her hands together, "Please make it back, Ulysses. I love you."

*

Suddenly Ulysses' eyes open. *This love will be your strength.*

His mind flashes back... "Let me give you something for your journey... it's an amulet, it will keep you safe, Ulysses," Delta said as she gave him a token of her heart.

Ulysses, struggling to move, slowly pulls the amulet from his pocket. "The love of all time exists within here," he whispers to himself.

He studies his surroundings. He knows that he has been in this exact place before on his recent trip to Sweden, while searching to discover the theory. He took a wrong turn and ended up in this very same town square. He remembers that the sun was directly above part of the square. It seemed so very bright as it shined in Ulysses' eyes. There must be a reason that he accidentally took this path in the future and that it made such an impact on him. It was synchronicity. A perfect design. Suddenly things become clear to Ulysses. Ulysses sees the order now; he must continue.

Ulysses stands once more, feeling a great power.

Orien's eyes open wide as he sees Ulysses. "My God, how could you stand after such a beating?"

But Ulysses says nothing.

"I admire your courage to fight, Ulysses, but you can't win. I've taught you everything you know," Orien says as he finally has Delta under his control. He moves the knife to her neck. She does not look at the blade or Orien, but simply at Ulysses. He is her only hope. Ulysses looks back at young Delta and realises that he can no longer simply defend, he must gather the strength to fight back.

"Yes, but there is one thing I have on my side."

"And what's that?"

"The greater force of the elements."

Ulysses spins the amulet around by the band and throws it in the air, high above Orien.

Orien looks up towards it.

The sky is cloudy. Ulysses cannot see any glimpse of the sun, but he trusts that he knows exactly where the sun will be, as he has experienced this powerful light before. Ulysses puts his arm forth and commands the sun to shine through the clouds. He uses an interconnected element, a great wind which suddenly blows past the town square. The clouds part and sunlight shines forth, its rays striking the amulet at the exact moment Ulysses wishes it to, reflecting a very bright beam of light from it.

The beam shines directly into Orien's eyes, instantly blinding him. He screams and drops the knife from his hand, releasing Delta, who drops to the ground, crying. The amulet continues to spin, the light of which creating what looks like a star. A star which has saved Delta.

*

Meanwhile, in this village in old Sweden, a member of Geno calls for the attention of others to look up into the sky, to see this bright light. They are amazed. *A star, in the middle of the day.* This signals that the prophecy has been completed. They can now fight back.

CHAPTER 83

DARKNESS IS NOT ALWAYS ABSENT OF LIGHT

ORIEN TRIES DESPERATELY, but all he can see is a bright light. He is blinded. *How could Ulysses do this? How could he command something as powerful as the sun?* But Orien does not wait for his vision to return. And nor should he – he has practised for this, to be able to see without eyes. He moves towards his knife.

But he senses something in the way. His vision slowly returns, and he discovers that Ulysses is standing before him, glowing from a ray of sun that shines directly above. He can see the power within Ulysses, vibrantly. It is like he has the power of a god.

"You ARE a chosen one," Orien whispers to Ulysses.

"Luke… it's over," Ulysses says calmly.

"I know when it is over, Ulysses," Orien says vehemently.

He knows that he is no match for Ulysses' magic as since he has gone down the path of being Orien his magical powers have greatly decreased. Possibly because he can no longer self-actualise. Possibly because not all his actions have the greater power of the universe on his side. He is not sure. All he knows is that the powers of The

Shadows pale in comparison to the powers the Geno members have. Instead, they rely heavily on brute force and psychological tricks. Psychological tricks such as The Art of Xiren.

"There is one thing you've never mastered, Ulysses." Orien moves his hands rhythmically, enchanting Ulysses. Ulysses' eyelids begin to blink, and his focus seems to become weary. Soon Orien is sure that he is under his spell. "Do not you know who Delta is, Ulysses?" And upon saying this Orien throws a jab with his left hand towards Ulysses' face. Suddenly, Ulysses stops the punch with his right hand which somehow amazingly glows with a bright blue light.

"Yes, I do. She's the girl of my dreams. Not even time can stand between us. And I will protect her," Ulysses answers with strength and conviction.

Orien is in awe of Ulysses' power. No one has ever defended against Xiren before. He quickly throws many strikes at Ulysses, but Ulysses blocks them all with seemingly very little effort, shining a blue light with every defence. He is at a level of fighting Orien has never seen before. Finally, Ulysses releases the blue light from his hands, which hits Orien in the chest, sending him immediately to the ground. Ulysses has finally fought back.

CHAPTER 84

BLESSED ORIEN

Ulysses checks to see that Delta is okay. Thankfully, she is not physically injured. But she continues to kneel, crying. *The poor girl.* His heart goes out to her.

He returns and stands over Orien who lies on the ground. Ulysses knows that he has the power to kill Orien in this moment. To be done with his influence on the world once and for all. To protect Delta and himself for all time that is to come. But Ulysses does not wish for Orien's death – instead, he feels great compassion. It was not long ago that Ulysses felt inferior to Luke. He saw Luke as being the perfect image of a human: highly intelligent, incredibly gifted and physically perfect.

He also empathises with Luke. Ulysses knows that he also could have become similar to Orien – that is, disenchanted with the magic of the world. On the day Ulysses believed that Delta unrequited his love, before he fell from the cliff, it felt to him that he existed in an eternal chaos. It would have been easy for him to go back to society at this point and lose himself in superficial goals to try to hide the pain of what was truly meaningful to him, as a sort of revenge on the world which seems so often cruel.

And because Ulysses understands Luke, he also feels that deep down inside there is still good within him. That perhaps this is merely a test for Luke to pass and perhaps once he does, he will see the order and become self-actualised again.

Ulysses closes his eyes and places a hand on Luke's shoulder as the sun shines directly down upon them, bathing them in light. "Please God, guide this man to be self-actualised," Ulysses blesses him. And as he does this blessing, he thinks of how goodness really does return to you. For it was Luke who taught Ulysses to bless his opponent after a fight. And now this good teaching has returned to Luke.

CHAPTER 85

THE MISSING PAGE

ORIEN LIES ON the ground, seeming defeated. Ulysses finishes blessing him, stands and turns his back on him. But what Ulysses seems to have forgotten is that there is the knife in between Orien, Ulysses and Delta. Orien knows that he has enough energy left inside of him. All he must do is reach towards it and make a surprise attack on Ulysses or Delta.

And so Orien stares upon this knife.

But he does nothing. Instead, he throws a piece of paper from his pocket. It is the missing page from the Geno journal.

CHAPTER 86

THE PROPHECY

THE WARM GOLDEN sun is beating down. Delta, ten years of age, kneels on the ground. Her village burns around her, the only home she has ever known. She strongly believes she will never see her parents again, for it has been destined by a prophecy.

The prophecy is written in Ancient Greek and inscribed upon a runestone. Translated into English it says – *There will be a girl without sin. A man who looks like no other will come and take her. You must allow this. This is all meant to be. Do not resist any evil on this day until the mid-afternoon, when a bright star shines in the sky and falls to the earth.*

Tears run from young Delta's eyes. She looks up at Ulysses, her heart in so much pain. He strokes her face with the back of his upper fingers. And he speaks softly to her things she doesn't understand: "I'm going to take you somewhere safe. It will not be easy but believe me, everything will work out. And while you'll be separated from your parents, always remember, *the love of all time exists within here*," he says as he points to the little girl's heart. She looks at Ulysses and whilst there is no way of removing her sadness at the loss of all that she holds dear, she understands a sincerity in his voice. One that she feels will forever stay with her.

*

Suddenly a group of ninjas arrive with black gis and cloaks. Some run to help Orien up from the ground. The others surround Ulysses and Delta. They do so with such grace that Ulysses senses they are slowing time. They all have the red triangle symbol on the breast of their uniforms.

"The Shadows! I can't fight them all," Ulysses says to himself.

Instantly, there is a loud bellow from the other side of the town square, from a man with long blond hair and a beard. He leads seven others, both men and women. And while their necklaces are not identical to that of his own, Ulysses notices that they have the Geno symbol. *They must be members of Geno from old Sweden!*

They rush towards The Shadows and a great fight ensues, one with martial arts and magic.

Ulysses sees the missing page of the Geno journal on the ground. He quickly picks it up and places it in his pocket. "Now is the time, Delta. We must leave!" Ulysses leads Delta by the hand. He then picks her up in his arms and rushes to escape out of harm's way.

He makes it to the edge of the town square and turns to have one last look at the battle. *Orien has also escaped.* But it is okay. Ulysses has what he came for: *Delta.*

Ulysses puts a time travel watch on Delta's little wrist. And they hurry towards old Geno.

CHAPTER 87

YOUNG DELTA

Nine years before the present day – Geno, Australia.

With a flash of bright light, Ulysses and young Delta land inside the Geno pavilion. A part of him was expecting to see his father, Emit and Delta all waiting for him. But as this is nine years in his past, no one is expecting them.

Now that they are out of danger, everything begins to sink in for Ulysses. He finds himself overwhelmed with emotion as he walks down the pavilion stairs with young Delta, holding her little hand. He feels sad that this had to happen. That she had to leave her homeland and hide in this time period.

When Ulysses was told of Delta being brought to the future, he always assumed that she first arrived at Emit's house on the Gold Coast. But he has made the decision to bring her to Emit's cabin at Geno. It will be less of a shock for her to begin here, surrounded by nature, near the Geno pavilion which may be familiar to her and with the lack of future technology. Emit can then slowly introduce her to the modern world.

As they walk on the Geno oval, he is reminded of walking outside the library with her on the Gold Coast, the very first time he met her. It was such a beautiful moment for him. She was familiar to him because of his dreams and although he did not realise it at the time, he was familiar to her because of these very moments in the past.

They walk along the dirt path and arrive at Emit's cabin. Ulysses gently leads her to walk up the stairs with him. He notices the same chalkboard on the verandah as in the future, however, it is void of equations. Ulysses knows what inspiration Delta will provide for Emit and that this chalkboard will be filled soon enough. He takes the time travel watch off her little wrist.

He holds her gently, just above where her elbow bends. "Geno will keep you safe. And I will see you in the future," Ulysses says, knowing that she probably doesn't understand English. He is hoping that somehow, beyond his words, she realises that he is trying to help her. That he is a force for good and there is good in the world, regardless of what she has just experienced.

Ulysses knocks on the cabin door and immediately begins to walk away. He looks back to see Delta still looking at him. She looks scared, unknowing of what her future holds. It devastates him to see her in this moment. He forces himself to turn away and continue walking. He does not want to. But he must leave her. He does not turn back again. And as he hears the cabin door open, the tears fill his eyes.

He knows that Delta will grow into the most beautiful woman. And his point of power with her is in the future, where he has promised her that one day he will heal her wounds. This is his quest. One which he must fulfil.

CHAPTER 88

BACK TO THE FUTURE

The present – Geno, Australia.

DELTA PRESUMED THAT it would be instantaneous for her. That Ulysses would return to the exact point in time in which he left, immediately after his departure. But it has been an hour and he still has not returned. As time goes on she becomes more and more worried.

"Emit, why isn't Ulysses back yet?"

"With the time travel devices, time continues to pass in the present while the traveller is in the past. Therefore, if Ulysses is in the past for an hour, when he returns it will be an hour after he departed."

Delta nods. She sits on a different blanket than usual, since her previous one has blood stains on it. And she continues to wait for Ulysses, her eyes focused on the exact point where he left, the pavilion.

Many hours pass. Delta seldom leaves during this time.

"Has something gone wrong?" she asks Emit as he passes her again.

"I don't know, Delta."

With every moment Delta feels more and more worried. Yet she does not give up hope. She brings her hands together in prayer, closes her eyes and prays for his return.

*

Finally, as the sun is setting, there is a flash of light. It is Ulysses! He returns to the exact spot where he left, in the Geno pavilion.

"Ulysses!" She sprints up the stairs towards him and kisses Ulysses with such force that it almost knocks him over. "You're safe!"

"It's good to be back," Ulysses says and returns her kisses.

Delta shouts out across the oval to let the others know. "Ulysses is back! Ulysses is back!"

Emit and Ioannis quickly arrive. They clap and give a hero's welcome to Ulysses. Ulysses walks down the stairs to join them. His dad hugs him warmly, as does Emit.

"I need another watch, there's something I must do," Ulysses says to Emit. Emit looks confused but nods and goes to his cabin to get one.

"But Ulysses, you've only just come back?" Delta asks, also quite confused.

"Delta, I'll be right back. I promise."

Emit returns with a time travel watch and gives it to Ulysses, who enters a time and date into the watch. He then steps up the pavilion and disappears once more.

This time he is only gone for a brief moment, and when he returns he has two people with him. A strong man with a blond beard and long blond hair and his beautiful brunette wife who has puffy eyes, particularly around the bottom of them, just like Delta. Delta recognises them immediately.

"Mum! Dad!" she says in her old language.

Tears well up in Delta's eyes and she instantly drops to her knees, just as she did as a little girl in the town square. But this time it is not because she is sad but because she is overcome with happiness. It is the first time she has seen her parents since she was ten. They are exactly the same as when she left them, the same age, even wearing the same clothes; it is only Delta who is different.

"Delta!" her mother calls.

Delta stands and runs towards her parents. They hug together in a group, kiss cheeks and talk excitedly in their old language.

Delta's parents make gestures which attest to Delta's physical beauty and say how beautiful she has grown to be and how proud of her they are for the lovely woman she has become. Delta cries with happiness. She has wished so deeply since the day of their separation that they would be reunited. And now, thanks to Ulysses, they have been. He promised to heal her wounds and he has.

Delta and her parents walk down the pavilion stairs, where her parents are greeted by Emit and Ioannis. And Delta walks to Ulysses. "Ulysses, not only did you rescue me as a child, but you've reunited my family."

"It's the least I can do for the girl I love."

"You have saved my life twice while I've only saved you once. But I'll save you again, if I ever need to. I promise." They share a deeply passionate kiss.

Ulysses hopes she will never have to. "There's one more thing, Delta."

"What's that?" she asks.

"One moment."

Ulysses takes a time travel watch from Delta's father. He adjusts the settings on the watch as he strides up the Geno pavilion. And with a flash of light, he again travels through time.

And not long after, he returns. This time with a majestic white horse. *Salt. He has brought Salt!*

"Oh my God, my horse! You have my horse here!" She runs up the stairs to it and pats it. She is joined on the pavilion by her parents and Emit, Ioannis and Ulysses. And together they all embrace and share this beautiful moment.

That evening they have a celebratory feast at Geno. Delta walks with Ulysses around the stone table as they fill their plates with food.

"I really don't know how I can thank you for this, Ulysses. It's a dream come true."

"I'm glad! The moment we shared at the waterfall was my dream come true, literally. I feel that if we keep making each other's dreams come true, then we are in for a great future!"

"Agreed!"

"But you know, there is a particular way you can thank me for this," Ulysses pauses while looking into her eyes.

"How's that?" Delta smirks mischievously. She assumes he is implying something sexual.

"One day soon, take me with you when you visit where you grew up in old Sweden. Show me the places that have touched your heart. I want to learn everything about you. What your childhood was like, even what your favourite tree was growing up. Everything."

"Ohhh, Ulysses," she touches his neck endearingly. "And I want you to show me where you grew up too. In Mount Isa." She leans over and kisses him. But Ulysses is not as affectionate as usual and is looking over at Delta's parents. "What's wrong?" Delta asks.

"Do you think your parents mind that I'm probably the same age as them? I mean, here you are so youthful and I have grey hair coming through."

"Grey hair? Oh come on! Where? And even if you did, I would find it attractive. It would reflect your maturity."

"Really?"

"Definitely! Besides, things like age and time don't matter to us. You know this. If time were an issue we would have never met in the first place."

"That's true."

"My parents will love you just for being you. So you can relax. And you know what's funny? I'm almost as old as my parents now too. It's kind of weird," Delta laughs.

"Yeah. And you were born in 877? That's right, isn't it?" Ulysses smiles.

"Yes, that's correct," she smiles, knowing what Ulysses is getting to.

"So, if we go off when you were born, you're over 1100 years older than me. We probably have the biggest age gap in history."

"Ulysses! Stop it!" She laughs and pushes his shoulder playfully.

Delta then sits next to her parents on the stone table and spends most of her evening simply laughing and speaking the old language with her parents. She embraces every little moment, all the time she has with them. But as the night goes on, deep inside she knows that her visitors from the past are not going to stay for good; they have a kingdom to rule over and a place where they belong. However, she becomes deeply contented with the knowledge that they can now visit each other, whenever they wish, as Emit gives Delta her own time travel watch.

CHAPTER 89

THE PAST IS WRITTEN

THE NEXT DAY, Ulysses walks to Emit's cabin. Here he finds Emit on his verandah, wearing spectacles, writing feverishly on his chalkboard. But it does not appear to be the usual physics theories Emit is working on.

Ulysses is unsure as to whether to interupt him, but since he only wishes a moment of his time, he decides that he will. "Uh hum," Ulysses gets Emit's attention, smiling.

"Ulysses," Emit welcomes him.

Ulysses draws a piece of paper from his pocket and walks up the stairs to Emit. "Emit, I found this. Orien had it. It's the missing page from the Geno journals. What does it say?" Ulysses asks as he passes the paper to Emit.

Emit reads the Ancient Greek. He then removes his glasses, places them in his front pocket and looks at Ulysses. "… It says what happened."

"That I saved Delta and defeated Orien?"

"Yes," Emit says as he takes a seat on the cabin stairs and motions for Ulysses to join him.

"So does that mean…" Ulysses asks as he sits next to Emit.

Emit nods. "Orien knew he would lose the battle all along."

"Then why did he do it?"

"Because it was written."

"I don't understand."

"Orien is still Luke, Ulysses. He's not all bad. This is why he went to old Sweden even though he knew he would fail. No matter how much it might not be his version of good, he believed that it was for the greater good."

Ulysses thinks back to his first night at Geno. As they all sat around the campfire, Luke mentioned how the greater good was something that he personally struggled with. Yet even with such struggle, Luke has selflessly travelled to old Sweden, knowing that he would suffer. "Will we ever see Orien again?"

"Perhaps. I don't know for sure. Orien is a time traveller so it's very difficult to predict when he'll appear next. But rest assured that he will not harm any of us in the past, as the past has already been written. The point of power for Orien and The Shadows is in the present. And thus, it is only in the present where we must keep watch. And on this matter, our sources say that The Shadows have a new Master. His name is Leucius. Second in command to Orien, he is both ingenious and ruthless."

"I don't fear Orien and The Shadows. I have synchronicity on my side. The force of all of the elements," Ulysses says with conviction.

"And you also have Delta to protect you. She's quite a good fighter," Emit says, smirking.

"That's true," Ulysses laughs.

"Is this all of the questions you have?" Emit asks, patting Ulysses on the back and looking back to his chalkboard as if he is eager to return to it.

"No, there's one more thing. How did this all come about in the first place? I don't understand. If you didn't invent time travel, then Delta wouldn't have come to the future. But contradictorily, you wouldn't have invented time travel if it weren't for the inspiration of Delta. We have a conundrum."

"Yes, we do," Emit smiles. "Only God knows the answer to this. But let me ask you a question before saying what I believe. What made you sure that Delta was the girl to follow when you first saw her in the library?"

"I dreamt about her."

"Precisely, Ulysses. You were helped to take this path by the system. I am guessing by God. For these things were always meant to be.

"Now, to answer your question of how this all happened... I have thought about time at great lengths. I originally considered that perhaps it was a process, where just as evolution often creates things which become more and more complex, history, time itself, has changed over and over until we have what we have today. If this is true, then there could have been a thousand different versions until our current situation finally came to be. Maybe I would have invented time travel even without Delta's inspiration. After all, God could have inspired me in many other ways. Maybe something else was written in the Geno book that led you to Geno. And after meeting me with my time travel devices, your recurring dreams inspired you to travel back to meet her, bringing her to the future. Maybe small changes happened over time, completing pieces of the puzzle, until finally, we have what we have today."

"But that's not correct, is it?" Ulysses looks at Emit curiously.

"No. I soon realised that if it happened in the past, then it would immediately change our present. And therefore, logically, everything had to be written at once. This is why we can't change the past. We can't even make small changes. What is the past, is the past."

"So, this is the very first time that this has all happened?" Ulysses struggles to take it all in.

"Yes. Time is, after all, just elements interacting. And the greater good always occurs one way or another. Whether through dreams, or synchronicity or by true desires, we are always guided towards the greater good. And so, with the help of God, somehow everything has occurred as we see it now. And as God is efficient, it happened all on the first time."

Ulysses nods. He finds it incredible that such an intricate adventure could so magically come to place. A great master really is at work.

Emit leans in with his upper body. "Ulysses, I've been thinking. I think the world is ready now for your theory. And to learn of Geno too. Geno has been silent on world issues for far too long. Particularly when it comes to The Shadows. But now that everything that was written has come to pass, the power for us at Geno is also in the present. We are to do our part for the greater good, and to help create this world's future," he says and then leans back to his original position.

"Are you sure?"

"Yes. It's time." Emit stands.

Delta gets their attention from the dirt path. "Ulysses, your father wants to meet us on the Geno oval."

CHAPTER 90

A FATHER'S LESSON

ULYSSES AND DELTA have been summoned by Ulysses' father. They all stand together on the dirt oval before the pavilion. Ulysses and Delta have an arm around one another. Ioannis stands before them, wearing a jacket, long brown pants and thick glasses.

Ioannis speaks, "I must leave Geno. But before I do, I wish to say a few words of wisdom, as a way to bless you both going forward."

"Sure," Delta says enthusiastically. Ulysses nods in agreement.

"I see you have something very beautiful. Delta, you're an incredible person. You're the one Ulysses has always wished for and I'm glad that he has finally found you. True love is real, you both encapsulate it. And I know you will continue to have the most beautiful relationship, equal to the greatest love that has ever existed."

Ulysses and Delta hold one another tighter.

"But you also must know a few things. Delta, you were perfect before you met Ulysses. And Ulysses, I've watched you grow. I know that you too have always been perfect. It's important that you know that you don't need one another to be perfect," Ioannis says. He looks at them both.

"Yes, we're already complete. The love of all time exists within here," Delta says as she points to her heart. "But still, even though we're already perfect, we can still uncover great love and perfections in one another."

"Exactly right, Delta. An element interacts in a system and creates. You are the elements. You have already created the most beautiful *once upon a time.* And now it's up to you to continue this fairytale and discover how deep your love can be. For staying in love forevermore is a choice.

"This is a choice which isn't always going to be as easy as it is right now. You may not believe this, but you will have challenges in your relationship. Challenges that often help your relationship to grow. They are the chaos that leads to the order. But underlying everything, regardless of the changes, I want you always to believe in your relationship. And do one simple thing: at all times, focus on the beauty that forever resides within yourself and the other. The beauty that exists in the time between time. Bring this beauty out. Keep filling yourselves with this love and sharing it with the other in the beautiful ways that each adores to receive it. Can you do this?"

"Certainly," Delta says, looking at Ulysses. "My love already exists in the time between time. My love for my parents. My love for Salt. It is strong and lasts all distances, through all time."

"You've certainly proven this," Ulysses confirms.

"And now my love for you too, Ulysses. And I promise to show you this and bring this out in each other."

"I promise too," Ulysses says.

Ioannis continues, "Good. Because your relationship needs to be kept powerful. Not just because you wish for it. But also because God wishes it. Your love is not only in the time between time, it also exists in the present as it is of the greater good. This is for a reason. You see, you both have a destiny together. Delta, from birth, you were born without sin. And Ulysses, you have been chosen. *For a reason.* Because together you will change the world."

"How will we change the world?" Ulysses asks curiously, with a half smile.

"Sometimes knowing your greater elemental purposes can come in the way of you achieving it."

"So… are you going to tell us?" Delta smiles, pressing him.

"All I will say is, you will see the order in time. Now go forth and change the world," Ioannis says, smiling cheekily. His lesson is over.

Ulysses releases Delta from his arms and moves closer to his father. He asks quietly, "How do I ever thank you? For all that you've ever done for me?"

"You have already thanked me more than you will ever know, Ulysses, simply by existing."

Ulysses smiles and hugs his father. "By the way, I've found out who the members of the Trust are now. Geno."

"That's right, Ulysses. There's a great deal of power that comes with money. Unfortunately, many of the world's wealthy are not putting this power into the right places. Geno, on the other hand, uses its wealth for the greater good. And you, albeit unknowingly for the most part, have been a great help in doing this."

Ulysses nods.

Ioannis continues, "There's so much you still don't know, Ulysses. But you will in time."

"I can't wait. By the way, does Mum know about Geno?"

"Possibly, I'm not sure. But now that the time has come to pass, she certainly will. And Ulysses…" Ioannis says, bringing some of his fingers onto his chin and slightly covering his mouth with them, as if he is about to say something he knows he should not. "… She doesn't think that I know, but she too has many great secrets to share with us. And so do your sisters."

"What do you mean?"

"Let's wait for them to tell us," he says with a mysterious smile.

CHAPTER 91

THE GREATER GOOD AND THE TIME BETWEEN TIME

In the afternoon, Ulysses walks through Geno. He can *see the order*. How everything has worked out perfectly for him. His whole life has been an amazing interconnected journey where he had to go through each part to reach the next.

If he did not have dreams of Delta, he would not have followed her and come to Geno. If he did not have the pain of Delta rejecting him, then he would not have fallen from the cliff and self-actualised. If Luke had not stolen the time travel watches, Ulysses would have never met Delta. Everything was meant to be. The bad times were not bad times. They were for the greater good. Everything was actually good.

Apart from one thing. Sophos. *She didn't have to die. Luke had a choice in that moment. It had not yet been written when he murdered her. It didn't have to happen.*

Ulysses, with a heavy heart, walks towards Sophos' grave and looks upon it forlornly. It has been three days since Sophos has passed and she is missed deeply.

As Ulysses looks upon her grave, he notices the rosebush at the head of it. It shines, shimmering with the sun, as if it is on fire yet the flames do not consume it. *A burning bush.* Seeing this bush reminds him once again of his conversation with Sophos by the campfire on his first night at Geno. She connected with him so deeply on this night. He still remembers her telling him that everything will one day be as simple as looking at a plant shining in the sun.

Suddenly while looking at this bush, he realises something. *It can't be...* But it is! On the rosebush is a flower, a white rose, in bloom above her grave! *Incredible.*

When Sophos spoke to Ulysses of foreseeing her death, she talked about this very rosebush. Her late husband planted it for her at Geno, but it never bloomed. And now, above her grave, it finally blooms. For the first time, a flower has opened!

It is a sign, a synchronicity. He knows that only a miracle could see a rose grow and open so quickly. Sophos promised Ulysses she would let him know that she has arrived in heaven. And she has. Through this rose!

On the third day, she rose again.

Ulysses touches the rose, his eyes becoming watery. "I have received your sign, Sophos," he says softly.

While he still deeply mourns that he has lost the particular embodiment of Sophos which he has come to know and love – a beautiful form that the universe made for a moment in time – he holds some contentment knowing that Sophos continues to exist in many ways.

She will live on because elements always exist, they purely change forms. And so, Sophos' physical form will become a part of other elements.

She will also continue to exist in Ulysses, where she has touched his heart. And through the many other elements she has touched through her time as Sophos. This effect will continue in some form, for all time.

And now, through this rose, he also learns that Sophos' eternal embodiment of beauty also exists in heaven. Where, possibly, the time between time meets the greater good.

CHAPTER 92

DELTA'S HOMELAND

887 – Sweden.

DELTA AND ULYSSES have travelled back in time to her homeland.

She rides through the green meadows on her white horse, Salt, and pulls the reins, bringing her horse to a stop. Ulysses extends his hand and leads her off her horse. She jumps on him, wrapping her legs around him. He spins her around and they kiss passionately.

They walk hand in hand through a beautiful garden. He has roses in his hand, cuttings which were sourced from elsewhere in Delta's homeland, as a gift for her parents. He hopes that they may wish to grow their own rosebushes. She looks up to see white doves in the trees. Suddenly Delta realises that this is from her recurring dream. The final part. It wasn't a dream of heaven after all, it was of her future, of her and Ulysses visiting where she grew up in old Sweden. It may not be heaven, but in a way, to her it is.

She thinks of how much adventure she and Ulysses have to come. And no matter what challenges they meet, she feels they will always be together, holding one another's hand throughout the way. For they have a true love that is forever, eternal. It cannot be overcome by the elements, for it exists in the time between time and is of the greater good.

Furthermore, she is committed to always making it work.

CHAPTER 93

THE FUTURE SHADOWS

The present – The French Riviera, France.

LEUCIUS IS BACK in his sprawling mansion with his gold pen in hand. Classical music echoes through the office. He looks up from his desk and to the man with a brilliant golden cane, emerald tweed blazer and magnificent moustache. The man bows before him.

"He's real," Leucius says.

"Who?" Anomonet asks.

"Orien. He exists after all."

"Of course he does! How could you even doubt this?"

"Save it," Leucius commands.

"Did you destroy Geno?"

"No, Orien interceded."

A look of understanding comes across Anomonet's face. His voice lowers. "Leucius, it is a hard lesson. But sometimes when you make plans, God laughs."

"My plans for the future of The Shadows remain unaffected! Everything is already in motion," Leucius says, his hands waving above some writing on his notepad that rests on top of a yellow envelope. "My plans were beneath your very eyes this entire time, you're just not smart enough to notice them unfolding. But you will see the order in time. Neither Orien nor Geno can stand in the way."

CHAPTER 94

RETURN TO THE BEGINNING

Gold Coast, Australia

EVERY DAY OFFERS new opportunities to experience beauty. Walk in your surroundings, notice the beauty everywhere.

Ulysses walks tall, confidently. He catches his reflection in a nearby reflective shop window, happy to be himself. *As long as you are happy with yourself, you can be content doing anything.* He passes a child running playfully with his dad as they hold hands. People are smiling. *The simple moments in life hold such beauty.*

He enters a bakery. The girl at the counter shows her physical interest in him. His psychic powers have become so strong that he can read her thoughts easily, thoughts of how his eyes are glowing with positive light and have captivated her. He receives some bread from the girl at the counter and leaves the bakery, passing a group of young men who sit at a table, one ruffling up the other one's hair.

He walks along a street parallel to the beach. His thoughts return to before Geno, to what was on his mind as he walked down this very same street, the very morning he discovered the theory: *The world around me, and everything it encapsulates, are like words of a sentence. Now that I've discovered this theory, I know how to read the sentence. But I still don't know what the sentence means; this I must decipher if I'm to tap into the hidden perfection of the world and live the life of my dreams.*

Now, eight weeks after discovering his theory, Ulysses feels he has the answer he needs: that he may never know the meaning of all that is. And he does not have to. Because the universe, God, knows. And this is good enough.

He reaches home and walks up his stairs. He hears a neighbour's music playing, which soothes him. A blue butterfly flies past him, a part of God's beauty. He enters his door and is greeted by Delta, who kisses him passionately.

Ulysses is loving existence. Everything has come together for him; his life is everything he has ever wanted it to be. He no longer searches for perfection. He knows that perfection is everywhere. It always has been, it just needs the right eyes to uncover it. And now, with this knowledge, he experiences perfection wherever he goes.

He feels deeply appreciative for his time at Geno. For being taught great wisdom and for the amazing gifts that he has been given. He is also appreciative to be allowed by Geno to finally let their guarded secrets of the universe out to anyone who seeks them. And so, with the wish that others will see the beauty of the world just as he does, he opens his laptop and begins to write a novel. The story begins on the morning he discovered his theory.

*

With only seven members left, Geno must now find another member – will it be you?

EPILOGUE

Ulysses answers his door.

"Dad!"

"My son." They hug warmly.

"So good to see you. I didn't know you were coming to the Gold Coast?"

"Yes, I'm here to tell you of your next quest."

Ulysses nods.

"You're to take the Geno book to its next location, which is listed on the page after yours, page 881… Oh, and you must learn Ancient Greek."

"Ancient Greek, why would I need to know that?"

"There is something I must tell you. There is a reason why I called you Ulysses…"

END

ABOUT THE AUTHOR

Photo courtesy of Nikki Brown
nikkibrown.com.au

Born in Mount Isa, George Sourrys now lives on the Gold Coast, Australia. He has a Bachelor of Psychological Science and has worked both in finance and as a model. George's passions are his life, his family and the natural world.

Please keep in touch with the author through the following links:

Email
contact@georgesourrys.com
Facebook
facebook.com/georgesourrys

Instagram
@georgesourrys
instagram.com/georgesourrys

Youtube
youtube.com/georgesourrys

Web Pages of Interest

Website:
georgesourrys.com

Blog:
georgesourrys.com/blog

Geno's theory (Sourrys theory):
georgesourrys.com/theory

The Perfect Mindset principles:
georgesourrys.com/perfectmindset

Printed in Great Britain
by Amazon